Bard FICTION PRIZE

Bard College invites submissions for its annual Fiction Prize for young writers.

The Bard Fiction Prize is awarded annually to a promising, emerging writer who is a United States citizen aged 39 years or younger at the time of application. In addition to a monetary award of $30,000, the winner receives an appointment as writer-in-residence at Bard College for one semester without the expectation that he or she teach traditional courses. The recipient will give at least one public lecture and will meet informally with students.

To apply, candidates should write a cover letter describing the project they plan to work on while at Bard and submit a C.V., along with three copies of the published book they feel best represents their work. No manuscripts will be accepted.

Applications for the 2013 prize must be received by July 16, 2012. For further information about the Bard Fiction Prize, call 845-758-7087, or visit www.bard.edu/bfp. Applicants may also request information by writing to the Bard Fiction Prize, Bard College, Annandale-on-Hudson, NY 12504-5000.

Bard College PO Box 5000, Annandale-on-Hudson, NY 12504-5000

COMING UP IN THE FALL

Conjunctions:59
COLLOQUY

Edited by Bradford Morrow

In *Colloquy, Conjunctions* will offer a major portfolio of never-before-published correspondence by William Gaddis, a towering figure in twentieth-century literature. These letters, which span the 1940s to the 1990s, offer an unprecedented view of this intensely private writer. Readers will meet the Harvard undergraduate making his first forays into fiction; they will see him struggling with his first book while scraping by in rented rooms in Panama, Spain, and Paris; and they will follow him as he comes to terms with his evolving status as an American writer and public figure. The selection includes his fan mail to other authors, passionate missives to his wives and lovers, tender and intimate notes to his children, frank and funny messages to friends such as David Markson and Saul Steinberg, and revelatory exchanges with scholars of his work. A mesmerizing glimpse into the creative process that produced his novels *The Recognitions*, *J R*, *Carpenter's Gothic*, *A Frolic of His Own*, and *Agapē Agape*, this portfolio will be essential reading for devotees of Gaddis, and will captivate anyone intrigued by the life of the mind. The issue will also include fiction, poetry, and creative nonfiction from today's most compelling emerging voices, as well as innovative new work by contemporary masters, including Edie Meidav, David Shields, Cole Swensen, Robert Olen Butler, and others.

One-year subscriptions to *Conjunctions* are only $18 (two years for $32) for more than seven hundred pages per year of contemporary and historical literature and art. Subscribe or renew online at conjunctions.com, or mail your check to *Conjunctions*, Bard College, Annandale-on-Hudson, NY 12504-5000. For questions or to request an invoice, e-mail conjunctions@bard.edu or call (845) 758-7054.

CONJUNCTIONS

Bi-Annual Volumes of New Writing

published by Bard College

CONJUNCTIONS is published in the Spring and Fall of each year by Bard College, Annandale-on-Hudson, NY 12504. This issue is made possible in part with the generous funding of the National Endowment for the Arts, and with public funds from the New York State Council on the Arts, a State Agency.

SUBSCRIPTIONS: Use our secure online ordering system at www.conjunctions.com, or send subscription orders to CONJUNCTIONS, Bard College, Annandale-on-Hudson, NY 12504. Single year (two volumes): $18.00 for individuals; $40.00 for institutions and overseas. Two years (four volumes): $32.00 for individuals; $80.00 for institutions and overseas. Patron subscription (lifetime): $500.00. Overseas subscribers please make payment by International Money Order. For information about subscriptions, back issues, and advertising, contact us at (845) 758-7054 or conjunctions@bard.edu.

Editorial communications should be sent to Bradford Morrow, *Conjunctions*, 21 East 10th Street, 3E, New York, NY 10003. Unsolicited manuscripts cannot be returned unless accompanied by a stamped, self-addressed envelope. Electronic and simultaneous submissions will not be considered. If you are submitting from outside the United States, contact conjunctions@bard.edu for instructions (please do not send International Response Coupons as postage).

Conjunctions is listed and indexed in Humanities International Complete and included in EBSCO*host*.

Visit the *Conjunctions* website at www.conjunctions.com and follow us on Facebook and Twitter.

Cover design by Jerry Kelly, New York. Cover art by Robert and Shana ParkeHarrison. Front cover: *Lowtide*, 2003. Black-and-white print on panel with acrylics and varnish, 50 x 60 in. © 2003 Robert and Shana ParkeHarrison. Back cover: *Marks We Make*, 2005. Photogravure, 24 x 20 in. © 2005 Robert and Shana ParkeHarrison.

Available through D.A.P./Distributed Art Publishers, Inc., 155 Sixth Avenue, New York, NY 10013. Telephone: (212) 627-1999. Fax: (212) 627-9484.

Printers: Edwards Brothers

Typesetter: Bill White, Typeworks

ISSN 0278-2324

ISBN 978-0-941964-74-6

Manufactured in the United States of America.

TABLE OF CONTENTS

RIVETED:
THE OBSESSION ISSUE

Edited by Bradford Morrow

Barney Rosset

May 28, 1922–February 21, 2012

Literary Publishing Pioneer

First Amendment Rights Hero

Inspiration

"I can't go on,
I'll go on."

—Samuel Beckett, *The Unnamable*

Clear Over Target, the Whole Town in Flames

Fiona Maazel

AND SO IT WAS THAT Nancy licked and kissed a gluten-free adhesive on the seal side of five hundred envelopes that should have gone out weeks ago. And so it was that this gluten-free adhesive was so rich with latex that Nancy, who heretofore had never touched a condom, surgical gloves, commercial diapers, balloons, a pacifier, or baby-bottle nipple, who had, in short, never reared a child from birth or had a lover she could not trust, so it was that Nancy mistook the tachycardia, hives, and respiratory distress of a nervous breakdown for a latex allergy that locked her in the hospital for a night while her stepdaughter, Tina, had a party.

Oh, Tina. Seventeen and a half, and seeded with resentments that prospered like ivy. For whom a night alone meant a night of trouble. On whose hope transatlantic boyfriend, Philippe Hoffman, had been flown over from Germany, never mind the revised allegiances of a boy loosed on the new world who would, at this party, mack on every girl in sight and flood his kidneys with drink so that when he woke up in the ER, in a bed next to Nancy's, with Nancy looking on him with a tenderness spurred to precaution thanks to years of having to alchemize similarly re: her stepdaughter, she said, "It's all right, Phil, you can fix this, and I know just how."

And so it was. Nancy was not a Calvinist—Augustine of Hippo, Pelagius, Elmo, they all had, for her, the same moral equity—nor was she mindful of the universe in terms of its hold on her. Character is fate, that's what she'd heard, and so if she had to name the punctum of her ethic, its name was defeatist. Her choices would always end badly, not because they yielded to a future she'd signed onto just for being born but because she had no judgment. Door number one, door number two, choice wrecked her life every time.

And so, the wreckage: an abortion at thirty-nine because she hadn't been married and what did a child sprung from your heart's only experience of love matter absent the approval of your father? Next up: her marriage, years later, to Sam Fleesenbach, who had proposed with a sock puppet because if she said no, the puppet could always be laundered of its grief. After that: her father, whom she'd chosen to take in despite alternatives, which were abundant and even palatable, for instance that place two blocks away that had a wait list longer than many of its applicants could outlive. Which felt, for its lighting and aroma, like an autoclave. Which welcomed, despite the list, despite his age, renowned allergist pater of Nancy Fleesenbach, but no, she had chosen to keep Leon for herself. And now Philippe, who said, "Uh, thanks, Mrs. F, but I think me and Tina are splitso for good," only he said it in German, which Nancy had chosen not to learn as a child, German being the language of hate and she was half Jewish.

"Wunderbar," she said and clapped her mitts. They'd swathed her hands in gauze lest she kill herself.

February 14, 1945, the Allies burned down Dresden. January 1, 2011, Sergeant Leon Kott succumbed to guilt. He'd flown that mission and had, every year since, spoiled Valentine's Day with its remembrance. Only this year, things were different. Leon was old and got lost in the apartment. He could walk into a closet and stay there, and because he was cusped on ninety but still had enough sense to know it, this year he wanted to apologize for what he'd done and to make a ceremony of it.

Nancy had been appalled. And then confused. Could you really be forgiven a holocaust on thirty thousand people just for saying oops into a microphone? And was this really the apology his feelings had worked him up to? Her father was mantled in remorse and unable to slough it off. How awful. But also: how excellent, its excellence a salve for the memories that hurt her most. But also: how awful! Her father was a great man, and, when Nancy was alone, with time to think, she clung to his greatness for ballast in the squall of failure that blew through her own life every day. Once, when she was a teenager, a journalist who'd come to interview Leon had touched her arm and said, "You are borne of genius." She had blushed, but propped herself up with that remark for weeks. If it made Leon happy, he should apologize for whatever he wanted, and to whomever seemed best.

There was, too, always the chance he would forfeit his joust with guilt or even forget the fight. A few weeks ago he lost memory of 1951: her birth, jaundice, every time he'd touch her skin, the contrails of rash he'd leave behind. But as the date neared, he didn't forget. And neither did she. And so: Philippe. Nancy didn't know anyone who'd survived Dresden, but she did know a kid from Berlin who could stand in for a city on fire.

Tina couldn't believe it. First of all: gastric lavage at the hospital? Like Phil had been to a spa? Had a cleanse, broke her heart? And now the object of some big apology when it was obviously Tina who needed succor? Wow, she hated him. And Nancy! A hippo could burrow in those smile lines. The skin of her face was fluted. Her cheeks, chin, even the fat of her forehead seemed to ooze down the hulk of her jaw because she had a man face no girl reared in its image could forgive. Tina's own mom, from the pictures, had been intuitive about makeup and clothes, had been effervescent in the outpour of her aesthetic, could, essentially, be draped in vomit and look good. But her own mom was dead, nine years now, and Nancy was Nancy and so Tina hadn't learned how to blush her bones until high school. And it was those Maybelline compacts with the labeled powder pads that taught her how to browbeat the other girls at the winter dance. But she learned, she did, and could, at 17.5, proxy for her mother at the same age. In other words: She was the most awesome girlfriend ever, what was Phil's problem?

It had seemed to her like this: Valentine's Day with Phil! In New York City, wellspring of opportunities to romance the part of her that felt weird about having to insist he come! He was eighteen and bused at White Trash, which served *die besten* steaks and burgers in Berlin, not to mention *die besten* bands, so of course he didn't want to leave all that, though once he serenaded her in Central Park, who would care. He was an awesome guitar player. He was awesome.

Nancy sang to herself as she reviewed the guest list. She used to sing professionally, but had given it up at her father's behest. She did not, after all, want to spend her life belting out folk songs for dimes, did she?

The guest list was to have been diverse but top-of-the-line. Her father had not treated Kennedy's asthma, Clinton's hay fever, just to repatriate his conscience for the janitor. The envelopes were stacked in columns, the plan to invite five hundred and hope four fifty were out of town. Nancy sat on the carpet with a sponge-cup moistener and purple nitrile gloves. She'd slapped her legs in cortisone and wrapped them in cling film to retain moisture. On hand, a Jet nebulizer, whose rumble, in a crisis, was as prophylactic as the medicine it fanned out. Her allergies seemed to ignite when it was just her and Leon in the house. Times like those, she made use of the nebulizer eight times a day. She made use of it now.

He could walk if someone helped him up. He had a cane. Glasses. Was not incontinent, could bathe himself, which meant life had chosen to surrender his faculties well before his body, though it was hard to know which was the more galling and for whom.

"Dad?"

"*Entschuldigung!*" he said, which he'd been saying for weeks. I'm sorry! the cry issued in an outage of hope that was always less abstract than Nancy expected, finding him, for instance, in the shower with the caddy fallen to the tile and the shampoo strafed across the curtain.

Today he was in the laundry room. He wore a red V-neck cashmere sweater and red gingham blazer, only neither was his or even designed for a man, which he seemed to intuit, but barely.

"Dad, it's all right," and she took his arm. "You look like a rock star."

"A star," he said, and he shook her loose. "How would you know?"

"Seen 'em on TV," and she steered him to the table.

"Now Phil?" he said. "That boy's got something."

She put yams in a blender. "He's resting, Dad." His glasses were steamed. "Sweet potato," she said. "Your fa-vo-rite."

"That Phil," he said, and gummed his lunch down.

The invitation was mostly news clippings: *Out of the west, 1,350 American bombers streaked their vapor trails into the dawn. Bombs away at 12:22. They were hours over a sheet of fire, a terrific red glow towered in smoke.*

Tina was upstairs, in bed. Downstairs: her stepmother and Phil, on yoga mats. Fold, stuff, stamp. Phil had moved into the guest room and it's not like Nancy would throw him out with the ceremony upcoming and the invitations still unsent. Also: With Tina's dad traveling for work nine-tenths of the year, Phil seemed to square the geometry of the house. They were listening to one of those live concert festivals from the sixties on box set, and though no one listened to that stuff anymore, Tina often thought wouldn't it be nice. Just to go to some field and dance barefoot all night without having to fear for your life because nothing was fun without consequence anymore, AIDS had put an end to that, death had put an end to that, so, yeah, what else was there to do but stay home, listening to the Byrds pipe up through the floorboards?

Her mother's death was: latent TB turned active in the presence of Acquired Immunodeficiency Syndrome. The story was: She'd gotten it in Tanzania, where she'd gone to ablate some bad, midlifey feelings, and to ink in their stead proof of the good, which motive ended in a tattoo shanty by Lake Victoria, and in this shanty: dirty needles, only who cared since everyone there was infected already. What the tattoo was no one said and Tina did not ask because most of her wanted it to be *Tina Tina Tina*, except for the part of her that didn't because, really, in the pursuit of *Tina Tina Tina* her mom got AIDS? It would not be hard to wrest from this sequence of events the kind of guilt that wrecks your life well before your first crime. Better to blame the friend who'd taken her along, James the family friend who had wanted to document the despoiled and corrupt fishing communities around the lake and who had wanted her mother to come. Course, he had died of AIDS a couple years later, so why hold a grudge.

"Man, such a good sound," Phil was saying. And then because Nancy laughed, Tina knew what he was doing, he was playing air guitar on a yoga mat while Nancy personalized five hundred invitations: *Not a single German gun was fired, the city was undefended; the attack was relentless, savage, selfish, and so comprehensive the city has never recovered.*

"I'm fine, I'm fine," Nancy said, her hands trembling and her heart punking out because maybe she was allergic to nitrile too. "Just a flutter. Not to worry. Dad?" she called. "This is gonna be great!"

"Entschuldigung!" Leon said, the ketchup fallen from the counter and bleeding all over the floor.

Tina flipped on her stomach with her mom's leather-bound journal open to March 14, 2001. On the subject of recrimination: How easy was it to accuse your husband of doing unto you what you have done? Vows obsolesce like an apple a day.

She went downstairs. Leon was still in the kitchen, wiping his pants and smudging Phil's passport, which he'd found in the boy's room, thinking it was his own.

"Pop," she said, "check it out. One stamp. He hasn't seen anything."

"Thirty-two missions," he said. "I've seen it all."

"I know, Pop. Here," and she swabbed his chin, the ketchup having clotted over his only scar from the war. A bailout over Pidley, he said. Did she know the story? She did. But tell me again, Pop. His crew had run out of gas on the way back from Dresden, their plane being a new B-17 whose fuel consumption was unfamiliar to them, two engines windmilling in the slipstream, and there was Sgt. Hendrix, who was the spot jammer, stuck in the aft bulkhead, only not so much stuck as unmoving because he alone understood what they had done to this beautiful city, those poor people, so that when the alarm rang, Leon was so busy yelling at Hendrix to move his hump, he had time to clip only the chest straps of his chute so that when he bailed, he took it on the chin from where the buckle held, all while their bomber went down and with it Sgt. Hendrix, who had a wife and newborn back home.

"I went to see his daughter almost every day when I was back, you know that, right? Nancy was just a baby. But Jill, she really turned into something, didn't she? A real star."

"Yeah, Pop," Tina said.

Apparently, Jill had come over once as a teenager to tell Leon to quit it. Now she worked quality control for a cat-food manufacturer. Sometimes she sent a card.

"Where's Nancy?" he said. "She's never around. If it's one thing you can count on, it's that my daughter is never around when you need her."

He drew up his blue eyes, blue but dull, like they'd been dipped in milk, and said, "Tell your mother to invite Jill."

The point of reminding Pop, for the millionth time, that Nancy was not her biological mother? Could never even approach the stardom of her biological mother? No point. None at all.

Nancy riffled through her stack of invites, and pawed at the wrap about her calf until it was pawed through. Christ, she hadn't invited Jill. Why hadn't she invited Jill? How about because when Nancy was little and her dad used to walk into the living room unexpected—he was home early, he was home at all—and if Nancy was already there, she used to imagine her heart popping out of her chest and, on little stick legs, scrambling across the carpet and beseeching her dad from this vantage, like one of those yappy, undersized dogs, a chihuahua, maybe, and watching him scoop up this little heart and press it to his own, and in her head, she called this routine The Jill.

"Of course," she said, as Tina drifted through the room, "Jill's on the list," and then she used a letter opener to score the hives erupted on the inseam of her wrist.

Phil looked at Tina, the mop of his hair parted down the middle just enough so he could see, and said, "No way that's allergies," to which Tina said, "Don't talk to me, fuckface."

Nancy smiled. Finally, the kids were talking, and talking in German, and this was nice because in German, people said *I'm sorry.* The proper phrase was *Das tut mir aufrichtig leid,* I am truly, truly, deeply, horribly sorry for everything I have ever done to you, but *Entschuldigung* was a start.

There were plugs of rash in the webbing of her toes. What looked like a hickey, but which was definitely not a hickey, at the base of her neck, her husband having not been home in three months. There were, in five hundred envelopes, five hundred photocopies of the same news clipping and, stapled to each, a photo of her father in his electric F-2 suit and harness. There was her father's address book and in it the pizza place, a barber shop, and a number for Jill Hendrix.

She fingered a clipping as she spoke. Voice mail. Her name and purpose, please.

Nancy and Jill were just five years apart. Only Jill's father had been immolated in a B-17, and Jill had grown up with his Purple Heart boxed under her pillow, and Jill lived in a one-bedroom apartment with cats who were more in temperament like dogs, who came when she called, who licked her face, who loved her in every way. When Nancy arrived, Jill had opened the door, but kept the chain on. She'd made Nancy say again who she was and also explain since when did not returning a phone call, or even several, mean come over? She relented only when the rosacea masked around Nancy's eyes began to blitz her chin and cheeks, and the pant of her speech, which had hitherto seemed thanks to the five-story walk-up, got wheezy and frantic. She'd left her inhaler at home. She hadn't known, but maybe she was allergic to cats too.

"Oh, please," Jill said. "Like there's dander in the hall. Now get in here," and she unhitched the chain. And when Nancy stepped in, palm to chest, wheezing, Jill said, "For God's sake."

The apartment, for its lack of decor, was forthright about Jill's life in a way that seemed embarrassing. No pleasures are enjoyed herein.

Blank walls, bare floors. Same went for her clothes—pink scrubs that looked more cardboard than cotton, and a button-down shirt that held across her chest like hands in the instant before they are torn apart.

"I can't breathe," Nancy said. "I shouldn't have come."

Jill took her by the arm and led her to the bathroom. Flipped on the hot water in the shower, and sat Nancy on the toilet, herself on the floor. Soon the room was congested with steam, and whatever awkwardness Nancy had felt for their proximity in a private place was lost to the proposition that out of sight was out of mind. She couldn't see her own hands, forget seeing Jill. The bunting in her lungs dissolved.

"OK," she said. "OK." She breathed in and out, and fumbled in her purse for the invitation, wilted and moist.

"Tea?" said Jill.

They went to the couch. Nancy's clothes were damp and shagged in lint. Jill's mug had a photo of a Maine coon mugged across the side. Nancy laughed.

"Hey," Jill said, shrugging. "When you don't have kids, people look at your life and find the next best thing to celebrate. You got kids?"

"A stepdaughter."

"Ha," Jill said, but that was it. She stood to readjust the elastic band of her pants, then plunked back down on the couch. "So what's this all about?"

It was noon, and, last Nancy checked, cold and bright outside, only here, light from the squiggle bulb overhead cast the room in dusk. She had not meant to come in person. She'd meant to leave a message and mail the invitation. But with the event a week away and the RSVPs totaling four including Phil and family, here she was.

"My dad thinks the world of you," she said, and then explained the rest, careful to lock eyes with the mug, the mug being neutral in expression, whereas Jill not so much.

"His star burning bright in the dawn of what?" Jill said.

"A new start."

"For whom? He's ninety."

"All the more reason. Every second counts."

Jill sat back and gripped the seam of her pants leg to pull one gam across her knee.

"Arthritis," she said. And then, "No wonder you're having panic attacks." And then, "Poor you."

"I'm fine. My dad's worked hard all his life. He was the most famous allergist in the country. Forgive the joke, but he was the Jimi Hendrix of his time."

"I haven't seen your father in forty years."

"But he's thought of you every day."

"Oh, Lord. Poor you!"

Nancy stood. "Look, the whole thing will be for nothing unless you're there. It won't take more than half an hour. There'll be food and drink. Lots of guests. Like a cocktail party."

"Let me ask you something: How do you spend your time? I mean, for a living. Do you work?"

"I used to sing. Folk singing. But my father didn't like it."

"Were you any good?"

Nancy smiled. "Actually, I was. But that was ages ago. I've made my bed."

"I inspect cat food," Jill said. "Maybe a thousand cans a day. So what I'm saying is: No one thinks the world of me but my cats."

Nancy leaned against the wall and hung her arms by her side. She could feel the blisters risen from the tissue-thin skin racked across her bones.

"You know that hives are mostly mental, right?" Jill said. "Maybe *you* should get a cat. I got plenty to go around."

"So will you come? It would mean so much."

Jill shook her head and sighed, less to refuse than to express that particular mix of incredulity and grief prompted by access to other people's lives. "OK," she said. "Done."

Phil stood in the doorway to Tina's room. Music leaked from his headphones while he squatted against the frame and cranked one arm over his midriff.

She was at her desk. "Can you stop?" she said. "Who you trying to impress? You have a real guitar, go play that."

"If I play, your grandfather will come watch. Yesterday, he just sat on the couch, staring like some groupie."

"Sounds nice."

"I'm having second thoughts about all this."

"Free room and board and all you gotta do is sit around while my pop says he's sorry? I pity your lot in life, I do."

He made for her bed and collapsed into the spread, which was baize green.

"Why's he apologizing to me anyway? And for what? Isn't it his friend who died he should be sorry about? Seems kind of stupid."

"Did I say you could come in here?"

"Whatcha reading?"

She closed her mother's journal. She'd read it many times over and had always managed to pull from its tides advice by way of example, though as of late this reading had come to feel more like dredging the sea for dimes.

"What do you want?" she said.

"It's Valentine's Day. We should go out."

He came up behind her and leaned over her shoulder. Pressed his lips to the top of her head. He'd been her first boyfriend of note, transatlantic or not, and her first hurt of note, and for these, her mother's journal had been abundant in the dispatch of her thoughts. But on the how of reconciliation?

He flipped the journal open. Jan. 20, 2000, her mom newly arrived in Tanzania with James, and visiting the lake towns one by one.

"Steamy," he said, and he stood upright. "So you want to go out? My treat?"

Tina had no idea what her mother would do in this situation. Her mother: beautiful, smart, loving, dead! Tina was all alone. Briefly she thought of Nancy—if Nancy could help—but struck the thought down with a ferocity she could have associated more with the rage of losing her mother than with Nancy's shortcomings, but which she never did. And so, she hoofed it alone. Had it really been so bad? Phil flirting with other girls? She stood to face him, was within kissing range, but just. "What's steamy?" she said and put his arms around her waist.

"Your mom and James? On Lake Victoria? Did your dad even know?"

She shoved him but because it was toward the bed, he mistook one kind of shove for another and grabbed her wrist before he went down and took her with him.

"'James is teaching me *everything*,'" he said, making air quotes and laughing in her ear, all while Tina struggled beneath his weight, the struggle ambiguous with intent because her mind was elsewhere, coming to awareness like a newborn who crowns into the world, screaming.

Finally she managed to throw him off. "Pig," she said, and bawled into her pillow.

He reached for her shoulder, but recoiled as if around the clench of her body had spread an unbreachable aura. He'd seen this happen once before. His kid brother, who had been a budding astronomer and who had the planets on his ceiling but whose cosmology could not actually accommodate change on a large scale—Phil had seen this same despair on his face and in his bearing in the weeks after Pluto's downgrade from planet to dwarf.

"Well, let me know if you still want to go out later," he said. "I'll play you a song," and he softly closed the door behind him.

Tina thought she might be sick. AIDS from a killer needle? How about AIDS from a killer affair.

And so it was that on Feb. 15, 2011, six people were gathered in the Fleesenbach home for canapés and white wine. Six or seven, if you included Sam Fleesenbach, who'd Skyped in from Montreal. Nancy had put the screen atop a vitrine in the living room so he could see over everyone's head to the stage area, only the effect was that no one could hear him and also no one bothered. He looked more bust than man.

"Nance?" he said. "When's everyone getting here? I have a conference call I gotta do."

He was in a hotel room, and behind him were the hotel tulips he'd said were for Valentine's Day and shown Nancy the night before.

Tina walked by and shot him a look of such hostility, it seemed to rebound off the screen and punch her in the face.

"What?" he said, and brought a bottle of beer to his lips, though Nancy had told him to get wine.

Jill approached Tina and thrust out her hand. "A ton of guests," she said. "I guess the ton's on its way."

"Whoa," Tina said. "The famous Jill."

Jill laughed. Pointed at herself. "Doesn't get more famous than me." She wore loose tan pants and a tan cardigan that reached to her knees. From behind, she looked like a body pillow.

"Don't say that," Tina said. "You're great," and she glanced across the room at Nancy, who was small-talking the widow who lived next door, and who'd come over to borrow some milk but who'd agreed to stay so long as she was home in time for her show.

"Wow," Jill said. "Just rolls off the tongue with you people. How many times you saying that a day?"

Tina frowned. "What do you mean?"

Nancy went upstairs. Tina tracked her across the room and made note of her dress with the muslin bodice and cross back straps in pearl white. She wondered where she'd bought it.

Jill drifted toward the front door and was sipping wine when Phil came her way. He wore a blue suit that cuffed above his wrists and ankles, though the double breast was enough to indicate it wasn't his. He said, "*Entschuldigung,*" and motioned to the door, as in, Excuse me, but I have to get out of here. She nodded, but did not move, instinct holding her ground seconds before she understood who this person was and why he could not leave.

Nancy pounded on her father's door, though just by way of making herself heard. She found him sitting on the edge of a chair in a houndstooth blazer and blue tie. He'd applied some kind of grease to his head, which was clowned with hair about the ears, but nowhere else. She noticed his shoes were shiny and uncreased, and that she'd never seen them before. What she had seen before was his mood. The day of her abortion all those years ago, he had dropped her off looking half as neat but just as pleased.

"Jill's here," she said. "Want to come down now? You're the star of this show, can't do it without you."

"Steroids," he said, looking her over. "You ever try steroids? A seven-day course and maybe you'd look all right. Where's your daughter? Is she with Phil?"

The point of reminding Leon, for the millionth time, that Tina was not her biological daughter? Could never even approximate the greatness of the biological daughter she never even had? No point. None at all.

Jill pressed her back to the front door. "No way, kiddo; nohow," as Phil kept saying, "Out, *bitte,* I go out?"

Tina stood by the vitrine, in which were citations of honor for her grandfather and his work on leukotriene modifiers.

"T," her dad said. "Seriously. What's with the angry looks? What did I do?"

"I am so stupid," she said. "How did you raise such a stupid kid?"

"Honey, I really don't know what this is all about, but probably now is not the time."

"You could have told me," she said. But why bother. When Nancy came down the stairs with Leon's arm linked through hers, Tina looked on her with new feeling, with admiration, even, which she furnished with what she knew: Nancy listened to a lot of hippie music, and that was cool. She was barefoot all the time. She had a perfect marriage, loved and cared for Leon, and, best of all, knew who she was, what she wanted, and how to get it.

There were fifty empty chairs half-mooned around a lectern. Jill sat two rows back. She thumbed through the program. A color ad for some novel about the burning of Dresden and a photo of young Nancy in a hospital gown—wide-eyed, shell-shocked. She thumbed to the back for an explanation but found only the suggested reading list, on which was *Apocalypse 1945*.

Nancy led her father to the podium and, when he seemed steady, with forearms braced on the shelf, she sat in the front row. Jill leaned forward and said, "What's that photo of you in the program?"

"I had an abortion," Nancy said flatly, without turning around. "My father's idea."

"Oh, Jesus."

"This is a big day for him," Nancy said. "Isn't that nice?"

Jill leaned in closer. "You know, a lot of people ask if my dad's name was Jimi. Just for a joke. If he was amazing like that."

"What do you tell them?"

"I tell them *no*."

Jill's voice was warm and wet and broke over Nancy's ear so that Nancy felt, for a second, underpulled into the dark and uterine calm of anything is possible. Like her father would get on that stage and apologize to her. Or just fall off the pedestal she'd put him on and stay there.

Phil sat down in a chair and when Leon began to speak, and appeared to speak at him, he assumed this was it and hung his head by way of forgiveness.

"A musical prelude," Leon was saying. "Just a little something."

Tina went to Phil. "Get up," she said. "Go get it."

"What?"

"Your *axe*. Pop wants you to play first."

"What?" Though the horror of this request was evident more in the snarl of his lips and the bell of his nostrils than anywhere else. "There's no one even here. No way."

Nancy understood what was happening and rushed back into her life. Squared her face with Phil's and said, "You will get that guitar of yours and play your friggin' heart out and be everything my dad thinks you are, or I will have you arrested for messing with my underage daughter," and she turned to Tina, who smiled so big, she could have blinded the sun.

He scanned her face for news of the joke, then blanched and scrambled out of the room. Only when he came back, for how slowly he plugged in his amp and searched his case for a pick, it was as if the guitar were albatrossed around his neck.

"Something mellow and sweet," Tina said.

"I can't."

"You can. I've heard you a million times. You play awesome."

He glanced at Nancy with pleading eyes, but she was already slouched in her chair and staring up at Leon like he was every plane in the sky.

"Phil Hoffman," Leon said.

Jill clapped. The widow in back touched a finger to the milk in her glass, which had gone warm. Phil shot Nancy one last miserable look, then hunched forward to see the fret board of his guitar and to mollusk his fingers into the right place, and when that was done, he dragged his pick across the strings and mumbled, "Hey Joe," first words to one of the finest rock songs ever.

"Oh, just start already," Jill said.

In the back, Sam could be heard saying, "Nance, I can't be here for this, I gotta go."

Phil reorganized his fingers and, toggling his gaze from pickup to board, eked out a few more chords. He paused in between each, and said, "Hey Joe."

Nancy's mouth fell open. Phil couldn't play at all? Leon began to teeter. Could topple over any second.

"Come on," Tina said, though really she was pleading. "Just play."

But he didn't. Instead he shook his head, said, "*Entschuldigung,*" and then did what he actually knew how to do, which was to unplug his amp and whale on his guitar and spider-crawl his hand up and down the finger board and then to sit down in shame.

Leon planted his chest on the podium, took a moment, and then said, "Great! You're really something, you know that? Great, too, is Ms. Jill Hendrix, who's been such a help and inspiration to me over the years."

"Oh, wow," Jill said. "What is wrong with you people? You know that even if my dad made it home, my mom was going to leave him anyway? That he was mean and abusive and had a girlfriend in every town he went?"

Everyone stared at her, but no one responded. Leon looked like he'd just lost the capacity to understand English. Tina waited for Nancy's reaction to know her own. But Nancy didn't move, so Jill tapped her on the shoulder because couldn't Nancy at least *feel* what was happening to her? "Hey, Nancy, your neck's pretty red. *Really* red. I think you need a doctor. I think you need to get out of here."

But no, it was way too late for that. Nancy had made her choice long ago. Door number one: happy. A successful artist with a twenty-four-year-old daughter, stay-at-home husband, and father who lived in a retirement home. Door number two: Nancy Fleesenbach, whose face was etched in fire.

The Woman Who Married a Cloud

Jonathan Carroll

HOW COULD SHE EVER tell him *that*? How could she ever look him in the eye and say, I'm sorry, but sex with you doesn't work. I don't like how you touch me. I don't like the way you kiss, and worst of all is your smell. She'd read once that if you don't like another person's smell it's because your genes are wrong for each other. An early warning system from the body, it's saying that if you get together with this person and have children, they'll likely be damaged—so don't do it. Maybe she could tell him *that* and make it sound like a biological problem: I like you, but our physical chemistry is wrong for each other, etcetera.

But he had so many good qualities too—funny and generous, thoughtful and patient. What more can you expect from a partner?

"I've been seriously thinking about calling in a Hate Writer."

Ramona closed her eyes and shook her head. "I was afraid you were going to say that. Is it really that bad? Isn't there any way of saving things?"

They were in that bar on Fourth Street with the good homemade draft beer and the handsome Dutch bartender who speaks five languages.

The two Candelen sisters, Lia and Ramona (Ray), sat next to each other. The bartender, Menno, stood directly across the bar from them and leaned on it with both arms extended. As always, he was happy to watch the two women talking together. He liked them both. He loved one of them. A moment before he'd brought them beer in iced mugs. They'd waited for him to return before continuing their conversation. Menno was Ray's husband.

After taking a small sip of beer, Ray cautiously asked, "How many times did you kill him?"

"Two. The last time I shot him point-blank. He was dead for like an hour, but then I walked into the kitchen and there he was—eating scrambled eggs."

Menno snorted and shook his head. "Does that guy ever eat anything *besides* scrambled eggs?"

Both sisters made almost the same face—exasperated amusement. Amused exasperation. It was true—it seemed like Patrick ate nothing but scrambled eggs.

"That's mainly my fault. It was the only thing I said he ate when I made him." Lia sighed.

"Yeah but you've already shot him two times, Lia. That's right on the border." Ray turned to Menno and took his hand. Across the top of it was a tattoo of a bull terrier. He'd had it done for her because she loved the breed and he'd recently bought her a puppy. "What was the most times I ever killed you?"

"Two."

She dropped his hand. "Get *out*! I never killed you two times. It never came that close."

"Yes it did, sweetheart. That was at the beginning. You were very hard to get."

Ray lifted her shoulders and covered her mouth with both hands like an embarrassed little girl. "That's *awful*! How did you put up with me?"

Lia interrupted. "Wait. We're talking about *me* here, not you two lovebirds. A little help, please."

A customer sat down at the other end of the bar and Menno walked over to take his order.

Ray slid her beer mug back and forth between her hands. "Is there anything else wrong with him that you can blame it on? Say you can't live with a tightwad—"

"No, I told you before—he's incredibly generous. That was one of the first things I checked on the application form: must be generous. Remember, this was just after Jason—"

Ray shivered and stuck out her tongue at the thought of that creature. "Blecch—Jason. No wonder you wanted a cloud after him. He was the world's worst boyfriend *ever*. I'm sorry, Lia, but, good Lord, how could you ever want to be with that man?"

"Because the sex was amazing. I told you a hundred times. End of discussion—next question.

"On the other hand, I don't believe Jason ever paid for anything—nothing. He'd have probably charged me for the sex if he thought he could get away with it even though he was living rent free in my apartment.

"So when I filled out the form for the cloud that was the first thing I checked on the list—MUST BE GENEROUS."

"Well, from what you've said, you obviously didn't check GOOD SEX on that list."

Lia hesitated and then said shyly, "I *did*."

"But you just said—"

Lia held up a hand to stop her sister from speaking. "If there was one good thing Jason did for me, he showed me how good sex can be. So naturally I wanted a great lover to replace him. The problem is Patrick doesn't . . . *do* it for me. Know what I mean? He's passionate, enthusiastic, and knows all the tricks, but it's not there between us as far as I'm concerned. And that's not even talking about his smell. I just don't like to go to bed with him, Ray. All the rest of the time it's great; he's the perfect guy for me. "She stopped talking when she saw Menno walking toward them, scratching his handsome chin. He was so good looking and such a nice, loving man. Ray was living proof that a person *could* make it work perfectly with a cloud if you just managed it the right way.

"I'm telling you I really have tried to make things work for us. But I'm thinking more and more that it's useless; time to call it quits and bring in a Hate Writer."

"I know, Lia, but—"

Menno looked at Ray and said, "Tell her."

Ray appeared to know exactly what he was talking about. "*Really*, Menno, are you sure?"

"Yes. I like Patrick very much. It'd be nice if they could work things out like we did. So, yes, tell her." He stared directly at his wife when speaking so there was no question he meant it. "Is it easier for you if I leave?"

Clearly embarrassed, Ray nodded and looked away. Menno left.

"What's he talking about?"

Ray ran a hand through her hair. She obviously needed a moment to bolster herself before she spoke. That only piqued Lia's curiosity because her sister was not by nature a reticent woman. "Ray, what's going on? Tell me *what*?"

"Menno smelled too. It must be part of their chemistry." Having said this, Ray blushed deeply. "He smelled bad and kissed like a twelve-year-old horn dog. I couldn't stand him. That's why I killed him two times. I knew it was two. I thought after the second time he'd get the hint and go back to his planet. Thank God he didn't."

That was part of the beauty of the cloud dating service. Before you met your prospective partner, the company issued both of you small flashlights the size and heft of a fountain pen. Press a button and it beamed a cerulean-blue laser light. If you were unhappy with your partner, you "shot" this blue light at him or her, which made the person disappear. But if the person thought the relationship still had a chance of working, he or she was allowed to return up to three times. However, if you "killed" the person three times with the light, it was finished whether both sides agreed to it or not. The final separation had to be formalized by signing release papers in front of one of the company's Hate Writers but that was just a legal formality. The most comfortable thing about it was that as soon as the final separation took place, both parties forgot completely about each other and everything that had taken place. It was as if your time together had never happened.

Lia was flabbergasted by Ray's admission about her earlier rough times with Menno. Her sister had *never* told her any of this. In fact, it was Ray's wonderful experience with the cloud that had made Lia, despite many misgivings, sign up with the company. She'd tried everything else by then—so what if he's from a different planet? Look at Ray and Menno. My sister has never been so happy or in love, which was saying a lot because the woman was a fucking *grump*.

No one knew the true history of the cloud because the company was very tight lipped about its origins. The story going around was some being in a distant galaxy that happened to be monitoring earth noticed all of the dating services popping up on the Internet. Then the being watched some of the many reality TV shows like *The Farmer Takes a Wife* and *Partner Search*. Bingo—light-years away the big idea was born—an intergalactic dating bureau! Earth was full of attractive unattached females. Space was way too full of unattached males, especially because of the slew of star wars in recent millennia that of course had decimated the vast armies of female warriors everywhere. The only problem was that these available males were not *human* but Zorgs, Nelmac, Chymeaneans, etcetera. So adjustments naturally had to be made. Aliens had to be willing to give up their natural-born selves and become human beings. That was no big deal for most of them, though, because they were from very advanced civilizations so that metamorphosis was easy. Life on many of their worlds was grim and getting worse; especially planets where there were no longer any females around to make things nicer.

Menno and Patrick were both from the same planet. On her application form, Lia had made sure to stipulate that. If she was going to go through with this, she wanted to start from the same place her difficult sister had found *her* ideal mate.

"But, Ray, you told me everything was perfect from the beginning!"

"I lied. It was bad. I killed him the second night we were together."

The second night! Lia wanted to strangle Ramona. All those glittery stories she'd heard and resented—about how perfect everything was from day one with Menno. How his touch sent Ray over the moon, that he was chivalrous, sensitive, funny . . . all the things Lia had never had with Jason or Guy or Steve or any of her former boyfriends. So what if Menno was from another planet where he might have had three heads or was some kind of unthinkable monster. On Earth he was one damned fine-looking man who treated her sister like treasure and would have been a lucky catch for any woman.

Half a year after Ray and Menno got together, Lia couldn't resist asking her sister, "I know you're really happy and all that. But doesn't it *ever* bother you even a little bit when you imagine what Menno was like on his planet? That he might be a sandworm or something else horrible beneath that beautiful exterior?"

"Nope."

"Really, Ray, never? Not once?"

"OK—once. Once he was in the bathroom when I was passing in the hall. He was making these *really* weird sounds."

"Like what?"

Ray shrugged. "I can't describe them. Just *really* weird noises, like nothing I'd ever heard before. But you know me and Menno—we have no secrets. So I asked afterward what he was doing in there—what were those sounds. You know what it was? He was studying. He was memorizing out loud some things he'd learned about being human. Like those kids who study at the madrassas in the Middle East. The ones who recite everything out loud again and again until they've memorized them? That's what Menno was doing, only in his own language."

"But don't you think that's kind of *creepy*? That when he's by himself he goes back to being, like, a Martian?"

"Shut up, Lia. You're just jealous."

It was true. At that point, Lia Candelen's love life was a fallen soufflé, a dull-throb toothache that never went away, and a big fat zero in her emotional bank account. Jason had gone from being a muse to mucus in less than a year and there was no end in sight to her heart's woe.

Then, to add insult to injury, she watched her self-absorbed moody sister transform almost overnight into a joyous songbird of love because she'd hooked up through an online dating service with an *alien* masquerading as a human being! Lia's initial pity at Ray's shocking, desperate move turned fast into neon-green envy when she saw the dreamy Dutchman and the enchanting way he treated Ramona. He even got a tattoo for her!

And maybe it was the tattoo that did it, the *foreverness* of it. That might have been the thing that finally pushed Lia over the edge and into contacting the cloud herself to ask for an application form.

On receiving the large envelope in the mail she took it to the kitchen table, laid it in the middle, and simply stared at the mustard-colored paper a while. Had her life really come to this? Good God, was she really so desperate, so squeezed dry romantically and emotionally that she was willing to let a space creature into her head, her bed, and maybe even her heart?

Yes, she was.

"What do they mean 'asexual'?" She was on the phone to Ray for the third time that night to ask about questions on the application.

"I guess it means you're not into sex and just want a companion."

"If I only want a companion, then why not just buy a *dachshund*?"

Ray, normally neither patient nor understanding, gentled her voice and said to her yelpy sister, "Just fill it out, Lia. Fill out the form the best way you know how. That's what I did and it turned out OK for me, right?" She looked at lovely Menno as she spoke. He sat across the room making funny faces at her. It was all she could do not to giggle. He thought it amusing that Lia had called so many times about the stupid application form. "The thing's a joke, can't she see that? All they're really asking for is her wish list. What kind of man do you want? We can become anything—just describe it. Tall, dark, and handsome? Check. Can dance like Fred Astaire? No problem. Tell us what you want and you've got it—simple."

Ramona shook her head, delighted by her smart husband's naïveté. "You're so wrong, sweetheart. You still don't understand human psychology. We want there to be mystery in our romance, not a checklist. We want this magical element of *chance* on a blind date. If we just make a list that we know is going to be filled, it's like going to the pharmacy to get a prescription filled. I go to the pharmacy for medicine; I go on blind dates hoping for a miracle."

Menno considered this, his expression grave and thoughtful. "But you filled out the cloud application form too, Ray, so you couldn't have been expecting miracles. From everything you've said about your state of mind then, you were looking for a sure thing."

"True, at that point in my life I was. But I didn't believe for a minute those cloud questions were anything more than window dressing. I thought it was like any other dating service: On every application form you check off the qualities you're looking for in a mate. Then the agency matches you up with someone who has similar taste. But what people say on paper and what they *really* want is usually worlds apart."

The telephone rang again and both of them knew who was calling.

Patrick walked into the bar grinning and rubbing his hands briskly together as if they were cold. His whole being radiated "I'm so glad to be here!"

His lovely Lia was sitting with Ramona and another woman he didn't recognize in a booth at the back of the bar. Both Candelen sisters were attractive but as far as Patrick was concerned, Lia had it all over Ramona because she was so unpleasant. It showed in everything she said and did. Even when she was in a good mood Lia looked cranky. And when unhappy she looked like she hated the whole world but most especially you. Patrick loved that about her.

He tried so hard to please his new girlfriend but usually to no avail. What a challenge! Patrick loved challenges. He disliked it when things were easy or went as scheduled. He enjoyed plotting and planning and preparing for a campaign. Reading maps and figuring out new, faster ways to get wherever he was going—bliss. If there had been a map to Lia Candelen's heart he would have memorized it long ago.

"Hello, ladies." He sat down next to Lia and stroked her arm once. He noticed that all three women looked gloomy. "Is something wrong? Did anything happen?"

"Patrick, this is Fionulla."

"Hi, Patrick."

No one said anything and the silence continued until it became uncomfortable.

Patrick thought he should say something to get the conversation going. "So, Fionulla, what do you do?"

"I'm a Hate Writer."

"Whoa!" He recoiled and then looked with great compassion at Ramona. "I didn't know you two were having *problems*." For the last part of the sentence he lowered his voice in case Menno was somewhere nearby and might hear.

The sisters looked at each other and then at Fionulla.

"I'm not here for her, Patrick; I'm here for you and Lia."

His face instantly lost all expression. That was odd because Patrick had the most animated face Lia had ever seen on a man. Whether he was happy or sad, there always seemed to be five things going on at once in his expression. His eyes told you one thing, his mouth another, even the way his nostrils flared, he licked his lips, or swallowed—all were signs that indicated what was going on in his head at that moment. Over time Lia had become very adept at reading both his face and body language. Now she read nothing there besides blank silence. She had never seen Patrick like this. He looked like a ninja or a stone-cold professional killer right before he struck.

"Why are you here—*for me, Fionulla*?" His voice was haughty and dismissive. He paused before saying the last part of the sentence. Then he spoke it with a kind of emphasis that made those three words sound both distasteful and in italics.

His eyes slid slowly from staring at his unmoving hands in his lap to Fionulla. Even she seemed nonplussed by the strength of his cold gaze. There was suddenly so much tension around them that without being aware of it, Lia started breathing differently—short, shallow breaths. She remembered with a jolt like a shove in the chest that her sweet boyfriend was actually an alien from another planet who suddenly sounded like he might do something scary right this minute.

Instead, he asked in a calm voice, "Is she here because of the smell?"

Fionulla glanced at Lia to see if she wanted to answer his question. Patrick took that as a yes. He turned to his girlfriend and asked, "*Is* she? Did you call her because of the smell? The way I smell?"

How could he know that? She had never said a word about it to him, no matter how much she disliked the odor. Unable to meet his eyes now, Lia stared at the table and murmured, "That and the sex."

"You brought a Hate Writer here for *those* things? Is that why you killed me twice?"

Lia nodded again quickly and vehemently, head still down. She closed her eyes and tried to magically will away this awful moment.

"So you lied before when you said why you killed me? It was really just because of the smell and the sex?" He didn't wait for her to answer before continuing. "OK, Lia—fair enough. All bets are off; the end of nice. Smell your hand."

Confused, she looked at him. "What?"

"Just smell your hand. *Now.* Do it."

He had never used that harsh tone of voice with her and it was very disturbing. Raising a hand to her nose, she smelled it. After two wary sniffs her eyes widened in alarm. She looked at Patrick.

"It's your smell," he said in a flat voice.

"What do you mean?"

"That smell is *your* smell. The one you don't like so much on me. It's actually yours—it's you."

"What are you talking about, Patrick?" she asked, indignant. But in between words, she sneaked another little snuffle off the back of her hand. There it was again—that all-too-familiar repellent odor. There was something metallic in it: metallic and strangely chemical. Also in that odor was the faint trace of something gone bad, *off*, like some kind of rotten food.

So many times when they were standing close or having sex or she turned in bed in the middle of the night, half awake, the first thing that came to her was that instantly recognizable unpleasant odor. At the beginning of their relationship when everything was going so well she thought, I'll grow used to it. But that had never happened. Every time it entered her nose Lia frowned or recoiled or winced or showed some other sign that she'd just bumped into ugly again and it was still dire.

"The smell is a combination of everything you don't like about yourself, Lia. All of it distilled down into that one tangy *stink*." Patrick rubbed a hand across his forehead before continuing. Part of him genuinely regretted telling her this. But he was so hurt and disappointed that she had called for the Hate Writer instead of first trying to work things out with him. Part of Patrick, some wounded very human part, wanted to strike back at Lia and hurt her.

The three women watched him and waited to see what he would do next. Fionulla had no stake in any of this so she was only interested in what would happen. She was there to do her job but always eager to learn new things. She could use all of this experience in her work.

Ramona Candelen knew some of what was coming but had hoped she would never have to tell her sister what Patrick was about to reveal.

"Where I come from, on my planet, we're optimists. Menno's like me in that way, right, Ramona?"

"Yes, he is."

"We have hope; we're a hopeful race. We honestly believe that things can work out fine if we just give it everything we've got. So when I came here and saw how unhappy you are, the very first thing I did was learn about the things you really don't like about yourself: the bad habits, all the reasons for your bad moods, where the mean thoughts come from that bum you out so much of the time. Why you're so *constantly* jealous of others, and your never-ending belief that life hasn't given you your due, your just desserts, even though down deep you know it has.

"I'll tell you why your life is shitty: because you're a sourpuss, Lia—a real *pill* to be around. You're basically a misanthrope who almost always sees whatever glass you're holding as half empty, even when it's filled with the best champagne." He took a deep breath, let it out in a whoosh, and continued. "Do you know what a 'nez' is?"

"No." She could barely breathe.

"It's the French word for nose. Perfume makers are also called nezes because they have to be so sensitive to different fragrances. In a way I was yours. I took all the things Lia Candelen doesn't like about herself and her life, mixed them together, and turned them into a very rare perfume: Eau de Lia.

"Then I put it on myself." Patrick held up one finger as if the point he was about to make was particularly important. "I wanted you to smell that noxious combination on another person; hopefully someone you cared about and wanted in your life a long time. A person important enough for you to overlook or even forgive some of his shortcomings, like his bad smell.

"I thought taking away some of the bad stuff from you and putting it on me would give you new perspective about your life and the way you've been living. Maybe you'd grow to accept it more, accept your life *as it is* as well as who you are, warts and all. Maybe *that* would lessen some of your constant unhappiness. Or if you *really* couldn't stand the smell, you'd change and then discover that the smell would too as soon as you did."

Aghast, Lia put a hand to her throat and turned to her sister. "Ray, is this true? Is this what happened with you and Menno?"

"Yes, pretty much. I changed because I loved him. Then his smell went away. Or I got used to it—I got used to *me*. Maybe I just finally accepted who I was so the smell was OK, like I was OK now, even with all my faults.

"I don't know which it was, Lia. I just know I don't smell anything bad anymore."

"But you also said Menno was a lousy kisser at the beginning."

Ray smiled. "He was, but that was something I could teach him and I guess I did."

Lia had to repeat what she'd heard to Patrick. "You took everything I don't like about myself and my life and made it into a *smell*?"

He nodded once. "And pretended it was mine."

"You can really do that?"

"Yes."

"And Menno too?"

"It was Menno's idea that I try the smell thing with you because it had worked so well for him and Ray. I'd tried so many other things by then and was at the end of my rope. I was desperate. I would have tried anything, Lia; I would have *done* anything to make our relationship work.

"I'm not a creative guy like Menno; I couldn't have thought up the smell thing myself, but I am absolutely *tenacious* when it comes to anything I want badly. And I wanted you; oh God, I wanted you. Even when you kept killing me I wouldn't accept it because I was positive I could make it work.

"But now you've ruined everything—you actually called a *Hate Writer*! How could you without talking to me? I was half of the dance! I had as much of a stake in it as you! I *never* would have done such a thing without talking to you first."

Looking at this good, sweet man so clearly hurt by what she had done, Lia answered without thinking. As if the thought had a mind of its own and needed to be expressed without any diplomacy or artifice, she just straight-out said it. "Maybe deep down I like the way I am, Patrick. Maybe I'm just a naturally grouchy person who likes holding a half-empty glass.

"I'm really not being arch or cynical. I *do* get sad and bitchy a lot but maybe I'm just happiest when I'm *not* happy. When I don't like what's going on in my world and there are all kinds of things to complain about." Having said this, she wasn't sure it was true but it felt true. It felt like her heart was talking.

Ramona and Fionulla didn't move.

Patrick made a disgusted face. "That's *perverse*." For a moment, an instant, a bright flare of fury flashed in his eyes. It said he'd like to throw her across the room. But it died quickly and then everything on his face went back to sad.

He turned to Fionulla, asked for the papers, and tapped a finger impatiently on the table while she opened her worn leather briefcase and extracted two white sheets with identical text printed on both. She slid one across the table to Patrick and the other to Lia.

"This is the standard cloud release form you were shown when you first signed with the company. You can take some time to review it now, or even bring it to a lawyer if you like. But you were already told everything about it when your initial applications were approved. I'm sure you remember.

"It says you both agree to formally terminate this relationship, which was originally arranged for you by my company. As soon as it is finished, the cloud takes full legal possession of your story to do with as it pleases. You relinquish all rights to it although once it is terminated, neither of you will remember anything that has to do with the other or this relationship. Nor will any of your acquaintances who are aware of your connection." Fionulla glanced at Ramona, who nodded that she understood and accepted that.

Patrick took out a pen and signed his paper quickly. He slid it back across the table to the Hate Writer. "Tell me again what happens to me now."

"Nothing. You'll be returned to your planet with no memory of this. You'll continue to live as before. You can reapply to the cloud any time you like so long as you accept the conditions."

As she wrote her name, Lia said with sincere fondness, "I hope you do try again, Patrick. I *hope* you find someone great—"

"Shut up, Lia. Please don't say any more. Just sign that paper and let me get out of here."

She finished and handed the paper to Fionulla. The other woman checked both signatures then nodded as she slipped both releases back into her case. Lia took the flashlight out of her pocket, aimed it at Patrick's chest, and, without making eye contact with him, clicked it on.

A month later the Candelen sisters were sitting together in that same booth late one rainy September afternoon. They had run out of things to say to each other and both were looking out the window at the gray world outside. Now and then they could barely discern the faint wet hiss of car tires passing on the busy street.

"So what are you doing tonight?" Ramona asked while sliding her empty glass back and forth across the table, impatient to leave.

"The usual—eating dinner alone and watching *Love Gone Wrong* on TV. But you know what's weird? I checked the *TV Guide* and tonight's show features a character named Lia who spells her name exactly the same way I do."

Ramona looked up, half interested. "Really? No one spells it that way. It's always L-e-a-h."

"I know. That's why I've got to watch. I love that show anyway;

I'm completely addicted. Everybody I know is. Everyone watches it—men *and* women."

"What's her partner's name?"

Lia shrugged, indifferent. "Patrick. That's a nice Irish name, eh? On this week's exciting episode of *Love Gone Wrong* my namesake has a failed love affair with an Irishman named Patrick from another planet. Be sure to tune in.

"I've got to go, Ray. Say hello to Menno for me."

Two Poems

Martine Bellen

HEY DIDDLE, DIDDLE

And the cat jumped over the Milk Moon, the Spoon Moon, the Sleepy
Mean Moon. Not the Flying Fish Moon. Or the Tiger Shark
Moon. Moon of the Terrible. Moon of the Raccoon.

Not the moon that swung atop the arboretum: the Peach Moon. Peony
Moon. The Moon When Trees Pop. The Lotus Moon, Mum Moon.
Raspberry, Blackberry, or Sassafras Moon. It was the pelican that
perched on the Crane Moon.

The cat never jumped over the secret moon peeping out of swift, high cloud:
The Bony Moon, the Windy Moon. The Hungry Moon. Moon of Ice.
Singing Moon, o Mulberry Moon
With a full-moon's might.

The maroon-colored cat jumped over the magnificent Moon of Horses.
The Moon When Geese Return in Scattered Formation. Moon When
the Calves Grow Hair. The Moon When Leaves Are Green. The Moon
When Leaves Are Gone.

Never the dreaded Dragon Moon. The Panther Moon. The Moon When
Horns Are Broken Off. Never the Twelfth Moon when a million
brilliant eyes light dense bramble
Below that most hallowed one:
The Moon When Eyes Are Sore From Staring at Bright Moon-Lit Snow.

Martine Bellen

CAT

The cat belongs to
Me. The cat belongs
To the house. The cat belongs to
The other cat. The cat
Belongs to itself. The cat
Belongs to the forest. The
Cat belongs to the bird and mouse.
The cat belongs to the mountain lion.
The cat belongs to no one. The cat
Belongs to nothing. The cat belongs
To everyone, everything.

The cat has a name
That I gave it. Everyone knows the cat's name
Is not its name. It is *my* name for the cat.
Sometimes the cat refuses to acknowledge
This name and sometimes the cat
Plays along with the life I've created for the cat.
Sometimes the cat pretends that it doesn't live in a realm
Different from the one that the cat and I
Live in together. The cat has needs that must be met
For the cat to live in my house, though most of the cat's time
Is spent elsewhere. I invite the cat to live with me
So I can perceive some of the "elsewhere"
In which the cat spends much cat time.
The cat shares what I can't see by maintaining
An existence in my house and by responding to
The name I gave the cat.

I know there will be a moment
In the circuitry of space-time in which the cat will discard
The name and forsake my house for good
And will exist only in the fields
I cannot see without the cat living in my house. On that day,
I might say, "The cat has moved full-time into the wild."
Or I might say, "Miau-miau has run away."

Philosophers

Sigrid Nunez

THE WHOLE WORLD CAN BE divided into those who write and those who do not write, wrote Kierkegaard. Not that I've been reading Kierkegaard. I found these words copied down in an old school notebook. The notebook I found while cleaning out the storage space I rent in the basement of my apartment building. Not a chore I enjoy: throwing out stuff I haven't looked at for years to make room for other stuff I know I won't look at for years. When I dump the old stuff in the trash, I am blessed with a moment's elation. But as soon as the empty space is full again, I feel a heave of something like nausea.

I once heard about a woman who watched her house go up in flames from a diner across the street where she sat wrapped in a blanket, drinking coffee. I felt the most amazing sense of freedom, she said. Like I could start my whole life over. In my head this woman sits in a niche alongside another woman I heard about (single, childless), who claimed that, in the space on forms where you're asked whom to call in an emergency, she put "Barack Obama." Women like these are my saints.

Not that I've never read Kierkegaard. The notebook is from a philosophy course I took when I was in college. I still have the books from that course. They belong to the part of my library—the far greater part—that I know I'll probably never read again and so plan to get rid of the next time the apartment is painted.

So I have studied Kierkegaard, and the chinless, slope-shouldered professor who to every lecture wore the same tan wide-wale corduroy pants and too-tight navy blue jacket stands out in memory. But when I think of Søren Kierkegaard, what's the first thing that comes to mind? That Danish mothers used to warn their children not to do something that might make them ridiculous by saying, "Don't be a Søren."

In high school I knew a boy who managed to get everyone to call him Ace, who often began sentences with some variant of There are two kinds of people in the world. Mrs. Mint, who was both our homeroom and senior English teacher, called him the philosopher.

There were two kinds of people in the world: those you trusted with your car and those you didn't.

Ace was almost two years older than the rest of his class because a near-fatal viral infection in childhood had caused him to start school much later than he should have. He drove a gunmetal Chevy convertible with oxblood interior that made me think of a gutted shark.

There was the kind of person who said, Let's split the check, and the kind who reminded you you'd had the extra beer.

What could have been annoying was charming, or, at least, tolerable, because Ace had the cuteness of a Brat Pack star—though this was many years before *The Outsiders*. If anything was annoying, it was Mrs. Mint repeating that Ace looked like James Dean, which just wasn't true, even if we knew she was really talking about his aura.

Mrs. Mint was an unhappy woman with tastefully teased hair and large, distracting breasts. Her aura was that of a woman whose husband had married her for those breasts and was now tired of her. She often sat on her desk with her shapely legs crossed, one foot jiggling nonstop. This too was distracting—especially if you'd heard it said that a person engaged in this nervous habit was unconsciously masturbating.

Whatever text we happened to be studying, Mrs. Mint seemed able to find an excuse to lecture us on the dangers of marrying too young, or in believing what we saw about love at the movies. She wasn't dislikable—compared to other teachers, she knew her stuff and had a pretty decent sense of humor—but being cooped up with her for a whole period on her darker days could be taxing. When the bell rang, you'd see an unusually large number of kids hitting the water fountain outside the room before moving on to next class.

Mrs. Mint loved her little philosopher, openly flirting with him, her foot going like crazy, and Ace ate it up, not caring how much he got teased for it. He didn't appear to be fazed, either, by the fact that he knew Mr. Mint, who owned Mint Condition, a repair shop that specialized in antique motor vehicles, and for whom Ace worked from time to time, hand-polishing cars. As a boss, Ace reported, Mr. Mint was totally cool, but of course that didn't mean he was a great husband.

Toward the end of the school year, due to what could only have been some act of magic, I got to date Ace, and the classroom flirting started to bother me. In fact, at that time, unhappily married women got on my nerves. They seemed to be everywhere, including at home, and I just wanted to shake them all and scream at them all, *Who forced you to get married!*

Ace came from what used to be called, hushedly, a bad home, one of those nice, simple descriptions—like nervous breakdown, or retarded—that society was about to decide shouldn't be used anymore, even though they expressed perfectly what they meant. The few times I was at his house his foxy, if slovenly, blonde mother was usually shut up in her bedroom, sleeping it off. Needless to say, there were two kinds of fathers in the world, and Ace made sure I never met his. There was a chubby, special-needs younger sister and a fluffy, snow-white dog that watched Ace's every move with the melting eyes of a new bride. Their prefab home listed like a houseboat and reeked of vanilla White Owls and unwashed dishes. I once saw a handgun sitting out in plain view in the living room. It's not loaded, Ace said, whisking it into a drawer, as if that had been my concern.

Unlike the rest of the house, Ace's room was the picture of neatness, the bed so tightly made you could have played jacks on it. That's not what we played on it.

Mrs. Mint was wrong, the movies were right. I was seventeen, and my sweetest dream had come true. I rode in that convertible kneeling on the seat: a queen in a chariot. One day, in homeroom, I caught Mrs. Mint looking at me as I anxiously watched the door for Ace, who was late that morning. Though her mouth smiled, I saw the wish in her eyes before she could hood it: The woman wanted me dead.

With love come new instincts. When I confronted Ace he shook his head as if he was disappointed in me, then addressed me in the slow, deliberate speech he always used with his sister. He and I were dating. He and I were not engaged. He and I were not even going steady (this, with a mocking cringe, for of course he was too old for such crap). And besides, he was leaving.

It was true, pretend all I wanted that it was not. While the rest of us had been filling out college applications or weighing other post-graduation plans, Ace belonged to a group of boys who knew that it was written: They were going to war.

The whole time Ace was explaining, he was stripping off my clothes. I would remember this: how he would undress me like a woman, and later, when it was time for me to go and I was too shaky and clingy to do it myself, he would patiently dress me, head to foot, like a child.

Years later, I would date a man who, as a teenager, had been seduced by one of his mother's friends and who was still brooding about it. When a woman had a story like his to tell, he said, everyone saw her as a victim. But a guy crying rape because an older woman had thrown her hot, experienced body at him ran the risk of being laughed out of the room. (*Don't be a Søren.*) As for Ace and Mrs. Mint, it was unimaginable that he would ever see himself as anything but insanely lucky, a young stud who'd made a spectacular conquest he would tell the whole world about if he could.

Where we came from you thought not twice but many times before you'd do anything that would cost someone his or her job. And, besides, who knew what Mrs. Mint's husband might do to her—and/or to Ace. (I had a pretty good idea what Ace would do to me.) It was fortunate that these were the last days of school. English was my best subject, Mrs. Mint had been one of my favorite teachers, the first person I turned to for a letter of recommendation for college. Now I could not look at her without seeing how Ace must compare us, the mere thought of those breasts in the nude like a knife twisted between mine.

But she's so old, I said, in a feeble attempt at bitchery. In fact, she wasn't that many years older than Ace. I cried to learn that when they were alone together she didn't call him Ace, she called him Frank. And yet in my broken heart I think I knew—cold comfort though it was—that he probably wasn't all that different with her than he was with me. Loving women to death was not the same thing as taking them seriously. A major concern about his future that he'd confided to me was that, although he knew for sure he wanted to be a father someday, he had a hard time picturing himself settling down forevermore with one wife. And that summer, working as a lifeguard at the town pool, he gathered a few more girls and women to his smooth, tanned chest.

It was understood that once he left for basic training it would be over between us. And that's when my own little world divided in two: first love, before and after.

Spring break of my freshman year, I was home from school so I got to see him one last time. And what kind of girl makes a guy wear a condom the night before he goes off to war?

It didn't matter whether I wanted the baby or not, my body was having none of it. I could not keep one Saltine down. The doctor said mine was the worst case he'd ever seen. My mother, who'd had the same problem in her day, guessed the likely outcome and persuaded me to put off telling Ace. She and my father had finally separated, and she and I had become each other's best friend. Two females bereft of their men, so helpless and abandoned. So scared. She explained that a miscarriage was sometimes nature's way of getting rid of a baby that, for whatever reason, would not have been normal and healthy if it had survived. I thought of Ace's sister, but instead of relief came atrocious spasms of want and love.

My mother had been fond of Ace. She made me see that to burden him with my own trouble—to lob this particular bomb at a man facing who knew what horrors at war—well, why would I want to do that?

Tell him later if you have to, she said.

I never told him at all.

He wrote me only once the whole year he was gone, a letter so lacking in information that I was left to imagine for myself what it was like in that burning land with "good soldiers and bad soldiers" and "two kinds of Vietnamese." And though he signed the letter "Love," there was no love-talk in it. The shame I felt because of his misspellings and other mistakes, a shame I hadn't felt before—nothing hurt worse than that.

I'd chosen a school only about a hundred miles from home, but in the way that can happen once you leave it, home—and with it the whole past, as it seemed—felt more and more like a foreign country. Nostalgia is a baffling emotion when you're still just a kid. You have no idea what to do with it. My memories of growing up were mostly happy, but rather than seek out old places and good old friends, I stayed shut in the house whenever I was back, feeling like a stranger in town, a stranger who might not be welcome. The way to live, of course, was to avoid looking back. To look back was to be reminded that all this—whatever you saw and touched and loved—would also change. Would pass. The way to live was as if you had just been born: a person to whom anything might happen. College—mine, anyway—turned out to be a serious, competitive place that asked you to see yourself as one to whom not just anything but something extraordinary could happen. Women, especially, were expected to reach high—for things that women before them could never have. Whenever I did look back, and saw how narrow an escape mine had been, my head swam. By the time I finished college, both my parents would have moved on—he, west; she, south—to new jobs, new spouses, new homes. I would stay where I was, first to attend graduate school, then to teach, and thus—not counting the three years I lived on fellowships abroad—would end up with deeper roots in this university town than in the town where I grew up.

I heard that Ace came back from his tour of duty, but he didn't get in touch with me, and the older, prouder woman I had become would not get in touch with him.

The rest of his story is quickly told. I was told it more than twenty years ago, by Mrs. Mint, in a letter signed "Amelia."

"First of all, I want to say congratulations on your book. I have often wondered what happened to you, and as your former teacher I can't tell you how pleased and proud your being a published author makes me feel. In fact, that was my dream too, once upon a time, to become a writer. (That, and living in Europe.) This was my main reason for writing you today, but I do have something more I'd like to share.

"Do you remember Frank Dugger? I don't know if you're aware that after graduation he joined the army and was sent to Vietnam. He was lucky, he came back safe and sound, spared both the bodily harm and emotional devastation suffered by so many others who served, including, it grieves me to say, a number of my own former students. You may be surprised to hear that Frank became my second husband. We had two very happy years together, which, besides other great joys, brought us a son, Christopher. Then a terrible thing happened. Frank became ill. He was so young and strong that at first we thought it couldn't be serious, but it turned out to be cancer and at a very advanced stage at that. In fact, from the time of his first symptom to the day of his passing was a mere ten weeks.

"I know this is very sad news for me to be telling you out of the blue. But I remember that you two were friends, and I thought you'd want to know. You might want to know also that although he suffered a lot he never lost his spirit, and he wasn't bitter about dying before his time. Frank was always a bit of a philosopher, and somehow he found a way to come to terms with how such a bad thing could happen to him. He didn't believe in God, but in the end, and in spite of all the pain, he died in a state of acceptance. I do believe in God, and for a long time I hated him for letting Frank survive the war only to take him away like that, when the happiest part of his life had just begun. But over the years I have learned acceptance too. Mostly now I try to be grateful for the wonderful time that we did have together. And I will always thank God for sending this beautiful young man to save me, by which I mean that, when I was so hopeless I could hardly face the day, he made me believe in love again."

It was the kind of letter in which you might expect to find inserted a photo or two, but there was none. Instead, the image that haunted me for days afterward sprang out of pure fantasy: Ace holding Mrs. Mint in his arms while she nursed Baby Christopher.

Those who write, according to Kierkegaard, write about despair, and if those who do not write were able to write, they would write about the same thing. "Little" Kierkegaard, people called him. A powerful mind in a weakling's body. He had a crooked back, comically thin legs, and an ugly, rasping voice. At twenty-four, he fell in love for the first time in his life, and at first sight, with a fourteen-year-old girl, Regina. When she reached seventeen, he proposed, and she, equally ardent, accepted. But to love and be loved proved too much for him. There followed a bedeviled engagement, during which he drove both himself and the poor girl nearly mad. After a year he decided that any marriage of his would be cursed. Over his loving fiancée he chose "my most faithful mistress melancholy." And, in a scheme that he hoped would let Regina down easier, he pretended that all along he'd only been deceiving her.

Though all of Copenhagen was scandalized at Kierkegaard's jilting of Regina, it was not this that made the name Søren synonymous with twit throughout Scandinavia. According to my notes, that was the result of something known as the *Corsair* affair. The *Corsair* was a popular scandal sheet that retaliated for an attack by Kierkegaard—who'd basically invited the paper to do him the honor of abusing him—with a yearlong barrage of lampoons and caricatures so vile that he could not leave his house without being gawked at and taunted, for everything from his writing to his uneven trouser legs.

Despite her declaration that she would die if he failed to marry her, Regina quickly married someone else. This was a blow to Kierkegaard, but his love survived. Once, he had hoped that, as his wife, Regina might save him by bringing him into the fold of ordinary human beings. Instead, she made me a poet, he said. She was his muse, his Beatrice. He never fell in love with anyone else, and he never married. Alone, he begat existentialism. He knew that he was doomed to a short life on earth, and he wrote and he wrote and he wrote.

The Cursed

Christopher Sorrentino

TWENTY-ONE MONTHS INTO his misfortune, which had climaxed (he hoped) the previous summer when he returned from a spectacularly unproductive residency fellowship in the Sonoran desert of Arizona to the Brooklyn apartment from which his girlfriend had removed herself, their son, and most of the furnishings, Nolan Dane sat with friends at a bar on Columbus Avenue, where they had come from a late movie near Lincoln Center. It was a little after one thirty, and they were talking about an interview Nolan had conducted two years earlier with the biographer of Frederic Constant, an underground filmmaker.

"Pissed Constant off," said Trish, who had worked at the magazine that published the interview.

"The bio," Nolan said.

"Oh, no doubt. But the interview, I mean. He wrote to Rebecca, demanding a retraction." Rebecca was the magazine's editor in chief.

"What did he want retracted, I wonder."

"Nothing, everything, who knows?"

"I guess he's supposed to be pretty reclusive."

"No, no. This is more like batshit. Way beyond even knowing how weird he is. He felt his privacy had been invaded. That was sort of the gist, I mean. It was more like, fuck you fucking fuckers!" Trish laughed, recalling the vehement letter.

The filmmaker's grievance struck Nolan as ironic. Constant was best known for an anecdotal history of old Hollywood scandals he'd published in the early seventies. A coffee-table book for people whose coffee tables, back then, had been old footlockers or the enormous industrial spools around which utility cable had once been wound, Constant's book was a campy glimmer of Jazz Age decadence to bedeck the improvised, pre-gentrified spaces of the urban Aware, and a common object in the households Nolan had frequented while growing up. Although many of its stories had been refuted, sometimes litigiously, the book remained in print. Still, over the decades, it had become as much of a curio as the art deco dildos and champagne baths that figured in its anecdotes: its presentation of envious resentment as lovingly acquired intelligence had been a fresh gesture when it was first published, but its louche voyeurism had passed into the mainstream, and it had the disquieting air of being the product of strange fixations, rather than tabloid insouciance. Nolan himself owned a copy. What a project, he thought.

"You kind of want to say he's just a sad lonely old guy," Trish continued, "but I swear to God, Rebecca was trembling when she read the letter. He told her he was going to put a curse on everyone involved."

"A curse?" Milo drained his drink and, leaning away from Trish and Nolan, tried to catch the bartender's eye.

"He does it all the time, apparently. Third eye on his letterhead. Occult. California. Who knows?"

Constant's films were full of symbols. The iconography was private, jumbled, intense—*occulted* was actually a pretty good word—and paired with midcentury homoerotic imagery: surfers, construction workers, cowboys. As with his book, there was an exaggerated old-fashioned opulence to them that masked the whiff of prurience. That was how Nolan Dane might have written it up—possibly even how he *had* written it up—for his brief introduction to his interview with the biographer: his own sparse and facile contribution to the small body of commentary on the work of Frederic Constant.

What he wouldn't have said was that when he watched the films he felt that the insistent inclusion of such stuff—the hamsas, all-seeing eyes, pentagrams, skulls, pyramids, etc.—was an anxious reordering of the confused and apparently shameful longings the films incarnated. Not often did Nolan mistake confusion for beauty. He was vain about his critical abilities. But in addition to being wary of publishing anything that might be used against him by one of his academic colleagues—evidence of wrong thinking, even of homophobia—he'd wanted to be kind. Nolan found that the works of a coterie artist almost always inspired a kind of indulgent sympathy in him. His own father had been a coterie artist, a fact that had been even more influential than Nolan's complete lack of creative talent in steering him from the artistic path and into academic criticism. If you were going to choose a life likely to yield small triumphs, it seemed saner to choose one in which large triumphs were impossible to imagine, or anyway were indistinguishable from smaller ones to ordinary civilians. His father had accepted his own obscurity with good, if not necessarily good-natured, humor. He wrote poems, he published them in little magazines and with small presses, he taught. He would not have characterized himself as "cursed."

Nolan instantly believed in the curse, and because of the kindness he felt he'd extended to Constant, he believed it to be unfair. Even if the curse was not *there*, it existed as ill will, more of which he didn't need. Nolan had had enough of that. He'd left his wife and children for the woman who'd eventually left him, and he was just well known enough in the inward-looking world he occupied for both events to place him, briefly and uncomfortably, at the center of its attention. This wasn't the extent of his bad luck, but who was counting? The debt and child-support payments that were crushing him, the fellowships he'd been denied, the teaching positions for which his candidacy had stalled at the finalist's stage, the pieces he'd sweated over that were then killed by pissant editors, and, most disturbingly, the echoingly empty rooms he'd returned to from Arizona. He was a sometime adjunct at four universities in and around the city, where his students fled the lecture halls in which he taught his courses in Film History: 1895–1930 as soon as he hit the lights. Oh, and a bunion was developing on his right foot. He was counting.

Nolan believed: The curse *was* there, invisible but real as radioactivity, arcing across space and collecting, a cancerous plaque, in his bones and sinew. Things clicked. What he might have regarded as a coincidental string of unhappy occurrences, or at most as a streak of bad luck, suddenly had a single cause, became programmatic and relentless, with premeditated effects. He noted in passing that the bourbon had hit him all at once. His movements became overly careful, but he failed to regulate his voice.

"Goddamn it!" he said. "That fucking faggot son of a bitch." Heads turned along the bar to look at the three of them. Nolan was tall, and bearish; he had gone without a haircut for too long while (according to the sad—more woe!—little handwritten sign posted on the locked door of the barbershop) his regular barber languished in the hospital, and he had recently grown a mustache and goatee that, in addition to forcing him to recognize his dead father's face each time he looked in the mirror, gave him a saturnine look. He was wearing a down jacket, now toward the end of its third winter of heavy use, that would have looked deflated and weary below Fourteenth Street, but simply looked ridiculous here on the Upper West Side.

"Relax," said Milo.

"What, relax? I just figured everything out."

"Figured what out?"

Nolan was surprised when others didn't immediately recognize and sympathize with the steady deformation of his life. They sometimes even seemed to believe that he was no worse off than other people, although he chalked that up to a quality of stoicism he didn't actually possess. The bartender moved unhurriedly toward them along the duckboards, then leaned on the bar and smiled in a friendly way.

"Hot topic?"

"He's just excited," said Milo.

"I just found out I'm cursed," said Nolan.

"Another?" The bartender indicated the two empty glasses.

"Sure," said Milo. "This'll be our fourth."

"But who's counting?" The bartender took the glasses and dragged them, in turn, through the trough of ice, then filled them. Placing the glasses in front of Milo and Nolan, he put his index and middle fingers on a twenty that lay on the bar before Milo. "Should I just take it out of this?"

Milo and the bartender gazed at one another for a moment. The bartender's look was calm and unconfrontational. "Yeah, fine."

The bartender took the twenty and rang up the drinks on the old cash register behind the bar. It was a heavy, antiquated, mechanical device and the bartender appeared to take great pleasure in operating it, whistling as he depressed its stiff keys with a flourish. He returned with four singles.

"Thanks, Nolan. That was our buyback round," said Milo.

He considered apologizing to Constant, but then went on the web and found photos of him, preening and posing, shirtless. It was powerfully sad. At nearly eighty, the man had finally granted himself permission to do certain things. It seemed essentially middle American, this twilit striving to release some sad approximation of a secret and dangerous self, like taking up skydiving in retirement.

The photos only served to deepen Nolan's feeling that he didn't want to communicate directly with Constant. They were already locked in communion. The curse had been wafted his way and he was suffering under its influence. To apologize would only acknowledge its power. The face in the photos was unforgiving; it held in its expression a vast ungenerosity. *You all will pay,* the face said. Nolan thought about how photographs of the famous often seemed to reveal this sentiment, contained and disguised, that of the ill-adjusted child who accepted adoration as the only palliative for his resentment.

The common thread joining a Keith Richards to a Richard Nixon could be seen in the obscured threat residing in their gazes. Constant wasn't even that famous; his look was compounded by his failure to conquer any world but the tiny celluloid ones he had made for himself. The curse, the act of placing curses, had to be compensatory. A terrible power that awed but did not ingratiate.

He stood facing the west: I am not cursed.

He stood facing the south: I am not cursed.

The next day he received a letter informing him that his seventh application for a Guggenheim Fellowship had been denied.

If we can't get what we want from the living, we try to get it from the dead. Nolan would sometimes sit on the couch and have conversations with his father, his own voice ringing out in the empty apartment. Since becoming aware of the curse, conducting these conversations made increasing sense to him.

"I can't get a Guggenheim," Nolan would lament.

"An error of talent selection. Happens all the time. No curse."

"You got one. You got *two*."

His father would chuckle. "They don't always err."

"*Two.*" Nolan was indignant. That the fellowship money had kept him clothed and eating as well escaped him.

"These are competitive fellowships. I'd bet that hundreds more are applying than there used to be when I was at it. Rise of the creative class, and all that."

"Creative class, my ass."

"Call it whatever you like, kid. Point is, look at those pedigrees: Harvard, Yale, Princeton—need I go on? These people have been applying successfully for prestigious shit since they were teenagers."

"So it comes down to me getting lousy grades in high school?" Nolan would say bitterly. "I'm forty-six, for Christ's sake."

"I did advise you to approach your schoolwork differently, if I recall correctly. But you had to do things your own way, as usual."

"I finished, I got my PhD—"

"That much is very true. And I'm proud of you."

"—but I can't afford to live."

His father would shrug. "What can I tell you? It was a brief historical moment. For about five minutes conditions allowing for a genuine bohemia overlapped with a public-spirited notion that individual artists and thinkers ought to be supported. Totally anomalous.

Everyone knew the jig was going to be up sooner or later. Mostly, we had cheap housing. The schmucks who work on Wall Street didn't want to live in New York then. You didn't see movie stars pushing babies around in strollers in the West Village when you were growing up, did you? Monica Lewinsky walking around Christopher Street? I'll tell you, she would've learned a hell of a lot about blow jobs if she'd been living there back in the seventies. Did I ever tell you about the time someone offered me their loft on Greene Street? Alto player, moving to LA to play in one of those West Coast bands. West Coast jazz, for Christ's sake. Don't get me started. Anyway, all I needed was ten thousand dollars in what back then they used to call key money and I would've had two thousand square feet right off Prince. But who had ten grand? It might as well have been ten million. This was 1969. Your mother and I were paying a hundred and forty dollars a month on Bank Street. We lived where we could afford. Did you think it was some principled commitment to the garret? You think your mother and I wouldn't have moved to Westchester if we could have afforded it? Grow up. Move to Staten Island, then call me and complain. Or maybe you want to live in Newark? Maybe they have subsidized housing in Newark."

"Who the hell wants to live in Newark?"

"Not me," his dead father would laugh at this rich joke.

"What about teaching? I can't get a teaching position."

"Listen to Chicken Little. Maybe you just don't come off well. Did that ever cross your mind? You're a good kid, and I've always loved you immoderately, but you're kind of impolitic. A pain in the ass, sometimes, frankly. Besides, these things have never been easy to come by, especially for certain persons I could mention who refuse even to consider spending a couple years in some podunk college town someplace. You know, now might not be a bad time to reconsider that. You're single again."

"Oy."

"But no curse. In fact, count your blessings. Twenty years I taught in California so I wouldn't die a broke old man. Then I retired and guess what? I died anyway. You think that while the cancer was eating me up I was thinking about how much money I'd managed to sock away? For Christ's sake. When I think of all the time I wasted in that shithole when I could have been here."

"But you just said that you would have moved to Westchester."

"Now you're noticing that I tend to contradict myself? *Now?* If it's even a contradiction. I should have stayed here. Funny thing is, I was never the sick one, it was your mother. One of the big reasons we went was for the health insurance. If we hadn't, maybe she would have died first, and I might have had a chance to get my ashes hauled once in a while. Instead she gets first-rate medical care for two decades and I end up with the cancer. Now she sits on all that money I put away and thinks, incidentally, about leaving a big chunk of it to your cousin Selena, who knows a lot more about how to be nice to an old woman of independent means than you. Sorry."

"But what about—"

"You're kvetching about material issues, sport. This isn't a curse. You just picked the wrong line of work. Not to denigrate your talents as a writer and critic, which are considerable. But if money's the problem, where'd you think the money was going to come from in the first place? Look, don't call me when you're broke. You think I have any use for money where I am? Call your mother, for once. She looks forward to hearing from you, believe it or not, but by now she isn't holding her breath. Call me when you're having a spiritual crisis."

"But my girlfriend left me!"

"So? You left your wife."

Around here the conversations with the dead would usually break down.

The available literature (i.e., that which came up in a web search) counseled against actively attempting to lift a curse. Mostly, it advised spiritual steadfastness, a positive outlook, and avoiding recriminatory thoughts about the person suspected of having placed the curse. Some sources suggested speaking with a clergyman, which seemed massively unoccult to Nolan. Even if he'd had a clergyman to speak with, he didn't need anyone talking sense into him.

He bought clothes instead, feeling the usual excitement at picking up winter items on sale as the spring lines began appearing on the racks and shelves. A new down parka, three pairs of corduroys, a cashmere sweater, a pair of boots. He wouldn't be able to wear the stuff for long, but when it got hot again he knew that he could equip himself for less than two hundred dollars: He'd worn the same summer uniform of cargo shorts, short-sleeved cotton shirts, and Birkenstock sandals for twenty years. It was in this outfit, freshly showered and standing before the mirror in his Arizona bedroom, that he'd received the news from his girlfriend that she had taken advantage of the opportunity presented by his absence to leave him.

It had taken him a moment to remember to sit down. The conversation had been brief.

"Do you want to talk later on, when you've had time to let it sink in?" She'd sounded solicitous.

"Yes," he'd said. "I think that would be a good idea."

Actually, the news had sunk in instantaneously; it was not an enormous surprise. He did not believe that she was having an affair. She was an easily dissatisfied woman who felt that the accommodation of another's sensibilities or habits was an infringement of her human rights, and Nolan's sensibilities and habits often demanded a lot of accommodation. He'd thought that their having a child would change things between them, an old story. They had argued a lot recently; often over her behavior toward his older girls: another old story. And then there were the money problems. The third and oldest story. He thought of his ex-wife, who had succeeded in accepting his decision to leave. It had been the most heroic emotional effort he had ever witnessed. That his decision would now be exposed as a stupid one made him feel terrible, as if he had fooled her. Yet she was the first person he called.

"Oh my God," she said. "Why?"

"I don't know exactly. She's been unhappy. She said that she feels like she's not inside her own skin."

"What does it feel like inside her own skin?"

"Better. Normal. Alone. Who knows?"

"Oh, babe. Are you OK?"

"Not really."

"Of course not. You're not going to do anything stupid down there, are you?"

"What would I do?"

"Don't drive drunk."

"You know me, don't you?"

"You shouldn't drink."

"I know. We'll see. It's not night yet. It might get hard at night."

"It's not your good time."

"'Night undoes the work of day,'" he said.

"Whatever. Just stay out of the car."

"Where the hell would I drive? There's nothing here."

"I thought you said that it was beautiful and you loved it."

"It was. I did."

*

It was and he did but he'd had enough of it now. Its washed beauty was like that of a dried bone. A few nights before he left, he caught a coyote in the headlights of his car as he pulled into his driveway, glimpsing it briefly as it disappeared into his backyard, a rangy demon animal slipping back into darkness. Days earlier a mourning dove had flown into his bedroom window, killing itself. Surely this was what had carried off the carcass in the night. Bones and beasts, and a beating sun that diminished everything to the condition of dust. He shouldn't have come. He'd gone to his desk each day, diligently attempting to work, but went at an even more plodding pace than usual. He felt guilty that he was not moved to work better—with more determination, with a sense of the opportunity in hand, the higher stakes. He would have to file a report with the foundation after he left, gratifying their sense of the value of their magnanimity. What was there to say? Now, dressed in his new clothes, he would know what to say, of course.

> During the period of my residency I planned to complete preliminary research on a book-length critical study of mythic forms in American cinema, to outline the book, and to compose at least one and possibly two chapters. Regrettably, I was unaware at the time of the existence (continuing through the present day) of a curse that not only impaired my abilities to reason, to concentrate, and to attain productivity by any means, but which actively worked against me, influencing events in my life so that the circumstances in which I found myself, and the conditions obtaining therein, made it impossible to put myself in a frame of mind conducive to creative activity. None of this reflects upon the generosity of the foundation, whose accommodations and largesse would have been more than satisfactory under normal, uncursed circumstances. Unfortunately, I have since learned that this curse has robbed me of all agency. I am in the hands of malign and cosmic energies, harnessed by a distant enemy I was unaware even of having. Fortunately, my enemy inadvertently has made it possible for me to become aware of his activities, allowing me to curtail my own, thus at least diminishing his opportunities to affect me. You may be certain that, had I been aware of this situation at the time, I would almost certainly have postponed or even canceled my residency, since it proved to be a waste of resources that might better have been directed toward a more capable, and luckier, recipient. For that I can only express my sincere regret.

He'd read a few books and articles that he'd intended to read for the project, but mostly he'd sat, as if in an uneasy reverie, in front of his computer. He read Swedish mysteries and watched Hollywood movies in a random and extremely unscholarly way. He also drank beer, wine, whiskey, and vodka in such alarming quantities that after a week or so he'd begun carrying the empty bottles, at night, to an overgrown field adjacent to his studio, tossing them into the high grass there where no one would find them.

Even if everything had remained exactly the same at home, by the time Nolan was ready to leave Arizona he had become so bored, so vexed by the foundation's quaint and romantic notions of what a comfortable and ideally equipped writer's studio should be, so filled with desire for the noise and crush of Brooklyn, so freshly impatient toward the writers he knew who insisted that silence and solitude were the only conditions under which they could pursue real work, that he felt pushed to the frontiers of desperation. What form might that desperation have taken?

Then he learned that his studio had once been occupied by Sandy Mulligan.

Although Nolan had been living in the studio for weeks, he'd had no idea that his predecessor there had been the illustrious suicide until Carl, the residency manager, mentioned it to him one afternoon when he came by to oversee the semimonthly maintenance work that was done on the property and its grounds. Alexander Mulligan III had not signed the guest book in which previous residents had entered their names. He had not left behind anything of himself; no trace of his presence, or of the tortured psyche that had led him, one afternoon while his wife and two daughters were visiting friends, to slit his wrists in a warm bath after nailing the bathroom door shut and throwing both the hammer and his cell phone out the bathroom window, as if to guarantee his resolve in the event of a sudden change of heart.

Nolan had not been particularly interested in Mulligan's work, but the novelist's sad story made an enormous impression on him. Mulligan had left his wife and daughters for a married woman who, a few months later, broke things off with him to repair her marriage after discovering that she'd become pregnant with her husband's baby while Mulligan was away on a magazine assignment. Mulligan had gone back to his wife, but eventually she had thrown him out of the house, and he had then drifted for a while, defaulting on a large book contract in the process. At the time of his self-murder he was indigent, and his now ex-wife had taken him in out of pity. He had slept on the couch in his old apartment.

One afternoon while Nolan considered Mulligan's "case," as he thought of it, during one of his regular walks, he wondered whether his having learned of Mulligan's occupancy had turned him against suicide or helped him decide in favor of it. He supposed he didn't quite know what he could hope to accomplish through suicide. Nolan already felt nonexistent. He'd felt that way before he felt cursed. When he got up he would dress himself in what he'd worn the day before. Sometimes he would shower and shave and put on clean clothes before the end of the day, but often not. He ignored the phone and refused to listen to his messages. E-mails piled up, unread. He'd bought some furniture, reshelved his books to fill the gaps that his girlfriend's departure had left, read until his eyes stung. Took his walks. So this was the young manhood he had sometimes yearned for while he'd been buried in domesticity: a life of reading alone in badly furnished rooms, inching toward a ridiculous PhD. He hadn't remembered the lonely boredom and, once he'd recognized it, it occurred to him that what had been essential at twenty-five struck him as stupid in middle age. It was this more than anything else, his habit of sitting for most of the day and night, unbathed and in soiled clothes, bent over a book, that lent texture to his feeling of dissatisfaction with the way he was leading his life. For the first time in almost twenty years, since he'd met his ex-wife, he was unaccountable to anyone. His tests of this lack of accountability invariably depressed him. If he returned home late, or drunk, or both, it wasn't freedom he felt but only that no one cared. Despite the chafing of the responsibilities that had contributed to his leaving his wife (he hadn't begun to feel them yet with his girlfriend, but they surely had been due to arrive sooner or later), they had tied him to a recognizable and substantive self that existed in the regard of others. Underemployment, and its gradual stripping away of duties and obligations outside the house, had hurt his ego and made him feel insignificant. But to return to an empty apartment made him feel nonexistent. Any sense of relief that he felt on returning home vanished after he closed and locked the door behind him, turning on the lights to be greeted by whatever scene had sat unchanged in his absence, awaiting his return to mock him. More and more often he imagined himself dead on the floor. Arizona had prepared him for it. An exaggerated state of solitude. Three hours from the nearest airport, sun hanging in an enormous sky until ten at night. But Nolan hadn't intended to be fooled by the desert spaces.

He felt not privileged, not convenienced, but *intelligent* to be living in an era of collapsed distances, a time when remoteness could only be experienced through deliberate self-removal, an exercise of the will. They'd informed him that he'd been selected to go, and he went, not intending to be fooled. He had his misgivings: space and isolation had never seemed like prerequisites for working well to Nolan. He could not imagine a neurosurgeon needing to withdraw to the Mojave in order to cut into a living brain, a distant passing truck raising clouds of dust; could not imagine a general requiring a remote cabin to grapple, amid birdsong and the drone of insects, with military strategy. But Nolan had done it anyway, for his "career." He was given a nice studio that looked like a Hollywood bureaucrat's dream of a writer's retreat; the place a man who'd made his money in software, some accidental tycoon with his heart stuck in the humanities, would have built to write the novel long congealed within his wealthy and thwarted soul. Nolan was practically afraid to sit on half the furniture. An octet of Agnes Martin prints on the wall: the same, again, the same, again, the same, again, the same, again. The light hit the prints in shifting stages each afternoon; each hour brought a different look to them. No, the desert spaces hadn't fooled Nolan: They'd simply asserted themselves with nature's candor. He might have had a cellular telephone set to the nation's official atomic clock, but the markers of time there were the most primitive, diurnal, clouds massing above the mountains and moving in each afternoon, thunder beyond the furrowed ridges. Sunlight tracking the wall, those prints—had Mulligan noticed also the way those sketchy, fretful lines had flared and faded when the sky changed?—as the world turned. Had the studio, too, been cursed? Could curses compound? Had Constant's curse guided Nolan first to that desolate place, and then to the single location, among six studios scattered there, where a suicide had spent a few weeks learning to be beside the point? But Mulligan had been different. Mulligan's fate hadn't been in the hands of a vindictive individual. It had been a matter of chemistry colliding with circumstance.

Nolan's actual report to the foundation ended up being simple and direct, incorporating a mild but genuine complaint about the studio's lack of a printer: That was the extent of the inflammatory content. Meanwhile, he became envious of the dead writer. In newspapers, magazines, and all over the Internet people wrote of Mulligan: tributes to his humanity, his humility, his sense of humor, his helpfulness, his aim to connect with the hearts of his characters and his readers. Students, colleagues, friends, relatives, people who'd met him once at a party—all wrote, apparently wherever the opportunity presented itself, of the dead man's humane decency, surpassing in its abundant quantity and transcendent quality. Could it really be? Nolan wondered. Wasn't there one undergraduate toward whom Mulligan hadn't been able to conceal his boredom and/or contempt? One supplicant whose letter to Mulligan went unanswered? One organizer of a literary festival whom Mulligan had brusquely turned down? One author whose book Mulligan had panned? Mulligan had gotten through an entire career without once pissing anybody off? There wasn't one person who was happy Mulligan was dead? Nolan had enemies all over the place, he was certain. It couldn't just be one senile old queen like Constant. He'd failed students, cut colleagues off at the knees on panels, named names in his essays and articles, chopped books he was reviewing into catmeat. It seemed like the only reason to become a critic to begin with: I am right and you are not; this is beautiful, that is ugly, and you are either ignorant or corrupt if you claim otherwise. Working to convince people, by any rhetorical means, that he was right. To save their souls, let alone to make them *feel good*, seemed completely beside the point—unless it was possible that he, individually and alone, was doggedly working against the grain of the age.

Suicide. The backlog of phone messages and e-mails continued to grow as Nolan read Alexander Mulligan for the first time, with care, finding premonitory references to the author's demise embedded, like large and projecting boulders, throughout the novels, essays, and stories. It was as if Mulligan had been *planning the whole thing* from the moment he'd started publishing. Going over his own output in his mind, Nolan took pride in his subtlety: He was certain that, after he himself had committed suicide, his future biographers would have to work very hard to find any foreshadowing of it in his work. Anything he'd written that was tinted by the various shadings of depression and despair he'd experienced was *far* subtler than anything of Mulligan's. But Mulligan had beaten the rap somehow. When Nolan himself died, who'd even show up? Where would they even sit? How would they manage, all the factions Nolan had created with his disastrous management of his personal life? Instead of the unanimous silence—broken only by a few audible sobs—of mournful admiration in a crowded public space, he imagined laughter, sniping, and, worst of all, the bored shuffling of feet that became discernible at readings and other tedious events. Fuck them! he thought. He'd keep on living.

I am not cursed.

I am not cursed.

I have to stop talking to the dead, Nolan thought. Is it normal to be so angry at them? He called his mother, as his father had suggested. As usual, the answering machine picked up, and, as usual, it was his father's voice that announced that no one was available. He wondered if the reason why he didn't call his mother more often was because of the ghostly message that always greeted him. Just as he might not have been able to recall his father's face in all its supple variability even while looking at a photograph, he couldn't really recall his father's voice while listening to the message, which was delivered in an even, uninflected tone from which nothing about the speaker could be divined. How had his father sounded when he laughed? How had his father sounded when he and Nolan's mother argued? How had his father sounded when they'd sat together in the upper deck at Shea Stadium and he had yelled at the players down on the field? He couldn't remember his father's voice. Intrigued, he hung up the phone without leaving a message and dialed again and again, listening carefully, intently, to the message each time. After six calls, his mother picked up the phone.

"Who is this? Why do you keep calling?"

She sounded old, and her voice broke with phlegm as if she hadn't spoken aloud all day. Nolan was silent for a moment. But he'd never been able to lie to his mother, let alone hang up on her.

"It's Nolan, Mom."

"Nolan, what kind of game are you playing? Just leave a message."

"I just wanted to see how you were. I know I haven't called for a while."

"No, you haven't. But I'm getting along just fine."

"No problem with the asthma?"

"Under control."

"How about the, what is it? Lumbago?"

"You mean my gout?" She said it as if it were an object she possessed. "Fine."

"Crohn's?"

"Fine."

Nolan couldn't recall the rest of her ailments off the top of his head.

"I have to say that I'm surprised to hear from you, Nolan. I'd about given up on you."

"Don't give up on me," he blarneyed. "I've just been superbusy." For the next few minutes he recited various imaginary challenges he'd encountered writing his book on mythic forms in American cinema.

"It sounds very challenging, Nolan," his mother agreed. "Now I have to get off the phone."

She hung up. She was comfortable being abrupt like that, while he was always standing there listening to people and then feeling guilty about finally having to excuse himself. Benefit of old age, Nolan thought. But he knew that he was telling himself a lie. His mother had excused herself long ago. Even when his father was still living, she had excused herself, although Nolan hadn't noticed at the time. As long as his father was alive—forcefully and unassailably alive—his mother appeared to be living as well. The existence that she had evolved entailed being responsive to Nolan's father and to no one else, and when his father had died, leaving no trace of his force and revealing himself to be all too assailable, she had faded into a vestigial being. They had, his parents, talked a lot about who was going to die first. It was a regular topic. Both were convinced that his mother would be the one to go, leaving his father saddened, alone, but free to write his poems, free to reach out if he wished, but mostly free of the chaos of another person. Instead, his father had been annihilated by cancer in eight months, and the widowhood with which his mother had been crowned seemed less like the sad consequence of living than it did an imbalance of nature.

And then Milo had cancer, "*Bad* cancer," as Trish told Nolan when she answered Milo's phone. Milo had left three messages over the course of the week, but it wasn't until Trish had sent him an angry text that Nolan had finally listened to them all.

"What happened?"

"He went to the doctor because he couldn't shake a cold. He figured he had the flu." She started to cry. "It's lung cancer, metastatic lung cancer. It spread to the lymph nodes, now it's just everywhere. Why the fuck didn't you call back?"

"I'm sorry," Nolan said.

"He's going to be dead in two weeks, you asshole. He wants to see you."

"Is he—has he had visitors?"

"Of course he has."

"Oh, good," Nolan said, relieved.

"He wants to see *you*," said Trish. "He loves you. God knows why."

He hadn't been inside a hospital since his father had died five years earlier. Same act, different theater: On one side, the terror of these failing bodies, existing most intensely in the crises enveloping them, utterly removed from their lives; on the other, the hive drone of bureaucratic routine. It was a site for processing paperwork to the accompaniment of people dying. He considered bolting, but pushed on. At the end of a corridor, an orderly was buying a Coke from a machine, and Nolan asked him the way to Milo's wing. The man put the can to his forehead while he gave directions, as if he was tremendously hot.

Milo was dozing when Nolan arrived at his room. The bedside table was covered with get-well cards—Nolan felt a brief surge of envy—and a copy of *Joy of Man's Desiring* was on the table. I should have brought something, Nolan thought, but then excused himself, blaming Milo for choosing a hospital so inconveniently located. He picked the book up and flipped through it while he waited for Milo to wake up. He opened the drawer of the table and found Milo's wallet and his phone. He opened the closet door and found Milo's clothes, his coat, his boots, and socks. The presence, the aura, of these empty garments actually forced him backward a step, made the illness serious. To see them hanging there was an alienating experience, not one of intimacy. It was as if Milo were dead already, these effects remaining to provide emanations of his essence. Nolan could see dying in an accident, being murdered—the sudden end that flattened everything and everyone within the blast radius—but this was surprisingly harsh; it had the gratuitous lingering sense of Now What? Was it possible they thought he'd get up and put these clothes on again, walk out the door? Now what. You said whatever you wanted to a corpse—he thought of his conversations with his father—but to a dying man, what could you say? Nolan again considered running away, but Milo spoke.

"Last book I'll ever read," he said, gesturing at the book. "It never would have occurred to me."

"It's not something you think about," said Nolan.

"No. It isn't." He shook his head. "The bitch of it is, I never read Giono before, and now I'll never read anything else by him. Really beautiful stuff. I haven't read anything like it. My tastes are changing, and for what?"

"Pleasure?"

"That's what's left, I guess. Not something I'm good at. All my life thinking, worrying, outlining, seeing the practical aspects, and now all there's time for is pointless pleasure. I don't even know how. It's like being rich all of a sudden. Except, of course, not." He paused for a moment. "I try to fool myself, to see beyond this, tell myself that I'll read the rest later on, when I'm done being dead." He covered his eyes with one hand and breathed heavily for a few moments. Nolan couldn't speak or move. Milo lowered his hand. "How's your curse?"

"Please." Nolan shook his head.

"Hey, I believe you about it. Soon as I got the diagnosis, I said poor fucking Nolan. Now he's going to lose his best friend too."

"Fuck you."

"I'm teasing you."

"Don't tease me."

They'd both been slightly older students, exempt from the residency requirement of their school and living together off campus in a ramshackle cottage near the freeway. They took their studies seriously. The friendship had developed slowly, but blossomed all at once when they returned to the cottage one afternoon and found that someone had broken in and disdainfully spray painted YOU GOT SHIT on their living-room wall. They found nothing missing. The legend remained on the wall until they moved out. They'd told the story countless times.

They talked until Milo started to seem tired, or a little stoned, or both.

"Hug me," said Milo. "You're not coming back."

"Sure I am."

"Oh, eat me. I can hear you kvetching in your head about having to schlep all the way up to the East Side."

"I might come back."

"Hug me anyway." They hugged.

"It'll get better, you know," said Milo.

"It'll get better." Nolan nodded. He kept nodding.

"For you, it'll get better."

"Can I bring you anything?"

Milo smiled, and shrugged. "What could you bring me?"

After Milo's funeral, Nolan sat at the dining table in his ex-wife's apartment, his own former apartment, watching her fold bedding. An old friend of hers had spent the week sleeping on the sofa. A lucky break for Stephanie, Nolan thought: an accident of timing had enabled her to crash the funeral, and her unexpected presence had made her its star, a role she assumed as if it were second nature. Now she was gone; she'd left for the airport directly from the service, from her appearance, while Nolan and his ex-wife had traveled together to Milo's father's house, where they spent a couple of hours before returning to Brooklyn. If Milo had died one day later, Stephanie would have missed a terrific opportunity to call attention to herself, Nolan thought. Afternoon sunlight came through the windows facing the street, and he sipped coffee. She probably wishes, Nolan thought, that she'd been the one who died. He sipped coffee. Then she could have been the undisputed center of attention, he thought. His ex-wife folded bedding.

"Poor Stephanie," she said, "she feels cursed."

"Does she," said Nolan, smirking with secret knowledge. In the fifteen years that he had been acquainted with Stephanie, she had suffered crisis upon crisis, although in her case it seemed that the world always gathered her up and soothed her, allowing her to retreat and heal herself far from life's sharper moments, albeit with unfailing broadband and cellular signals with which to relay news of her recuperations and relapses. She fell in love and as quickly into disappointment. She had, in a dramatically recounted financial misadventure, bought and renovated an old farmhouse upstate, then rented a pied-à-terre in Brooklyn six months later to get away from the isolation of the farmhouse, and then had withdrawn to Yaddo for months, bitterly complaining about the noise and distraction of the city, apparently having forgotten about the farmhouse. She moved to Paris and hated it, moved to Los Angeles and hated it, moved to Austin and hated it. Inevitably, amid such adventures she would meet her heart's next deceitful thief. Yet money and opportunity always seemed to fall out of the sky to rescue her and subsidize the latest calamity. Stephanie was not cursed: Bad luck for Stephanie invariably meant that some inexplicably disproportionate stroke of good luck was steadily heading her way. Even better luck, Nolan thought, than the opportunity to make an unexpected appearance before all their friends, and at the funeral of one of their own, as Nolan had overheard Stephanie put it. His ex-wife folded bedding. Stephanie had done little, Nolan thought, to discourage the notion some people had that she had dropped everything to fly in to make her appearance at Milo's funeral. He sipped coffee. In this way, she had become not merely the *star*, but the *hero* of the funeral. As if he were introducing some sinister fact of which he was the inordinately proud discoverer, Nolan announced, "I'm sure things will turn her way soon."

"Oh, they have," said his ex, tucking a comforter and a pillow under one arm. "She got a Radcliffe Fellowship that starts in the fall. She's just not sure where she wants to live between May and September."

She put the linens away and they started bundling up to go outside; it was almost time for her to pick up their younger daughter from afterschool and she had invited Nolan to accompany her.

"She'll be thrilled to see you."

"Don't I see her enough?"

"That's not what I meant," she said.

He walked through the streets of his old neighborhood at her side. They'd picked it together, the neighborhood, back when nothing had felt like a curse, when he had lightly worn the most discouraging setbacks, when the idea that there might be any "place" in the world he was supposed to occupy other than the one at her side would have been alien to his very conception of self. He had just started as a lecturer at the School of the Arts and the hour-long commute from a Brooklyn rental seemed preferable to living in one of the tiny, dirty apartments they'd looked at uptown. The chair of the film division, a man not much older than he was, had invited the two of them over for drinks at his own elegant, university-subsidized apartment on 111th Street, and Nolan had observed in passing that, with its high ceilings, ornate moldings, parquet floors, and spacious, light-filled rooms, it was nothing like any of the places they'd "viewed." But only in passing: Life was about nothing but moving forward, and there was still so much territory left into which he would steadily advance. Now he couldn't figure out if he had been too dumb or too smart to be envious. Now, as they walked the few blocks toward the school, the renovated brownstones loomed on either side of them, lining streets that had become prosperous in the intervening years. Houses and homes. Middle-aged men and women with dogs and children, toting sacks of groceries and soft leather bags and car keys, talking into their phones and making plans. They looked like him, but they were nothing like him. When they left the house in the morning, someone somewhere expected them. When they returned in the evening someone was waiting, or they themselves would wait expectantly. They owned property. Their credit cards worked. Their money made money. Their parents flew in from the suburban greenswards, sprightly in their white sneakers, for holidays and extended babysitting stints. They had elective surgery, the kind that left them with bandages and braces that had the effect of making them look fit, rather than injured. They abhorred smoking, drinking, passing out on the subway late at night. And none of them was cursed. Dungeoned in the human breast, Nolan reflected, doubtless secrets lie. But if that quotation had ever consoled him, it didn't today. He thought it very likely that not a single one of them would ever sit on a bed, hair still wet from the shower, to be informed that everything he had assumed would be in place, even had taken for granted, had changed, vanished. Not one of them would ever feel the particular dread of pausing before the door of his apartment, key in hand, trying to prepare himself for an encounter with the emptiness waiting inside. Not one would ever walk into his home to confirm that it had indeed been stripped of the people and things that belonged there. Not one—except for the patient woman who walked beside him: the patient woman who had seemed to him a nag, the patient woman who had seemed to him to always misunderstand, the patient woman who had finally begun to bore him, the patient woman who, abruptly, had not been enough. They were two of a kind, as fully so as he once had imagined them to be, when they had first fallen in love: Together they walked through the streets, the streets they'd chosen together, and together they saw all the people living the lives they should have lived.

He decided vaguely that he wanted to speak to her, to discuss things with her, so he hung around until she invited him to stay for dinner.

"I'll buy another," he said, after he'd drunk most of a bottle of wine standing up in the kitchen talking to her as she prepared the meal.

"Oh boy," she said.

He walked to the liquor store, where he bought another bottle of white wine, and a pint of whiskey that he put in his coat pocket, for later. When he got back to the apartment, his ex-wife had just put the food on the table and was rousting the girls from where they and their belongings were sprawled around the living room. It took a while. He opened the second bottle, poured glasses for himself and his ex-wife. He should have bought a third bottle as well—this feeling didn't register in words, but only as a tension that pressed steadily upon him until he remembered the whiskey in his coat pocket.

"We have to eat at the table?" his younger daughter asked.

"Don't you usually?"

"Not always," said his ex.

"Never," said his older girl. "It must be for you." She said it as if she blamed him.

"Yeah, what are you doing here anyway?" the younger daughter said.

"Oh my God. Oh my God. We don't have to go to your house tonight, do we?" The older girl delivered this line staring into the middle distance as if at an unimaginable horror.

"No."

"So why? Are you here?"

"Mommy and I had to go to a funeral today."

"Who died?"

"A friend of ours. Milo."

"Daddy's friend, mostly."

"What'd he die of?"

"He was cursed," said Nolan.

"He had cancer," said Nolan's ex, ignoring him.

"Mmmm. This looks good," said Nolan.

"Bleucch," said his younger daughter.

"Just eat it," said his ex-wife.

"I agree," said Nolan, authoritatively. "Your diet is shrinking to practically nothing."

"No lectures, please, Nolan."

"Just trying to back you up."

"I can handle things here," she said.

They ate mostly in silence. By the end of the meal, the wine was gone and Nolan was eager to get home to read and start on the whiskey. He couldn't recall exactly what things he'd wanted to discuss with her. The acute nostalgia that had taken hold of him that afternoon had dissipated as the familiar and stultifying rhythms of his former life had forced him into step with them. No, he didn't want this. It was yet another thing he liked the *idea* of, the *idea* of a once-perfect marriage, the *idea* of these children. And Nolan wanted only to be able to claim them as his own, to stop being nonexistent, to have something more than an old man's spiteful curse as the measure of his significance. He wanted only that: *ideas*, once instantiated, were good only if they could be stored in a drawer to be taken out occasionally and admired in all their unchanging beauty. Then put back, sold, given away. *Things* didn't have histories, they only had provenance, chains of ownership. *Things* weren't wary of him, as his ex-wife and children were. No heirloom wept in its cabinet, no masterpiece resented its neglect. These *people* indicted him with every glance, intentionally or not.

He helped clear the table and helped cajole his younger daughter into the bath. His older daughter settled back on the couch and disappeared behind the screen of her computer. Nolan put on his coat and paused by the door.

"Well," he said, "thanks for dinner."

"It was nice to have you," his ex-wife said. "I'm so sorry about Milo."

They paused awkwardly for a moment. He kissed her on the cheek and left. What else could he have said to her anyway? "Hello, I'm cursed"? What could it even mean to her? He'd thrown his ex-wife into a pit without a moment's warning and she had managed on her own to climb out of it. He did not flatter himself with the thought that their good relations were any reflection on his own virtue. After he had returned to Brooklyn from Arizona she had come to his apartment and brought him two folding chairs, a kitchen knife, and a colander. It was an opportunity for her to point her finger at him and laugh, and she'd brought him housewares instead. Was he now going to insist that she take that opportunity? Cursed? His ex-wife liked him. His daughters were healthy. All was well. He was welcome, sort of. *I am not cursed,* he said.

After Nolan got home, he found that his girlfriend had called for the third time that day. His—their—home number, this time. He relented, and listened to the message, pouring himself a glass of whiskey. In a slightly put-out tone she asked him to please call back as soon as possible. It was a scheduling matter, having to do with their son. Nolan managed to forget for long stretches that he now had a third child with whom he did not live, although whenever he was reminded of it he had no trouble remembering for a while. Still, although he missed his son, it was his girlfriend he missed most grievously.

What had she wanted, really? Nolan couldn't remember: She'd

always claimed that he hadn't been listening, maybe she was right. Now she was free, apparently—he wasn't sure. Whatever it did feel like inside her own skin, he knew that she was as alone in there as he was, and he knew that, as much as he missed her, as disturbing as her exit had been, he was at home in the clear space left by her absence. Letting go of her as a force in his life had been easy, just as, in the end, it had been easy to leave his ex-wife's apartment tonight. The chaos of another person. And yet. And yet.

He'd been invested in Constant's curse, but he saw now that Constant's curse had a distinctly unsatisfying, incomplete feel to it. What could Constant have known of him? The generic questions he'd asked his biographer? The biographer had gone on to receive an award for the book. Constant's films had subsequently been issued, for the first time, in a boxed set of DVDs, remastered to bring out every grainy detail of his various sixteen-millimeter obsessions. Rebecca had received a National Magazine Award for General Excellence for that year. These things hadn't occurred in a vacuum. They certainly hadn't occurred *in spite* of Nolan's labors. He'd read the book, he'd watched the movies. Then the two of them, critic and scholar, had met, one yammering at the other for a couple of hours, filling the room with a stuffy, overused atmosphere. This was what Constant had based his curse on? Boilerplate? Self-satisfied comments from inside the smug-bubble of the overeducated? Nolan refused to believe that his life had fallen into ruin not because of something he'd done that was the product of his mind at its most fertile or creative or devious, but for something he'd done mechanically and formulaically. Suddenly it struck him with the force of a great idea. This was perhaps how it went. Through your very own prescription, the mechanism of your compulsions and rotten habits, your prejudices and phobias, you led yourself to your own destruction.

He lay down on the couch and closed his eyes. He tried hard to pray, to ask for help from a God he'd never been certain about. He was rewarded with a vision. Rilke wrote that one carries one's death within him, "as a fruit its kernel"; Nolan's reward was a vision of that death. He saw himself in his seventies. It was undoubtedly his own face, seamed and pouchy, framed by long—longer than he'd ever worn it—thinning gray hair and a patchy gray beard. His eyes were querulous. He wore old jeans and a turtleneck with a sagging collar under a heavy flannel plaid shirt that looked like, that might even have been, the very one he wore around the house now. It was his apartment—darkened and vague—but he knew it was his with the certainty of a dreamer. He gazed at himself as he might have gazed into the depths of his own reflection: He had appeared before himself as suddenly, and as alone, as he might have appeared in a mirror. Was he alone? He stared at himself; angry, hurt eyes stared back. He wanted to be looking into a mirror because he was afraid of the vision's extending past the boundaries of a mirror's edge. He did not want to see whatever, or whoever, else was, or was not, in the familiar, run-down rooms lying beyond. This was not a face that he could associate with success in any sense of the word. This wild hermit's face was enough to tell him what he needed to know. He was frozen, fearful that if he moved, the totality of all that was yet unknown would become clear to him.

On Repetition
Elizabeth Robinson

Have I imagined

what it means to lean

against?

Have I got the melody fully within my head,

my literal head, not a mind, but bone

and hair and the tune

recirculating before it loops

toward the throat, intercepted

by the tongue that pushes it forward—

was it pushed forward

of the mouth

through the lips

to be said (and not sung)

again?

Wasn't the obsession other

than a body? It was a chair

that one sat in, and another

tried to sit in as well. Wasn't the chair

rigid enough to pull

the clothing

off, to turn the

face to the table, a meal there—

one and the other that the

lips push forward—

food and furniture,

rivals who wait

an arm's length away,

melody, like hair, tugged

to its protein, fed its

body to the place it

sat, this out-

of-reach structure.

Can a repetition interrupt itself?
Can a map be the repetition
of where a body has been?
Can the body perspire on the
basis of memory? A tune
embeds itself in muscle, hair,
tongue. Does

the gesture remember itself
as return, as repetition
even when the hands tug a different
shirt on or off?

Was memory a question that was liable
to betray?

The chair left a bruise on the leg,
didn't it, and by this the body repeats itself,
and states that it wants
to repeat the climbing back to
what it wants, to a structure
that is too rigid to hold it.

Elizabeth Robinson

Doesn't the question repeat itself
simply by being asked, even the first time? Does the shirt fit
as it peels away from its torso, shoulders, arms? Didn't

they walk a long way, separately and
together? Is the chair a garment
the way a pair of pants is, that both
cover the body and so hold it together, and
does a lover also hold the body while

instead uncovering
it and, in that way, is a lover a chair? Did
they walk to the chair, did they climb
into it, did the
tune leave a little bruise on
the thigh?

Were they moving or holding, holding
nakedly, to the tune, a tune endlessly
subject to interruption?

Weren't they exhausted with their own
creaturely protein and bone, breath, tongue, and hum,
as it failed its own pattern?

Had they followed this route before, many
times before, would they have found
themselves also afterward, as they were, straining
against the furnishing that says a question is sweat, that a refrain
is sweat against the curve it wants to make, because

wasn't it memory that they wanted to recur? Didn't
being out of tune mean stepping outside the tune
while still remembering what, in truth, the tune is?

I Get Her Up in Daylight

Andrew Mossin

IF DAYLIGHT THEN I. If daylight then I must be with her. I must be with her in daylight when she is waking and I am alone with her. I must go down with her in daylight and wake her until she is with me again, and the gloom of winter parts, and her eyes open again. I can see the light in her eyes, I want to see the light in her, each eye when she is awake and I have been sleeping, the light still dirty on the floor of our house where we have been sleeping. The last days are these and she is sleeping beside me in my arms. The last days are these and we are sleeping in each other's arms. I hear her waking in my arms, the body she is and the body I have become, sleeping in each other's arms. The light is stretched thin across the line, and when she wakes and sees me there is a crayon lifted into the sky and the color is like no color we have seen, drawn onto the surface of ash-blue sky, like the first days of fall when she woke in my arms and held me close to her bosom, the color held like that between thumb and forefinger, so that she and I lie beneath the lines of color in the smooth grass and there is no one else on earth who can comfort or console us and no one we will know in time who can offer us a way out. But I will come to her as I always have. And if she wakes before me I will come down the stairs and lead her back to me, as the daylight moves into spaces where it wasn't, no one awake but us in the early-morning shell of daylight. No one is awake when she comes forward in the light, a body partway mine, comes forward and leans into the light, a sweetness to her withdrawal as she and I form a trinity from which one member is always missing. The sun is a cage of light, and when she opens her eyes, blue to green when she opens her eyes, I come and sit by her awhile, distilled by what comes to us, the light in its season, summer or spring, she is waking with the light in season, and we dream together of the seashore, its patterns forming sunless night in mind as we come back to it and walk its shore together, just before dawn in the blue light of dawn walking together as we have all our lives. In the water there is the blue and unsettled light of late night, then its bluing formation around the edges, a precision to the way we encounter each other, the place we make in time with our bodies. Her body that rests upon mine, nearly my own, like this hand I am extending to this day, out of myself, and hers that comes back through the fine-knit light of morning. We come back and forth through the long slope of water, a line pulls taut, and we come through it again. She is always telling me my wrists are still quite strong and I can lift her, carrying her body down a dreamlike state, a dream of water we can have together. She is telling me the surface of the ocean is bright with color, there are discs in the water, she has gathered them up and put them before us. The light is like a cave enclosing our bodies, smudges of shadow where she was dreaming, where she and I were standing together. In daylight facing the shore, she is less able to say it, to frame the words when the words won't come. Now and again there is the pull of the flame across her ankles, sense memory that is oblique when it occurs. There will be winter again, she counts on her hands how many winters she has known, how many are left, she counts on one hand how many are left and waits with her hands on her knees that are bare, she counts to the rhythm of the seasons left, and she hears what she has always heard, the internal rhythm of the days and hours left to her, she will count them back as she did at night when she couldn't sleep, until falling into it finally she realizes she can't remember his face any longer, its contours and concessions, she can't form an impression in mind of what he will look like when she goes. I wait with the kettle downstairs, hot then cold again, the water that was once blue is turning copper, she is waking in the light when I come inside the room, it's warm where she was, now she is against it, and I take her by the hand. In the water she says there were stones floating in circles, the stones were floating then she was working her way across each of them, paraded through the light, she is telling me the first time she went in it was cold, he took her, in daylight he took her to the sea and they stayed until dark, fish 'n' chips by the water's edge, he bought her a small memento that she keeps on the dresser with his portrait. The man is nameless but I know him by sight, the man could be my father, I know him by sight, he is standing near her, in the picture they are together and I am not there where they are standing but apart from them. One after the other they go into the sea and I see them going away from me, then returning, and he is like my father but not and she is like my mother but also not, and I lean into the light where they are going away, a sloping surface of water, she slides into him and away from me, I slide underneath them and hear the crack of her ribs when she hits the wave, and it is altogether one force of water that pulls him away from her, she and I where he is not.

When she wakes it is half past one in the afternoon and the light is coming in and the street is quiet, the street is always quiet, and she tells me there was no need to hide or be hidden, there was no need to be seen or unseen, the world of events she says to me is happening in accord with God's plan, it is a plan she says, plain and simple, God will make the way clear to us if we attend. And she recalls me as I recall her, and it is nearly a pattern of making like shapes in pure air. I can tell the difference between a triangle and a circle, can tell the difference between a rhombus and a sphere, we are learning the forms of things while she tells us it is always better to tell the truth, it is always better, the form of telling the truth is always better she is saying than not telling the truth. When she rises from her place she says it is smooth where she goes, it is smooth and delicate and without form and part of what we know is that it must be without form. Silence is what we see of death, it is a form of death, she is telling me, but not death itself that has no form, it is like no other thing we have seen or tasted or touched, it is this thing without form that we need to give form to. And I am sitting on the floor all this time and by her bed is a copy of what she has been reading for ten years, the blue-green binding of the collected plays, she has been reading them for ten years, and I push the binding back into place where it's been torn, small tear in the binding, and she takes the book from my hands and places it back underneath the bed, ten years underneath the bed she has been reading the plays backward and forward when he is not there, she reads and I sit by her side and listen as she reads, the words in stray syllables forming shapes in the air I catch, don't catch, as she reads what she can and I sit by her on the bed and listen.

When the visions come of her they are often like this: parted lips, small childlike glances across the room to find me where I am standing and waiting for her to beckon me nearer. She is resting and I am resting near the small white pillowcase, a heart-shaped pillow on top of another white pillow, she is resting with them, and I see her lifted on her back and the stones underneath, stanching the flow as in childhood her mother had said to her when it got bad the best way was to lie down in a cool bath and let it bring the flow down into the white cold sea, white against the flesh. When she lifts her eyes and holds my hand, she tells me it's like she's going into the sea and the pain lessens and she can't feel her legs when they go under and she is going under into the sea and my mother is this close to death I think and this far from coming back to me, and I listen as she reads out the lines from her blue-green book of plays and the whistling sound of trees in a wind brightens, then ceases, her words brighten then cease, and it is all she can do and all I can do to remember how many seasons are left. She can't recall how many there were, how many she had left, what the plan might look like at three o'clock or if there would be another three o'clock like this one, the one that had just passed, so that when she looked up she was looking toward the mantel and the clock and her face had no expression at all, blank as a root of white balsa in the palm. Sometimes it is crooked like memory, other times it is soft celluloid crumbling in the hands. Each instant is a variant of one instant that repeats. Iris. The eyelids shut, the eyelids open, like a doll's eyes she opens them to me. She is lying in the layer of linen he has put down for her, I have put down a layer of linen for her, and her flesh is the book I am writing on, the sheets of her body fall through my hands, the words do not appear at first, at first nothing appears, then the arching of the t's and u's and the wide-mouthed opening of the o's, she leans down to kiss my hand, the stenciling is imperfect, everything we have done has come to this, the memories are imperfect, their design is like that of a calendar thrown into water, the pages ballooning out in the water, months collapsed smudged in water as the tide moves them again until the form of the months vanish, rectangles of color vanish, her hands vanish in the smooth water, the hands can't catch all that falls away, what falls away falls of its own accord, there is the simple reality of such events, superreal as if displacing everything that comes before or after, as if one day there had been this thing she started to say, and then it stopped, midpoint, stopped just as the writing started to say who she was, vanishing into layers of unsettled grass, bright uneven ripples of water.

In visions, she says, I understand how we came back, I understand how we moved toward death and then came back from it, and went toward it again, like a summer storm overwhelming the landscape, then just as quickly gone, so that when you woke it was past what you remembered, and what you carried inside your pockets, small things you took from your room, they too were like talismans, bright bits of something you thought were important at the time and could count on as you could on rope to cut into your wrists or light rain to drench you in its smooth falling pattern. She wants now, she says to me, mostly to understand the body that moved her, that moves, as it does, into these rooms again. What matters she is saying is what we made here, the detached period between fall and summer, the period between winter and spring, she wants to remain attached here, she wants to say it was sufficient, there was a plan and we held to it, then kept the bargain as if one ever could do differently. It is to this we are bound like bodies to wild horses, she says it is not death that enters the system but the potential for death, the way light will move across a landscape in summer and you can stand almost beneath it, almost beside it, the light moving across the landscape, and it is mirthless and irreal and someone may come back and place his hand on your shoulder, turn you to him, and his body will affront yours and complete the cycle. There is always the pattern moving between things, the bodies held like captives in periodic dissolution, one is moving along the side of a house in sunlight, the perfection of a dream she is having, while the boy I was is standing beside a woman in her late fifties in a small garden in back of a house and I am watering the peonies and she is not there yet always there, and later she will come out to see me and tell me the peonies are white as balloons, white like her mother's hair whitened in the English sun, and she will lie down with my flowers on the ground beside her, smooth fleshlit flowers she will hold one then the other of them close to her, a wall of color will rise from between the sides of the garden and some appeal will be made, she will appeal to me to lie down with her and I will rest on the walk where the colors are dimmest and she will hand me the flowers one by one, magnolia and peony and bright daffodil, she will hand them to me as a stranger hands flowers to another in passing, a day in passing, she will say it's what we do, it's the lesson we make here, to keep these things between us, a mother and son she will say are two bodies placed in proximity, nothing else may be done, but they are placed here, in proximity to shield each other from the wall of color that surrounds them.

Days pass and she is walking at an even pace, the days come and go, she says it is enough to know they are behind us now, there's no need to regret what we did or didn't do, you could carry the weight of the world that way, there wasn't anyone to consider or bear ill will toward. The mornings were most painful, she hadn't been able to sleep well in more than a month, then another, now and again the glass shards piercing her soles, jagged edges of glass that cut into her, so that she would ask when will the bandages come off, when will the flesh heal itself. If she had been dead and brought back to life, the meaning of the act, if she had never gone who would be left to remember who was here. *Don't believe he had said to her once don't believe everything you are told it might simply be that a woman goes down as you are going falls apart this way and there is nothing and no one to help. It may be he is saying to her you may wake up and not be alone and want to leave this person and you do and then so you are alone and it is quiet and you decide in such a moment what you have already done already decided and later there will be someone else standing in front of you asking you what for and why but it won't matter you won't hear them.* When she wakes I pour the warm water onto her arms and legs and bathe her until she is clean, I am ready she says to go down and meet your father, there is no one alone, there is only the sound of the passing truck, then a bus moving distantly up another street, and she tells me she couldn't do it alone, she needed to know he would come in time, when he comes to her in time she'll be ready to let go, she'll be ready because he is there waiting for her and that will make all the difference. She is proud to tell me I am like no other, in the storm's movement when she wakes I am sitting exactly as she has left me, there are candles in a row, the beach walk is long and narrow, she is fifteen years old the first time it happens she tells me, her voice is like wood against my back, it wasn't with a stranger or anyone she didn't know, there was another fire along the beachfront and he said lie down beside me on the stones *the exact location of his hands I can tell you they were on my neck and breasts and he was pushing me down and the ferry was passing in front of us and the people leaning out to see like flags in a row on the water and his face was hot as it came down the sun high up and his hands high around my thighs pushing up* and when she woke it was always the same inside the long room with them while they undid her bandages and put salve on her ankles and heels. The burns would take time, there was a time, she said, I wonder how the world will look after, if I come back this way how will the world look, the light is not as I recall it, the light comes back down and I can feel my way to the staircase landing and move up the stairs like a child you said, like a child of another era and history, you are with me, I am hearing what has passed, and I wonder if you can tell me how it was I came to be here, what will the world look like when I go *his hands I felt them pushing up and one thumb pushed into my cunt and spread me on the stones and the light was hot in my eyes I saw him grimace his come grimace and he knelt down with it in his hands bent over it a sight of it like a broken piece of doll covered in a white film.*

Silence is the perfection of self, she tells me later when she wakes and I have come back to find her in an afternoon as if lined with paper and reconstructed from scraps of wire, flat pierced linen, small wax beads melted then dried on paper. I was sure that she would wake in time, the day was half over, I was cleaning in the kitchen, making myself useful, then saw her in the corridor like that, pulling at her bandages and the blood smeared on the walls, and when I came back she was sitting with a rag in the hallway and cleaning the walls behind her, bloody smudges reddening under her cloth, and her hands were cut from where the glass had cut her, and I helped her stand up again and she was white in the face and nearly fainted and I put my arm around her and took her to her room and laid her back down on her bed and didn't say anything and turned away and I went back with my rag and washed the trail of blood away, handprints of blood I washed away until my father came later in the afternoon and said it was enough, nothing more needed to be done, and he took me with him away from her as the light flooded the front porch in ashy tones and her voice came back calling for us, I could hear her calling, and coming back inside the house she was still lying asleep and he looked down at her and said *Let's go she's asleep no one is going to wake her now.* And we left her in the safety of strangers, in the safety of dreams we left her, and when she woke a little past one in the morning she called out to us and there was a tree moving against the glass and her hands felt for her lighter and she saw it was nearly over, the reds and blacks had faded, she saw there was no one near to catch her, and she felt her way to the staircase and looked down the way she'd fallen and saw the boarded-up window like a gash of shadowy light sprung to life before her, and it was as if she had come to find her way back across a walkway lit by streaming flares, glass bits cracking beneath her soles. And in the light she was walking with a stranger, he knelt down, he pulled her to safety, the nets were thrown, fish nets thrown into the water, green then blue she dove in under him and let him finger her in the dark, let him take her in the dark she said to herself *There's safety in his arms there's no one to see me go under when he takes me there is no one else* she was carried into the room, almost drowned, the first time she felt him she was in the clearing with him on white sand and his hands were up her dress when she fell down and the blood rushed out, she hadn't yet but now he wanted to again, between her legs the fire, she saw some spots of light, the way light eventually will cut into a landscape, and he curled around her ankles and pleaded with her to let him come back inside her and when she did she said it was nearly over before it began, his tanned skin brown against her pale skin, she said he closed over her like a storm cloud and passed until it was impossible to repeat, impossible to say what had happened in the sea that day when the man who had been a stranger followed her there and offered her his hand and she took it as a proffering of trust, as brief respite she said from what was yet to happen.

The second time was years later, he had known she would return, she needed to return as he needed to find her on the way back, strange that the face of a person could resemble no other's, strange that it was her face that meant all to him, as his to hers combined with others, forgetful, not forgetting. The days were lit up by what wasn't there, she knelt on the porch floor, his hand came around her waist and drew a figure on the floor, and later she was dreaming when he woke next to her and took her again, he had such lovely hands, she wanted to know the circumference of light as it entered her bloodstream, he was working with rhythm, a child against her belly, aching for what she wouldn't give, the dream was clothlike, burrowing into it she found her habitat, later in the skyline he undid her blouse and licked the moist crease between her breasts, he was pleased to have her this way, she said *I'm in no shape for anything and want nothing from you* the words dull in his ears *I'm in no shape for you and want only for you to go against what I have given.* The sea came to her in dreams while he stood near the bed and emptied her bedpan of urine, from one part of the house to another was perhaps forty steps, there was no system, no way to know for sure how it would come out, her voice calling for him or not, the days went past, one forgets to count, one forgets there is another beside you, there are just these twinges, nearly unnatural, as if you could cry out their names and have them all be with you again, like one waking beside her who took her hand and drew a figure with her blood, a sustaining vision of one then two inside her. So many are left wanting, so many don't see where it goes, she said to herself again and again I see where I am going it is not frightening I see the strands let me pull them together let me emerge without stain, and when he freed her that second time she knew it was also a pact made within herself, irresolvable, muted, shelterless as a bird may sometimes fly in the opposite direction from where it intended, coined sunlight enclosing leaf and wing in a rain of coded signals. Yet what did she remember of any of it, a day like this one when he slid into place like the possible figure of a man she had once called husband. Or was it entirely possible that no one was there after all? The man at her bedroom door or the boy inside the basement cabinet where he hid for seven summers before being discovered. Did she hear laughter or was it his muffled cry downstairs, the vision of him laughing or crying, the claustrophobic density of his body near hers. Was it an appeal she heard, the boylike cry crimson in blue nights, and then the boy become nearly a man, then not a man, the clockwork dissolution of their bordered boundless figures as if he were always present and always impermeable, a bell lifted down into the waters and submerged, and she became wordless as he spent his days near her, like a body of sulfur she spent her days near him, envisioning a world rent by lightning, summer storms, the purity of thunder forming in the sky, lightning bolts across the cobalt sky, she waited for them as he went back inside her dream. And it was years before that she saw another man, fatherlike, nonparental but familiar, a man with flowers in his hands, extended, as she had once written him *knowing their meaning to me and their cost I'm surprised you hadn't thought of this earlier* and he hadn't yet refused her, perhaps never would, when he laid the flowers on the table and she was preparing for dinner and saw him out the corner of her eye and he said *Iris Iris Iris* over and over again he said her name and she thanked him for what he didn't know and she said *I want to visit your home* and he said *It's gone it was destroyed* and she took his flowers and knelt near his leg and felt his woolen trousers with her palm and left the flowers on the floor and knelt at his side for their first night out in more than three months and he said *It's quiet the streets are quiet Iris we can go the streets will be deserted* and she looked through the windowpane onto the Kensington street and saw it was nearly over as the lightning formed a bridge between them and he was standing in his army uniform, a soldier stateless yet somehow proud of his bearing, and he hadn't yet gone into hiding from her and he wasn't yet able to refuse her and there was something blackened and strong and febrile in his gaze and she said *You are the haunted boy aren't you* and he looked away and took her hand and pressed into her palm a rigid palm leaf in the form of a ring and said *It can be for you to keep* and she had already risen from the table and seen the light shift and knew it was coming time to go.

Everything is distinct when she comes back, she is telling me it was all as it had to be, the regularity of their lives together that no longer possessed a center, a form she could read clearly or rely on. Even the notes she'd kept to forfend such misreadings were of no use. They lay like so many note cards on the floor, each one bearing the imprint of her hand, embossed in warped tinlight, serenic black legend scrawled over the top of one then another piece. Had she intended them that way she would have intended them that way. In the first days following the accident she could hardly breathe, she says it's likely she wanted to die, but couldn't bring herself to the end, it was an ending she couldn't have seen yet saw as one part of the plan. Hidden not destroyed by what was nameless. Hidden not deterred by what was impervious to change. It was always a possibility she said, the way we receive bad news, telling ourselves it was necessary for it to be like this, the hands make trivial gestures and the eyes dart back and forth over the closed room where once there had been some sign of life. But the sign is itself a forgery and the life long ago ceased to make a difference. So it was and wasn't an accident. It was and wasn't possible to say how many days she might have waited for it to pass over her like sea foam passes over a body and the hands rest and the torso rests nearly below the waves nearly above the waves, everything comes to rest where it must, and if you're gifted you can rely on pure instinct to get you back safely but sometimes you wait too long and the breathing goes shallow and you can take yourself under it a while and know that surely you will be found in time surely you will have the recovery necessary. The light shifts back to blue-black and the storms pass overhead and in one room she is standing without her son near her and in another I am watching from the doorway as my father and I gather her up and place her on the bed and help her as best we can. It is July 23, 1967. My mother is not dead. My father is with us then not with us. He is wearing wool trousers, a white shirt, a black belt, his hands are clean and hard scented from Clorox and he has gone back downstairs for more bandages. I inspect her like a wounded vessel, keeping watch for more blood, and I take my index finger and run from her shinbone up to her inner thigh and trace the muscle that has gone slack and kneel in to taste her thigh flesh and it tastes of piss and blood and when I come back she is still lying on her side and my fingers can't find her pulse and I think she's gone but hear her breathing and go back on my knees and wait for it a bit longer, the way we do when we know we can't be found out, and when I get up I take her clothes off the floor and find some new clothes for her to wear when she wakes, and I push the piss pot to the side of the room and stare at the circle of yellow briny liquid and see floating atop it a length of gray-red hair and it floats there like a branch floating in a small pond and I lean into it and catch a reflection of my face and peer down the hall and wait for him to return. He enters the room from the left and closes the door because he's used to having it closed and his arms are halfway up in shirtsleeves and he cuts open the bag and takes out fresh gauze and wraps her ankles in white gauze and the bandage is soon soaked through emulsifying like a print and he says to me that she will have to go to the hospital and he unwraps the bandage and cuts another length and rewraps her ankle and heel where she cut her foot on the glass from the window and it too congeals with blood and as I rest next to her I hear him moving downstairs. And I am aware of nothing else but the sulfuric odor rising from her limbs as she lies three more days on the bed before on the third day we come to find her nearly awake and I take her clothes from the closet and bring them over to her, the daylight she says hurts her eyes *close the blinds Andrew Christ close them* and it's half past one when she gets up and her cheeks are pale and her arms and legs are white and unsteady as she comes down the hall into my room, and she makes her way to my bed and lies down beside me and I can travel the length of hall back with her so that when she arrives and lies down and rests her mouth next to my ear I have already re-seen her, the images are stitched together so finely. And when she lies down and pronounces my name *An-drew An-drew An-drew* it's like a mirror being placed to my ear my name bent back over itself, flexed, renounced, and as her voice enunciates my name the syllables break apart to reveal her figure carrying a basin of warm water to my side and she lays the washcloth across my forehead and I see how everything has led us to this moment, it is common time we share, so that when she turns to face me I hear not one voice but three moving past us moving away from us and they are saying *The days and nights can't go on without something happening, there's no one waiting for us, no one cares, why don't you rest darling why don't you rest here your mama is here* and when I lean into the light her body releases its pattern like a body's breath going out of itself.

What cannot be remembered must be reconstructed, hands must build from the ground up, soft earth, trees must be aligned with the living mechanism of sight, as birds move through the sight lines of their history, the birds moving now one then two, the light has a history to it, the birds in the trees felled by what brought them here, to the garden outside the fence, the days passing, one then the other, to the third and final day when she appeared. He was writing with his left hand when he saw her in the garden, so much of what I recall can't be pinned down, a little later she came in and brought flowers to the table, the whiteness of her wrist as he lifted it like a broken stem into his palms, and I stopped and put down my pen and looked over to her, writing this at such distance from her body it cannot be communicated, the way she feels is the way she has always felt, her belly when I was young and lay with her on the bed, someone waits or doesn't wait down below and the places where she has taken me are beyond recall. When the daylight comes she is waking near my hand, I get her up, with my bare hands I lift her and her face is privileged and sad near the end of it, and I raise my arm with her arm, my leg with her leg, she is moving as I move, the bodies of mother and son, moving as they do, there is no other movement but this she says *I waited for you at the side and saw you the light was bleak but still there it was when you appeared and my mouth opened to hear you and my fingers curled around you and if there was another I didn't know him and if there is no other I will not keep him from you.* And the tale is woven rewoven, so there are parts inconstant parts that can't be told any other way, as if he and I and she were moving through the weave of our times apart and together, and what I heard is what he heard, and what he hears she has meant to tell him, she was not denying him anything, there was no one else for her to be, no other woman she could have been, motherless as she had been, now fatherless, and when she spread her palms on the sheets at night to show him the way it happened she showed both of us, my father and me, what it meant to have lost her when she was beginning to understand the force of her nature that had drawn her back to him then to no one. And it could be in that vision she had near the end she was alone when the light came through the window and she saw her father and knelt by him in the living room of their house and when he rose to go she went with him, a child barely seven years old in morning clothes she went out into the garden with him and walked to the gate and watched him go and heard behind her in the house behind them her mother calling for her to come back, and years later she would say it was the last time she saw him alive, he went and that was all and years later it was still all she could say or do in the face of his going, to see it happen that way as it would and did. And if she made appeal it wasn't to him or to any other, perhaps not even to herself, the days were passing, she let them pass one after the other, a lifetime of short spans of time held together like a rubber band holding pages of a book together, and to see it all happen again was part of it, so that the room would be once again crowded with color, light beams in midsummer, and it was the two of us in front of the light and her head was sealed in light and lying near her without words, with words but no voice, I heard myself talking in the circle of light that enfolded us *I will be there when the sun comes in, I will be there when the sun goes down, I will be here when the wind is high, I will be here when the wind is low, I will be here no matter what, I will be here no matter when.*

And it would be days going like that and the backward and forward of time is a jetty on which I rest, and the years are posts in the sea, and I am settling into it when I hear her on the landing again, the day before she falls, the day before the day after, and she is wearing her white sundress with pale roses printed down the bodice, her legs are newly shaved, and we are alone in the house and it is like summer but not quite summer, and she has come down from her room and a smile seems to show itself on her lips, then disappear, in her eyes there is an absence of emotion, and if we were in the sea I think we would be fine, we wouldn't need any words, the sea would settle around us and then we could go under together as we had once as children. She is in the room now and it is the afternoon before the afternoon after, and she pours the lemonade and sits on the sofa where the light has taken her, and she takes me to her side and asks me if I want to help her, and she pours out the rest and says it's done and I haven't got any more and so we'll go and get some more, she says the day is this long, and it feels almost like summer but isn't and isn't that always the way of it, as the heat of summer simply comes in suddenly like this and one's never ready for it and when you get the fan out in front it spins patterns of light on the walls behind you as the ale-colored sunshine strokes out beneath a windless afternoon and it feels a century old the heart can't begin to recover all that it was told. And she is sitting on the landing near the last pieces of our story, I am eight years old in the picture I have stored next to other pictures and thinking back how sorrowful that she must go away, if there is a way she can return will she come back to us, and then she is walking again through the garden gate. *Look* she says *what I've brought you my little man* and she holds me close to her and kisses me on the neck and her mouth is wet and hard on mine and she pulls me tightly into her body and says *This is the only day we have this is the only hour* and later it seems providential but at the time without meaning like a clapboard house passed on a road you'll never get back to and the day passes just like any other and its location is no different than what it was yesterday or what it will be thirty years hence. You wouldn't even notice it, one day passes so you don't even notice it's gone, and when they find us I am standing outside and the light is falling and I see as I never have my place inside of it.

The Last Film of Alan Smithee
Gabriel Blackwell

AFTER ALL THAT, I CHOSE the avatar that looked most like me: similar build, similar features. I gave him my name, Alan Smithee. I gave him glasses. I felt relatively certain that my wife would have recognized this, at least, as progress. There had been so many choices of what to be—round bodies, flat bodies, flabby bodies, tan, pale, or liver-spotted bodies, bodies with long arms or skinny legs, triangular noses, dimpled chins, jug ears, or thin lips. So many choices. Now it was done. Once, she had opened my cabinet in the kitchen and stood next to me, silent, while I looked in. Six identical rows, seven cans deep—three weeks' worth of meals. She had opened my closet. Six blue Oxford shirts with left pockets; next to them, a row of plain-front khaki slacks. I had one gray suit that I never wore, though this was never remarked upon. There was no time in my schedule for a job. It took me hours to get dressed. I thought about what I had to do that day. I tried different combinations. I had long ago ceased to eat breakfast—by the time I was dressed, it was lunchtime. I stood in front of the open cabinet in the kitchen, scanning the rows. I could not allow lunchtime to pass in the same way as breakfast had, but I always bitterly regretted my choice, closing off as it did other, very possibly better, choices. Having fewer things to choose from had made these decisions somewhat easier, though of course the smaller differences in each item—of circumstance, of memory, of effect—meant that a high degree of care was still required. In the game, some of these choices had been made for me. I gave my avatar the khaki slacks. I gave my avatar the blue shirt. I gave my avatar the brown shoes. I chose the haircut that I had had since the age of eighteen. My wife had it styled once, the day we got married. I wore a tuxedo in our wedding photographs. People asked if it was me when they saw the photographs. I considered laughing. I considered who was speaking to me. I considered what they would want to hear. I considered answering seriously. I considered making a joke. I considered answering with a question of my own. I considered changing the subject. In time, they moved off.

*

I spent two days on the Internet looking for a strategy guide, a walk-through, an FAQ, anything at all about how to proceed in the game, but I could not find anything. I spent half a day in front of a screen that asked me to press a certain button if I wished to proceed. I was unsure. I knew that I would have to finish the game if I pressed the button. I did not know if I had the time to finish the game. I did not know anything about the game. I did not like that I did not know anything about the game. Without being aware of it, I had already spent so much time on the game, and I had not even yet begun it. It seemed now that I had no choice. I pressed the button. I regretted it. Alan Smithee was by himself in a house. Nothing happened. I did not know how to proceed. The game seemed to be an open-world game, a game without predetermined paths to follow. I had always avoided these games. They had none of the advantages of the other games. What was the right thing to do first? What was the right thing to do next? One entered situations thoroughly unprepared for them. One might go through the entire game in such a state, never feeling prepared for anything one had encountered. How does one proceed when there is more than one right way to proceed? What if one had to go back in order to proceed? What if one had to take on obstacles or challenges in a certain order but this order was never made clear? One was always made conscious of possibilities closed off. One was always made conscious of optimal strategies, of the importance of preparation and an advanced state of readiness. One could never be too ready. Unless there was no way to make ready.

In the game, there was a gaming console with a game already in it, ready to be played. I could not find any other games. I could not think what else to do. After deliberating and searching the Internet, I commanded Smithee to play the game. From what I could gather, it was called *Time Out*. I paused the game. I queried a long string of search terms beginning with *Time Out* and including the words "walk-through," "strategy guide," and "FAQ," without any results. I unpaused the game. I still did not know how to proceed. Smithee's wife entered their living room, standing just inside the door. I do not know if she had a name; I had neither clothed nor named her. I could not see the expression on her face because of the angle of the camera. I expected a cutscene, but there was no cutscene. I still had control over my avatar. I could not decide what to do. I longed for the cutscene, if only as a way of easing the burden of decision. I thought perhaps if Smithee spoke, this would trigger the cutscene, but the speech interface used by the game was so clumsy that he could not. Each word had to be picked out letter by letter, through a laborious process of using the joystick to control a cursor hovering over a huge and confusing list of symbols and letters that had been arranged in an order I had never seen used anywhere else. If a single wrong letter was chosen, the entire sequence had to be performed again. I stood Smithee up and walked him to the opposite wall, where the television hung. I had intended to turn off the console and the television, but he would not approach the console or the television. He faced them, inert no matter what button I pressed. *Time Out* seemed to be paused. It was difficult to tell—nothing had happened in it yet. Smithee's wife stood near the doorway, her hair and shoulders bobbing. Perhaps the cutscene could only be triggered if Smithee approached his wife, I thought. I paused the game. Smithee faced the wall. I searched the Internet again. My query began with the word "wife." The search engine suggested dozens of possible endings for my query. None of them included the words "walkthrough," "strategy guide," or "FAQ." I had trouble choosing one, so I erased "wife" and started over. This time I tried the word "walkthrough" first, but none of the choices included "wife." I cycled through endless queries. I came up with nothing. I unpaused the game. I tried to turn Smithee around, but he would not turn. The camera overcompensated, turning my commands to him to turn around into commands to stay facing the wall—if I thumbed the joystick left, the camera turned past him to the right; if I thumbed it to the right, the camera rotated left. Alan Smithee slowly turned around the room, always facing away from the camera, away from the center of the room. The cutscene I had been waiting for began when he had almost reached his wife, still not facing her. It began with a close-up of the mirror that hung next to the doorway where Smithee's wife had stood a moment before. The mirror's silver was warped. It showed the room behind Alan Smithee. The television was in the center of the mirror—"Press A to continue," the screen blinked. Then Alan Smithee stepped over to the left and appeared in the center of the mirror, the game screen behind him warped now and the text there indecipherable. I could not see the resemblance between us anymore. I thought at first that it was not my avatar at all. I moved the joystick on the controller. He moved with it, disappeared into the warp, and then reappeared. I tried to turn him so that he faced the camera; was this the avatar I had chosen? Was this still Alan Smithee? The cutscene ended, but by then Smithee's wife had left the room, and there were other things missing too. The plant next to the couch was gone. One of the pictures that had hung on the wall was gone. The rug was gone. There was a ring of lighter-colored wood where the rug had been. There was another, smaller lighter-colored area next to the couch. There was a rectangle of bright white on the wall.

I did not seem to be advancing any, and did not seem to have triggered anything of consequence. I had only the challenge of finding a challenge. I felt that Smithee lacked an item or piece of information, and I commanded him to look through his house again and again, hoping to find something, anything, that would tell me what to do next. Nothing ever turned up. I searched the Internet again and again. I despaired of accomplishing anything at all. My Internet search queries got longer and longer. Then they began to contract. Every time I unpaused the game there was something else missing from Smithee's house. The books on the bookshelves were gone. Then the bookshelves were gone. The armchair was gone. The game console had been transferred to a card table. The other rooms were just as bare. In the breach, I established a routine for Smithee. I showered him in the morning, spent some time dressing him, then played *Time Out* for a few hours while waiting for something to happen. Then I prepared and ate lunch. Then I returned to the game. Then I ate dinner. Then I returned to the game. Then I went to sleep.

Time Out began with a cinematic sequence. The player's avatar, named Bill Connor, is in a bar with his coworkers. He has just been passed over for a promotion. He is complaining about it. Connor had a haircut very similar to Smithee's. He had a set of pixelated features very similar to Smithee's. He was wearing a gray suit and a red tie. After the bar sequence, a load screen came up, presenting a choice of "New Game" or "Saved Game." There were three entries under "Saved Game." Someone had already played this game and advanced its story. The choices were: "Vichy," "KKK," or "Vietnam." I did not know which to choose. I searched the Internet again and again. I searched Smithee's house. I sat in front of the game, with Smithee sitting in front of *Time Out*, waiting for the right choice to become apparent. After two days of this, *Time Out* shut off, and I was returned to the main game. But nothing had been happening in that game for quite some time. Still, I envied Alan Smithee a little. He had those saved games, whole sets of choices already made, to work from. It remained to him only to choose the saved game that had progressed the furthest, the densest agglomeration of choices. He would be relieved of so much. I saved my progress, and I considered whether to turn off the console or not.

I slept uncomfortable sleep when I slept. The springs under the couch cushions and a burden I could not seem to identify kept me awake. I did not feel myself. I found myself talking to the screen, telling Smithee what to do even as I failed to make him do it. "Smithee, you do-nothing son of a bitch. What are you doing? You aren't *doing* anything! There must be something more to this than staying at home. There must be something more to this than playing a video game." But it was useless. The suit in his closet could not be put on. I could put on any of the other clothes hanging there, but the suit could not be put on. I thought perhaps it was that Smithee was too out of shape. Getting into shape, though, would mean spending hours and hours on the treadmill. It would take weeks to get into shape. I would have to set up a routine to get into shape. I would have to exercise at the same time every day. I would have to exercise before I showered in the morning, so that I was not wasting water. I would have to wake up even earlier. I would have to go to sleep even earlier. I would have to exercise in a new set of clothes so that I did not ruin those I already had. I would have to go out and buy a new set of clothes to exercise in. I could not be sure that the treadmill would be there once I had decided on a set of exercise clothes and had worked out the changes to the schedule. Things had disappeared from every room in Alan Smithee's house. The shelves and cabinets were now bare. The bed had gone. Footsteps were louder when he crossed the rooms. And there was almost nothing to interact with. Nothing, other than *Time Out*. Smithee turned it on. The same cinematic sequence played. The same load screen came up. I scanned the buttons on Smithee's controller. I considered which was most likely to prod him into action. Smithee chose "Vietnam." It was last on the list, perhaps closest to the end of the game. There was another cutscene. Connor, in the suit from the bar, was now in a mangrove swamp. There was a Vietcong patrol passing him. He hid in the mangroves. A snake swam past him.

Smithee paused the game just after the cutscene. Smithee checked his house. There was no new information. The couch was now missing. There was less information than there had been before. The game's clock had disappeared, corresponding with the clock that had formerly hung on the wall, but which had disappeared in the interval between pause and unpause. I had no idea how much game time was elapsing. I could not tell when to stop *Time Out* to prepare and eat lunch. I could not tell when to stop *Time Out* to have dinner. I could not tell when to stop *Time Out* to sleep. I began to worry that I had involuntarily caused a glitch in the game by having Smithee choose, by the fact that he had then chosen "Vietnam." I thought about resetting and starting over. But I could not make that decision. I would have to play this game through to the end. It was time to prepare my lunch, I thought, but I could not seem to get the game to save, and so instead of saving and turning it off, I paused it, or so I thought, and prepared and ate my lunch.

When I returned to the game, Smithee had carried on without me. I didn't understand how this was possible. I sat and watched for a minute before I realized what was happening. It was not that the game had come unpaused in the interval when I was preparing and eating my lunch: In that case, things in the game would have gone on, but Smithee would not have been able to act, he would only have been acted upon. But on the screen in front of me, Smithee had left his house somehow and walked to a pawnshop. When I picked up the controller, Smithee had a gun in his hand and was exiting the pawnshop. I do not know what he could have pawned to get it, as almost everything of value had already disappeared, but I took control and steered him back to his house, only because I was sure that this was what the game wanted me to do: There was a police car cruising the boulevard, shining a spotlight on the storefronts I had only just passed. I was tempted to bring the gun back to the pawnshop, but I could not reach a decision, and I instead got Smithee home and had him stay there. I had Smithee unpause *Time Out*. The soundtrack blasted "Purple Haze." American soldiers approached, and Smithee, perhaps in desperation but certainly not as a result of my command, commanded Connor to yell out to them. They fired in his direction, but he was not hit. It seemed I had no control over Smithee at this point. Was it a cutscene? It did not seem to be. Still, I watched as Smithee commanded Connor to take two young Vietnamese children hostage. I watched as he commanded Connor out to the paddy, holding these two young children in his arms. I watched as Smithee commanded Connor into the middle of the paddy, underneath the American helicopter passing overhead. I commanded Smithee to jerk the joystick in the direction of the swamp. Helpless, I watched as Smithee commanded Connor to yell up to the gunner in the helicopter. I watched as the helicopter was hit in the fuselage by an explosive launched from the village. I watched as the helicopter canted over and its blades severed Connor's head from his body. I watched as the screen went dark and the words "GAME OVER" came up. I felt a small measure of relief. I watched as Smithee pointed the gun at the television. The noise of the shot was deafening. He pointed the gun at the console. As the camera continued to zoom out, I noticed that the table was gone. Smithee had only gun, television, and console. And now the television and console were inoperable. My options were thus limited. But this was how I preferred it. This world was so large, its interactions so complex, it seemed best to limit one's options. Smithee had reminded me that there really was only one button, one action. I felt almost ready to reach a decision. I had had as much preparation as I was ever going to have.

Proposals for the Recovery of the Apparently Drowned

Michael Sheehan

IT HAPPENED AFTER DINNER, as they walked from the recently well-reviewed restaurant on St. Mark's toward a club whose facade suggested it was one of a litter of overlooked Chinatown markets, the types of places that still had empty pallets or overturned wooden crates sitting in front of the glass door crosshatched with iron and whose streets still smelled of fish, the residual fishstink you assume from generations of mongering there, but whose interiors were a slick and lowlit chic that boasted New York's brightest and yet most underground DJs including tonight's unannounced but widely circulated appearance of DJ True Identity and whose dance floors had the usual admixture of hot bodies in motion and those who cluttered the dance floors hands filled with drinks not dancing but simply being there and whose bartenders were the speakeasy variety whom you told simply to give you something with top-shelf ingredients and just watched them invent; they were somewhere between the two, having elected to walk rather than cab it when, taking a step perhaps a little hurriedly to keep up, or maybe she was as she often felt just clumsy, but it was right around Second Avenue and First Street that she stumbled there on the sidewalk within sight of the kabob cart and the glowing red light of the next block. The fall was not all that hard. It was immediately more her hurt pride than any physical pain that radiated through her, but radiated through her fiercely, the shock of the fall slowing time and making her suddenly, acutely self-aware—it was as if she could see herself falling as she fell, could know the ridiculousness of her awkward gait and gangly frame spilling down like a clatter of drinks splashing tumultuously off a tipped cocktail tray—and so as she hit the sidewalk, she let herself go. It was not the type of fall that leaves you with abraded palms, scraped chin, or cut knees; not even the type that results in a twisted ankle or a snapped heel. More accurately, as she came down against the sidewalk, she froze. It was not exactly a willed or conscious thing, though certainly it later felt almost as if it had been. She let herself just stay there, stay down, didn't move or cry out or in any way indicate any sort of life to her at all.

This was not the first incident like this, a fall, as indeed it felt she was constantly making one type of blunder or another around her coworkers, family, and friends. These friends indeed were coworkers, Aisha and Julie and Cab (who claimed to have been named after Cab Calloway but was evidently named for some family member who'd borne the unusual name Cabbowell and who either took some gentle ribbing almost every time someone mentioned a cab, as in NYC taxi, or had in fact initiated this joke himself, it was unclear) and the various others, all of whom had been with her at dinner and before that work and had witnessed her fallings or blunderings before, though far less than she herself had witnessed them. In truth, they overlooked her more than they mocked her for any perceived social or physical awkwardnesses, and it was just this overlooking, this simultaneous worry that she was unnoticeable and invisible and without any worthwhile qualities unique to her person combined with her acute desire to avoid—above all things—standing out and becoming the center of attention, the subject of the gazes and stares of others, that caused her such extreme pain upon such a stupid, ridiculous thing as falling while walking on the sidewalk, perhaps because her attention was too keenly tuned to what Cab was saying to Emily, the new girl with the great calves.

In the eighteenth century, when doctors first discovered and sought to prove the existence of "suspended animation," many in the public—including medical professionals—were skeptical. The idea that a patient could exhibit no signs of life, could instead present as not just paralyzed but dead, devoid of all life functions, and yet still be recoverably alive inside sounded absurd. But the argument focused on the slow heart rate, breathing rate, and altered states of those who had undergone extreme physical trauma, for instance drowning or near drowning, and how not all of these who exhibited lifelessness posttrauma were in fact irrecoverable. Certain patients, it was argued, were instead in a sort of liminal state, what we would call a coma. Their report on this "suspended animation" sought to gain ground through calling on the compassion of other doctors by highlighting the numberless souls needlessly lost throughout all time and in all civilizations because an understanding of this recoverable near death was lacking. Even as early as the eighteenth century, the belief existed that through understanding how patients could be recovered successfully from near death, frozen, suspended-animation states could lead to the possibility of intentionally freezing a subject, slowing the life process down, and reviving the subject at some later time, perhaps every hundred years, thereby gaining immortality and insight into the totality of human affairs.

Once on the sidewalk, of course, there were the inevitable laughs and calls and jeers, but this lasted a very short time only. Her friends, led mostly in this by Aisha and Sami and Julie, teased her and laughed and then chided her and called for her to get up, come on, until after what seemed like several minutes of an acutely tense, panic-level self-awareness but was in truth no more than one minute, Aisha asked, Are you all right? and was kneeling beside her. Then things started to change. Cab was there, and Emily and the rest. They gathered around her limp body, still splayed like something spilled there on the sidewalk.

Amanda?

Are you all right?

Oh my God, what's wrong with her?

She's probably just knocked out.

Is she unconscious?

Hey, no, you're not supposed to move her; what if her neck is broke—

And Cab rolled her over, and her eyes were open—she could see, was aware, but had sort of willed herself into a state of suspended animation, hiding as it were deep inside her own self, acutely aware still like an actress onstage in the lights without her lines on opening night—and they were calling her name and she was breathing, they observed, and Julie started to freak out as Julie tended to do, and Emily was consoling Julie—she was actually consoling her in the midst of this—and general confusion reigned and oh God was Amanda so acutely embarrassed and self-conscious and both just wishing this was over and unable to find any way past this other than for the moment to ride it out.

We should call an ambulance.

What's wrong with her? Is she hurt?

Maybe she's in shock. Amanda? Amanda. Aisha snapped her fingers distinctly in Amanda's face, as in directly at her open eyes (how much easier it would have seemed if she'd closed her eyes, but the level at which she had frozen was such that she emptied her every limb and muscle and nerve of automation, had willed paralysis of a sort) and the natural response is to blink or wink or flinch or in some way respond and to let the snap happen without responding was startlingly difficult and yet, again, it seemed time had slowed and she watched the snap happen without attending to it, her concentration focused intently on being and remaining frozen and paralyzed and limp. (Lying there, her head near Cab's bent knee, was not unlike playing dead; she wasn't holding her breath or trying to do anything extreme like that—she hadn't died from such a fall—but it was similar to the intensity with which one plays dead, tries to hold perfectly still despite whatever attempts are made to revive her.)

This thing with time slowing was not new either. It seemed every time she did or said something stupid and goofy and dumb and laughable it felt this way, like her own inner experience of time had slowed and dragged and thus the embarrassment and the raw real burn of the attention being focused her way, the laughter, the derision was all that much worse, as it seemed interminably slow.

The continued stress of lying immobile combined with the extreme self-consciousness and embarrassment and humiliation she felt with her friends gathered around, staring at her, touching her, trying to get her to snap back out of it and wake up and move and respond (at once indicating they believed in the paralysis she was evidencing there before them and seeming to suggest they did not in fact believe anything was wrong with her, were convinced if they just said her name again, or snapped their fingers, that that easily she would revive and they could presumably rib her and tease her and point out how dumb and goofy and ridiculous and embarrassing her fall had been) was acutely, unnameably painful. Their attentions only made the situation that much worse and intensified the self-consciousness and embarrassment, which in turn demanded even higher degrees of willed inaction and immobility, which meant focusing closely on everything they were doing, which made her even more embarrassed. And so on. Oh God, Aisha was rubbing her legs, literally massaging her thighs, and explaining to someone—Sami?—that this was what she'd seen done to people who'd passed out when drunk.

Philosophers and poets of the eighteenth and nineteenth centuries used the idea of suspended animation in various ways, including Coleridge's criticism that modern media created a sort of suspended animation in which we existed at all times, our minds beaten back by the ready delivery of information—traveling libraries—we received passively, without the required mental action. He saw such states as what we needed to be shocked out of; contemporary life was anesthetizing us, our inner lives locked off and inert. Keats, however, believed states of suspended animation were the only way to achieve a sense of commune with consciousness in the midst of modern society, and that such disconnection from the physical world was essential for attaining alternative ways of thinking and perceiving and being. He considered suspended animation a sort of ontological or spiritual tool, necessary in silencing the cacophony of the world outside.

The ambulance arrived after seventeen minutes. By then passersby—including notably the man from UAE who had been leaning casually on his kabob cart and smoking who kept asking the same questions over and over, This your friend? She on drugs?—had gathered into a crowd, pretty much forcing her continued lack of animation and necessitating even greater attention focused inward on simply staying still, being limp, not reviving, and not even thinking but only sensing, if at all, and were offering help and speculations as to what was wrong with her, and then the paramedics cleared the area and had knelt and crouched around her, gently massaged her head and neck—evidently looking for any contusions or noticeable breaks or damage—before lifting her head gently, shining a light into her eyes, taking her blood pressure, and asking many questions of her friends—She on any medications? Anything at all? Has she been sick recently? Been drinking? How many drinks? Eat anything that could have caused—

For whatever reason, along with the ambulance, two police cruisers and fire trucks also arrived, all double parked, lights ablaze, drawing an even larger crowd. God, how embarrassing, this scene, as Amanda lay there, inert but aware, her essentially motionless eyes' pupils contracted automatically with the flashing lights, every ounce of her interior being bent solely on not responding, on not showing that she was aware of them all, that she was hidden here in plain sight. She willed herself rigid, near dead, empty, and struggled intensely to continue this unbroken self-silence. More and more people were gathered, and the police were directing people around, away, she could hear the crowd murmur and the periodic orders of police. There was some discussion now about whether to move her. Julie was totally freaking out, weeping, her head buried into Sami's shoulder. The man from UAE from the kabob cart was talking agitatedly with someone farther away about young people and drugs. Cab was standing over her, directly in her line of sight, though her eyes were unfocused and it wasn't like he would think she was seeing him—she wasn't exactly, her eyes had him as an object, but she'd turned the true seeing part of herself intently inward, like some inner part of herself had spun into a defensive crouch, turning its back toward the world outside, huddling around its own most vulnerable core, an ostrich with its head in the sand; she was gone. Aisha had her hands over her mouth, sort of drawn together with the fingers on the bridge of her nose, her mascara smeared with otherwise invisible tears. Amanda wished this had not happened. She couldn't move, couldn't take it back, not now, but she wished this had not happened. Withdrawing deeper and deeper into herself, forcing her body to stay limp as people prodded it, shined lights at it, held her wrists for a pulse, listened to the blood moving beneath her skin—could they tell if her heartbeat changed? Could she will her breathing slowed, will her heart to rest?

And then they very gently and carefully lifted her onto a stretcher and loaded her into the ambulance, Aisha and Cab asking if they could ride in the ambulance with her and being told they could follow behind in a police car that had also responded. An officer was aggressively telling bystanders to mind their business, keep walking, clear out the area, as Amanda let herself be settled into the ambulance, and listened very attentively to everything that was happening and now started to have some distinct thoughts about what she was supposed to do—she wasn't hurt—which came from the parallax awarenesses of finally being out of the eyes of her friends and the others who'd gathered on the sidewalk (and thus she'd achieved some sort of respite from the humiliation and the embarrassment and the acute and painful self-consciousness) and but also now being treated with serious medical concern, albeit confused, loaded into an ambulance with really nothing wrong with her as far as anyone could yet tell, but worries the paramedics had spoken quietly among themselves—all the while a woman with untidy bangs and white gloves kept speaking to Amanda, asking, Can you hear me? Amanda? Let me see you move your eyes if you can hear me, and assuring her, It's all right, it's going to be OK—ranging from some sort of bleeding or swelling on the brain or even a rarer case of sudden paralysis, which evidently could and did sometimes happen (which Amanda took what could perhaps be called pleasure in hearing, insofar as this analysis erased even the fall from her, suggesting she had stumbled not out of clumsiness or goofiness or anything of the sort but rather because her body had given out beneath her as part of a dramatic and extremely rare and tragic event) and so she had managed to see this through far enough to feel slightly relieved at the transition of shame via tragedy and yet her ability to get out of this position seemed ever more complicated—at this point, her thoughts showed her that she had succeeded in making herself an object of tragic concern rather than comic derision, but she now needed to figure at what point she could revive while maintaining the sense in others that she had undergone something terrible, and this is when the deeper and farther-ranging ramifications started to make themselves painfully clear to her. If she were to revive now, for instance, in the ambulance, would they realize she had been faking and that nothing was wrong with her, not really, and that she had just tried to fool everyone by freezing and staying still in order to avoid being mocked? That would naturally only result in greater and more terrible mockery. Her friends from work would never hang out with her again. And she would have to continue, day after day, arriving at work and going through the motions, desperate not to be seen and yet known by everyone to be the crazy girl who had faked paralysis after a simple stumble on the sidewalk in order to try making people concerned for her—she'd have to quit and try finding some other job; there was no way she could continue with them all thinking and knowing and believing this about her. And were there legal implications? If she revived now, in the ambulance, would she go to prison for lying and pretending she was hurt when in fact there was nothing wrong with her? During all this time, her attention remained acutely focused on her inner self, on not responding in any way to the stimuli all around her. And even if her friends did indeed believe she had some serious trauma, some unidentified medical problem, things could never be the same. Going out, just as they had tonight, if anyone even asked her to go out they'd be asking her out of pity, out of some innate concern for the weak and the infirm, or they'd want to show her they didn't care, didn't mind having a friend who'd suffered such a weird episode in the middle of the street on a Friday night; they'd be asking her as a form of derision, of mockery. And they'd worry about her the whole night, and worry and wonder if maybe she shouldn't have another drink or shouldn't eat fish or red meat or curry or whatever and ask her if she was OK but do it in a way that seemed to suggest they were trying, for her sake, to be subtle about it, asking her if she was feeling all right and how was she but by slipping aside with her, touching her elbow gently to ask, or following her into the ladies', or falling behind the group a step or two while they walked. She wouldn't be able to bear the shame. She'd be either a pariah or a potential paralytic, everyone wishing to take turns nurturing her and showing their concern.

The ambulance ride seemed to take impossibly long. She had never been in an ambulance, but she'd ridden in cabs and trains all over, from midtown to Brooklyn nightly, and this seemed like the longest ride she had ever endured. The siren sounded the whole way there while the paramedics in the ambulance talked agitatedly to one another. Though she knew they were speaking rapidly about her, her condition, it felt like riding in a cab with one of those obscurely Middle Eastern drivers who wears a Bluetooth and talks impossibly fast into it, never pausing or breaking even when he shifts from talking into the Bluetooth to talking to you there in the backseat telling you to swipe your card and then dipping into clipped, hyperspeed Farsi without even a breath and how humiliating when they did this and you didn't notice they were suddenly asking you something and they turned and directly to your face repeated themselves, indicating what an airy, idiotic person you were, how they saw you as unutterably stupid and beneath them, even them.

She wanted it to be over. This was the only desire she knew, other than to will her body to stay still, to not respond at all to anything.

In what is commonly called "locked-in syndrome," it is possible for a patient to be completely physically paralyzed and yet, internally, retain full brain function. In some instances, very minimal motor functions may remain: the ability to wink or blink, sometimes simply the ability to move the eyes or an eye, perhaps the power to flex a finger, wriggle a toe. There is no definitive way to decide whether a patient does have full brain function in such a case, particularly without the patient retaining some physical ability to express thoughts and alert medical staff to her continued mental presence. This is also a common recurring idea in nightmares, where the dreamer is immobilized and yet aware, the nightmare's content being mostly devoted to the dreamer's attempts to move or cry out or simply wake herself up.

*

They stopped abruptly, the woman nearest Amanda's head shot a hand out and grabbed the stretcher's little side rail, jostling Amanda. She was still extremely uncomfortable, this paralysis still stressful and agonizing, but yet, she was finding a sense of place in this. The rear doors to the ambulance were flung open, and it was surreally light. She was finding some sense of calm, deep inside herself, willing her body limp and empty and motionless and withdrawing every bit of her true self inside, away, acutely aware of everything around her and through this awareness focused more and more on nothing but staying still, hidden. The legs of the stretcher were extended as she was wheeled into the emergency room. It was not unlike one of those movies, seeing the blurs of passing fluorescent ceiling lights flash Morse messages, the straggly bits of nose hair clearly visible in the male nurse's nose. She was becoming relaxed maybe. But, still, this was not over. They were talking over her head, talking tests and she was wheeled—not hurriedly—into a private room. Oh God, would they take her clothes off? They would have to. This was all too much. She had to will herself away, allow time to pass. They would know, they would be able to tell there was nothing wrong with her. Distantly, someone said shellfish-poisoning paralysis. A nurse lifted her left arm. She focused again, aimed every bit of her thoughts on the problem of staying inert, staying frozen: What would she do if they started stripping her down, pulling her clothes off? Why would they? What if she had to pee? Variously, she heard fragments: history of periodic paralysis, signs of trauma? no prior medical conditions that would indicate, nondystrophic myotonia, blood clot, circulatory function appears normal, oxygen deprivation to the brain could maybe result in pseudocoma? no evidence of flexibilitas cerea, stroke or hemorrhage could perhaps. The nurse slipped a needle into the vein in her forearm. Again, time was slowed, though everything inside her was moving now incredibly fast, and so the snap and white flash of pain that came with the needle's entry—she hadn't been paying attention—did not cause her to even flinch, or cry out. She wanted to cry. This was too much. When could she let it go? When could she flinch and scream and move again and tell them it was all right and tell them she was sorry and just scream?

The nurses were talking quickly, and she was trying hard to follow without listening but more and more now she was unable to do the work of both listening and watching everything and exhibiting no signs of life or listening or watching. Someone said allergic reaction. Though the fall had not been all that hard, this had become unbelievably painful. They were still touching her, the needle the nurse put in her forearm had drawn some blood and was withdrawn. What felt like a man's thick, dry, rough hand was palpating her stomach's fleshy parts, pressing softly on her insides. Someone said spinal trauma. Where were Cab and Aisha? What would they think? If she sat up now, would everyone be relieved? Someone said catalepsy. Someone said signs of overdose? She now hoped just to ride this out long enough to earn the sense of a tragedy evaded, a very close call, she had had a rough fall but was OK now, and no one would laugh and no one would think differently about her or act differently or worry when they went out again after work as they did most weeks and she could overcome this whole thing.

In 2006, the condition of Rom Houben, who at that point had spent twenty-three years in a vegetative state after a 1983 car crash, was revised to locked-in syndrome using modern brain-imaging technology. However, the evidence suggesting consciousness and an ability to communicate remains the subject of dispute, and some of the original claims about his communicative abilities were retracted after inadequate evidence and a failure to repeat the findings. However, his doctor still claims Houben is conscious, a ghost in the machine, sparking debate about how doctors diagnose locked-in syndrome versus a persistent vegetative state and also about withholding certain medical treatments and procedures from patients diagnosed as vegetative. Imagine, for instance, if for all these paralyzed years Houben really were conscious, the inexpressible terror he lives with.

She was now starting more clearly to regret staying down when she'd fallen. Why had she? She started wondering, as the nurses did indeed open up her shirt to place something—a heart monitor? those little suction cups?—on her chest. She pictured her eyes completely empty. She wished she'd at least closed her eyes. But they would probably open them anyway. The shock of all the attention, the tops of her breasts above her bra now cold against the air, combined with the exhausting effort of willing herself away, numb, empty, made her feel sort of stunned. Perhaps she hadn't chosen to act paralyzed when she'd fallen—though it now seemed she had. Perhaps she had indeed suffered some acutely real injury, something physical rather than psychical, something she herself did not know the name of and that she was only fooling herself did not really exist other than in her mind. The nurses and maybe doctors around her had quieted, and now there seemed to be just two. She couldn't tell from this angle where they all were, whether they were still watching. One was sort of pinching Amanda's right wrist's inner vein. How would she know if this was not just in her head? But she did, she knew. She was aware she had been so humiliated and ashamed and embarrassed she had just gone still, played possum, acted like something terrible had happened to escape the shame and to make others feel pity for her. This was true. This was objectively the case. But how would she know? How would she know she could move her limbs but was choosing not to unless she tried and confirmed the movement? The temptation was suddenly terribly strong, just to flinch, twitch her arm. Both nurses were now gone; the room above her was totally quiet and empty and still, though brightly lit and distantly filled with sounds and a sort of electrostatic hum.

The physical pain was nothing compared to the psychical pain. Physically, the pain was just to the outside of you, and you couldn't control it. She'd fallen, her body gave way and hit the pavement hard. That was not up to her, was not something she had power over. The fear of that pain, thus, was misused: Despite the fear, you couldn't really do anything about it. It would hurt, that's all there was to it, but it would only hurt on the outside. The pain would be strictly on the level of neurons warning the brain or whatever. But the psychical pain, the anxiety? That was something else. Instead of being pain *to* you, something that hurt you, it *was* you. The pain on the inside that filled you up, that was something really to fear. That was when everything you were became an element causing harm to your own self. You made yourself feel pain. Amanda, lying here, she was the cause of her pain, and it was way worse than when her body hit the ground. If she could figure out a way to be unafraid of what was inside her, as she felt now much less afraid of what was outside, the pain that happened through her senses, if she could somehow become calm, let the anxiety and self-consciousness become something like just being really aware, wide awake, that seemed like maybe not altogether such a bad thing.

Soon she would have to act, though. There was no way she could keep doing this. What was she thinking? How embarrassing this all would be. If instead she could somehow figure a way to wait for everyone to leave and maybe try just slipping up and out of bed and hurrying herself away, buttoning her shirt closed over her exposed skin and going home, laughing this off later. She was not the type who could laugh this off. There was no going back now. How would she ever face her coworkers again? They would all want to know what happened, to understand at some root level what had caused her body to empty out like that, had caused her to lie lifeless that way, and she would not be able to tell them. What if the nurses and doctors and whoever could already tell? Was it obvious? Had she actually moved when the nurse put the needle in her arm? God, how humiliating. And would they have to contact her family, call her mother, if she didn't act soon? Amanda focused herself again inward, let her body go and pulled her self inside, willing herself not to cry, not to make any motion. She was now extremely uncomfortable both inside and out, with the shirt half open and the self-consciousness sharp and real and radiant even when no one was looking.

Since 1962, approximately two hundred people have undergone cryonic freezing, with the hope of radical advances in medical technology being able to bring them back. Among other techniques, one of the currently impossible but speculative technologies involved in reviving the apparently dead is known as mind uploading or mind transfer or whole brain emulation, in which a mind is mapped and transferred, or uploaded, to a computer. Conceptions of whole brain emulation appear in many popular science fiction works, including *The Matrix* and William Gibson's *Neuromancer*, in which an "infomorph" helps the protagonist in exchange for the promise that he will afterward delete her consciousness, effectively ending her technological immortality by assisting her suicide.

Her consciousness was now fluttering between an acute awareness of where she was and her body and the space it occupied and the need to simply stay still and a sort of disconnected, inner-aimed awareness that felt separated from her body and the room she was in and the feeling of the paper sheath on the vinyl emergency-room table beneath her. It was quiet now, the room. Emptied, or so it seemed. She let her eyes remain open, and tried to control her breathing, slow her heart. This was such difficult work. She pictured herself falling, replayed the moment once, twice, no longer in first person but in third. Her body stumbling on nothing, knees clacking, buckling, crumpling beneath a feeble flick of the wrists outward as her purse came off her shoulder and her face showed true horror. She pictured this, and pictured it, and pictured it. Distantly she heard voices, perhaps outside, in a hall, perhaps at the foot of the bed. She understood at some level that despite what it felt like to her, it had really not been all that long since she had tripped, stumbled, fallen; half an hour? perhaps less? Her eyes, unfocused, looked straight up at what was meant to be a soothing image of birch trees, golden coins of sunlight spilling through their leaves, their trunks stretching up at an exaggerated perspective, like she was on her back on a forest floor, these endless, nearly branchless trees extending from her off to infinity. The voices and the continuing hum of what she assumed was some machine continued, but she felt less agitated by them. What would she do? How could she ever live down such shame? She'd gone completely numb, empty, when her humiliation had tripped her up. But regaining feeling would only let the hurt in, would only let the others laugh. And wasn't her accident not a tragedy but a farce waiting to be acknowledged? Once Cab and Aisha got here and the doctors and nurses told them there was nothing they could find wrong with her, wouldn't they all guess? When she finally sat up, when she showed them she could move all along? How long would she have to stay still to lose the stigma of embarrassment and convert it permanently into unmistakable tragedy? She knew once she got up, this terror would be over. She would not have to stay in her head anymore; she could be free. And she also knew once she sat herself up, turned her legs to the side and let them drop off the table, crinkling the paper sheath, settling her hands' palms on the edge of the table, readying her easy ascension, at that exact moment whatever humiliation she'd tried to bypass would return just like the supposedly mysterious recovery of feeling in her limbs, her friends seeing her goofiness and clumsiness and awkwardness all bringing her to such a silly state, cataleptic on a city sidewalk, comatose and in the emergency room, all as the result of a stupid stumble, a turned ankle, a missed step. She had no way out. It was all or nothing. She had no idea what all or nothing really meant, here. The sound of the voices started to grow louder. It was time. She had to move now, she had to recover while they were not looking, be better when they returned, sit up a little, play confused, perhaps cry, yes, she would cry, and they would be real tears though not for the reasons others would think, because if she didn't move now, they would catch her at it, she would not be able to stay so still, no matter how hard she tried to will herself away, to disappear, let all the life ebb from her body like the bad energy her yoga instructor would describe while they lay in corpse pose, seeping out of her appendages, total relaxation and calm filling her like high tide coming in, and all these thoughts she held in her head.

For Tamara
Sarah Lang

Basil is very temperamental / I'm sorry I have no idea how to make a TV. / Find a library sweetheart, please. / Intact.

If all resources fail: bleach. / Learn to can / fruit, vegetables.

Flamingos, / to read, / that we love you, / Rhinoceroses. / Poplar trees have sunscreen (SPF15) on the south side.

The sun rises in the east and sets in the west. / The longest day of the year is June 21 / shortest December 21.

Your city was so glorious, but not so much as this sky.

You need songs. You can make your own (which I know you can). / I hope there are books. / I hope you find this one.

It is OK to cry. / Just say you need one to five minutes to cry. / Then you are going to take care of shit.

Learn to hunt. / Your mum and dad have been vegetarians, but never for the sake of your life. / Arrow and spearheads.

Then there are the stories I can't tell you. / Lying under a piano listening to Satie.

My Darling Dearest, first-aid kits are frivolous until you need one. / I'm sorry. / Eat strawberries (I dreamt about them last night).

She's my kid: She's going to start her life by looting a Safeway.

Tamara, I trust you will be strong enough. / Eat eggplant, it's good for you.

Sarah Lang

If I could be alive for you, I would. The thing that bothers me most is that I've let you down.

Don't get angry with ppl for being human. / Just help; / and I know you can. / No use in screaming.

I'm so very sorry I'm not there to tell you. / I'm sorry I'm a bad teacher.

I can't draw you the map you deserve. / Remember pineapples though, OK?

Sweetheart, your mum took pretty great photos. Find them.

I can't write down all our jokes, but remember to make them.

I think I'd like to name you Tamara.

Maybe Mum isn't going to make it, OK, My Darling Dearest?

We made those choices for you. / We are sorry if they were the wrong ones.

You need to tap into everyone's skill set and push them further. / You can do this as you are of my blood.

It is like waking up in a strange house / and all I want to do is go home. / Which means before all this. / Which means you.

Your mum is writing with a broken thumb. / This: for you.

When you plant seeds, leave about a two-finger space between them.

T.: Yes this responsibility sucks. / Feed yourself. / Take care of them (I know you can).

Humans are gross and annoying. / Take care of them anyway. / Learn about all types of birds and bugs.

I was just trying to draw you a compass for the world, / for right now. / But I should just make you one. / Iron (Fe) filings and all.

We're setting up a hospital here. We can't take everyone because we just can't. Our choices aren't going to get any easier.

I never wanted to ask you to do this, but I'm trying to keep us all alive, OK? I need you to do this.

We imagined creatures that swam through space: They didn't need a ship. (Your mum is writing you a fairy tale, she's sorry she's so busy.)

In a tornado: Hide under the stairs in the basement. / Your dad loved you and me so much; he is sorry he can't be here.

I know this isn't by the book. / But, Darling, we've run out of those. / Trust your mother. / This works. / I'm teaching you to make painkillers.

Fevers run in your maternal line. You're probably fine up to 104. Other ppl 102. / Yes you will hallucinate, but you'll live.

Love ppl for their faults, aka humanity. / All their quirks. / Boil water for three hours to be safe.

Seriously, T., if you sleep when I sleep, everyone wins.

Tamara, I have this vision of you running toward me in the kitchen and it is . . . extraordinary.

Sorry for the spelling. But it is the end of the world and Mum is going to do whatever she wants. She's going to use that excuse a lot.

Mum's sorry she can't play more, but one day you'll be doing her job. / Wash your hands.

Don't tell anyone I sing to you in Ukrainian.

Those tomato seeds will be food, save them. Save all seeds.

Don't worry it didn't hurt. / I'm sorry I'm not there anymore. / But at least when doing medical stuff, put up your hair, OK?

Sarah Lang

Your mum wishes you could have your own bedroom, but she promised to take care of these ppl.

You run at me so happy with this red hair. / I've told you to cut. / That is my last memory.

I remember expecting someone to be there when I woke up, other than you, of course, My Darling Dearest. / Yes, I miss your dad every day.

I know you saw me die and I'm so sorry. / But you're made of me and will keep doing a job I wouldn't wish on anyone. But, Darling, you have to.

It has been eighteen days. / No help. / You're going to have to do this yourself.

Your mum really wants to tell you tomorrow will be better, but she hates lying.

Don't let people see you cry. / Let them see you mourn, but not cry. / Tamara, they need your strength.

Don't always try to fix problems. Sometimes just listen and say you understand. / But fix the ones you can.

Your dad was, is, awesome.

OK, I need you to board up the windows. / You make a latrine.

I don't want this to be the world you're born in. / Please let there be books and pictures.

Oh My Beautiful Idiot. / Which I stole from a TV show. / If I ever get to see you again I will be so happy.

A few days before this / your father and I argued about him leaving (again). / Love someone for who they are. / That was part of who he is / to deny him that would be cruel.

You want to be forgiven, but you did nothing wrong. / Nor did Mum and Dad. / This just happened. / Shortwave radio.

Your grandparents taught me how to be strong enough to do this. / And meds, electricity, space, and cooking, and . . . / I wish they were here.

How to do CPR. / Cancer runs in my paternal line. / Grow potatoes. / Find a great partner. / How to make a poached egg: Get water to a slight boiling temp., add a bit of vinegar, crack the egg into water, and coax it together.

Thyroid meds. / I'm so proud of you.

I so do not want to tell you about making babies and birth. / But I have to.

Part of me doesn't even want to tell you about what it was like.

Pick someone who loves you for what you do, and you're crazy, OK? And don't ever forget what I said about gardening.

We are ruthless, but we don't hate. / Hate is a word like evil: It never did anyone any good.

Sweetheart, you need to figure out how to make a beacon for other survivors. / I'm dealing with these ones, can you do it?

I never cried until I lost my first love. / I'm sorry I won't always be there to help you.

Secret: Your mum hates being understanding all the time. / So she knows you do too. / But do it anyway. / Like vegetables.

Lick your wrist / then smell it. / Fruity equals infection, / that sort of thing. / Our bodies are better machines than we will ever be. / Trust them. / They will tell you what you have to know.

Why doesn't matter anymore. / They're dead and we're not. / So do your job.

Sarah Lang

B/C it started on a normal day.

Mum wants you to write books. / She wants you to have the time. / Eat bananas.

Darling, I hope to do this for you, but if I don't have a chance. / I need you to calculate how much water everyone needs /wk, OK?

We need to set up a perimeter, fortify it, and set up an alarm system that runs back to the house. / Not just noise, we need advance warning.

I wish I could come up with something less cheesy / tell your grandparents.

As a baby you weren't as quiet as your grandmother said I was. / And you did grow up to be so headstrong.

The well water here should be OK. / I wouldn't wish your job on my worst enemy.

And that was me. / But without you I couldn't have come as far as I did.

I'm drawing you pictures of how it used to be. / But you save those 'til the end.

There used to be these cities and they were remarkable. / They had parks and hot-dog vendors. / And buildings so tall. / Much taller than you.

I was built to care about / for these people. I hope you are too. / Either way you're strong enough to do it.

I'm sorry I'm going to always be needed elsewhere. / You're still beautiful. / As are you, My Beautiful Idiot.

I want to tell you how it used to be. / Sit up straight.

Don't tell anyone, but sometimes Mum wants to give up too. / Go practice your letters.

This house isn't built to deal with the cold without a furnace. / We'll figure something out. / And wear layers. / Corn stalks.

Chop down trees to make the barrier. / How I do not want to give that order.

I know you're busy, but I want you to plant flowers, OK? Try tulips. / They're easy.

I saw whole cities being destroyed. / T., I never want you to see that, ever. / Rebuild, always. / At least my thumb is healing.

Tamara, I never wanted kids and then all this happened and you were here. / Thank you. / Remember what I look like.

Mum doesn't want to have to teach you to fight, but she will. / And you will teach others.

I realize I haven't taught you much history. / Part is that I don't want to remember what it was like even a few years ago. / Part is where to start. / And no idea if that will change a thing.

Stockpile paper. / I'll teach you to make more, but it is going to take some time. / And ink, of any kind.

To triage you have to rule in/out the worst first: head wounds, fever . . . / I would love to teach you how to fly a kite instcad. / To open a jar that has a seal: rubber gloves and /or turn it upside down and hit it against something hard. / It will pop right off.

The best thing you can do about the weather is understand it.

Use that table, I don't care. / Keep the globe. / It never rains this much.

Celebrate Earth Day and your birthday. / I'm making time to write you fairy tales. / Don't overcook your vegetables.

I watched the windows blow out. / I used to watch romantic movies on Valentine's Day. / I hope you get to eat watermelon.

He's why you catch me wearing my wedding ring. / Your dad would be here if he could. / So brilliant and beautiful.

Weaving. / There are paper and if yr lucky electronic copies. / How to protect yrself.

Find yr grandfather's radio that says "Fisher-Price" on it; those things will outlive most other tech. / Good luck with finding batteries.

Tarama, ppl are going to have all sorts of mental problems. Just figure out if they are dangerous. / Most of the time they are just hurt ppl.

This isn't how I pictured things. / Not for you or me. / This is the last sheet of paper until I teach you to make more. / In this house / right now / all I can do not to cry: you & your dad. / This house had a TV. / I wish I could check to see if your father even tried to contact us.

In some ways this is the best love letter / I could have ever given you. My Beautiful Idiot / I know it is supposed to be for T. / But you are her / and don't ever forget it.

I don't have the ability to write you a surgical textbook. / I'm sorry, b/c you're going to need it. / Sterilize everything.

Types of plants. / Some plants that grow here are medicinal. / I'll make a list.

How to nurse a baby. / Don't worry if you can't, or it is hard. / This is common. / You find someone to do it for you. / You just do.

Don't think yr mum didn't cry when she saw all this. / You have the strength she had to help and salvage and make the best of it.

I need you to loot a hospital. / For any and all supplies: gauze to analgesics to anesthetics to needles to basic surgical equipment.

No, I don't know where Dad is, but I know him. / He is safe and helping. / Maybe not the way we are. / But he is helping.

Earth was green and famously blue; white clouds. / But we have brown and red too. / And neon yellow, don't go near that.

Do what you may—no, you have to just destroy the dead. / Too many diseases. / I'm sorry.

We're not sure what happened. / The lack of airborne disease spread leads us to think probably nuclear attack. / No idea from whom. / There was a light.

T., you need to make sure you quarantine parts of the house for the dying.

Mum wishes she could have a glass of wine. / That doesn't mean you shouldn't brush your teeth.

Dad's in some gov't bunker somewhere and I know he wishes he could be here. / He has really important things to do. / Just like us.

Tamara, while I want you to be understanding, set boundaries. / The world I wish you were born into. / I am so very happy, and proud, you learned to play catch.

You put your fingers in everything. / You want to be a part of everything. / I think yr grandparents would be proud.

Mum doesn't want to work until 4:00 a.m./0400. / But she has so much to tell you, and it isn't like a baby book. / It is how to survive. / I should be making ink prints of your feet or some crap.

A government is like when Mum and her friends decide what food to grow, but bigger. / We try.

What you love becomes a part of you. / Yes that sounds like a Hallmark card (I don't even know if you'll get that). / But I have to go feed people.

Tamara, you're going to see so much death. / I wish I could tell you it ends. / That there was a reward. / But you have to do this.

Be careful with your water supplies. / Clean, at least. / Dying of dehydration is both ugly and unpleasant.

I taught you to spell on a Scrabble set. / I don't know which way the wind was blowing that day. / I'm sorry.

Try not to be too hard on them. / And listen to other ppl. / Mums used to luxuriate in making their own organic baby food.

People will have withdrawal from all sorts of things: caffeine, nicotine, benzos, SSRIs, narcotics, alcohol. / Do the best you can.

Bathe. Check for lice with a fine comb. / Lice will freeze, but you need ice. / Comb through hair the best you can.

I want you to find chalk. / Try schools. / You need it for toothpaste. / Trust me, we can't make you new teeth.

Before all this, we sent people into space, to the moon even. / We had pictures of the earth from the moon. / Very pretty, like you.

T., there is so much I want you to know about world history. / Geological, a bunch of -icals./ Great civilizations. / Mistakes.

T., that space I call a "backyard" is a fortified courtyard. / There were playgrounds. / I don't even want to tell you what those were.

Yr mum believed in forgiveness and nonviolence and not-dying. / Recruit (ex)military personnel. / Don't let them take over. / Find a real doctor.

I have a fever, don't I? / Forget the tools & trust yourself. / Put the back of your wrist to my head, / if you feel it is too hot, / you are probably right.

I know you want to see your dad. / I do too, my dad. / But there are other grown-ups here. / They are OK, right?

That is a bit of a drive. I would also argue that unless we know that location is secure, it may have been a target.

I wouldn't say no, I'd say we have to think about it. Right now, there are military facilities within walking range. We check those out first.

No one will replace you / My Beautiful Idiot. / You and T. have to know. / I'm doing the best I can.

People! There is a line of wounded outside our door. / Unless you step up & help out, I will pass out. / Intake: obvious wounds, depth, organs, head injury. / Ask what meds taken. / Ask about everything from caffeine to sleeping pills to vitamins & supplements.

She's adorable. / This adorable brat, and nightmare. / She's beautiful.

We don't have the machines or meds to diagnosis cancer. / A violin. / Piano.

Shh: As much as your mum is a doctor, she is a killer, an assassin. / That is how it works. / Both ways, always. / Be strong.

No, Tamara, my daughter, I don't take good enough care of myself. / That's your job right now. / To remind me.

I never thought I'd order anyone to loot fruit cocktail. / Turns out your grandfather was right / that stuff lasts forever.

We can't grow orange trees here. / We have to can what we have. / Make sure there's a seal.

I can still remember those cities. / I think we have a bird nest. / Yr grandparents would be so annoyed. / Do you want to see?

You need to know about clouds and weather and how I know by the sound that is a nest. / You need to be able to track animals.

I'm so rushed, drawing these maps for you. / I'm sorry. / I know I say that a lot. / I still am. / Yr mum knows more than she thought.

I worry so much that I'm not a good mum. / I take care of all these ppl. / That I skip you. / The most important one.

Sarah Lang

Someone told me to turn on the TV. / I didn't believe it. / I wish you didn't have to believe me.

Mum's computer finally died. / I know that doesn't mean much to you. / It does to Mum, OK? / Here my computer won't work. / One day our pens won't work. / Yes, Mum is annoyed.

May you never know what a Money Mart is. / A mall. / We will find a way to make you balloons.

Yr mum really wants to sleep. / It is 1:00 a.m./0100. / But someone needs a basic abdominal exam. / I thought I taught this already.

Yeah, remembering teaching you to spell w/Scrabble. / In like five writing systems. / You practice.

Don't grow a lawn. / And yes, Mum is scared of wind, OK? / But she will never tell you.

There is still magic in the world. / Why I tell you stories. / Pictures. / Why you eat your vegetables.

Being sick on yr own is really hard. / But we both have the skills to do this. / Don't be stupid enough not to ask for help.

Don't carry a weapon that could be used against you. / Cheerios have remarkable nutritional value.

I need you to hold yr hand above yr heart, head even. / Apply pressure. / I'll go get the kit. / Yr going to need two stitches. / Keep applying pressure. / Keep yr hand above yr head.

Clams at night when the tides are low. / Vines and blackberries to start fire.

Just decided to burn the dictionaries instead of the medical books. / I can't believe it. / I'm so sorry. / I had to. / Save any spare paper.

I need you to get all med supplies. / We are not the best, but we are the best here.

These are your guards. You are the info. This won't be the last place you hit. You are there for your knowledge. Think: We need antibiotics. I need you to pick the best ones for likely infections.

Make sure the bodies are buried away from our water supply. / Just burn them.

The taste of strawberries. / Like people, not literally; just wholly knowing someone that way.

I can't believe the last thing I thought of you was that I was mad / your hair wasn't up.

Magnetize iron (Fe) filings to make a compass. / Or learn your stars.

Tamara, you should know how to make a book now, young lady.

How am I supposed to teach you all this? / It took my parents yrs. / They knew I could handle myself around a bear or a herd of deer.

Stay still, back away slowly. / Never get between a mother and cubs. / Deer can really, really kick. / They knew I knew about weather. / That I could swim. / That to get out of a riptide you swim sideways and then to the shore. / I'm sorry I'll ever underestimate you.

I hope you get to see the sky again.

Turns out Mum will take painkillers so she can help others. / Yes, she knows it is stupid. / And she does her job anyway.

Keep that mercury thermometer. It is far more accurate and doesn't require batteries. / Yes I can tell the most serious cases by touch, but I'd like to be a step ahead. / Shake it down.

You want a chronological description of what happened. / That is one fairy tale I won't be writing.

I never had the time and time doesn't even exactly work that way anyway. / You know our math works with time going backward or forward?

Sarah Lang

T., you should have been starting school. / I know we started a basic one here. / Not the same.

I wish I could tell you if you didn't want to feel so bad about your life, turn on the news. / The fact you can't is worse.

I never believed in guns—nor did your grandmother—so no, I have no idea how to put that thing together.

The smell of a Mayday treee. / Tea roses. / Me.

I wanted a supply list of meds and weapons. / Secondly, I wanted someone to paint a cross on the house to mark it a hospital (help me board it up).

Dad is working on helping us all. / I promise. / Right now, eat those carrots I grew.

Hot soap and water is key. / Bathe. / Wash the dishes, cutlery.

Postal System: an infrastructure designed to send from and deliver to physical materials, like letters, from sender to recipient.

The explosions were brilliant, blinding. / Then clouds. / We'll never know.

The Flatbed

Joyce Carol Oates

—For Henri Cole

She liked to envision him in this way.

Some sort of flatbed. Like the kind hooked behind a small truck.

And he's on the flatbed in some kind of arrangement of chains securing his wrists and ankles so he can't move.

He's sitting up, chained. An awkward posture that must strain his back, neck, legs.

His head is lifted, his eyes are alert and aware.

The flatbed is being hauled along the interstate.

Wet snow has begun to fall. No wind, the snow falls vertically out of a gunmetal sky, mostly melting on the ground.

Who is driving the truck, he can't see.

He's trapped there on the flatbed. Can't move except to jerk his shoulders and head and tug against the chains making his wrists and ankles bloody. He has screamed—but no longer. His throat is raw, he is exhausted.

Snow on his face like melting tears.

Would G. know where he was being hauled, on the flatbed?

Would G. guess it was to a slaughterhouse?

He said, Is it me? Must be.

He was N. who'd come into her life unexpectedly.

He was one in a sequence of men. Most, she eluded and rebuffed and found reasons to dislike, or they suddenly disliked her—one of them said bitterly, *A beautiful face doesn't give you the right.*

She hadn't had to ask, *The right to what?*

Or suddenly she was afraid of them, of what is called *leading a man on.*

For no man likes to be *led on.*

But N. was different, she had no idea why. N., she found herself thinking of, often. Maybe it was an ordinary sort of female yearning. Maybe it was her fear of being left alone or discovered to be a dirty girl, that's to say a badly dirtied girl, past redemption. Or maybe (this was a thought she could hardly acknowledge) she was falling in love with N. as a young woman might fall in love with a man.

A normal young woman. In love with a man.

But now, it had gone wrong. She was stricken with guilt, shame.

For again it happened. Again, her body resisted the man. It was a subtle stiffening of her body, the tension of one poised at the brink of a dangerous action: diving from a high board, for instance.

It was not an obvious rejection of the man, or a rebuff. It was subtle, yet unmistakable. Every molecule in her body shuddering, *No no no.*

And she began to shiver. The shivering was convulsive, and unstoppable.

Her way of combating it—the convulsive, ridiculous shivering in her own bed, in the man's arms—was to clench her jaws tight. If relaxed, her jaws would tremble, her teeth would chatter.

What chagrin, her body shutting up as it did. Like the body of a frightened child.

And the chattering teeth, with another as a witness, so intimate.

She said, No. It isn't you. I . . .

There was a pause. N. was listening to her intently. His breathing was hoarse, harried.

She could not bring herself to say, *It isn't you, I love you.*

He said, Well. Then there is something you haven't told me.

She said, I don't think so.

Amending then, for this sounded too defensive, I—I don't know. I don't think so but I don't really know.

Something you haven't revealed to me yet.

His hands on her, tentative, caressing. As you might lay hands on a frightened and shivering dog, to comfort; to contain, calm, and comfort; and in the strength of the hands, a certain confidence, assurance.

Somebody hurt you, I'm guessing. D'you want to tell me about it?

How many times she hadn't wished to count.

There had been the mortifying first time, when she'd been nineteen years old—*old* for a first-time sexual experience. And there'd been a second time, and a third—and each time baffling, humiliating.

This was perhaps only the fourth time. But it seemed to her the final time. She was twenty-nine years old: She would have no more chances.

As a young girl she'd been diffident about sex. She'd been uncomfortable hearing other girls talk about sex, her friends had laughed at her.

As an older girl she'd become adept at avoiding sexual circumstances. She grew to like the company of boys and men, and they liked her company usually—but it was not a good idea to pursue this attraction, she'd learned.

To mislead another is cruel. To entice, and to repel—this could be dangerous.

For she could not anticipate the reaction of her body. Even if she'd had a few drinks. Even if she felt *loving*.

The clenching of pelvic muscles involuntary as the blinking of an eye when the eye is touched. The panicked withdrawal, recoil.

As if the man touching her, seeking entry into her body, was an instrument of harm, torture—to be repelled.

The panic reflex. The convulsive shivering. She was helpless in thrall to a terrible suffocating fear as the sexual part of her, that had seemed so alive, so yearning, as if thrumming with desire for the man, had shut up like a fist.

No. It was her body's mute cry—*No.*

An aroused male would have the right to be seriously pissed. Seriously offended. He'd have the right to extricate himself from the female, throw on his goddamned clothes and depart and not return.

She could not protest. She could barely murmur, *Sorry.*

At the bottom of the pit she lay helpless. Her body was a child's body, in terror of violation. Clenched tight, shivering.

N. was saying, Will you tell me? Who has hurt you?

She told him no one. Please.

No one? I don't believe that.

She'd managed to control the shivering. Clenching her jaws tight so that her teeth couldn't chatter. *That* was an accomplishment, in these mortifying circumstances.

Until at last N. said, Hey: it's OK. We'll be fine.

N. spoke genially, with a kind of forced cheer. For this, she loved him.

Though he was somewhat mysterious to her—not a man she knew well, except intimately.

She'd calculated that he was at least fifteen years older than she was. She'd gathered that he was the father of children; divorced, and the children near grown. Some bitterness—personal, legal—regarding the ex-wife. And there'd been a domestic tragedy in his life—the death of a child.

To which he'd alluded but of which he had given her to know he did not care to speak, just yet.

Just now he'd seemed to understand, and to forgive. Her body's clenching against his touch was not a clenching against *him*.

The last man who'd touched her in this way, who had tried to make love to her, whom she hadn't liked so much as she liked N., had been sulky, sullen—rudely asking if she'd seen a doctor about this—*problem*.

Asking if it was a *problem* she'd had in the past?

What measures had she taken, or tried to take, to deal with the *problem*.

Sexual frigidity. Fear.

Sexual terror, phobia.

Can't breathe. Can't bear it.

Sorry sorry.

No man wanted to think that it was he whom the woman's body was rejecting. It was necessary to think that the woman had a *problem*—physical, mental.

Yet N. was saying, We just need to go slow, I think. Slower.

Through a buzzing in her ears like cicadas she heard herself murmur *yes*.

I'm a big man. I'm heavy. Heavier than I look. Maybe I scare you. Maybe your body thinks it's being crushed. We can figure some other way. When, you know—you think you're ready.

Heard herself murmur weakly *yes*.

We have plenty of time, right? There's no urgency about any of this.

No urgency! She wanted to think so.

Except: *I am twenty-nine years old not nine years old. I want my life to begin.*

She and N. had known each other for approximately eighteen months. Not as lovers nor even as friends but as acquaintances brought into contact through a professional association in which she, the younger, the female, was a new employee and he, the elder, the male, had a position of authority.

Not that N. was her boss. N. was her superior, of course, but the chain of command didn't link N. and her directly.

The intersection between nonprofit and private. *He* was the private.

Was it true, there was no urgency between them? There is always an urgency to sexual love.

He would find another, she thought. There were so many women. Young, unattached. In the early stages of their careers.

And there were other women, single, divorced, even widowed—a man like N. would not have to look far.

Yet N. had seemed to be attracted to her immediately. A shrewd-hunter look had come into his eyes, when he'd first approached her at a reception. She'd come alone, in black: black silk skirt falling to nearly her ankles, sleeveless black silk top and over it a black velvet jacket that fit her narrow torso like a glove. Her ash-colored hair she'd braided and twisted around her head. He'd greeted her, and peered at her quizzically—he hadn't recognized her at first as one of the young women of the arts foundation, too junior to have a title other than assistant. Then, he'd seemed embarrassed. He said, I'm sorry—I thought you were someone else.

Wittily she'd said, Yes? Who?

Between them something seemed to have been decided. Though they'd spoken to others at the reception they met again as others were leaving and N. said, Have dinner with me? Hey?

She wanted to think that N. was right: There was no urgency between them.

But when they tried to make love another time and her body recoiled—what then?

She was deeply ashamed of her sexual shyness. If that was what it was.

She had never gone to a therapist. The very thought was repugnant to her, such *weakness*.

It was wonderful to her, that N. seemed to forgive her. Kissing her, and caressing her, comforting her and trying to warm her, so that she stopped shivering. Wonderful, this man was on her side.

She'd heard N. had a quick temper. She had not yet witnessed it but she'd heard from others at the arts foundation, who'd been astonished and impressed at the way N. was capable of speaking at meetings, cutting off slow-speaking individuals, interrupting or contradicting others. One of his favored words was *Bullshit*. Another was *Fine!*—meaning the discussion was ended.

It was said of N. that he never attacked younger employees but only individuals of his own approximate rank.

It was said *You wouldn't want to cross him*.

In N.'s arms she lay shivering, less convulsively now. The panic fit was passing.

The bedclothes that had been freshly laundered when she'd made the bed earlier that day were now humid, sticky. A ceiling fan turned wanly overhead. It was an unusually warm autumn. Their bodies were naked and hopeful—or had been. Now they clutched at each other like exhausted swimmers washed to shore.

She felt the fatty flesh at N.'s waist, and at his back: sinewy little knobs of flesh, and bumps and indentations across his back. Sparse, coarse hairs scattered on his back, in striations across his sides. How strange, to be caressing the naked body of a man whom she scarcely knew, yet imagined she might love!

All love is desperation. This is our secret.

Her fingers groped for his penis, which had been so hard, a minute before; now limp, soft skinned, and vulnerable; and his fingers closed over hers in what she felt to be a kind of rebuke, gently pushing away.

Saying, Maybe we need a drink. Maybe that would help.

She wasn't sure that she had anything to drink in the loft. A friend had brought a bottle of red wine to celebrate her moving into these new quarters in a refurbished warehouse overlooking the river but that had been months ago, she'd never opened the bottle and wasn't even sure where it was.

Drinking was not a solace for her. Or, drinking would be too wonderful a solace, she had better not begin.

He had urged her to drink. A little sip of his drink. On their walks, a stop at a *taverna*, as he called it, or a *bistro*, and how delightful, the little girl sipping from the older gentleman's wineglass, until she began to cough, choke.

Then, he'd given her chocolate mints. To disguise the smell of the wine.

Our secret. Just the little darling and me.

N. said, Tell me what you're thinking, Ceille. Just now.

She couldn't recall. What had she been thinking?

She said, I love the sound of my name when you say it. For the first time, I love my name.

Neither made a move to detach from the other. N. would fall asleep kissing her.

That the man so trusted her, felt comfortable with her, after even this clumsy episode, was deeply moving to her.

Badly she wanted to sleep, in the man's arms. It was very late: nearing 2:00 a.m. But she was not so comfortable. Her skin chafed against his. His thick-sounding breathing would keep her awake though she was relieved to hear it close beside her as if this were N.'s bed in N.'s life and she had been taken in by N.

Her brain was alive with thoughts: brittle, darting thoughts like nails that flew about to no purpose. Often in intimate situations this was the case, with another person.

Fear of the other. His strength, and the surprise of what he will ask from you.

What he will execute upon you, without asking.

And still she was cold. Her fingers and toes like ice.

Huddled against the man's warm body, a solid, sizable body, taking up more than half of her bed.

So cold! Bone-marrow cold!

As if her life, a still-young life, were veering to a premature ending like a runaway vehicle on a twisting mountain road where you can see only a few yards ahead for the way is blind, and the descent from the road steep and irrevocable.

Wanting to plead with this deep-slumbering man in her bed, *Love me anyway—can't you? I think—I can love you.*

She'd never told anyone. Not ever.

She'd known better. Already by the age of—had it been seven? eight? ten?—that it would be a mistake to *tell.*

For once you *tell*, you can't take back what you have *told.*

In the household, in the family. And it was a large family.

A family so large if you shut your eyes and tried to assemble them all in the living room, standing and seated in a half circle around the ceiling-high Christmas tree, you could not.

For always there are shadowy figures, vague and undefined at the periphery of the scene. Always, tall male figures whose faces are just slightly blurred.

You could identify them perhaps. But you could not truly see them.

Sometimes, these figures are sitting. In fact, sitting on the floor.

In some juxtaposition to the glittering Christmas tree. The astonishment of the Christmas tree, that so glittered and gleamed and the fragrance of its still-living needles so powerful, just recalling makes you want to cry.

Eyes filled with moisture. The trip of a heartbeat.

Want to cry but will not cry. Not ever *cry.*

For she was a shy child. Shy, and shrewd. You might mistake shyness for slowness, reticence for stupidity, physical wariness for physical ineptitude, but you'd have been mistaken.

He had counseled her, *This is our secret. These are good times but secret.*

He had warned her, *This is our secret. These are good times but secret.*

And so, she had not ever told.

(For who was there to tell? Not her nervous mother, not her irritable father. Often they smiled, startled, seeing her before them as if she were a surprise to them, a happy surprise, amid so many other surprises that were not happy; as if somehow they'd forgotten her, and the sight of her was a happy reminder; for she'd been led to believe from a young age that she was the one happy thing in their lives, despite being an "accident" in their lives—*I think we were burnt out almost—with the marriage—playing house—we'd had our kids, we thought: four of them! Jesus! And then—our darling. . . .*)

(And later, in grade school, when still it was happening to her, still she was in thrall to him-whose-identity-she-could-not-reveal, she could not have told her teachers, nor could she have told another child, even her best friends—especially not her best friends. From the experiences of others who'd had far less significant secrets to reveal she'd learned how *telling* flew back in the face of the *teller* like spitting in the wind. Forever afterward you were the one who'd *told*, the *tattletale*; and what had been done to you would be irrevocably mixed up in the minds of others with *you*.)

No one knew. No one wished to know. No one asked *her*.

The family was large, and well-to-do. The name *Bankcroft* was attached to a downtown street and a square and a dignified old office building. *Bankcroft* exuded an air of satisfaction, pride.

Brothers, sisters, cousins, aunts and uncles and grandparents.

These were highly sociable people. Most evenings there were visitors in the big old Victorian house.

In such circumstances you would think that a little girl so frequently singled out for special attention by a (male, older) relative would be observed. But you would be mistaken.

Our baby. Our darling. I'm shamelessly spoiling her—she's my last baby.

Everyone adores her! They just can't help it.

Her mother certainly adored her. But mostly when others were present. At the start of dinner parties she was shown off—her curly ash-blonde hair, her special party dress and fancy little shoes—then carried away upstairs by a nanny hired for such purposes.

To have *told* her mother! She could not.

For she could foresee: the look on her mother's face.

Surprise, hurt, disbelief. *No no no no no*—this could never be.

To have *told* her father! Absolutely *no*.

All this, she would have to explain to N. If she did not, she would lose him.

And if she did, very likely she would lose him just the same.

Yes, of course, as a child she'd been taken to a doctor periodically.

A (male) family doctor, pediatrician. An acquaintance of her mother's and so during the visits, in the examination room, her mother and Dr. T. chatted.

The examinations were routine, perfunctory, nontraumatic. The examinations did not involve an inspection of the child's body inside her clothing for why would one do such a thing? With the child's mother present, friendly, and sociable?

Visits to Dr. T.'s office usually involved a "booster" vaccine, possibly earwax removal.

She who was her mother's *darling* endured these visits to the doctor stoically. Young she'd learned the strategy of being mature beyond her years.

Later, as a young adolescent, she'd had to endure the ignominy and pain of a gynecological examination.

Here, the doctor was her mother's (female) doctor: obstetrician, gynecologist.

The examination of her small, hard breasts had been both painful and humiliating but she'd managed to bear it without resistance only just biting hard on her lower lip, to draw a little blood.

The pelvic exam had been so brutal, such a shock to her rigid-quivering body, in horror and disbelief she'd begun to cry, laugh, hyperventilate—this could not possibly be happening to her, that which was happening to her—*worse, far worse, more painful and more terrifying than what had been perpetrated on her as a child, which she'd begun to forget*; the examination had had to be terminated for the delicate-boned girl was squirming, thrashing, kicking in hysterics, in danger of injuring both the examining doctor and herself.

Her mother had accompanied her to the gynecologist's office but now that she was fourteen, and so seemingly self-composed, she'd asked her mother to please remain out in the waiting room. Now, her poor shocked mother had to be hurriedly summoned into the examination room by one of the nurses.

It took some minutes to calm the hysterical girl. Her blood pressure had been taken at the start of the examination and had been one hundred over sixty; after the bout of hysterics, her blood pressure was one hundred thirty-five over sixty.

The doctor who was her mother's friend was both concerned and annoyed.

Telling her mother to take her home. The examination was over.

She's had a shock. She's extremely sensitive. Maybe some other time I can do a pelvic exam. But not today.

She'd had to comfort her mother, on the way home. Assuring her mother that she would have no "traumatic" memories of the assault.

And afterward she'd overheard, by chance, her mother telling her father, in a rueful tone, *At least we know she's a virgin!*

Yet, years later, when she was living alone, and went alone to a (female) gynecologist, for a routine examination, virtually the same thing happened: shock, hysterics.

Except then, for God's sake, she'd been twenty-three years old.

Though technically still a virgin but no longer a skittish young teenager.

Usually, she avoided doctors. She was in "perfect health"—so she believed. But for medical insurance purposes, in connection with her new employment, she'd had to have a routine physical examination and this included a gynecological examination.

Again, she'd managed to endure the breast exam. But the pelvic exam was as brutal as she'd recalled. The gynecologist was a young Chinese-American woman, very skilled, soft spoken; she'd explained what she was doing, as if to mollify her tense patient; she'd shown her the speculum—was that the word? the very sound of it made her tremble—which was an instrument of torture to her, a crude caricature of the male penis, unbearable. Involuntarily, on the examination table, feet in stirrups and knees raised and parted, she'd recoiled as she had at the age of fourteen; her lower lip would ooze blood afterward, where she'd almost bitten through it.

The young woman gynecologist had been concerned. She couldn't complete the examination, she hadn't been able to get a Pap swab, there was no way to know if the young woman shivering and shuddering on the examination table had a vaginal infection, or—something more serious.

I'm so sorry! My God. Please forgive me. We can try again.

It was the voice of reason. Her best self. But the child self, quivering with hurt, in dread of further hurt, was always there, waiting for the collapse of the best, adult self.

But she'd managed. She had gripped the edges of the leather examination table and held her trembling knees parted as the gynecologist reinserted the speculum, to open her vagina, to open it terribly as a delicate flower might be opened, exposed to a harsh, killing sun.

What relief then, the speculum was withdrawn!

Am I bleeding? But bleeding doesn't last.

It's normal to bleed and the blood to coagulate.

Yet, there was more to the exam. The gynecologist had not yet finished. Inserting her rubber fingers into the young woman's vagina, pressing against her lower abdomen, to determine if there were tumorous growths, irregularities. And, at the end, a rectal exam—swiftly executed, and less painful.

In the vagina were scars, fine as hairs, faded scars—and in the soft, moist walls of the uterus. So the gynecologist said, puzzled.

Have you had an illness, an infection? This would have been some years ago, perhaps.

Shook her head *no*. Did not know.

Or some sort of—accident? Or . . .

There was a long pause. An awkward pause.

Until Dr. Chen said, It's healed now. Whatever it was, it has healed. Do you have pain with sexual intercourse?

Shook her head *no*. Frowning and vague as if to suggest, *That is a private matter, Doctor!*

The gynecologist regarded her with an expression of—was it sympathy? Pity?

She thought, *This woman knows. She is my sister.*

Carefully Dr. Chen said, Do you have any questions to ask me? We will receive the results of the Pap test in a few days and we will call you.

The dreaded exam was over. In triumph the shaken young woman sat up on the leather table, tissue paper bristling beneath her buttocks. A smear of lubricant, a barely visible smear of blood on the paper.

Thank you, Doctor.

She'd gone away smiling. Whistling.

These good times no one will know. Our secret.

*

The Pap test came back negative. It was a confirmed fact, she was in perfect health.

No need to see any doctor for a long, long time.

N. said, We have to talk.

Gravely and profoundly N. fixed his gaze upon her. He'd urged her to sit down, to be still. For there was a need for her, in N.'s presence, to be always moving about, to a window, for instance, to glance nervously down into the street. The sound of a phone ringing, in a neighboring loft, was distracting to her.

Wanting to tell him, to amuse him, that she'd had a "stalker" once—when she'd still been a university student.

Foreign born, dusky skinned, lonely looking. He'd waited for her in stairwells, on the sidewalk in front of the residence hall. (He'd been a graduate or postdoc, she thought, in something unimaginably difficult—molecular biology, computational neuroscience.) She'd smiled at him in her careless way and he'd followed her home and thereafter for much of her senior year he'd hung about with yearning doggy eyes and her roommates had been concerned for her. *Aren't you worried? Shouldn't we report him to security?* And she'd laughed, saying, *Don't be silly. He'll give up soon.*

Through a rustling in her brain N. was saying gravely, Look, I love you. We have to talk.

Love you had the air of a mild rebuke. He was chiding her, as you would a small, stubborn, self-destructive child.

Frowning, N. said, You aren't being honest with me. If you care for me, as I care for you, we have to be honest with each other.

Care for me. Care for you. These words were giddy in her ears, she was stricken to the heart.

She'd never *told*. She could not begin now at her ridiculous age.

He had never threatened to hurt her, exactly. The tall (male) figure of her childhood. She was sure he'd never hurt or injured her, it was bizarre to suggest that he'd inserted something into her tiny child's vagina so sharp that it had left miniature scars; her mother, or one of her older sisters, would have discovered bloodstains on her panties, and all would have been exposed.

Though this individual, this tall (male) figure so predominant in the life of her family, alone of his (older) generation insisting upon sitting on the floor, Indian style on the thick carpet in front of the Christmas tree, with the kids. An individual whom her mother greatly respected, adored, and to a degree feared; a man whom her father greatly admired, though G. had never been particularly friendly to him.

Which was a mystery, since G. was her father's father.

Good times our secret. Ours.

And so, she'd never told. In recent years when she tried to recall what *it* was—exactly what had been done to her, and with her; what sorts of things he'd shown her, and spoken of to her—she'd discovered that she remembered very little at all.

There was such banality to it—"recovered" memory.

Or was it "repressed" memory?

She'd never tried to explain to any man. Never to any of the boys with whom she'd been friendly in high school. Boys who'd been attracted to her in ways flattering to her even as she understood, *They don't know me. How disgusted they would be, if they knew me.*

But she could not. She could not *tell*. Not only was she repelled by the prospect of *telling*, she would have faltered and fumbled for words. For, when she'd been a little girl, and entrusted to this tall dignified relative, a kind of blindness had come over her, amnesia like a fine, pale mist—she could not really remember clearly what he'd done to her, only the air of furtive excitement, anxiety, and elation. *That he was getting away with it. Under the noses of the family. His family! That was part of the attraction.*

All that she could remember of those years was both faded and overbright, like a photograph of an exploding nova. You understood that there was something inside the blinding light but you could not see it. You could not identify it.

He'd given her gifts. Countless gifts. He'd taken her to *The Nutcracker* each year at the War Memorial. And to *A Christmas Carol*.

He'd taken her sisters and her brother to some of these occasions, as well. He'd given them presents. He'd pressed his forefinger against his lips, smiling. *Don't be jealous, darling! It's to make them think that they are your equal though we know better.*

He'd been clever. He'd never been suspected—not once.

She'd been made to know that she was special. That was the secret.

And now, she did not want to acknowledge herself as a victim. In this era of victims, "survivors." She could not identify herself as one of them. She was too accomplished a young woman, and too promising—in her career in which she had an excellent job helping to oversee the funding of arts projects, if not in her private life. If she'd been visibly wounded, crippled—she would have stubbornly denied it. For she did not want pity, nor even sympathy.

She would explain to N. That she could not tell him who he'd been, the man who had despoiled her life. She could not share with him such memories.

And of course, she wasn't certain. She remembered—some things. But in patches, like broken clouds.

Broken clouds blown swiftly across the sky. You crane your neck to observe, as the clouds are blown away and disappear.

Oddly she did recall G.'s voice, sometimes. In others' voices, she heard G.'s voice. His grunted words. And pleas—she remembered pleas. (But these were not his. These were hers.) In the speeches of politicians she heard the thrilling timbre of his voice, the voice of a public man, even when he'd retired from public office.

The fact was, G. had been a locally renowned man. *Bankcroft* the revered name.

All of the family was proud of that name. She too had been proud of that name except in secret she'd been ashamed of that name for it was *his* name, as it was her own.

She would not tell N.: a ten-year-old child is capable of considering suicide.

Killing oneself isn't such a secret now. Not such a taboo. A child is well aware of suicide attempts, and of successful suicides. As a child is aware of death generally. And betrayal.

She'd moved three hundred sixty miles away from *Bankcroft Street, Bankcroft Square, the Bankcroft Building.*

Yes, she'd been proud that G. had so favored *her*. You would have been proud too.

They'd sung together, on their walks. G. had taught her *"You Are My Sunshine," "I'm Dreaming of a White Christmas," "Tea for Two."* Jaunty tunes were G.'s specialty. Hand in hand. She had not ever tried to run away. She had not ever tried to wrest her hand from his, and run away.

Through the cemetery she might have run. Run run run until her little heart burst and she fell amid the weatherworn old grave markers striking her head, cracking her skull so the bad memories leaked out like black blood.

He had not ever injured her. His finger inserted inside her to tickle, that was all.

Tickle tickle! That's my good little girl.

Of all that G. had told her, the stream of words, chatter and banter, teasing and cajoling, years later she would recall virtually nothing.

The grunts, she did remember.

And when they'd been alone together (when he'd managed to arrange that they were alone together: could be a visit to Cross Memorial Cemetery to the grave of his dear departed wife who'd been buried beneath a shiny salmon-colored grave marker) he hadn't felt the need for words.

His hand gripping hers had been sufficient. No need for words.

Plunged to a place beyond language where even his careful, cautious demeanor dissolved, spittle gathered in the corners of his mouth and his eyes rolled white beyond the dignified gold-rimmed glasses.

N. said, You're thinking of him now. You're remembering.

She denied this. Guiltily, weakly she denied this.

No. You're thinking of him now. Tell me who he is!

N. was becoming impatient, angry. She had not guessed at the start of their relationship how aggressive N. might be, how possessive of her.

She would have risen, walked quickly away. But N. seized her hands in his, and held her in place.

Tell me who he was. What happened.

Her hands, gripped by his. She felt a swirl of vertigo.

Whoever it was—the bastard! Tell me.

She was not adept at lying. Bold, frank, outright lies. She was no good at such. But she'd become adept at another sort of lie, shrewdly nuanced, ambiguous. The lie that is an omission, a failure to totally recall.

Yet even this, she could not risk. For N. seemed to see into her innermost heart.

Someone hurt you. Sexually. Or—in some other way, as well as sexual. Tell me.

I did tell you! I told you *no*.

Something that went wrong, something that left a wound. Not a scar that has healed. A bleeding wound.

I am not a—bleeding wound. Don't do this to me.

N. was smiling at her. But N. was not smiling with her.

He was more than a dozen years older than she was: yet not old, only just in his early forties. A still-young, vigorous man. A man whose physical being seemed trapped, or in any case contained and repressed, inside his proper businessman clothing: expensive suits, shoes.

His background had been, he'd said, working class.

Or maybe just a little lower.

Immigrant grandparents, and his father had worked with his hands most of his life, and had wanted to be, for a few years in adolescence, a professional boxer.

He, N., had tried boxing at a neighborhood gym. In high school.

He'd loved it. Hitting, and even, to a degree, getting hit. But there were guys in the neighborhood, black kids, some of them built like Mike Tyson at age fifteen-sixteen—they'd discouraged N., you might say.

So, he'd quit. Probably just in time before he'd gotten seriously hurt.

His hair was thick, sleekly brushed back across his furrowed scalp. She could see the boxer-hunter in him now: the way his eyes were fixed upon her.

She was frightened of him, in that instant.

She'd thought him husbandly, fatherly. But there was something else now, a deeper and more primitive being.

She said, I—I can't remember . . .

What? What can't you remember?

. . . what happened, or . . .

When? When was this, that you can't remember?

Not recently. Not for a long time.

And who was it?

Who was it?—no one . . .

Fuck that! Tell me.

Oh, he's an old man now—he isn't the man who . . .

She was laughing. Her face was bright as a flame, her very hair seemed to stir on her head, like upright flames. He was staring at her in triumph, he had won. He had overpowered her, he had obliterated her opposition to him. Never in her life had she uttered such things—it was unbelievable to her, she'd said so much. Secrets snatched from her, irremediably. Her burning face she hid, she wiped at her eyes. Bright laughter fell from her mouth like broken glass.

She'd twisted her hands out of his grip, but now she seized his hands, his large hot hands, and held them tight.

In a lowered voice she said, I never told anyone.

He said, Until now.

He deserves to die. Anyone who harms a child.

But you promised!

Fuck my promise. That was before.

*

And then he was saying, I promise not to harm him. But I would like to talk to him.

She called home. A rarity in recent years.

She preferred e-mail. Though she did not often write to her parents, either.

At once her mother heard something in her voice. Her mother asked what was wrong, why was she calling so late in the evening, was it an emergency?—sounding both frightened and annoyed.

A mother's first thought is *Pregnant!*

She said, No! It is not an emergency.

She said, The emergency was years ago. Not now.

Her mother said, Emergency? What are you talking about, Cecie?

Tell me how G. is. I don't hear about G. much any longer.

G. was Grandfather. Or, as he'd liked to be called, with a French flourish, *Grandpapa.*

He's—well. I mean, reasonably well, for his age. He's just returned from—I think it was the Amalfi Coast. He'd gone on a tour, with friends. He's still involved in politics, behind the scenes. You know how the Bankcrofts are! He comes to dinner here at least twice a week and sometimes after mass, we have brunch at the High Bridge Inn. I wish he and your father got along better together but he just—sort of—ignores Matt. He asks after you. . . .

Does he? Does he ask after me?

Of course. Grandpapa always asks after you.

What does he ask?

What does he *ask*? Just how are you doing, your work, are you engaged, or seeing someone—the usual questions.

He wants to know if I'm "engaged" or "seeing someone"? And why is that his business?

Your grandfather asks after all his grandchildren, now that so many of you are scattered and living far away.

But me, he asks after *me*?

Why are you asking me this, Cecie? Why now?

I think you must know why.

What do you mean? I—I don't know why. . . .

Why didn't he ever remarry, after Grandma died? Wasn't anyone good enough for him? All those rich widows!

Why are you asking such questions? Why about your grandfather? You sound so angry, Cecie. . . .

No. I'm not angry. Why would I be angry?

I have no idea, Cecie. You've always had this way about you—this unpredictable short temper—first you call late, you must know a phone ringing past 11:00 p.m. usually means bad news, and now—

She interrupted, saying, I think I will hang up now.

Please, wait—

I'm sorry to disturb you, Mother. You're right, it is late. Good night!

None of them knows. None will guess.
Our secret is safe, little darling, sealed with a kiss.

She told N.: It isn't an issue in my life. I never think of it, truly.

Bullshit. You think of it all the time.

N. touched her. His warm, broad hand across her belly, a lover's casual caress, and she stiffened at once.

All the time you are thinking of it. I could see it in your face, before I spoke to you.

She wanted to protest: She was always so much more than whatever had been perpetrated upon her.

A fact she kept to herself to nourish herself like something warm—a heated stone, or medallion—a kind of shield—pressed against her breasts and belly, secreted beneath her clothing.

She took pride in all that she was, which had nothing to do with the naively trusting little girl she'd been more than fifteen years ago.

For instance, she was a swimmer: almost a serious swimmer. In the dark of winter she rose early to swim in the university pool, for which she paid a yearly fee since she'd graduated from the university with a master's degree in social psychology.

In the shimmering water, her body dissolved into pure sensation, the strength of her muscled arms and legs to keep her afloat and to propel her forward. Once, N. would observe her swimming in the university pool, in the early morning, and would stare in surprised admiration. For her body was sleek, slender, and yet strong—this was not the body of a female victim. *If you've been thinking you know me, you are mistaken.*

And she took pride in her professional career. Such as it was.

(And was G., too, proud of her? She had to suppose so. Her mother continued to forward greetings from G. to her: occasional cards, presents. He'd learned her latest address in order to send her a lavish bouquet of two dozen yellow roses in celebration of her appointment at the arts foundation; she'd shocked friends by gaily tossing them into the trash.)

She had her job. Her new position. She loved books—nineteenth-century novels, classics—her favorites were *Bleak House*, *Middlemarch*, *Tess of the D'Urbervilles*, and *Jude the Obscure*. She could reread these, late at night when she couldn't sleep; or she could watch the late-night Classic Film Channel—Cary Grant, Greer Garson, Spencer Tracy, Katharine Hepburn, Humphrey Bogart, Clark Gable, Rita Hayworth. Their faces were comforting to her, like the faces of distant relatives.

Several times she'd seen *The Red Shoes*. Mesmerized, and deeply moved.

She felt a perverse sympathy for the murderous lovers of *Double Indemnity*. Each time she saw the film, the ending came to her as a shock—for it might so easily have been another kind of ending.

She went to gallery openings. She went to poetry readings. She bought books for the poets to sign that she kept in a special place in her loft apartment, on a windowsill in the sun.

What are these? N. asked curiously.

She selected one of the slender books, opened it as if casually, and read lines of surpassing beauty and wonder:

What a fine performance they gave!
Though they didn't know where they were going,
they made their prettiest song of all.

N. asked what did this mean. Was it a happy poem?

She said, I think so. Yes.

Another thing about her, another special thing, to set her off from the pack of other good-looking young women, Ceille dressed exclusively in black.

*

She told him about the flatbed. A man chained on the flatbed behind a truck hauled on the interstate.

He whistled between his teeth. Where's the man being taken, to a slaughterhouse?

Yes. To a slaughterhouse.

But do you get that far? In the dream, I mean.

No. It's just the flatbed behind the truck, and him on it chained and knowing where he's being taken. He has plenty of time to think about where's he's being taken and what will be done to him then.

But you've never gotten that far.

He seemed to be goading her into saying, *Not yet.*

They were lying together on her bed. On the rainbow afghan on her bed. There were ways of intimacy, ways of avoiding her sexual fear, they were learning, in compensation.

In each other's arms not fully undressed. As a parent might comfort a fretting child so N. comforted her. Kissing her forehead, the hot pit of her neck, which made her laugh wildly, and squirm.

It wasn't your fault, Ceille. I hope you know that.

She knew. She wished to think so.

A young child, an adult—there is no way that a child can "consent." The law recognizes this. And the moral law.

She smiled. She laughed. For he'd quoted a German philosopher to her once, in one of his playful extravagant moods in which he pretended that she wasn't a little girl but an adult and an equal—"*The starry sky above, and the moral law within.*"

Why G. had quoted Immanuel Kant to her, she had no idea.

Only that he was a highly successful public man who tired of being public and accountable and responsible and adult and so at these secret times he was playful and extravagant and could not be predicted in his behavior as he could not be reined in, or controlled.

He smelled of a sweet cologne dabbed on his clean-shaven jaw. You wanted to smile at this fragrance, or you wanted to hide your face and cry. His *tickle finger* was a special finger and the nail always kept clean and filed by G. himself with an emery board carried in his pocket.

You're thinking of him now, Ceille? Tell me.

She bit her lip. She would not.

It makes me sick, Ceille. When you think of him. When you're with me, like this, and goddamn, you think of *him*.

She wanted to console him. *Yes. It makes me sick too.*

His name? Who he was, to you?

He was—he—

Her heart beat painfully. She was frightened she would faint.

—he was very clever. No one ever knew, or suspected. In all those years—six years. He was *trusted.*

And did he victimize other girls? What about your sisters?

No.

No? Are you sure?

She tried to think. She was laughing, this conversation was so ridiculous, years too late to matter.

Oh no. I mean—yes. I'm sure.

He hadn't adored them. They were older, less attractive.

I was his little darling!

It would be premeditated. Therefore, it would have to be skillfully executed.

N. had a law degree. He'd practiced law for several years. He told her to contact the relative who'd molested her for six years and to arrange to meet him in a neutral place.

Quickly she said, *No.*

Unless, she said, *The cemetery.*

N. asked if it was a cemetery where people would be likely to be visiting, where they might be observed.

She said no. Her grandmother had been buried in a part of the cemetery owned by the Bankcroft family and this was at the edge of the cemetery near a pine forest.

You won't hurt him? You will just speak with him.

That's right. Just speak with him.

G. must have thought it was strange, at last she called him. It had been years since they'd seen each other for, of course, she had avoided family gatherings as soon as she'd left home.

Cecilia! Is it you?

The shock in his voice. Yet the old warmth beneath, she'd forgotten.

She'd been very clever. She'd learned G.'s current telephone number in a circuitous way so that the fact that she'd sought out the number might not be immediately evident. She had not asked her mother or her father, for instance.

She heard herself say, I miss my old life, Grandpapa. I am having some hard times now. I am very lonely, Grandpapa.

Grandpapa. This had been the magic name.

Pronounced as if French. Emphasis upon *grand.*

Blithe and bright, she spoke to the astonished man at the other end of the line. Asking to see him, so that she might introduce him to her fiancé, who was a secret from the family.

Secret? But why?

When you meet him, you will know. I will trust in your intuition.

This was flattering to him, she knew. This was the silver hook in his fat wet lip that would doom him.

In Cross Cemetery. We can meet there.

In Cross Cemetery?

Yes. Please.

But—why don't you come to the house first. . . .

At Grandma's grave, we can meet. Where we used to walk, Grandpapa, remember?

Of course, I remember, darling. How could I forget?

Truly the old man was flattered, hypnotized. This slow hour of his old-man life and the phone had rung and it was his *little darling* calling him who had never in her life called him before.

I've kept up on your news, darling. Your mother keeps me informed. I know you've moved. I know you have a new job that sounds important but I would guess it probably doesn't pay much so if you need some money, darling—just let me know.

That would be very kind, Grandpapa. We could talk about that.

Before hanging up the phone, she said suddenly, Oh I miss you, Grandpapa! So much.

Each would be away for the weekend. N. in New York City, Ceille in Washington, DC.

So they told friends. So N. told his near-grown children.

In N.'s SUV they then drove west to Rochester. It was a clear sunny vivid autumn morning in October.

She'd had a sleepless night. She warmed her hands at the dashboard heating vent as N. drove.

She was distracted by a pickup truck speeding ahead of them. The flatbed of the truck, piled with what appeared to be lumber.

And the lumber secured to the flatbed by chains.

She said, as if she'd only just thought of this, He's older now. He isn't a danger now. I'm sure.

(She was not sure. She was certainly not sure of this.)

I've heard he has had medical problems. I think cancer of some kind—prostate, probably.

(Of this she was more certain. Her mother had kept her advised of her Grandpapa Bankcroft knowing how much he meant to her, far more than he meant to his other grandchildren.)

N. said, Of course he victimized other children. Before you, and after you.

N. said, You didn't tell. He'd terrified you, and you didn't tell. And so, another little girl was victimized after you. That is the pattern.

N. was not accusing her. Carefully he spoke, sympathetic.

Now we're breaking the pattern. This will end it.

She wasn't hearing this. She was thinking maybe it had been a mistake to have confessed to N. For now, the secret had been revealed. She'd unfurled a precious garment to be trampled in the mud.

She laughed, shivering. She was very excited!

Playfully she warmed her icy fingers between his legs.

N. pushed her hands away. Don't distract me, darling. I'm trying to drive.

He'd made a reservation in a high-rise upscale motel outside the city, eleventh floor overlooking the interstate and, in the distance, the serrated skyline of the city of Rochester. They were registered under a fictitious name as *Mr. & Mrs.*

Her love for N. was no longer a separate thing she could detach from her and hold at arm's length to contemplate.

Her love for N. had burrowed deep inside her. Her love for N. was inextricable from her fear of N.

In Cross Memorial Cemetery they saw him: the lone tall figure, still erect, well dressed, with a head of thick, white hair. In his right hand he gripped an ebony cane in a way to suggest that the cane was mostly for show, not really needed.

He is only seventy-two or seventy-three, she said. He is not *old*.

Grandpapa had brought a pot of golden mums to the grave. The grandmother's grave.

It was famously known, locally—how grief-stricken G. had been, how heartbroken at the end of the long, good marriage of forty-six years.

So good then, G. had had his family to console him. His young relatives, grandchildren.

On the graveled path they approached G. It was afternoon, the sky was amassing with clouds blown down from Lake Ontario. The last visitors were leaving the cemetery.

Now G. had sighted them. G. was alert and staring at them. At her. Slow, happy recognition came into his face like candlelight.

Hi, Grandpapa!

Cecilia!

He moved to her, just perceptibly favoring his right leg. He would have taken her hand extended to him to squeeze her hand in greeting—but N. stepped between them.

Don't touch her!

White-haired G. stiffened. His smile faded.

His face was fine creased, clean shaven. He was a handsome old man who did not look his age. She felt a touch of vertigo in his presence.

N. was addressing G. calmly. Yet you could feel the mounting anger.

N.'s anger was inward, secret. Like N.'s love, which was indistinguishable from possession.

G. began to stammer, to N. Foolish words were shaped by the old-man lips, and wattles in the old-man face trembled.

She stood a little behind N. She saw that her grandfather had forgotten her in the confusion.

I—I have no idea what you are talking about, sir. Keep your voice down, please.

G. was indignant but G. was pleading. She was remembering how she and her family had heard G.'s voice frequently on the local radio news; they'd seen him often on television. He'd been a politician—township council, US congressman on the Republican ticket—in the prime of his career.

G. was backing away from N. now. G. was visibly shaken—this was not the reception he'd anticipated.

His favorite granddaughter and her fiancé!—her secret fiancé.

Introduced to *him*.

Wanting a blessing from *him*.

With a shaky hand G. was tugging a handkerchief out of a pocket, dabbing at his nose.

A red-veined nose, this was. Still handsome and still youthful but broken capillaries marred the clean-shaven skin, and the alert eyes were ringed in creases.

He said, I have no idea what you are talking about, sir. If you don't desist, I will call 911.

N. spoke further. N. was accusing G. of certain acts—"repeated statutory rape"—"sexual assault upon a minor."

G. said indignantly, What has the girl been telling you! I did nothing to be ashamed of.

He said, Those were lost years. The girl was lonely.

Turning away with a look of wounded dignity. And the fear beneath.

Turning away on the graveled path clutching at his cane hoping that the confrontation had ended, he would be allowed to leave; that N., the girl's fiancé, advancing upon him, was going to let him go.

I want him to shit his pants. To be that scared.

The savagery of these words shocked her. She had no idea where they had come from.

She was hanging back, very excited. The shivering had begun, her teeth were chattering. She saw the chagrin, sick guilt, yet righteousness in her grandfather's face. No! They could not let him walk away.

He would have walked away except N. sprang after him. The joy in N.'s face as he grabbed the fancy shining-ebony cane.

Sir! What are you—

Fuck you, old man! You're not going anywhere.

Foolishly G. tried to retrieve the cane. N. swung the cane at him, striking his head, his shoulders. Swift and deadly and unerring and paying no heed to the old man's pleas.

She was hiding her face. A little girl peeking through her fingers.

In the parking lot the last of the cemetery visitors were driving away. This was a good-luck sign: a blessing.

She was telling N. it was enough now.

N. paid not the slightest heed to her. He did not hear her at all.

With a kind of sick fascination she held back. She saw her lover N. striking G., who'd been *Grandpapa*. She wanted to cry, *No! Stop! He did love me.*

Within seconds the white-haired man had fallen. Still N. continued to strike at him, cursing.

The white-haired man on hands and knees in the grass. Desperately trying to crawl, to escape amid the gravestones.

N. stooped over him, now striking him with his closed fist. You filthy son of a bitch. You disgusting old pervert. Inflicting yourself on a little girl—you bastard! She shut her eyes, she could not bear to see the white-haired man so humiliated, broken.

Yet there was pleasure in this: so swiftly happening after the stasis of years.

And still G. was pleading. Not to her but to N., whom he had never seen before in his life and whose taut, furious face would be the last face he saw.

She should have intervened. Beforehand, she knew she would feel this way afterward.

Yet she did not move. Eagerly her eyes were fixed on the fallen man, the bright exploding blood from his scalp, his flailing hands.

You're filth. You don't deserve to live, you filth.

The old man whimpered. The younger man cursed him.

A beating of several minutes. You thought it would cease, yet it continued. Such a deliberate beating can't be rushed, or careless. Even N. was staggering with exhaustion, he'd broken the ebony cane across a grave marker and flung both pieces at the fallen man in disgust.

When they left the cemetery, walking without haste on the graveled path, not wanting to attract attention, they checked another time and saw no one: Cross Memorial Cemetery was deserted.

From the parking lot, no one was visible in Cross Memorial Cemetery. Within a few hours the sun would sink beneath the horizon, for dusk came early at this time of year in Rochester, New York.

They drove to the motel where they were *Mr. & Mrs.*

Eleventh floor of a high-rise building overlooking the interstate and already headlights were shining out of the gathering darkness.

N.'s breath was still quickened, hoarse. She'd discovered that he was asthmatic, to a mild degree. As a boy, he'd suffered more seriously from the condition.

Wryly rubbing his knuckles. Though he'd worn thin leather gloves, yet his knuckles ached.

I hope you didn't h-hurt him badly. I hope . . .

Goddamn! I hope I did.

N. had opened the minibar. N. poured a tiny bottle of scotch into a glass for Ceille and a tiny bottle of scotch into a glass for himself. Laughing, they struck the glasses together, hard. Ceille steeled herself, lifted the glass, and swallowed.

They fell onto the absurd king-sized bed. The size of a football field, as N. described it.

Drinking, and laughing. They were so happy suddenly.

N. kissed her, protruding his tongue into her mouth. She could not breathe, she was so very excited. The man kissed her breasts, her belly, he tugged open her clothing, she could not restrain him. In the cemetery G. was dying of an artery broken and bleeding into his brain. She seemed to know this. She was touching N.'s penis to guide it into her, or against her; gently nudging between her legs, the sweetest of caresses she felt with such intense pleasure, she could scarcely bear it. And he, the man, whose name she had forgotten in the exigency of the moment, shuddered and moaned in her arms, as she held him, as tightly as her arms could clutch.

In the cemetery miles away the old man would not regain consciousness. The beautiful white hair was soaking with blood. The skull like an eggshell had been cracked and could not ever be repaired.

A trickle of sensation in her groin, she began to shudder, it came so strong. She shut her eyes seeing the trickle of blood seeping into the old man's brain. She would have wept except N. was kissing her mouth and his tongue filled her mouth.

No one will ever know, she thought. *Our secret.*

That Obscure Object of Desire
Ryan Ruby

TIME HAD LONG SINCE left me in the lurch, stood me up, hung me out to dry. So all I can say for certain is that, by the time I found myself in the subway station at DeKalb Avenue, I was neck-deep in the nth hour of an obsessive mania. Already there had been a sleepless night, a foodless day, innumerable cigarettes, half a dozen cups of coffee. The telltale symptoms of incipient madness—anxiety, delusion, suspicion, and yes, *a voice*—were staring me down, hands raised. Schoolman that I am, I dutifully marked each one "present" on an imaginary roster with quick synaptic flicks of the wrist.

A homuncular percussionist, you see, had installed himself in my chest, where he was playing my pulse in odd time signatures. Instead of a motley assortment of paint cans and plastic tubs, he was using my heart for a snare, my stomach for a ride, and the two hemispheres of my brain for his toms. I paced the platform, from one end to the other, incapable of standing still. I watched familiar objects like trash cans, signboards, staircases, backpacks, and human faces dissolve into hideous shapes and colors. No joke was necessary to elicit from my lips a dry cackling. Unidentified vermin flew across my path and disappeared. *Was it that they were moving too fast? Or that they were not there at all?*

When it finally came, the Union Square–bound Q wore an inviting expression, lascivious and merciful as a nun's. Through the vivid neon whiteness of the car's interior, I stared far longer than is considered polite at my fellow passengers, swearing in each instance that somewhere, sometime I'd met this or that unfortunate victim of my unbreakable gaze.

Meanwhile, my autonarrator was on autopilot, slurring his words, having selected as his imperative speed rather than sense. *How had I contracted this lunatic!* I wondered, crumpled-up, dirty fingernails to throbbing temples. Of our cannonball journey across the Manhattan Bridge, he pontificated: *Ligature is a training pants of moolvee like a stringency of beadledom; and as we pass through them they prove to be many-colored lentigos which paint the world federalism their own huff and each shows only what lies in its own foetation.* Which observation was punctuated by a series of tourettic ejaculations, a half a dozen *plips*, *knuffles*, and *screes* that hardly deserve, even by the low standards of this crushing avalanche of logorrhea, to be called speech. *This*, I thought, *this must be rock bottom.*

To every obsession, its object. In my case, it was a book: *Inferno*, by August Strindberg.

Why this particular object and not some other?

That it should have been a book doesn't surprise me in the least. Bibliomania is as congenital as suicide and schizophrenia: My father has it and so does his father, as do a number of my aunts, uncles, and cousins. Some men measure their lives in coffee spoons; mine is measured in page counts. If, however, you were to mean by the question: why Strindberg's *Inferno* rather than *some other book*, the answer, I'm sorry to say, isn't entirely clear. Probably Patrick Harrison is to blame. In all likelihood, the precipitating cause for my *Inferno* crisis was his offhand remark about the novel during a monologue about his plans to stage *The Ghost Sonata* in a run-down hotel in Prague, over our dinner of pancakes, eggs, and bacon at a diner in Williamsburg. At least, it was upon coming home that night that I began searching for and failing to find *Inferno* online.

Still I wonder: Would my desire have mushroomed into such a cloud of fixation had I not discovered that Strindberg died on May 14, 1912—*exactly* seventy-one years before I was born? Without having received the day before a letter from Olivia Olsen postmarked Tegnérgatan 55, Stockholm, *exactly* seven hundred and ten meters from the Blue Tower, the house in which Strindberg spent his last four years? Would the desire have gone viral in my nerves if the posters advertising Alan Rickman's staging of *Creditors* at BAM were not still hanging in the bus stops in my neighborhood? Or had I not come across the correspondence between Strindberg and Nietzsche in the book I was then reading? Or had I not, along with Olivia's letter, found in my mailbox a red envelope with my roommate's name on it containing a biopic she had ordered about Strindberg's sometime comrade, the painter Edvard Munch? Or had I not overheard, on the subway ride to Kellogg's, an allusion to *Miss Julie* in a debate between a pomaded mustache and a pair of yoga pants about the persistence of misogyny in contemporary dating culture?

It is impossible to tell. The truth is that the reasons hardly matter:

The initial choice of an obsessive object is always, in a certain sense, perfectly arbitrary. The only necessary criterion is that it should prove difficult to obtain, for, to an obsessive, the pleasures of frustration are always far greater than those of satisfaction. Which is no doubt why the *loci classici* of monomania are beautiful women, white whales, and utopian political orders.

Justifications come, but only later. When they do, they pile up high and deep and with incredible speed. The resulting mental state is not irrational, but what amounts to the same thing: a hypertrophy of reason: a pole vault over the bland bar of the real into an empyrean vision of order, purpose, meaning, and design where at best there is only suggestive chaos. All of the above coincidences are easily interpreted by susceptible minds like mine as coded imperatives from the universe. *Find buy read!* the universe was commanding. *Find! Buy! Read! Findbuyread!*

Online, I was able to locate a Penguin Classics paperback first published on April 26, 1979. Twenty-one copies were available on Amazon, none of them in particularly good condition, the cheapest of which went for a criminally high $24.33 plus shipping, more than double the list price, a number that represented, at the time, fifteen percent of my total worth. AbeBooks, Alibris, and Powell's were no better in terms of cost or selection. The library at the college where I work didn't have a copy; the New York Public Library, the largest public library system in the world, and to which I owe quite a bit in late fees, only had two—and these could only be read on-site. Needless to say, none were available at Barnes & Noble or at Borders, and none among those independent bookstores who have managed to catalogue their inventory online. Neither Labyrinth—I simply refuse to call it Book Culture—nor the Community Bookstore in Park Slope, nor the 18 Miles of Books better known as the Strand even had an entry for *Inferno* on their websites (in the end, this didn't prevent me from visiting these stores anyway, either out of an obdurate refusal to accept the evidence of my senses, or out of futile protest against same).

Google Books had an old 1913 Knickerbocker Press edition that could be read in limited preview, but limited was not enough for me. By the time I'd clicked on that link, the mania that would soon overtake me had already been kindled in my brain. It would prove to be a mania for ownership rather than for information, a mania for something I could hold in my hands and not just for something my eyes could pass over, a mania that the vanguards of progress embodied in the latest technological developments would prove incapable of satisfying.

That night, after I'd closed my laptop, my eyes exhausted by the singeing light of the screen, I lay in bed, neither awake nor asleep, my limbs pinned to the mattress, staring out the window at the starless sky. A lit cigarette dangled dangerously from my apathetic lips. Over the cluster of rooftops, an oblong tuft of fog was floating toward my window. "What the hell is that," I mumbled, dislodging an inch of ash from my cigarette, which formed a small pile on my chest.

Icicles began to form along the window frame as the freezing fog placed its palms against the glass and peered inside. Though I could now see that it was dressed in a pinafore, I couldn't tell at first whether the figure floating in the fog was male or female, so deeply was its face distorted by putrefaction. Clumps of black flesh were all that remained of its cheeks and brow; sporadic shocks of gray hair rose like smoke from a peeling scalp; tears of iodine flowed from the empty sockets. Only the mustache and soul patch that bookended its wrinkled purple lips led me to conclude that it had once been a man.

The figure passed through the window, but terror didn't manage to rouse me from catalepsy. Hovering a foot above my bed, where I was now shivering violently, it introduced itself to me in herring-scented English. *Hommelette I am your friar's skillet!* I could see its orange tongue, the only thing about the figure that suggested health, warmth, and vigor, glowing through the windy caverns between the rail-thin points of its decayed teeth.

Here then is what my ligature adds up to, it told me, though I hadn't asked. *A signalment, an excardination destined for the impudicity of others: a launderette set up to demonstrate the vaporescence of celestiality and the family circle; a launderette to teach the younkers what waylands of ligature they should avoid; a launderette that believed itself a propinquity and found itself unmasked as an impresario. . . .*

Hours later, when the figure came to the conclusion of its mad monologue, it removed the cigarette from my lips and, without warning, buried its tongue deep into my astonished mouth.

Burning. Unspeakable burning. As if I had swallowed dry ice. Or a blade that had just been lifted from the forge. My eyes flew open. It was ten o'clock. My alarm was going off. All across the city, bookstores were opening.

In the bathroom, I nicked a jowl trying to liberate an august Strindbergstache from the brown block of my beard; in the closet, I got on my hands and knees to find the wing-collar shirt and waistcoat that had fallen from the crossbeam shortly after Halloween, the last time I'd worn them; before the small mirror on my dresser, I noosed up a patterned tie.

Brimming with purpose, I walked out into the world, ready to violate the one rule known to every book buyer: Never go to a used bookstore in search of a specific title, especially if it's extremely rare. Used bookstores are for aimless browsing, or for finding cheap copies of widely available works. Anything else is needle-in-haystackery, a quixotic quest at the end of which lies only disappointment and delirium.

My method was simple. First, I'd check the Fiction section, where *Inferno* ought to be shelved; then Drama, in case the bookseller found it more profitable to group an author's lesser-known writings in one genre with his better-known works in another, as when, for example, Baudelaire's *Artificial Paradises* is shelved in Poetry, though it is technically a collection of essays; after that, in Memoir, Biography, or Belles Lettres, on the off chance that the bookseller was even less rigorous in his distinction between fact and fiction than Strindberg himself was.

How my heart leapt every time I saw the letters "ST—" on the spine of a book! How it sank again when I saw them followed by the letters "—EIN," "—EINBECK," "—ENDHAL," "—ERNE," "—EVENSON," "—OKER," "—OPPARD," "—OWE," "—RACHEY," "—RAUSS," "—ROUT," or "—YRON." Confronted by their names in store after store, on shelf after shelf, I came to loathe these authors, some of whose books I'd enjoyed in the past, but which now existed only to taunt and torture me with the brute fact of their not-being-by-Strindberg. For all I cared, Tristram Shandy could fail to get born, Julien Sorel could be granted an eleventh-hour pardon, and Dracula could suck Transylvania dry. For all I cared, Queen Victoria could be deposed, every last Joad could starve to death, and Sophie Zawistowski could give up *both* of her brats to the Nazis.

Fiat Inferno *pereat mundi* for all I cared.

As a last resort, I checked with the bookseller. Stumbling and mumbling my way to the counter, I'd begin, "You wouldn't happen to have *Inferno* . . ." At which point I was invariably interrupted by such looks of contempt, superior sneers that said, Of course we do, Ignoramus! Any bookstore worth its salt carries at least half a dozen translations of it! With a simple knowledge of the alphabet you could even find it at one of the chains! ". . . by Strindberg?" At which point, the bookseller's aspect changed to one of two new expressions. Either blankness followed by total befuddlement: You mean Strindberg *the playwright*? Or, among the true aficionados: Ah, yes, we sometimes get that book in, but rarely, since no one who'd had the good fortune to own such a book would ever think of selling it back. These latter looks, though misty, inflamed rather than dampened my desire.

Empty-handed I entered the doors of the Community Bookstore, Unnameable Books, Atlantic Books, PS Books, Spoonbill & Sugartown, Book Thug Nation, Housing Works, Mercer Street Books, the Strand, Alabaster Books, East Village Books, Left Bank Books, Westsider Used and Rare, Brazenhead, and Labyrinth; empty-handed I exited them again. I gave all of these booksellers my name and phone number with instructions that, should the book wash up on their shores, I was to be called immediately. Some refused, until I insisted, and then obliged me, perhaps to get me out of their stores. Others took my information so willingly that I began to suspect it was out of pity. Finally, behind the counter at Mercer Street Books, the barrel-chested bald man with a thick Brooklyn brogue told me that it was totally useless to take names. Booksellers, it seems, have better things to do than compare their recent arrivals with a list of requests, which would only net them between five and ten dollars for their efforts.

After these first fifteen failures, I lost control of my method, simple though it was, and delivered myself over to momentary whims. I paid visits to Bluestockings, McNally Jackson, Unoppressive Non-Imperialist Bargain Books, Biography Bookshop, BookCourt, and Greenlight—with full knowledge that they wouldn't have what I was looking for—just because I happened to be in the areas. I revisited certain stores several times a day, because, to paraphrase Kafka, hope springs eternal. When homeless men asked me for change, I asked them for *Inferno*.

From a café in Fort Greene, I sent two incoherent emails. (At least I assume they are; I haven't yet mustered the courage to click on "Sent Mail" and reread them.) The first was to Olivia in Sweden, proposing that, as soon as possible, which is to say at this very moment, she should find and translate *Inferno*—from the French or the Swedish, for she knew both languages—and overnight me a nicely bound, private edition. The second was to an editor at Penguin Classics, demanding that he expedite the long-overdue reprint of Strindberg's novel. I threatened and cajoled; I begged and pleaded. My sanity—no, *literary culture itself*—depended on it, I probably said. Both literary culture and my sanity depended on quite a bit more than that, he doubtlessly surmised, as he pressed "Delete."

Brain boiling, I slammed my laptop shut, and walked to the Q at DeKalb Avenue, to once again prostrate myself before the remainders in the carts outside the Strand.

The next day I was scheduled to help a friend, Ana Fitzner—"Fitz," as I call her—with the art direction for a short film. The film tells the story of a young British woman, L, who is spending the summer interning at a fashion company in New York. L rents a set of rooms from an elegant American woman of a certain age, who invites L to join the weekly dinner parties she throws for her three girlfriends. Work goes well for L, but not romance. Though she has an attractive face, a sweet disposition, and a charming English accent, none of the men she goes out with ask her out for second dates. Viewers are led to assume that male callowness and fecklessness are responsible for L's dating woes, until the final scene, in which it is revealed that her landlady has been killing, cooking, and serving her suitors at the dinner parties. (Were he alive today, it occurs to me, Strindberg would read the script as a barely allegorical portrait of the war between the sexes.)

The film was being shot in a beautiful three-story mansion on the Upper West Side, a block from the park. My primary job was to help move valuable pieces of art and furniture into a storage room, wrap the banisters in blankets, tape cardboard along the floorboards and corners, and cover the glass windows in the doors, so that the house would be protected from any scuffs and scratches that might result from the moving of the camera, lighting, and sound equipment. It was rumored that the owner, who paid for his vacations by renting out the house to film crews like ours, did research for a best-selling author of historical novels. Whether this generated sufficient income to afford such an enviable piece of real estate, or whether the owner had purchased the mansion with alternate funds, through inheritance, say, or through the income of a wealthy spouse, was something the crew speculated about over lunch.

The work was physical, repetitive, simple, and even relaxing. It required no thought whatsoever: If someone told me to move something, I moved it; if someone needed fabric cut, I got out a pair of scissors; if someone asked for the roll of blue tape, I passed it along. After more than two dozen hours of sustained mania, I was grateful for it.

I was scissoring the fringe off a roll of brocade that was being used to replace the wallpaper in the room where the dinner scenes were to be shot when Fitz asked me to come upstairs to help her move a television, mammoth as it was ancient, down a steep flight of stairs. The television was located in the library, on the top story, opposite a large leather couch, behind which loomed wall-to-wall, floor-to-ceiling bookshelves. Entirely out of habit, like an old cat burglar who can't enter a house without casing it, I scanned the shelves in search of the box of jewels.

It wasn't a promising collection. The mansion's owner had organized his books more or less by genre, but not alphabetically, with the first editions of the novels he'd done research for prominently displayed on a shelf in the center, next to pictures of his family and other personal trinkets. Beneath these were biographies, mostly of writers, but also of various English and French monarchs, American presidents, and Robert Moses.

On the shelf nearest the wall were tall monographs on art and architecture and interior design, no doubt overflow from the coffee table, spiral-bound books that I assumed were screenplays, reference works, books by now marginal political figures on issues whose expiration dates had long passed, and cookbooks representing every culinary fad since *Joy of Cooking*. On the shelf nearest the entranceway lived what I'll call works of the imagination, since fiction, poetry, and drama had all been mixed together. It was a strange *quartier* in this disorderly borough of books, where scrappy paperback *grisettes* and best-selling *demimondaines* indiscriminately rubbed covers with the morocco *doyennes* bearing the gilt seals of Harvard or the University of Chicago.

Then, just as I was about to turn my mind to the task at hand, I saw it.

O, Ryan! O ye of little faith! On the bottom shelf, sardined between a dog-eared movie tie-in edition of *The Lord of the Rings* and an untouched, ornately bound gift edition of *The Complete Stories of Edgar Allan Poe*, there appeared—*lo and behold!*—set upon a black spine—*wonder of wonders!*—above the colophon of the Knickerbocker Press—*miracle of miracles!*—seven letters—

burning unconsumed!—in luminous halo, in gold leaf shining:

I-N-F-E-R-N-O

"Watch out, Ryan!" Fitz yelled. It seems I'd nearly dropped the television.

Three excruciating hours later, after the director, the DP, and the principal actors had arrived, while everyone was crowded in the dining room to watch a run-through of the film's final scene, I snuck back upstairs, tote bag over my shoulder. But standing again before the book, I hesitated to pluck it off the shelf. Though I was a prentice purloiner, my sudden irresolution had nothing to do with the morality of theft or with the fear of getting caught. I had come to the end of my search. What I had wanted I was about to possess. Like an Israelite about to enter the Promised Land, like a career cadre on the eve of the revolution, like a persistent suitor being led at long last to the room where the stuffed animals and laced pillows are hidden, I wondered whether the consummation of my desire was worth the price of its disappearance. True, this obsession of mine had brought me to the border of mental instability; nonetheless, I had come, perversely perhaps, to cherish it. Surely, there must have been one or two Israelites who declined to follow Joshua across the border into Canaan, preferring the flat bread of a nomad's life to the milk and honey of nation building. Perhaps I also wasn't quite ready to stop wandering in the desert.

"Can I help you?" someone asked. The mansion's owner had appeared in the entranceway to the library. He was eyeing me suspiciously.

As if to explain away the look on my face, which any anthropologist will tell you is, from the remotest jungles of Malaysia to the highest skyscrapers of Manhattan, universally interpreted to mean you've-caught-me-doing-something-I-shouldn't-be-doing, I put a hand to my chest and exclaimed, "You startled me!"

"What are you doing here?"

His contemptuous tone proved decisive. What was I doing? How could I begin to explain? *For starters, jackass, I'm stealing your book. No, liberating it—from the philistine company with which you've had the nerve to surround it! I'm busting it from the prison of your awful taste! Giving it the home it deserves, where it will be appreciated: by someone who knows its value! Maybe the wood on the shelf won't be as expensive as yours, but at least it will be on the top shelf, where it belongs! Hell, I'll give it its own goddamned shelf! At least there it will get looked at, not to mention read from time to time!* What actually came out of my mouth was:

"I left my . . . totem pole here . . . when we were moving the telium."

"Excuse me?"

"I said, 'I left my tote bag here when we were moving the television.' "

"Well, I see you have it now. The rest of your crew is leaving."

"I'm aware," I said impudently, although, of course, I wasn't.

As soon as his back was turned, I dropped to a crouch, allowing the bag to open as it slid down my arm. Passing a finger along the sensual lip where the pages meet the binding at the top of an old hardback, I stealthily slipped *Inferno* off the shelf, stuffed it into my bag, readjusted the bag's straplike handles around my shoulder, and followed the owner down his cardboard-protected staircase.

To my horror, the stolen book was glowing through the tote's thin black canvas. I tried my best to hide that rectangular-shaped admission of guilt beneath my arm. (This must have been successful, since no one commented on the strange orange light that was clearly emanating from my armpit.) Outside, I stammered quick thanks and goodbyes to Fitz and the rest of the crew, and walked as nonchalantly as I could to the corner. Turning it, I ran until I reached the subway station, flew down the steps, through the turnstile, and onto the train that fate had so thoughtfully furnished for my glorious getaway, just as its doors were closing. I slid regally into an empty bank of seats, breathing heavily, smiling crookedly, my foot tap-tap-tapping to the horn-heavy Sinatra song that, were my life a film, would then be playing for everyone, and not just me, to hear. Ultimately, I think it was the giddy flush of my triumph that caused my scruples about satisfying my desire to disappear. At that moment, the book appeared to me less as the holy grail of a frantic, desperate quest than as the radiant trophy of my first theft.

Without giving it a second glance, I pulled the book out of my bag and opened to the first page.

You can imagine, no doubt, the looks of disgust, pity, and alarm on the other passengers' faces when they witnessed my howling reaction to what I read there: "Midway on our life's journey, I went astray from the straight road and woke to find myself alone in a dark wood."

I Would Never Do These Things
Stephen O'Connor

IT SEEMS THAT THIS STORY is actually happening and that I am one of the characters in it. I am at a vacation resort—rattling fan palms, turquoise harbors, chickens everywhere (crowing, making fretful clucks)—and a gigantic golden cloud is making its way toward us across the ocean. This cloud, gleaming sublimely in the vacation-bright sunshine, is death—but not just death; it is the end of the world. No one seems to know what brought this cloud into being or why the world is ending, but there is no question: When the cloud finally rolls onto our shores it will be as if none of us, and nothing we have done, seen, heard, or believed in will have ever existed.

Apparently, I am on vacation with my secretary (although I know neither her name nor the nature of the business we work in), but I am passionately in love with the farm girl up the hill, who sells us chicken eggs. Her name is Pelagea, and her eyes are exactly the blue of a vacation-blue sea when the sun is not yet even a rose possibility in the east. She slides her red-tipped fingers under chickens and removes the perfect ellipsoids of their eggs, which she gives to me in a wicker basket. We have met once or twice in the night, and, although I am not entirely sure what went on between us, fevered and fragmentary images from those nights relentlessly pierce my thoughts. I can't stop thinking about her.

The strange thing is that this story is being written by Chekhov. Every now and then he is there and I can talk to him. "Anton Pavlovich," I say, "why are you writing this story? It doesn't make any sense." But he just looks at me as if I am the one not making sense. He averts his shoulder and hurries down the sidewalk. He wears a brown velvet jacket, and is much smaller than I had ever imagined he would be. As he rounds the corner, chickens cluck and turn ill-coordinated circles in his wake.

I am on the beach with my secretary. Our faces are yellow tinged from the golden cloud, which is still many miles distant, hardly more than a brassy blurriness between the sea and sky, and seeming to move on a different wind than the one driving those galleon puffs of white (yellow tinged on one side) above the turquoise sea.

My secretary seems a nice girl. She is about twenty-four, I imagine, and I am forty—which qualifies me as "old" in a Chekhov story. I like my secretary. She is generous spirited and a little sad. Even when she laughs there is just the faintest hint of sorrow in her cola-brown eyes. She is nice looking too: Her hair is also cola brown, shoulder length, surrounding her face in appealing arcs, dips, loops; and her figure (bikini clad) is a minutely puffy version of petite. She looks as if she would be very comforting to hold in the night. I still can't remember her name, however, although I am much too embarrassed to say so, given how well we know each other—or, at least, how well she knows me. She seems, in fact, to know a great deal about me. She knows, for example, that while we are lying on the cream-colored sand, my wife, Olga, is undergoing treatment for pancreatic cancer.

"I know you are worried about her," my secretary says tenderly. "I can tell." She rests her fingers on my forearm and looks me in the eyes—the sadness in her own eyes accumulating in such a fashion as to make her seem courageous and wise; clearly she has already endured considerable hardship during her brief life. "You don't have to feel bad," she says. "On my account, I mean. If you feel that you have to go back home and be with her, I'll understand. Really. You don't have to prove anything to me. I can see how miserable you are."

Her words are shocking to me on a number of levels. The first is that I have no memory of Olga, nor of being married. And, in fact, I am not wearing a wedding ring—although there is a pale, hairless band at the base of my left ring finger. But what shocks me most is that I would abandon my wife at a moment when she must be enduring incalculable pain and fear, and that I should have chosen to so betray her with a woman who—whatever her many merits—reminds me of nothing so much as an orphaned chipmunk, and whom I am betraying, in turn, with Pelagea, the farm girl up the hill. Can I possibly be so two-faced, hapless, and cruel? How have I allowed myself into this intolerable situation? How am I going to get out of it?

My secretary kisses me on the cheek. "I love you," she says. "Nothing can change that."

Perhaps it will come as no surprise to hear that, with such awful realizations circling like leering jackals inside my brain, I am incapable of speaking.

I do notice, however, that my secretary has overplucked her eyebrows. They seem to have been drawn by a carpenter's crayon, and the skin around them is pale, stubbly, and swollen looking. In fact, her nearly bald brow ridges make her look as if she once took a beating in a boxing match . . . and maybe that's it. Maybe the reason she seems so courageous and wise is that she was once in love with a man who abused her.

With this thought, another leering jackal joins the circle inside my brain: If my secretary could love a heavy-fisted brute, then maybe I am part of a pattern for her; maybe she is drawn to me precisely because I am such a loathsome specimen of humanity.

I can't meet her eyes. I am looking out at our doom glinting yellowly on the horizon.

"Why do you think," I say at last, "that the end of the world should look so beautiful?"

"Because it is death," she says, with a wise and courageous smile. "And death is a part of life."

"But it is *not* a part of life. It is the antithesis of life. It is the erasure of everything we live for, everything beautiful, desirable, sublime."

"And of everything hideous, despicable, and cruel," she says.

Once again I am incapable of responding. My secretary smiles poignantly, and I want to run from her as fast as I can. I want to fling myself into the surf. I want one of those enormous toothpaste-green waves rising every few seconds out of the turquoise sea to sweep me up to its foamy crest and smash me down onto the pebbly beach bottom.

My secretary's hand is still resting on my forearm, which she gives an encouraging squeeze.

"Without death," she says, "there can be no beauty. Death itself is beauty. Because it is perfect. Because it can't be changed. You can see that, can't you?"

"Anton Pavlovich," I say, "this is a preposterous story. It is utterly unlike anything you have ever written—"

"Nonsense!" he says. "Must literature pluck only pure grain from the muck heap? Shall none of our trees have yellow leaves? Preposterous, indeed! If you can find a single banker's daughter in one of my stories who cannot easily trade places with a cart horse, I will hang myself on this spot!"

I search my memory of Chekhov for a banker's daughter, but none comes to mind. Then I realize I can't remember *any* of Chekhov's stories. Is it possible I have never read him? Is it possible that I know him only by reputation?

We are on the beach. Chekhov is lying on a brilliantly colored tourist towel, illustrated with arching palms and leaping dolphins. His swimming trunks match the towel so exactly it is hard to tell where the trunks leave off and the towel begins. His skin is the color of Ivory soap, and his body is virtually hairless, except for a wiry black nest between his pectorals. His only adornment, apart from his swimming trunks, is his pince-nez.

"But that's not what I mean," I say at last. "I only mean that in this story . . . Well, as the protagonist, I guess I do feel a little funny saying this, but—"

"What makes you think you're the protagonist?" says Chekhov.

"Uh . . . I just assumed—"

"All of my characters make that assumption," says Chekhov.

He snatches a Kleenex from the box beside him, works something around inside his mouth, and tongue-shoves it into the Kleenex, which he releases to the breeze. All down the beach, carnations of crumpled Kleenex tumble over sand humps. Most of the Kleenexes are cloud white, but some are dabbed red.

"I hope that's a lesson to you," Chekhov says, although I am not sure whether he is referring to his previous statement or to the Kleenexes.

Before I can think of a suitable response, Chekhov has sprung from his towel and is trotting down to the water. Without troubling to remove his pince-nez, he high steps through the sliding foam and dives into the toothpaste-green maw of a cresting wave. He emerges sleek and white from the far side, and proceeds to plunge and leap dolphin style from one wave to the next, as if he were stitching them together. After a few moments he saunters wetly back up the beach, his pince-nez still in place and drip free.

By the time he has resumed his position on the tourist towel, I know what I want to say: "What I mean is: Why are you even bothering with a story like this? With all of your genius, I don't see why—"

"*Why, why, why!* Why are you always asking me why?" Chekhov is so incensed by my question that he sits up on his towel and gesticulates wildly with both fists. "Life is too short for why! I never trouble myself with why! And I never have a clue what I am going to write until the words are already trailing behind my pen. Why can't you understand that!" He is shouting now. "Why can't you leave me alone!" His white face has gone purple and his eyes are bloodshot. "I don't have time for such stupid questions! I have a living to make, in case you haven't noticed!"

I am sitting on a wooden stool under the heavy roof of Pelagea's house. Pelagea is on the stool beside me, and we are holding hands. Coals make soft clinks in the huge white oven, tiered like an early skyscraper, that takes up at least a third of the room. The heat is unforgiving. Pelagea's grandmother is perched on the dark house's one elegant piece of furniture: an oriental divan entirely covered with Persian carpets, much like the divan that once graced the office of Sigmund Freud. She is lumpish, dressed entirely in black, and her potato-shaped feet do not touch the floor.

I believe she is talking to me, but the words she is using seem drawn from a language boulders might grunt to one another in the lonely middle of the night. I understand not one syllable.

The grandmother has lapsed into silence and Pelagea is looking at me incredulously. After a moment she pinches her brow and lowers her chin in a manner that indicates I should answer her grandmother. I can only hope that the bafflement on my face will make the nature of my predicament clear, but it seems to have the opposite effect. After a prolonged silence, an indigo spark of irritation flies off Pelagea's magnificent eyes, and then, smiling at her grandmother, she says to me, "New Jersey, right?" As my vocal apparatus continues in its state of paralysis, she adds, "That's where you . . ." She shrugs, frowns, and lowers her chin one last time. It is clear that I am now entirely on my own.

"Yes," I say. "New Jersey . . . I grew up in New Jersey. On a farm. Like this one. Well, not exactly like this one. We didn't have chickens. Or eggs. Or cows either. And we didn't really grow anything. Except grass. And weeds. In fact, it wasn't a farm. Just a farmhouse. Or a farm-style house. In the middle of a suburban development. All the houses were identical, in fact. . . ."

I stop there, not having a clue what to say next, and having wholly fabricated everything I have just said. I have no memory of my childhood, and only the dimmest idea of what New Jersey might be like.

Pelagea's grandmother is delighted, though, and shows her delight by laughing and loosing an avalanche of boulder-speak in my direction. She hops down from the divan and duckwalks over to the samovar.

Returning to our side of the room, she offers me a tea in a gilded glass, and a silver tray heaped with sugar cubes and topped by tiny silver tongs.

Pelagea is smiling too, but looks cold, despite the stove's unforgiving heat and the tropical weather outside. When I meet her eye, she looks away.

Her grandmother offers her tea, but she shakes her head: no.

Later, Pelagea and I are in the moonlit yard, chickens roosting in the dust on every side of us, making plaintive burbling noises in their sleep. She lifts up the skirt of her dress, takes my arm by the wrist, and places my hand flat against her bare belly.

"Do you feel it?" she says.

I feel her body warmth. I feel her belly's convexity and its drum tautness. Perhaps I feel the tiny tremblers of her digestion.

"Feel what?" I say.

"Deeper," she says.

"Deeper?"

"Inside. Can you feel deep inside?"

I feel her extraordinary beauty. And I feel the effect her extraordinary beauty is having on me. I see the mushroom paleness of her skin in the moonlight. And I see the elbows of her pelvis casting their deltoid shadows just above the elastic of her underpants. Then I feel how very pleasant and easy it would be to slide my hand down just a bit. And then I think that maybe this is exactly what she meant by "deeper." But then, as I angle my fingertips so they might make their passage beneath the elastic of her underpants, she lets go of my wrist.

"It's too late for that!" she says, turning away in disgust.

Chickens squawk, outraged at their interrupted slumber, as she darts across the yard and down the long hill to the beach.

I am all by myself beside the black mass of her heavy-roofed house. Even in the moonlight the cloud out at sea is golden. It looks clearer, I think. And maybe closer. Yes. Closer. Very definitely.

In the early morning a golden mist of insecticide billows from spritzers on the back of a golden tank truck, and rolls across the lawn of the vacation resort, murdering mosquitoes and filling our throats with an acrid sweetness. My secretary and I have snorkel masks on our foreheads and flippers on our feet. We are waiting for the van to take us down to the beach.

I gesture at the tank truck with my chin. "Why are they even bothering to do that, with that cloud out on the water getting closer every day?"

"What else are they going to do?" my secretary says. "It's not like anything's going to stop the cloud. And they can't just sit around and mope. Think how crazy that would make them feel! And besides, doesn't the fact that everything is going to be taken away make everything seem precious?"

"Even bug spray?"

"Why not?"

My secretary is smiling one of her wise and sad smiles. She winks at me, but then a tear dampens the peach down on her minutely puffy cheek, and I do my best to believe that her tear is only an allergic response to the insecticide.

I am sleeping next to my secretary. Her sleep breathing makes a noise like a feather being drawn first one way across broad-ribbed corduroy and then the other. But I am also hearing another sort of breathing. It is Pelagea's. I look over, and her head is resting on the pillow beside mine. She stops breathing and places her index finger across her puckered lips. I have no idea how she has gotten into the bungalow. The doors are all locked. The windows are shut and fortified by festive ironwork. I place my hand on that webby spot between Pelagea's pelvis and ribs, and then I slide my fingertips around and down. Her lips are against my ear and her whisper sounds inside my head. "No," she says. "You can't possibly do that. Not here." But she is wrong. I can't control myself.

In the morning my secretary looks rested, but perplexed. We are sitting at a table on the vacation-resort patio. I am on my fifth cup of coffee. I can't touch the eggs on the plate in front of me. Their very smell revolts me.

"Penny for your thoughts?" says my secretary.

I can't even meet her eye.

"Action is character," says Chekhov.

"That's not true!" I say. "I would never do these things you have made me do. That's not who I am!"

"Suit yourself."

We are in the vacation-resort bar, and international vacation-resort bar music does its tinselly percolation in the space between invisible speakers. Chekhov does not look well. His skin has gone fatless, and hangs off his bones. It flaps a bit when he moves or speaks.

"But it's not just me," I say. "It's my wife, Olga. She's dying and in pain, and I'm not there. That's not right."

"Why do you care?"

"She's my wife!"

"Actually . . ." Chekhov falls silent. A thunder-green storm cloud crosses his brow, and is even visible in his eyes. Then he says, "Well, never mind. That's neither here nor there."

"Answer my question," I say.

"What question?"

"Why am I here when I should be with my wife?"

"You answer my question: Why do you care?"

"She's *dying*, for Christsake! What kind of a ridiculous question is that?!"

Chekhov looks bored. He takes a sip from his mojito, then says, "You haven't had one single scene with her. You don't know what she looks like. You don't even know whether she deserves your love. For all you know, she may be cheating on you with every actor in Moscow."

"Moscow?"

"Maybe. I'm still thinking about it."

"But she's got cancer!"

"So what?" says Chekhov. "She's not dead yet, so she can do whatever she pleases."

Clearly I have reached an impasse. I take a new tack. "But what about my secretary? She's the kindest woman I have ever met, and she has already suffered so much! And then there's Pelagea! What about Pelagea? I am passionately in love with Pelagea, but I never know what she is talking about! Why have you gotten me into this awful mess?!"

Chekhov shakes his head wearily. "It's always the same."

"What's always the same?"

"You people," he says. "My characters." He dips his thumb and forefinger into his drink, pulls out a mint leaf, and starts to chew on it. "You always imagine yourselves to be impossibly virtuous, impossibly boring, and utterly unbelievable."

*

The mopers are in the shanty bar down by the harbor. They are the usual denizens of such places: the loud and lobster faced; the grinless twentysomethings, halfway between keg-party blackouts and a twelve-step program; the grizzle-headed losers, happy that near senility has liberated them from all expectations; the terminally isolate, whose gazes anchor in the middle distance and never budge. None of these people are actually moping over the golden cloud, of course, but some of its radiance is reflected in their shifting or shiftless eyes, and lends a certain nobility to their grunts, shouts, and guffaws.

I am well into my second margarita when I hear a surge of murmuring in the corner. I walk over to find Chekhov at the center of a crowd. He has shrunk to half his normal size, and is lying, eyes closed, in a half-size bed, with the covers drawn up to his goatee. He is wearing seersucker pajamas and the rattling of his breath in his throat is indistinguishable from the rattle of a water-clogged snorkel. His chest heaves slightly at the end of every breath, and the insubstantiality of his stature and of his bed makes the crowd around him seem composed of giants. Perhaps I myself seem a giant to those opposite me, though I can't rid myself of the feeling that they are all much bigger than I am.

"What's going on?" I say, but their murmuring continues without the faintest alteration that might be construed as a response. I have no idea what they are saying. More boulder-speak, perhaps. But their voices are so soft, I can't even tell.

"Excuse me," I say, and repeat my question. Then I try again: "Excuse me." Then, a little later and a little louder: "*Excuse* me."

In the end it is Chekhov who answers, but without turning in my direction or opening his eyes. "I'm in a coma."

"Are you dying?" I say.

"I don't know. It's hard to tell."

After that he is silent, and no one else ever seems to hear my questions.

I have discovered two entries in my cell-phone contacts list: "Home" and "Olga." As I have no idea what I have told my wife, I plot out a variety of apologies that I hope will cover all possibilities. The main reason I am calling her is to say that I will be catching the next plane home. There is one problem, however: I don't know where home is—

which means that, somehow, without revealing my ignorance, I am going to have to get her to tell me.

Moscow? I wonder. Did Chekhov mean I live in Moscow?

The bungalow is spinning around my skull; my fingers are greased with sweat, and my heart is going "dum dum dum" in my ears when I hit the "send" button for one number and then the next. But the result, in each case, is identical: three punitive screech tones followed by a message informing me I have reached a "nonworking number."

I stagger out of the bungalow into a paradise of sideways-gliding pelicans and foot-long caterpillars, and can't figure out why my failure to get through to this woman I have never even set eyes on should leave me so heavy of heart and head. It is all I can do to keep from falling face-first onto the sun-blanched sod strips of the lawn.

The golden cloud looms higher over the palm forest surrounding the vacation resort. Does that mean the cloud is closer, or only that it has gained altitude? It is very definitely more resplendent, however, and seems no longer merely to reflect the brilliance of the tropical sun but to have a luminosity all its own. I begin to wonder if my secretary might be right: Can the golden cloud actually be beauty itself? Is it possible that perfection is exactly and only equal to zero? And would that mean that what awaits us out there on the water is not so much our undoing as our purification?

I am snorkeling, and seem to be alone—at least for the time being. I am listening to the hoarse hee-haw of my own breathing, the tick of tiny bubbles beside my ears, and the muted squeegee squeak of my flippers as I coast past reefs that seem half fungus extrusions, half crud-encrusted moose antlers.

All the fish are neon yellows, blues, greens, and turquoise—turquoise especially; pink too—except for the backward-skimming squid with tinfoil eyes thumbtacked at the base of their wiggle-finned heads, and their clumped-together tentacles trailing neatly behind. And those fish that look like rocks: cavity dwellers, with blunt faces and jaws fanged like staple removers; pocketbook-shaped bottom-feeders, piloting their rigid bodies with fins like insect wings. And the fleets of surface-sucking abstract fish, like so many infinity signs, or like the stainless-steel car ornaments favored by fanatical Christians. Endlessly. Everywhere I look. Every instant: creatures utterly unlike any I have ever seen before. Poking, darting, plunging.

As I flipper in and out of coral cul-de-sacs with my hands extended, I feel, for the first time, as if I am truly in a world imagined by Chekhov. This is all too fevered to be real, too intensely vivid and enveloping. There's genius in it, though. I can't deny that. Only an extraordinary mind could have cooked up a world so visceral, so phylogenetically elaborate, and yet so blatantly impossible.

I hover under a quicksilver sky. When I dive, almost all the sounds go away—at least after the last bubbles have glugged out of my snorkel—and it becomes harder to distinguish that part of the world I think of as myself from that part which is the water through which I am moving. When my ears start to hurt, I hold my nose, force air into my sinuses, and then can dive a little deeper. After I have done this two or three times, I feel as if I can go on forever.

The world keeps growing darker, bluer, simpler. As depths open in front of me, I slip into them—because it is so easy. Because there is nothing to stop me. Why not? I keep thinking. Why not? Although every now and then it does occur to me that it may not make much sense to keep on doing something merely because I can.

It is only when my hands are another variety of the gloom into which they are extended that I realize I have gone too far and for too long. The need to breathe is now suddenly so ferocious I feel that, were I to yield to it, I would gasp myself inside out. The quicksilver surface has become only a pale disk, flickering far overhead like the mouth of a well. As I watch, it recedes, then recedes some more, until it is less like the mouth of a well than a coin tumbling heads over tails to a well's bottom.

I want to rise, but I seem to be sinking ever deeper under the water. And that is when it occurs to me with something like certainty that I have come, at last, to the end Chekhov is imagining for me—and has been, perhaps, from the very beginning.

Then everything changes. I am no longer on the sea bottom, but belly-up on the surface, a full moon whitening the fog smears on my snorkel mask. Has Chekhov had second thoughts? Has he made a revision? Or is it that he has been sinking ever deeper into his coma, and has now, finally, just this instant, died? If that is the case, and—as seems evident—I have not ceased to exist myself, does that mean I am no longer ruled by Chekhov's imaginative predilections, that I am finally free to lead my life as the person I actually am?

I right myself in the water and, bicycling my flippers in the cold and dark, slide my snorkel mask up to my hairline. A breeze blows over the restlessly fragmenting valleys and peaks of the waves. It cools my face. It fills my lungs with salt sweetness, and my head with lucidity.

I haven't gasped. I haven't turned inside out. I'm not even panting.

The golden cloud looks even higher than it did this morning, and it covers one quarter of the whole sky, though maybe that is only because I am closer to it out here. It is motionless, in any event, like a stilled tsunami, or like the pomaded forelocks of a brass-blond giant.

Someone is calling my name—or what I think is my name. Only now do I realize I have never heard my name spoken before.

I reverse in the water and see a pale figure on the beach, waving. At first I think it is Pelagea, but then it seems clearly to be my secretary. Another figure arrives, and this one too seems to be my secretary, or Pelagea. Then there is a third waving figure. Could she be Olga? All three figures are standing together on the beach, jumping up and down, and shouting my name.

As I swim toward them, I become afraid. I have no idea what it will be like to be in the presence of all three of these women at once. I have no idea what I will say, or what they might say to me, or to one another. I only know that, if I am not wrong, if these three figures are who I think they are, then this is a moment I cannot avoid, a moment in which the whole of my future is waiting.

Other people have begun to arrive. First there are ten or twelve; then instants later thirty, maybe forty. They swarm onto the beach, from both ends and over the tops of the dunes. They are running. Leaping. The shadows they cast are so profoundly black they seem cut out of the sand they wobble over. But the people themselves are brilliantly illuminated, at first, it would seem, by the arc-welder white of the full moon, but eventually by the softer, yellower light of a dawn. It is not dawn, however. The sky beyond the beach palms remains star pierced and blackout black. But the yellow light grows ever brighter, ever more intense, until the people clustered on the shore, jumping up and down and waving their arms, begin to look like the individual flames of a conflagration.

They are shouting. All of them. And they are all looking in my direction. Is it possible that they are shouting my name? I'm a stranger on this island. Nobody knows me. And why would so many people call out to me, even if they did?

I can no longer tell which of the figures on the beach are the ones

I thought might be Pelagea, my secretary, and Olga. All I can do is keep my eyes fixed on that place where I first saw them. Sometimes I rise so high on the sea, or sink so low, or I slide so far to the left or right, that it is hard to be sure I really am looking at that place where I saw them, or even to know whether I am actually drawing closer to the shore. I just keep swimming. I have no choice. My arms chop and my flippers oscillate, and a swaying path paved by flecks of yellow fire flickers between where I am and where I want to be.

Children Love Color

Lyn Hejinian

CHILDREN LOVE COLOR, BUT even more they love sculpting—whether they do it by pushing and patting sand, or plucking handfuls of grass, or by squeezing soft food, or collecting pebbles or buttons or Legos or pyracantha berries in a bucket, or by carving patterns into pudding. This must be primordial behavior. Each continent sits in its own separate sea, one of wine, one of cream, one of melted butter, one of lime juice, one of vinegar, one of tea, and one of ever-falling rainwater. Those who are native to the continent surrounded by cream traditionally worship cumulus clouds, which they regard as divinities, continuously changing form. I know this is sad, but sadness is a pervasive, though perhaps strange, form of continuity. A divinity may be briefly an exhausted soldier, or a rumpled gray calf at the udder of a diminishing cow. And now for a few days the current batch of political candidates have disappeared from the front page of the daily newspaper, replaced by coverage of spreading drought and mandatory water rationing (we are required to reduce our water consumption by nineteen percent), a devastating earthquake in China, the deteriorating postcyclone situation in Burma/Myanmar. Mikhail Epstein has coined the word *chronophilia*; it refers to compulsive attention to the continuous flow of broadcast news, producing in the chronophile the sense, if not the reality, that he or she is a witness to events. Of these events, however, chronophiles, within a day or two, can remember nothing. They pass through chronophiliac temporality without adhering to anything. The chronophile's time gets filled up and remains empty. The sun is a locked door. The weather is warm, a pigeon flying from one roof to another utters a peep with each beat of its wings, someone in the neighborhood is deftly wielding a hammer, striking with regular blows. The nail goes neatly into the wood and the board is bound to the stud. Here's a typical bit of fiction: Jane walked down her front stairs onto Russell Street, worrying that the phone message from Timmy's school was summoning her to be informed of yet another "problematic concern." Across the street, James, thinking about the beginning of his shift, noticed her coming out of the house and waved. He was surprised when she didn't acknowledge his greeting. Who could possibly know all this? The "omniscient voice" of narrative fiction is the most bizarre invention still at play in the arts, and, despite its frequent deployment in so-called "realist" fiction, it unfolds at an unfathomable distance from credible cognitive realism. It's fantastic! But what if an author doesn't want to reach the audience in the expected way? The major north-south streets running through the center of the city are an Earlier Street, an Improbable Avenue, a Later Avenue, and a Remarkable Boulevard. Crossing these run various smaller streets, given over to residential buildings and small shops: an Erstwhile Lane, a Systematizing Street, an Uncompromising Street, a Possible Alley. Coming from work, I find that my usual route home along Closest Road is cut off by police activity—black-and-white patrol cars block access. I don't know what has happened and want to. In Bernadette Mayer's *Memory*, there is always a hint, a suggestion, a possibility (none of which are proper to memory as we conventionally think of it but nonetheless so to speak haunt it) that she is preparing to rob a bank or stick up a convenience store. But to a large degree, the world of everyday life is independent of invention; it's given. Christa Wolf (in *One Day a Year*) speaks of "the growing uneventfulness of modernity" and "modern man's neediness, which is often hidden, even from himself."[1] Everyday life is lived at a mesocosmic level—it's almost never viewed close-up (in detail) nor from a distance (as a set of changing patterns). It is said that hummingbirds migrate by riding geese. This isn't true. For a writer of bourgeois inwardness, the highest achievements are dreams. Reading through the first issue of a xeroxed literary journal published in Ciudad Juárez, I find half the pages covered with a language I don't understand, but I imagine I can. My demons tell me that the heart stands guard in fish over those who breathe. Nothing is incidental. If everyday life can't be invented, perhaps it can be inventoried. Here is an alphabetical index to some local billboards:

Authenticity, choose
Billboard, this isn't a
Car, America's most fuel-efficient
Chuck, talk to
Fees, death by a thousand
Happiness, don't keep bottled up

[1]Christa Wolf, *One Day a Year: 1960–2000*; trans. by Lowell A. Baengarter (New York: Europa Editions, 2003).

Hippies,Yuppies, and Yippies and, full coverage for
Motherland, fresh from the
Outlet, everybody needs an
Plant, it's not a power
Results, call us for great
Savings, big
Twist, give your summer a
World, oceans are part of your

I pass some doors that open onto other hallways; the names of the rooms available via each door are etched on them, but I can't find the access to Room K. I go back outside and walk down the street toward a large department store, Kissiwick. Room K. And my bag is empty—completely empty; I've been pickpocketed. My black leather backpack is completely empty. There is a degree of happiness very close to unhappiness but not quite it yet that comes to the dutiful, the obedient. The soil holds the roots of the plants, the plants hold up the sky, and we walk through it—this is how it was described. The world of fish is an imperfect analogy to it. Viktor Shklovsky says, "It seems that in order to have a new society there has to be a shipwreck."[2] Is this what George Oppen was thinking when, in his poem "Of Being Numerous," he speaks of "the shipwreck of the singular"? A jay squawks, birds twitter. One can't look at the sun unaided, one has to use something intermediary whose function is precisely to partially obscure the sun. The next morning's predawn pink tint is not a source of light but its seeming destination, and as the tint receives the rising sun it fades—or retreats—or doesn't fade but is obliterated. Everyday life might be compared to the carnival game in which, one at a time and at seemingly arbitrary and certainly unpredictable moments and places, targets pop into view and then drop back out of sight, though not so fast that one can't take a shot at them. The trivialization and debunking of the ordinary and everyday is a product of the aftershock of "make it new." Between Ashby and Russell, walking north and all but imperceptibly uphill along the east side of College Avenue, one first passes the Elmwood branch of the Wells Fargo Bank, then Boss Robot (a tiny model and toy shop, specializing in remote-control toys and mechanical toys from Japan), then a storefront under renovation (formerly Elmwood Hardware), Elmwood Stationers, the Gem Gallery (a jewelry store), Bill's Trading

[2]Viktor Shklovsky, *Energy of Delusion: A Book on Plot*, trans. by Sushan Avagyan (Champaign, IL: Dalkey Archive Press, 2007).

Post (specializing in Native American jewelry and artifacts), La Tour (a hair salon), Elements (a clothing shop), Treehouse (another gift shop), the Beanery (a coffee shop and bakery), Sweet Dreams (a toy store), La Foot (a shoe store, specializing in athletic shoes), Village Shoes (a shoe store), Body Time (a knockoff of the Body Shop, selling soaps, ointments, bath supplies, hair clips, etc.), Cotton Basics (a clothing shop), A. G. Ferrara (an Italian delicatessen), Sonam (a Tibetan gift shop), It's Party Time (a party supply shop, replacing Teddy's Little Closet, a children's clothing shop), and finally Sweet Dreams (a candy shop, affiliated with the toy store down the street). The approaching Marching Homeland Band is unimaginably vast, with its five hundred drummers and what are rumored to be several thousand trumpeters along with frightening phalanxes of men and women with trombones whose slides they thrust and pull and thrust again upward like golden sabers or scythes, and it is coming over the horizon toward us, crushing the winter grass and spring flowers and future melons and playgrounds. "These details, which are incorrectly termed little—there being neither little facts in humanity nor little leaves in vegetation—are useful," as Victor Hugo says.[3] In this context, dreaming is an act of disreputable profundity. In response to criticism (that it's useless, a waste of money, etc.), the managers of NASA's Mars *Phoenix* mission, which is exploring a polar region of Mars in search of vestigial evidence of once-existing life, have replied that the mission's purpose is to find us "a new home." Despite the "economic downturn," there has been a huge increase in the number of tourists in San Francisco, and in the amount of money they are spending: Sixteen million visitors were here last year, and they spent $8.2 billion (a 6.2 percent increase over the year before). And more and more US soldiers are committing suicide. Victor Hugo and Leo Tolstoy were writing their respective epics (*Les Misérables* and *War and Peace*) at more or less the same time. It took Victor Hugo fifteen years to write *Les Misérables*. He began it in 1845 but three years later his work was interrupted by politics (the uprising of 1848, in which he participated; the short-lived Second Republic; his opposition to Napoleon III and the coup d'état that brought him to power; his subsequent flight and exile). He finished the book in 1860 and then went back and added to it. *Les Misérables* was published in 1862; an initial draft of *War and Peace* was published in 1863 (though Tolstoy

[3]Victor Hugo, *Les Misérables*, trans. by Lee Fahnestock and Norman MacAfee (New York: Signet Classics, 1987).

then went back and rewrote the work, which came out in its final version in 1869). *War and Peace* covers an eight-year span, from 1805 to 1813 in Russia; *Les Misérables* covers the approximately twenty-year-long period in France beginning just after the Napoleonic Wars and Napoleon's exile. Hugo, in other words, shows us France in the wake of the defeat it has suffered in the Russia of Tolstoy's novel. "What would art be, as the writing of history, if it shook off the memory of accumulated suffering?" Adorno asks (at the end of *Aesthetic Theory*). For the mouth, neither death nor candy nor lumber from felled trees used to frame the windows set in the walls through which one crawls into the artists' quarter of a city and hence into the future belongs to the students or to the pigeons that politicize them; death, candy, and lumber belong to the emperors of global capitalism. Adorno remarks that "art reaches toward reality, only to recoil at the actual touch of it."[4] (It is equally plausible to claim that art *delights* in reaching reality; it depends on the nature of that "reality," on whether it is the site of the catastrophe of human history that Adorno, with justification, thinks it to be or whether it is, rather, an unjudged simple suchness—of, say, today's beautiful weather, the red chair in which I'm sitting, the ambient household sounds, etc.) Art reaches toward an ontological reality and encounters historical reality—perhaps this is why it recoils. Looking for my dark glasses, I find several left around the room, and I try them, one by one, but each in turn blurs the things around me until I put on a pair through which I can see fine. I look around: Here are various spoons, bowls, a four-burner gas stove, etc., and a window, this one unfortunately looking out over a narrow alley onto the facade of the building next door and into the neighbors' kitchen. A spark falls to the floor and burns a hole clear through it. I catch a glimpse of a microcephalic cow, and then, apparently kept in the same pen, a turkey-headed cow steps into view. The imagination has, in Walter Benjamin's words, "remarkable propensity for structures that convey and connect." For the writer of everyday life, even to the extent that she deploys some of the strategies of the diarist, memory comes into play (though it takes various, sometimes minor as well as major, roles). But, even if she doesn't record things at the precise moment they occur but only does so later, her chronicle will be configured, rather than, in the conventional sense, plotted. Or rather, it is plotted but as land or a map

[4]Theodor W. Adorno, *Aesthetic Theory*, trans. by Robert Hullot-Kentor (Minneapolis: University of Minnesota Press, 1997).

is, with elements placed here and there. The resulting paratactically configured work keeps first her and then our attention on present particulars in the present tense, since that is the tense of cognitive time. It is the temporality, too, by the way, of encounters with the dictionary, since almost no one moves through a dictionary from front to back. What would an alphabetical ordering of the sentences in the paragraph preceding this one look like? But a digression inserted at this point would be less entertaining than irritating, though of course the author may intend to irritate; why should she feel bound to entertain? A digression would produce something like the situation of the three young peasant soldiers, a woman and two men, who are making their way into enemy territory: Someone shouts "your fly" or "the fly," referring to a missing insignia on the woman's jacket, and afraid of being exposed (afraid that they've already been spotted), the three young soldiers disappear into a crowd of people swarming into a department store. For an instant the sunlight coming through the open window picks up a stain or shadow on the floor so pale and transient I'm not sure what I'm seeing, and in just that way a memory is haunted by doubt and an event by a fly.

The End of the World

Julia Elliott

"MONSTROUS PACKS OF FERAL DOGS," says Possum, "one thousand curs strong, sweeping through gutted subdivisions, their dead instincts raging, high on the scent of human blood. And hordes of ex-cons who've spent years fermenting in testosterone-drenched prisons—I'm talking twelve-hour-a-day iron pumpers, black-market juicers whose bodies can survive on instant mashed potatoes and rancid Hi-C."

Possum, a weight-lifting lawyer who subsists on cigarettes and power bars, resembles a corroded action figure. He paces in expensive motorcycle boots. Hyped on Red Bull and something pharmaceutical, he keeps plucking rocks from the road and hurling them at birds. Like a voluptuous harem woman, Tim reclines in the grass sipping a Schlitz. Green mountains swell around us. We're waiting outside Bill's barbed-wire fence, having driven up to his cabin only to find him gone.

"Where the hell is he?" I say.

"Maybe he's out hunting for his supper," says Tim.

"There would be no hope for you, Tim," says Possum, "as fat as you are. You'd die without air-conditioning and cable. And the second your life-support arsenal of Benzos ran out, you'd be a quivering mess."

"Unless he found some postapocalyptic warlord who needed a jester," I say.

"Well," says Tim, "a guy with hepatitis C's sure gonna kick some butt in an anarchic dystopia. Won't your liver fail when your meds run out? And like you're not addicted to Xanax and Adderall."

"I use Xanax recreationally and the Adderall only to write briefs, an activity that would be obsolete in the latter stages of anarchy." Possum gazes out at the mountains. "Besides, I've got a twenty-year supply of everything in an industrial freezer."

"Liar," I say.

"Plus, I can make the hep C work for me. Nobody's gonna want my blood spurting all over them. But let's talk about what will happen to Lisa."

"I'll get kidnapped by some greasy road pirate and ravished," I say, opening another beer.

"Dream on," says Possum. "With the whole courtship economy collapsed and taboos blasted to hell, every neo-Attila will want a teen concubine. The value of the adultescent thirty-something will plummet like the dollar, and her life, sans cosmetics, out in the raw elements and carcinogenic sun, will turn her into a crusty troll in no time."

"This is bullshit," says Tim. "Nothing's gonna change. We'll die in front of our televisions."

"Don't have a TV," says Possum.

"That's why you spend hours in front of mine," says Tim. "If civilization as we know it is about to collapse, why bother driving up here?"

"A man should always have several plans of action," says Possum. "And who knows: If *Loser Bands of the Nineties* goes viral, and the American Empire declines slowly, we could spend the rest of our thirties parodying our twenty-something personas and retire at age forty by pimping our nubile selves."

"That makes my head hurt," says Tim.

About a month ago, I got an e-mail from Possum titled "The Child Is Father of the Man." In it he quoted Heidegger and filled me in on the results of his latest liver biopsy. And then he informed me that this rich guy he knows from his LA aspiring-writer years is producing a record called *Loser Bands of the Nineties*. A trust-funded dabbler whose dad just died, the man wants our single "Scorched Tongue." He knows somebody at Howlhole Records. Plans to hype the release with a farcically glitzy commercial. And he aims to film our old band Swole in high cliché, rocking on a roof or brooding by some kudzu-smothered railroad tracks.

"Bill will never agree," Tim says again.

"Don't know," says Possum. "Bet you he's sick of that Unabomber shack."

The shack. There it sits, beyond a flurry of trumpet vines, a cedar-planked cabin with a new tin roof. Its front porch boasts a solitary lawn chair, and the relief I feel upon noting this detail takes me by surprise. I peer down the road again, tensed for the sight of Bill's green truck. It's been two years since I've seen him. It's been a year since his last letter appeared in my mailbox. Six months ago he called from the only pay phone in Saluda. Christmas Eve. Midnight. He'd drunk a bottle of cough syrup and walked down the mountain on the ice-crusted road.

We avoided certain subjects. We talked about the habits of beasts in winter, where they slept and what they ate. We speculated on the delirium of hibernation, bears dreaming of sparkling fish, the moist static inside frozen reptile brains. He asked me if I missed the snow.

"Here comes somebody," says Tim.

But it's not Bill. It's the Donkey Man in his fat white truck, carting a trailer of exotic asses: miniatures, albinos, and shaggy Poitous. The Donkey Man waves, smiles like he might remember that time he gave me a lift to town.

"I like to fool with donkeys," he'd said, gesturing toward his empire of slapdash barns.

I'd climbed into his truck for the experience—to ride with an authentic old-timer in the rich fall light. I expected yarns and tall tales to stream from his ancient lips. I expected advice on planting by the phases of the moon. But the Donkey Man had said nothing the whole way to town. He seemed to be shrinking as he drove, scrunched down in his Carhartt coveralls.

"What the hell?" says Tim.

"Donkeys," I say.

"More like mutant poodles," says Possum.

Possum is also preparing himself for Bill. What started off as a game last winter has become a key obsession for him. In the thick of a dystopian-film marathon, after Tim had fallen asleep during the endless last stretch of *Zardoz,* Possum started speculating about apocalyptic scenarios and what would befall particular friends of ours within each. It was fun to imagine Tim, for instance, in the quivering throes of Xanax withdrawal, hurling a hand-whittled spear at a cat. It was hilarious to picture Tim skinning the tom and roasting its carcass over a fire of burning trash. It was fucking sidesplitting to envision Tim sprinting though a blighted urban landscape with the last bag of Fritos clutched to his chest, a mob of starving mutants hot on his tail.

Whereas Tim and Possum used to maintain a constant stream of abusive banter, Tim has grown quieter ever since he had a kid. Bill has vanished into the woods. And now Possum, who's neck-deep in law-school debt, and who financed three ghetto properties with credit cards during the height of the real estate bubble, never sleeps.

"Superviruses," says Possum. "Postmodern plagues. Rogue nanobots that tinker with your neurons and turn you into a raving lunatic."

He flashes a cryptic grin, lights his hundredth cigarette. The clouds above the mountains are turning pink. Possum regards their softness with bloodshot eyes.

I wonder if Darren, the landscape painter, is out in some meadow with his easel. I wonder if his wife, Willow, the grief therapist, is meditating on their fifty-foot deck.

The first night we'd moved to Saluda, Bill and I were still hauling boxes into our rented cottage when Willow and Darren showed up with an asparagus quiche. Their dog snapped at me. And Willow, in her aggressively gentle therapist voice, explained that Karma was working through some issues. They'd researched dogs to find the sweetest breeds, settling on a golden retriever/lab mix for its loving, docile qualities. But Karma turned out to be vicious. She once chased me into a creek bed and nipped my calf.

Our house, designed as a summer cottage for our rich landlord's parents, perched on the dark side of the mountain. We had a ridiculously pastoral view: angora goats and llamas, milling about in a green valley, their picture-book barn poised on a hillock. I was writing a dissertation on female mystics. Bill got a job at a bakery in town. That winter, as I pored over microfiche printouts of medieval manuscripts, Bill read books like *The Permaculture Bible*. He dreamed of lush gardens as snow blanketed the mountains and valley. From late November to early May, our world was frozen. All day I sat cocooned in a comforter, drinking green tea and reading about the visionary fits of my mystics. Every night, after Bill came chugging up the slushy dirt road in the truck, we'd start up with the red wine.

One morning a blizzard curled around our house like a great white beast. The light was a strange pink. Bill stood in the doorway holding our old four-track.

"Look what I found," he said.

We had a vintage Wurlitzer, three guitars, a cheap violin, and a broken flute. Bill could play anything, while I could get by on the Wurlitzer. But I could do things with my voice that he couldn't do. At 11:00 a.m. we opened a bottle of wine and embraced the delirium of winter. Crouched by the woodstove with his guitar, Bill strummed demented Appalachian riffs.

"Gronta zool nevah flocksam lamb," I sang, half joking, half ecstatic.

We chanted nonsense like snowed-in half-starved monks. Howled like Pentecostals. We layered weird shimmering harmonies and attempted authentic yodels. After we'd had three or four glasses of wine, we couldn't stop laughing at the exquisite absurdity of it all. We stripped off layers of thermal fleece and wool. We groped on the couch, the woodstove ablaze, combining our selves in yet another way.

All winter we made plans for the summer, where the garden would go and what we'd plant and how sweet and abundant our organic vegetables would be. In the spring, mammals would crawl from their musky holes. Insects would hatch. The landlords would shave dirty wool from their goats and pregnant mothers would drop steaming kids into the straw.

It's that strange time between day and night when lightning bugs sway out from the woods. Possum has driven off to replenish his arsenal of cigarettes and power bars. And Tim's up, talking about his infant daughter, about the skull-splitting rage he sometimes feels when she cries all night. When he sees the dainty spasm of her yawn, his exhausted nervous system surges with the purest love he's ever felt. But then the fatigue after that is even more intense. And she'll start screaming again, an amazing roar for such a small person, with her moth-sized lungs and tensed fists.

"Does Bill even know that Violet exists?" Tim asks.

"When I spoke to him last Christmas, I told him Jenna was pregnant."

"What did he say?"

"Nothing, really. You know Bill."

Tim has known Bill the longest, since high school, when they were both pimply creatures learning to play guitar. Bill had mastered the instrument in two months, with astonishing proficiency. Tim, demoralized, had switched to bass. They kept up this arrangement all through college and formed Swole their junior year. And then Possum and I stepped into the picture. As Bill regarded me through silky black bangs, I thought him the most attractive boy I'd ever seen. I loved his huge eyes and the scars on his cheeks, which saved him from being too pretty.

We played dense, frenetic music, a rabid mutant of punk and prog, each of us striving to worm in a quirky rhythm or micromelody. I had to howl like a manic monkey just to be heard. When I listen to our old seven-inch, I'm amused by our naive arrogance but impressed by our relentless energy—the essence of hormonal youth, splooged and shrieked.

"Remember when Bill didn't speak for a week?"

"I'm very familiar with that tactic of his."

"He'd come to practice, do his thing, but not utter a single word. I think that was right before you two started dating. He thought Possum and you were some kind of thing."

"He was an only child," I say, "raised in that house surrounded by goat pastures."

I gaze down the road again, see a billow of dust. But it's only Possum.

"What if he's dead in there?" Possum says. His grin tenses into a grimace. He scratches his head as we stare him down.

Tim squints at the cabin and shakes his head.

"But then his truck *is* gone." Possum's voice quavers into damage-control mode. "Which means he's not dead, that he's off gallivanting somewhere. Fucking frolicking. Full of happy Bill thoughts about sweet potato harvests and apple cider."

"What if he parks his truck behind the cabin?" I say. "Or it could be back by his garden, full of manure or something. And then he might be, you know, in the cabin."

"But we've yelled for him more than once," says Tim. "Wouldn't he come out?"

"Maybe he can't come out."

"Let's scale the fucking fence."

Possum has already inserted his left foot in the chain-link mesh. Now he's almost at the top, where barbed wire lies coiled, ready to tear his tender lawyer hands or disembowel him. But he somehow hoists himself over in a single maneuver that resembles a movie stunt. Lands like a ninja, dusts himself off, and smirks. Possum strolls over to the gate.

"Ha!" he says. "He left it unlocked."

"That doesn't sound like Bill," I say.

But Bill has indeed left the padlock open, which makes me think he's on the premises, down in the pit he cleared for a garden or holed up inside, perhaps peering out at us, perhaps chuckling, perhaps scowling and twitching at the threshold of craziness.

It's almost dark. The cabin, I know, has no electricity. But I have a penlight in my purse, and we slip onto the porch like thieves. I point my thin beam of light: at a basket of kindling, at a dusty box of canning jars, at *Mushrooms Demystified*, splayed on the seat of his plastic chair.

"The door's unlocked too," Possum whispers.

"Knock first," says Tim. "He might go Rambo with his air rifle."

Possum knocks, a loud knuckle rap on the door.

"Yo, Bill," he says. "Open up." But Bill doesn't answer.

When we step into the cramped darkness of his cabin, I'm overcome by the inexplicable smell of Bill: a clean animal musk tinged with cinnamon and dust. A hint of cumin. A vague plastic smell like Band-Aids.

I remember Bill's letter about digging out a tree stump. The earth had collapsed onto a fox's den, a nest of keening pups. According to Bill, their lair had smelled of milk and piss, something dark and sweet like overripe yams. He didn't touch them. He sat in his camp chair drinking beer, waiting for the mother, who appeared near dusk, a jolt of gleaming red fur, to move her pups one by one. When she snatched the puling creatures up with her teeth, they went limp and silent. Every time she darted off into the woods, she'd look back at Bill, meet his eyes to make sure they had an understanding.

"Imagine all the middle-class dog walkers," says Possum, "gentle eaters of Sunday brunch, roasting their radioactive pets on spits."

"Or eating them raw," says Tim. "Tearing frail Chihuahuas apart with their hands."

"We would resort to cannibalism," says Possum. "How could we not?"

We sit on the dark porch, still waiting for Bill. Katydids and crickets signal frantically for mates. I'm pretty sure Bill still has the insect recordings we made our second summer on the mountain. I'm pretty sure he still has that box of cassettes and CDs in chronological order, spanning the early days of Swole all the way up to our third summer when I left in a silent rage. And perhaps he has other recordings, brilliant and mysterious, that he made after I went away.

After I'd gotten the job in Atlanta and Bill had retreated to the basement, I'd meant to duplicate all those recordings while he was at work. But every time I stepped down into the moldy basement, with its damp Berber carpet, sweating walls, and deceptively innocent toothpaste smell, I'd feel a wobble of panic in my heart. I'd rush back up into brighter air.

Millipedes had invaded the basement bathroom our second summer on the mountain. Every morning Bill found two dozen slithering around the dewy toilet base. He'd smash them with a hoe. Their crushed bodies smelled like toothpaste. Flecks of brown chitin littered the carpet. The woods that enveloped us were practically a rain forest, and the summer humidity didn't let up until first frost.

That fall, the landlord's daughter, off at college for the first time, suffered from food allergies, and when the health center treated her with steroids, she had a mental breakdown. She went jogging after a star, followed it all the way out to an interstate exit where the police found her, dehydrated and chattering about astrology. They sent her home. Every time she had a squabble with her parents, she'd run off into the woods.

I'd be gazing out the window at the autumn leaves, when she'd dart by our house, a whir of pure anxiousness and flowing hair. And the landlord's llama Zephyr started spitting. I'd be strolling though the goat pasture when Zephyr would rush up, a flurry of black fur and dust, and attempt to spit a reddish jet of puke into my face.

That winter, Bill turned vegan and lost fifteen pounds. He wanted to live off the grid, he said, away from bourgeois pretenders in a small cabin that would meet our basic needs. The landlord's daughter was still having episodes, wandering the woods behind our house. Zephyr was still a dark, furious presence down in the goat pasture.

I got an instructorship sixty miles away, would drive off into the mountains and return exhausted just as Bill got back from his stint at the bakery. We'd throw a meal together, open a bottle of wine, talk about the cabin we planned to buy that spring, though we could never agree on how big it would be and whether or not it would have electricity.

Fifteen pounds lighter, Bill could never get warm. Huddled by the stove, he wore two layers of thermal underwear, a dingy mustard snowsuit, a wool cap with a special cotton lining he'd sewn in himself. In the flickering firelight, his cheeks looked ghoulish and his enormous eyes brimmed with strange fevers.

"I have a sinus headache," he said one night. "Because you didn't clean the cheese knife."

"What?"

"You used it to cut vegetables. All it takes is one tiny particle of dairy to make me sick."

Bill winced like a martyr and turned back to *Mysteries of Beekeeping Explained*.

*

By summer our arguments had swelled luxuriant and green, like the poison-oak patch behind our house. We spent entire nights screaming our throats raw. Sometimes the landlord's imbalanced daughter, out prowling, would pause at one of our open windows to listen, an ecstatic grin on her face.

In July I got a job offer in Atlanta and Bill moved down into the basement with the millipedes.

One warm, shrieking night, waking in a ruttish fit, I drifted down to the basement. I planned to climb upon Bill and kiss him all over his face. He lay prone on the moldy sofa he'd covered with a sheet, one arm flopped onto the floor. I could hear his thick breathing, louder than the silvery pulse of the katydids. I could smell the strange minty scent of crushed millipedes. I straddled Bill. He opened his eyes. When I leaned down to kiss him, his thin black tongue slithered out of his mouth—a millipede, I realized, its underside feathery with a thousand moving legs. I floated back up the stairs and out of the house.

Only when I was hovering high over the trees did the sadness of his transformation hit me. I woke up and e-mailed the English Department at Georgia State.

"Brain-computer interface," says Possum. "Wetware made of insect parts and frog neurons. Telepathic cockroaches creeping around your house, gathering data for marketing companies."

"But I thought everybody had a crystal implanted in their head and voluntarily broadcast all brain farts to the mainframe," says Tim.

"They do, but the cockroaches are looking for microtrends, subthoughts, unconscious motivations."

When Possum is deep into the bullshit intricacies of postmodern surveillance, and he has lit his thousandth cigarette, and Tim has drifted, once more, to the edge of the woods to take a leak, Bill arrives.

It's 10:10 p.m. An owl offers an ominous hoot in his honor, and then flutters off to snatch some clueless rodent into the howling air.

Bill must be surprised to see us, but by the time he kills his lights and opens his gate, eases his truck into its spot, and emerges, with a cloth bag of groceries, he has composed himself. He's a slight figure, moving through darkness toward the porch, and I find myself gripping the handles of my chair.

"Well, well, well," he says.

If I could see his face it would show only the faintest quirk of shock, I'm sure—an eyebrow twitch, a shifting of frown lines—the same look he used to get when he spotted yet another millipede gliding across the damp linoleum of our basement bathroom.

"It's us," I say, shining my penlight at Possum. "And watch out for Tim. He's creeping around your property somewhere. Please don't shoot him."

"I'll try not to," says Bill. "I've upgraded to a Savage Mark II, a big improvement on the old Beeman."

"Killer," says Possum.

"Been doing a little hunting." Bill steps onto the porch, puts down his groceries, stands warm and humming a foot away from me. "Though I do keep it under my bed at night."

During our second winter on the mountain, on a sunny day after the first snow, alone in the house, I'd gotten caught up in a three-hour frenzy of vacuuming. With fierce efficiency, I'd vacuumed the walls and the baseboards and every square inch of floor. I emptied closets and cupboards and drawers, probed with my sucking wand under furniture and behind appliances. I vacuumed until I reached the ecstatic state of a fasting medieval nun, feverish with holy purpose.

When I squatted beside our bed to peer beneath it, I saw dried roaches, floating balls of filth and hair, a wool sock coated with dust. I saw Bill's machete, the one he'd bought to harvest heirloom grains, stashed under his side of the bed. He'd never mentioned that there was a weapon under our bed, poised within easy gripping distance.

I cleaned the machete with a damp rag and placed it exactly as I'd found it. I went to my office and dug a box of Camel Lights from a drawer. I smoked only one, out on the front porch, as the iced branches near our chimney dripped.

Possum's pacing out in the front yard, in light as crisp and tart as a Granny Smith apple. His black boots gleam. His goblin grin has erupted in its full glory, thanks to two cans of Red Bull and a half dozen cigarettes. He walks circles around Tim, who's reclining in a broken lawn chair he found stashed under Bill's cabin.

"Why not directly into their nervous systems?" Tim yawns. "Computer-calibrated microdoses for intricate mood adjustment, released by nanobot teams in the brain."

"Not drugs per se," says Possum, "but drug technologies. They might use bacteria or viruses or bioengineered parasites, for example."

Bill has disappeared again.

This morning, in the dark chill of the cabin, I'd heard him getting dressed. As a bird warbled outside the window, I thought I was in Atlanta, waking up to a car alarm. But then I smelled Bill, the cedar of the cabin, the glandular odor of small game animals. He actually sells their pelts on eBay, drives to the local library to check his account and download pics. The walls of his cabin are soft with patches of fur.

Last night he told us that hipsters in Brooklyn will pay sixty dollars for a coonskin cap. That the Etsy crafting crowd can't get enough of his bones. That's why his industrial shelves are lined with the bleached craniums of foxes and coons. That's why he has tackle boxes packed with the delicate skulls of birds. Some girl in Philadelphia dips them in silver and strings them on vintage chains.

"But I only kill what I eat," Bill said, describing the taste of fox as wild, with a hint of brassy urine. "You have to soak the meat in vinegar."

"Trap or shoot?" Possum asked.

"Both." And then Bill told us about the ingenious bird traps he'd made of bamboo. He described the thrill of hooking brook trout, the sadness he'd felt when he shot his first rabbit and heard it scream.

Last night, in the guttering light of kerosene lanterns, we drank warm beer on the porch. Our cooler had run out of ice and Bill has no refrigerator. Sometime after midnight, Bill dug out the shoebox of old Swole cassettes and played them on his boom box. The music was ridiculously fast, as though calibrated to a hummingbird's nervous system. And we marveled at the thrill we'd felt back then, when we were enmeshed in every last bleep and sputter.

Though we could get no drunker, we drank more beer. Possum and Tim finally swayed off to sleep in the car. And Bill put on a CD of our mountain music, the stuff we'd concocted in the midst of a blizzard two years before. We sat on the porch as psychedelic crickets pulsed over a moaning Wurlitzer. And then: six meticulously layered violin tracks, silver smears of flute, and our voices—so many different versions of both of us. Moans, howls, hums, grunts. Lots of chanting. We circled each other, overlapped, fused, and retreated. We cleaved and melded and darted away.

"How are your mystics?" Bill asked me.

"I don't ever get to read them. Too busy grading freshman essays."

"Do you miss them?"

Of course I missed my scrawny, passionate mystics, who starved themselves until their brains caught fire and Jesus stepped down from the ether, right into their freezing cells, his pink flesh so warm it almost burned their crimped fingers.

"Yes," I said. "I do."

How could we help falling together in the darkness? How could we help giggling as we tripped over each other on the way to his futon? I still hadn't gotten a decent look at him. But as we rooted in the dark, I could smell pure Bill, his hands musky from the little animals he killed. He tasted different from eating meat. And he seemed denser yet lighter, stronger yet somehow more nebulous, Bill and not Bill.

This morning, as he moved around the room getting dressed, making small domestic noises that were painfully familiar to me, I felt self-conscious and faked sleep, burrowed down under the blanket so that he couldn't see my face. When he finally left, and I emerged from the covers to take a deep breath, I saw neat rows of animal skulls, white as industrial sugar, eyeless but somehow staring right through me.

"Lisa is lucky," says Possum. "Within ten years she might be able to clone herself, implant the embryo in her own uterus, and give birth to herself."

"And when my old carcass finally wears out," I say, "I could put my half-mad brain into my daughter's exquisite twenty-year-old body."

Bill's still gone and our hangovers have reached such a nasty pitch that we've popped open our first round of beers. My stomach's empty, and the first five sips translate into instant giddiness. The woods look ethereal, the perfect medium for frolicking elves. Birds twit and fuss. And Bill comes strolling through the speckled light with four gleaming trout on a string. He's even whistling, absurdly, and I wonder if he's rehearsed this scene in his head. I wonder if he's imagined that moment when he, the handsome outdoorsman, emerges from the woods bearing game he's caught with his own clever hands as his decadent urban companions laze around drinking, our faces pasty from last night's debauch.

But Bill himself looks a bit green under the gills—way too skinny, I see with a catch in my heart—so skinny that his pants hang from his pelvic bones, his eye sockets jut, his neck resembles a delicate stalk, hoisting the overlarge bloom of his head. I note eye bags, the kind he used to get when he couldn't sleep. I see flares of gray at his temples. And he seems pretty eager to crack open a Warsteiner himself.

"Rainbows?" says Possum.

"Just brook trout," says Bill. "But they're tasty grilled."

We walk around back where a stone patio overlooks his garden. He's got a hand water pump set in a square of concrete, a hibachi grill, a Coleman camp stove. His kitchen is protected from the elements with a tin-roofed shed and furnished with a salvaged picnic table.

As Bill guts fish on a concrete block, Possum hunkers down beside him. Teetering like a manic Weeble Wobble, he watches Bill scrape off scales and slice each trout from anus to jaw. Bill chops off heads, pulls dainty wads of guts from cavities, tosses the scraps into a plastic bucket. He rinses his hands and tells us that grits are simmering in his solar oven, which is down in the clearing behind his chicken coop. His beer can is flecked with silvery scales. His patched khakis, held up with a strand of twine, look adorable. And when he takes us to see his chickens, four coppery hens strutting behind a split-sapling fence, I want to kiss him again.

We gather eggs and pick arugula and carry the pot of grits back to the patio. Bill puts trout on the grill and makes a salad of baby greens and wild blackberries. He has a little raw cheddar. He has cilantro from the garden, a nub of organic salami, some bread from the bakery.

As Bill makes scrambled eggs with cheese and salami, we have another round of warm beers. Birds flit through the woods in search of food. Birds scratch at the black forest floor. They peck bark for larvae and snap up glittering dragonflies, thrust their beaks into the throats of flowers and suck.

It's after two. Tim and Possum have gone on a beer run. Bill and I sit at the picnic table gazing down at his garden, which isn't getting enough sun.

"I spend five hours a day grinding through scrub trees with a chain saw," he says. "But one day, I'll have a view. One day, I'll be able to see the Blue Ridge Mountains from here."

"You're turning into your dad," I joke, remembering stories from his youth, how his father, who suffered from obscure sinus issues, became obsessed with mold and waged war against the woods. After working eight-hour shifts at a nylon factory, he'd drive thirty miles home to his rustic property and fight the encroaching brush until dark. That's why he surrounded their house with flocks of goats.

"Now I know exactly how he feels," says Bill, "though I've only got three acres of unruly wilderness to control."

"But you seem to be doing OK."

Bill shrugs. "How's Hotlanta?"

"The same filthy, sprawling mess it's always been. I sit in my apartment grading papers most of the time, making the occasional excursion to the neighborhood hipster bar. But I've got Tim and Possum to entertain me."

"You don't have to live that way. I think you know that."

"A temporary solution."

"Solution to what?"

"I'm still figuring some things out."

"Can you be more specific?"

"My bowel situation is getting too dire for specificity." I smile. "Now where is that composting toilet I've heard so much about?"

Bill has a nonelectric, waterless composting toilet in his garden shed, sitting right beside the tiller we bought four years ago.

On a giddy September day, just when the weather was starting to turn, we'd driven to an area outside Asheville where an old homestead was tucked between a Target and a Bank of America. The farmer's family had owned the property for five generations, and over the last twenty years, the world had crept up to his door. High on a hill where his grandparents' house was collapsing into ruins, the farmer told us about the time his aunt shot a goat that stank so bad it kept her awake at night. He told us about the first time he walked into a supermarket at age nineteen. From our vantage point, we could see an Applebee's sign rising beyond the farmer's double-wide. We could see the carbon haze hovering over the paved valley like swaths of mist.

I find Bill in the cabin, stretched out on his bed with *The Goat Handbook*, the room awash with forest light. I crawl in beside him and rest my head on his shoulder. I can see myself drifting into this life, doing garden chores and reading in the afternoon, learning to hunt and churn butter, creating strange music at night. But then I imagine the stuffiness of the cabin in winter, the smell of pelts, the funk of wool-swaddled bodies sponge-bathed with bowls of heated water. I imagine the endless snow. I see myself pacing around the woodstove, chattering as Bill sits in silence, burrowed deep in the mystery of himself like a hibernating mammal curled nose to belly.

But still, we kiss. Still, I peel off his ancient T-shirt. I run my fingers over his abdomen, which is covered with chigger bites. I reach into the humid darkness of his boxer shorts and feel the familiar scruff with my fingertips. I glance up at the rows of skulls and laugh.

"When the Chinese are buying American mail-order brides," says Possum, "blonde and luscious and sweet sixteen, we'll be the ones riding our bikes everywhere."

We're on I-85, leaving Commerce Georgia, kingdom of the outlet malls. We're exhausted and rumpled and our mouths are smeared with grease. Stopping to grab a pizza an hour ago, we'd smelled middle-class aspiration in the air, faint and acidic like burnt plastic. We'd seen it in the hungry-eyed families, clustered amid shopping bags, slurping corn syrup from soggy paper cups.

I need things (new sheets and a decent set of cookware) as does Tim (a stroller and a better car seat), but we're too hungover to make sense of the staggering abundance—to choose from among twenty different types of skillet without reading the consumer ratings first. So we're back on the road in the exurban hinterlands, which, Possum insists, will fall into wilderness when the oil runs out.

Like a lover with a pure flame of passion in his heart, ready to burst into a tiger-orange blaze, Possum speaks of peak oil with wistful longing. When we pass a gated community called The Hollows, Possum falls into a rapture of speculation. Tim, waking from a nap, fires up a cigarette and joins him. The End of the World is something they can toss between them like a fraternal football, a prosthetic appendage that enables them, two troubled men, to touch each other.

By the time we reach the blighted outskirts of Atlanta, they're both giddy, speaking a notch louder, finishing each other's sentences the way Bill and I used to do.

Traffic is slowing. The air is smoky with the smell of fresh-laid pavement. And they keep on dreaming up new nightmare worlds.

We haven't moved for ten minutes. I see a twist of smoke rising beyond an overpass, probably from a wreck, and I wonder what Bill's doing. When we left him this morning he'd calmly descended into his garden with a tray of pepper seedlings. I noticed that his left tennis shoe had been repaired with duct tape. I noticed that his hair was thinning. I noticed that the sight of his thin, childish neck still made my heart feel sprained. In less than a month, I'll see him in Columbia,

SC, our old stomping grounds, where we've agreed to shoot the lame video for *Loser Bands of the Nineties*.

"I'll do it," he'd said last night at his cabin, which had surprised us all. Huddled together in the depths of drunkenness, Bill had played our mountain music for Possum and Tim. Steeped in its strangeness, they sat smiling. A sweet flicker of something moved between me and Bill, and then all four of us, and we started talking about the lost days of Swole, when we were all glowing idiots with youth to burn.

"Imagine dosing a whole city," Possum says. "With some neuro-pharmaceutical a thousand times more potent than LSD."

"Sounds groovy." Tim yawns. "You could live-blog the craziness."

"The CIA did it to Pont-Saint-Esprit in 1951."

"I saw that on AlterNet."

"Acid in the local bakery's bread, but you could hit the water supply."

"Or the air supply."

"Great name for a band."

We're moving a few feet every five minutes, approaching what I assume is a wreck. I imagine iconic five-car pileups, crumpled metal, the apocalyptic stench of smoke. I imagine mangled travelers moaning on stretchers, their blitzed faces discreetly covered. Mushroom clouds swell. Helicopters dart like wasps. Just over the horizon, alien life forms swarm in spaceships as sleek and black as insect eggs. I imagine the world ruptured, angelic screeches flying around my ears, my heart finally opening like a rose.

When we reach the overpass there's nothing on the roadside but a piece of fender and some shattered glass. Traffic picks up. And soon we're bearing down upon the city, navigating through a mess of orange construction cones.

Eight Poems

Robert Fernandez

drinking the blood
back into itself—

ever weak willed (black eggs

for Christmas)—
desire is not

insatiable tall salt, not anything that
tumbles out of us and smacks
of inevitability

red roe
pouring from us

in soft slow
clusters

red roe at
the height of my life

like a wall
of wildflowers

*

Robert Fernandez

happily I explore
bunches of

cherries under the
happily I explore

bouquets of paradise
roses inside of

happily
from Paris

their son a
little bunch of roses

*

I am shrill,
barking through

a waterfall
at black rock

these odalisques
on the moss

take their color
from the falling water
& the sky

take their color
from the snakes
that cool themselves

& drink
between the rocks

take their color
from the fine
mist,

the rainbow's
light

*

one is not to cower

one is to stand straight

one is not to cower

not to ease or

release

one is to grip straight

one is to tense right

one is to grit

the straight teeth

one is to tense

& arc the blood

one is to style

& tense the blood

one is to grip right

*

to hell with those that
hand themselves over

the vents are warm
to hell with those that

hand themselves over
to me to hell with those that

hand themselves over

to hell with those that
hand themselves over

to me
that warm themselves

in me

*

we all

have something to say
how soft

we all
have screen doors

to press our
light through

to press our
soft

money through
we all have

holes, souls,
black-widow

hourglasses
to pass our

winsome lightnesses
through

*

who floods
loosens us

who can blend
release me from my

often I am chittering
& swayed

often bright Christmas tree
budding in the veins

often I am permitted
to ultra-

violet
funnels

I can bend light
I can drink heat

I can disembowel
my seeing

*

& am seeking
the bleeding vent

get me on my feet,
help me stand

the roads are black,
the roads are iced,

the roads are
choked with snow

the roads are
staggered meat,

fresh rib cage
of a deer

what is meat
to common

"shall suffer"?

what is meat to
sides of venison

covered in moths?

Counting Sheep

Brian Conn

KATRIN LIVED ON A SHEEP FARM located so far away from anything at all that she had to be schooled by shortwave radio. Her father was busy all day with the sheep, because he had made it his mission to claim the world's record for the most sheep owned by a single individual. He believed that a man lives exactly as long as he has some mission.

"That's all you need to know, Katrin: your mission. Figure that out and everything else will make sense."

He owned about three thousand sheep, which was not really very many, so he was confident that both his mission and his life would last a long time. But he never knew precisely how long, because he had never been able to learn just what the current sheepholding record was. Certainly he was nowhere near it yet, but he worried that someday he would achieve his mission without knowing it. Would he then continue to live? Would everything still make sense? Every evening at the dinner table he asked Katrin whether her lesson from the shortwave had happened to include any information about particularly large holdings of sheep, but it never had.

Katrin's mother was a biogeochemist in the nearest city, which was much too far away ever to visit. She and Katrin's father were divorced because he had called science undemocratic. Katrin never saw her, except for one time when she, the mother, came to live in the attic of the farmhouse for two weeks to research a monograph on a rare millipede. On that occasion she became very sunburned and began to insist that the whole house and all its demesnes were underlain with aluminum—she seemed to mean aluminum foil—which had saturated the water and earth as well as the meat and wool of the sheep, and which, if Katrin's father succeeded in growing his flock and dominating the market with aluminum-adulterated sheep, would make all the world demented.

Neither Katrin nor her father was sorry to see her go. When Katrin went to clean up the attic room, she found a few old bones under the bed, a little too big for sheep bones and not the right shape, but not quite like human bones. She threw them in the trash pit, but later came and got one out again and wrapped a leather thong around it and hung it on her wall. Her father sat her down for a talk about nihilism, but Katrin was only imitating Doggett, one of the men her father engaged to help with the sheep, whom she had sometimes seen wearing a small bone on a leather thong around his neck.

Doggett was the only one of her father's men whose name Katrin knew, because her father used to pretend to mistake him for a dog. He had a pronounced slouch and a large mouth that turned into a rectangle when it opened, like a letter box. Katrin did not like Doggett, but she had begun increasingly to fantasize about putting something into that mouth of his—a sandal, maybe, or an alarm clock. That was the closest thing she had to a mission. She never spoke to him and he never spoke to her.

Once when Katrin's father needed more men to look after the growing flock, Doggett said he knew a man named Lars. Lars came to meet Katrin's father, and when Katrin's father asked where he came from, he said, "The mountains."

"What mountains?" said Katrin's father. "This is a plain all around. There are no mountains."

"Just the mountains," Lars said, as though it were an abstract concept he came from and not a specific locale. Then Katrin's father asked him why he'd come down from "the mountains," whatever he meant by that, and Lars said, "It was necessary for my mission," and after that Katrin's father felt he understood Lars, as any man with a mission understands another man with a mission, even if that man claims to come from the mountains. Lars and Doggett went off right away to see about some sheep, and Katrin, in the living room, left the shortwave for a moment to watch them out the window. Lars had a way of walking wherein he kept his body perfectly straight from the backs of his knees to the crown of his head, but bent the knees themselves considerably, so that most of him was rigid but at the same time leaning back at a steep angle—an attitude somewhere between that of a partially paralyzed man trying to lie down in a hammock and that of a man who has been transfixed with a spear through the crown of his head while preparing to limbo.

That evening at dinner Katrin's father asked her not only whether she had learned anything that day about large holdings of sheep, but also whether she had learned anything that or any other day about mountains that might exist nearby. It occurred to Katrin that she didn't know where the voice on the shortwave originated, so even if it had talked about nearby mountains, those same mountains might nevertheless have been very far away from the sheep farm, but she thought that idea would be too complicated for her father. "No," she said.

"What does the blasted thing tell you about then?"

"Canals," said Katrin, and her father had to admit that there might be some value in learning about canals. "After all, we may need one here someday," he said. "The amount of sheep around here, we may need just about anything."

"You mean the number of sheep," Katrin said. "Not the amount. 'Sheep' is a countable noun."

The next morning, Katrin moved the shortwave nearer to the window so that she could watch Lars come out of the bunkhouse while she listened to it. It seemed to her that there was something very strange about Lars. He was a man who chewed tobacco and ice cubes together at the same time. Katrin had never heard of anyone doing that before, and her understanding of how tobacco was chewed didn't permit her to understand the mechanism of it, but nevertheless it was his habit. He would come into the kitchen midmorning, throw open the icebox, scoop out two cubes of ice—he had long, narrow hands, like a sloth—lean his head even farther back than usual, and dangle the ice cubes over his mouth for a moment before dropping them in, one after the other. Then he would crunch the ice, throw in some tobacco, and do something with his tongue that made a slushy sound. Katrin hated this performance, which she watched carefully every morning. After he'd done the thing with his tongue, he would look her over silently from head to foot, as though monitoring her growth, and if Doggett was there he would make some remark, such as "She is intensely private," or "Note the development of the suborbital ridge."

And there was this: One time when the voice on the shortwave had told her to draw up a plan for some canals to use in her own household, and she had gotten out her graph paper and compass and straightedge and sat on the porch for a long time chewing a pencil stub and then finally gone inside and made a mutton sandwich, when she came back out she noticed that her pencil stub was chewed more than she had chewed it, and also the end of it was wet and brown, and it smelled like tobacco. And there was a little piece of ice sliding down the little metal part that goes around the eraser—*still frozen.*

When she told her father she suspected Lars had chewed her pencil, he just said, "They probably do things differently in the mountains." In fact, after having worked with him for only a short time, her father would tolerate no criticism of Lars. The flock was booming, he said, sheep were popping up all of a sudden out of nowhere, and he attributed this state of affairs to certain ideas Lars had implemented for "organizing" the sheep, in order to "stretch them a little farther." He wasn't able to explain Lars's ideas to Katrin, but then again organization is always hard to explain. At dinnertime he asked Katrin less and less about mountains and prominent sheep holders, and more and more about organization, as though it were a commercial product, like a flea dip. Katrin mentioned some methods of organizing canals, and they had conversations that went nowhere and ended with her father staring into space and tracing little boxes in the air with his finger.

"How many sheep are there right now?" Katrin asked.

"That's the trouble," her father said. "They've become difficult to count. Lars says to really organize them I need to know how many there are, but to know how many there are I need to organize them. When you have a serious mission like mine you're bound to come up against some problems."

When she went back to her room that night to work on her canal plan, Katrin noticed that the bone on her wall, the not-quite-human bone that she had found underneath the bed her mother had slept in while she researched the millipede, had been replaced by a different bone. This new bone was just a normal sheep femur, similar in size and shape to the first bone but of no real interest. Katrin didn't mind the loss of the bone itself, but worked herself into a rage at the thought that someone had thought it appropriate to come into her room without asking and replace an interesting object with an uninteresting object. She decided she would balance an open can of something, for example, tomato soup, on top of the door frame, with a piece of string tied between it and the doorknob, so that if the person came back again he would get tomato soup dumped on him. She wouldn't be able to go out the door herself once she'd set up the tomato soup, but she could climb in and out the window.

She had fetched a can of tomato soup from the pantry, and was standing there with it and looking up at the door frame in a speculative way when her father came in to ask her something more about organization. When he saw the tomato soup he asked about that instead, and Katrin thought this was another situation that would be too complicated for him, so she lied and said the tomato soup was for a canal project. She said she had to model canals in clay and the tomato soup would be the water. He asked her why she didn't just use water for the water, and she panicked and said you couldn't use real water as model water because a substance couldn't be a model of itself. Water was just actual water, you needed something else to be model water. Katrin wasn't very good at lying. Her father said of course a substance could be a model of itself, it was a common and even desirable practice in modeling to use a substance to represent itself, there was probably even a word for it, and then he started driving himself crazy trying to think of the word that meant using a substance as a model of itself, but the closest he could get was "synecdoche."

He went away to look for a dictionary, and Katrin put away the tomato soup and went to bed early to avoid talking to him. He wound up calling her mother in the faraway nearest city to say he'd found their daughter mooning over some tomato soup and a sheep femur, and he didn't know how to explain to her that whatever she was planning to do with the tomato soup and the sheep femur you just don't do that kind of thing. The mother said she had probably just been trying a recipe, and the father said little girls didn't try recipes anymore, they tried black magic; and the mother alluded to aluminum and called him a public health risk, and they ended by simultaneously hanging up on each other.

The reason Katrin was such a bad liar was that the shortwave had gone through a fairy-tale streak when she was young and she now believed that any lie she told would eventually come true, but with some diabolical twist. For example, now that she had lied and said she had to build a model canal system, she felt that she was likely to fall sick and sicker with fits until finally she had to be taken to a doctor far away in her mother's city, whose extensive modern tests would reveal canal-like patterns made out of mysterious lesions on the surface of her brain. To avoid this kind of outcome it was necessary for her to make any lie she told into the truth as soon as possible, in her own way and on her own terms, thus neutralizing its potential. Under the present circumstances, then, she found herself obliged to build some model canals out of clay and fill them with tomato soup. She began this project immediately, on the living-room floor by the window, where she could both listen to the shortwave and watch Lars as she modeled.

The other advantage of the living-room floor was that her father was likely to see her, because her father's acknowledgment of the canal model would definitively establish its truth. Her father, however, had become entirely engrossed in the problem of determining the number of sheep he owned. The flock's astonishing rate of increase was giving him terrible difficulties in this respect. He would count a group of sheep and as soon as he turned his back there would be more. It didn't matter how small he made the groups; he could count a pair of sheep and it would turn out there was a third sheep underneath. He started painting numbers on them, and that helped for a while, until, late one afternoon, he discovered two different sheep painted with the number 7,955.

He went pale and fell down. "This is my doom," he said. Some of the men carried him into the house and laid him on the couch, and Katrin had to leave the canal model and turn off the shortwave so that she could moisten his lips with a sponge. She had seldom missed a shortwave lesson, and it occurred to her that the voice might even now be reciting the world's record for the most sheep owned by a single individual, but it also occurred to her that if her father had lost hope of determining the number of his own sheep, then the number of any competitor's sheep was of no further interest. His mission had neither succeeded nor failed, but become unresolvable.

Katrin was afraid he would die in front of her. "You just need a new mission," she said when at last he regained consciousness. "Something resolvable." He tried to bury his head in the couch cushions, but couldn't muster the will for it, and ended up with his neck outstretched and one eye staring blankly, like that of a fish.

Katrin phoned her mother, who said she had always known this would happen and that she was prepared to deal with the situation through hypnosis.

"Hypnosis?"

"Your father is extremely susceptible to hypnosis. How do you think you were conceived? I'll convince him there never were such things as sheep."

"There are a lot of sheep here," said Katrin. "If he sees one, won't he remember?"

"Then I'll convince him there never were such things as numbers. He won't see any of those—they're abstractions."

"Should I dangle something shiny in front of him?"

"Don't be provincial, Katrin. This is modern hypnosis. Just lay the phone over his ear and go do something else for half an hour."

So Katrin propped the phone against her father's ear with some pillows and went to sit on the porch and think. She had gotten as far as worrying that if her mother succeeded in making her father forget that there were such things as numbers, his mission would become not only unresolvable but also incomprehensible to him, when she noticed Lars and Doggett standing close by.

"We were led to believe in a canal," said Doggett. "Going from this spot."

"A channel," said Lars.

"To the mountains," Doggett added.

"Your father said you know about this."

These were the first words either of them had ever spoken directly to her. Luckily she knew what to say: "Canals don't go to the mountains. A canal is flat."

"Flat and broad," said Lars.

"And high," said Doggett. He started to say something else, but Katrin, who had never been this close to him before and might never be again, and who was still holding the sponge with which she had been moistening her father's lips, chose that moment to reach up and drop it in his mouth.

She had always thought that something special would happen on the day she finally dropped something in Doggett's mouth, but he only swallowed it and began to choke. Lars pounded his back, but he kept coughing, and eventually they went away together to get him some water, Doggett still coughing and Lars still reaching out to pound his back but now repeatedly missing, both of them thin and ephemeral in the dusk, as though made of paper.

Her father came out of the house, looking completely normal, and said, "Your mother wants to talk to you."

"Your father is fine," her mother said. "But don't mention any kind of number to him. He'll get confused. If you talk about sheep, say, 'a sheep' instead of 'one sheep' and 'some sheep' instead of 'two sheep,' and if you need to refer to distance, say, 'the length of a sheep' or 'the distance a sheep walks in a day.' Do that for the rest of his life."

Katrin found her father looking at his profile in the full-length mirror in the hall. "Life is a real thing, Katrin," he said, "as real as tomato soup. The right and proper thing to do with tomato soup is to eat it for the nourishment of your body. The wrong thing to do with tomato soup is to use it as a model for water. What I'm trying to tell you, Katrin, is that I'm fort—I'm some years . . ." He clutched his head and seemed to be struggling with something.

"You're substantially aged," Katrin supplied.

"I'm substantially aged and I've been using my life as a model for water. Life isn't a model, Katrin. I've learned that. From now on life is life."

And with that he strode out the door and across the plain toward the nearest group of sheep, and toward Lars, who happened to be sitting in front of one of them, massaging its sternum.

Katrin didn't exactly understand the details of what her father had said, but she thought that was probably just a side effect of the hypnosis. At dinnertime he no longer talked about organization, but started instead to talk about *re*organization, which was, if anything, even harder to explain. Aside from that, he seemed older, and had trouble distinguishing a dessert fork from a dinner fork, but at least he wasn't collapsed on the couch.

Moreover, since his attention was no longer fixed on the number of his sheep, he finally noticed Katrin's canal model, and even started helping her with it. Katrin was glad at first, but he didn't understand the idea of multiple canals forming a system, and only wanted to build a single canal, impractically large. When Katrin corrected him he ignored her, and when she reminded him that she knew more about canals than he did, he reminded her in turn that he knew more about sheep.

"What do sheep have to do with canals?" said Katrin.

Her father grew serious. "It's about the size of dreams," he said. "The scope of a mission." He put down the putty knife and made her turn to face him. "You know what my mission has always been."

"Sheep," said Katrin cautiously. It was the first time he had mentioned his mission since it had become incomprehensible to him.

"The increase of sheep. And what I've been doing all my life—frankly, it's baffling to me, but it doesn't seem to have contributed to the increase of sheep. I was aiming too small. Now that I've discovered reorganization I'm making progress, but I don't want to see you waste your time like I've wasted mine. Find your mission soon, Katrin, and in the meantime practice making everything big."

Katrin wondered whether something special would have happened after all if only she had put something bigger than a sponge into Doggett's mouth. "Can we just make the canals like they are in this drawing?"

Her father gave her a measuring look. "Maybe you're not ready for big dreams."

After that Katrin worked on the canal model alone again. Through the window she watched as her father and Lars and Doggett built a new shed and took some sheep inside, for vaccination, Katrin thought, or some other thing that was ordinarily done to sheep; but shortly thereafter she started noticing some extraordinarily large sheep around the farm, and before she knew it the three men had built a second, bigger shed, and Lars was bringing the big sheep into the big shed while Doggett brought the normal sheep into the smaller shed, and her father paced back and forth between the two; and soon after that Katrin began noticing some sheep that were *very large indeed*, and when she paid careful attention to the sheds and the sheep and the size of the sheep, she saw the way things went: Two sheep went into a shed, and one larger sheep came out.

At dinner her father asked her if the shortwave had happened to mention anything about the world's record for the largest sheep owned by a single individual.

"What do you do in those sheds?" she asked.

"Reorganize the sheep," he said. "For their increase. But you don't want to hear about that; that's not a size of dream you're comfortable with."

Bigger sheds went up and bigger sheep appeared, until one forenoon Katrin heard a panicked bleating outside so loud that she thought at first that this must be what was meant by an air-raid siren, and when she looked out the window she saw all the men gathered around a capsized juggernaut of a sheep, which kept heaving up and then falling down again, like a flaccid hot-air balloon flapping in the wind.

"Her legs snapped," her father said when he came in. "As it turns out, the mass of a reorganized sheep increases faster than the strength of the legs."

"What if," said Katrin, who had been thinking about it, "you reorganized the flock instead of the individual sheep?"

"That is dilettantism. The point of a mission is to pursue it, not to trade it in for something easier at the first sign of trouble. With modest projects such as you enjoy, Katrin, everything works out in a week, although I notice that it is taking you an extraordinarily long time to finish that model. If you had a great mission, as I do, you too would be compelled to struggle with great forces, such as gravity." Then he said it again, "gravity," as though pleased with himself for having run aground on something so famous.

Katrin longed to tell him that it was only since his mind had been crippled for his own safety that he had begun thinking in this way, but she remembered how he had lain on the sofa with his eye like the eye of a fish, and stopped herself in time.

In the days that followed he made increasingly frank remarks about the pusillanimity of her dreams, especially when he saw her working on her canal model, and in the end he became so insufferable that she started working on the model only very early in the morning, before he was awake. But he started getting up very early in the morning too, in order to badger her, and she had to get up earlier still, and one morning she got up so early that when she looked outside, she saw the moon shining on Lars and Doggett, who were working in a narrow trench under the window, the bottom of which appeared to be lined with aluminum foil.

She went outside and asked them what they thought they were doing. Doggett closed his mouth and kept it closed, but Lars said: "We are making a canal."

"Canals are not made with aluminum foil," Katrin said.

"This is not the canal itself," Lars clarified. "The canal will be electrical. This metal extends under the plain, and once we have configured it properly, it will create the electrical canal, which will return us to the mountains."

"There are no mountains," Katrin said. "This is a plain all around."

Lars rummaged inside his shirt, which was strangely lumpy, and drew out the bone that had disappeared from Katrin's wall.

"Then where does this come from?"

"From my room," said Katrin, who had always really known that Lars had taken the bone.

He brandished it triumphantly. "This is the bone of a creature that lives in the mountains."

"It's my mother's bone."

That stopped him. "Is your mother from the mountains?"

"Not a bone from her body. A bone that she had in her possession. She's never been to any mountains. It's just a bone of something."

At that, Lars quite unexpectedly began to weep, and wept so hard that he had to sit down on the edge of the trench. Doggett tried to comfort him, but still wouldn't open his mouth in Katrin's presence, so the best he could do was pat Lars on the shoulder. Then Doggett began to weep too, and they both took their hats off and looked so tragic, two grown men weeping over a bone at the edge of a trench before dawn, that Katrin sat down beside them and said, "You'd better tell me all about it."

When his tears had stopped, Lars told her that modifying the subterranean aluminum foil to create an electrical canal had been merely a plan of desperation—that although he and Doggett knew that they had come from the mountains, their home seemed to become more remote every day, even unreal. Did she know what it was like to struggle to believe in her own home? "The bone gave us a little hope. We took it for the bone of a mountain creature—and it does look like one." He turned the bone over in his hands. "We thought you had been to the mountains yourself, perhaps on an educational trip."

"And brought back a bone?"

"In the mountains a bone is a common keepsake," he said, "as best we can remember. Doggett wears the bone of a ground squirrel as a keepsake of the plains."

Doggett took off the small bone that hung from his neck and threw it away from him.

"You and your father have been very good to us," Lars said. "It's just that we would like to go back to the mountains."

When Katrin's father got up, she recounted all of this to him, and he said it was rather remarkable, because he himself had had a dream vision of the mountains the night before, featuring clear air and friendly bears and, most importantly, a reduced gravitational field, these being very high mountains.

"With a nice light gravitational field like that, the relative leg strength of a sheep would hardly matter. Why, a man could safely increase his sheep by a factor of—" He clutched his head.

"The sheep would increase dramatically," Katrin said.

"Right."

"But there are no mountains," said Katrin. "The reason Lars and Doggett have trouble believing in their home is because they made it up."

"We would have to make the electrical canal big enough," her father said, "so that we could fit the sheep at their current level of increase. We don't want to lose ground."

He ran out and called to Lars in the bunkhouse, and later that morning he found a bulldozer somewhere, and soon everyone but Katrin was engaged in digging trenches and reconfiguring aluminum foil. Katrin told her father she didn't think this was how canals worked, or how electricity worked, for that matter, but he said this was how a real mission worked, a big dream—and anyway he was surprised to hear her arguing against a canal, which was an idea that she herself had introduced to the farm, and which thus represented as much of a mission as she herself could be said to have and the only thing keeping her from descending immediately into a kind of stygian half-life. Katrin said these trenches constituted neither a true canal nor a feature of any credible mission, and that anyway she had finished the canal model yesterday and filled it with tomato soup, not that he cared, and moreover the shortwave had long since stopped talking about canals and moved on to talking exclusively about itself, that is about shortwave technology, not that that mattered either, except that it was one more way in which he was wrong. But her father couldn't hear her because he had climbed to the top of the old windmill, where Lars was directing the work with signal flags.

"I won't go to the mountains," Katrin called after him. "I'll stay here! My mission is to stay here!"

That he heard, and climbed back down the windmill. "Your mission," he said. "You've found it?" And Katrin nodded. "This is the happiest day of my life." He embraced her.

As she embraced him back, Katrin knew this was a bigger lie than any lie she had told before, and therefore even more likely to turn on her and come half true in the worst possible way. She tried frantically to think of some harmless mission she could give herself to head it off.

"What is the mission?" her father said.

"It's complicated."

"I knew it would be. You have always been complicated. I will think of you in the coming years, when I am in the mountains."

"Oh," said Katrin, realizing she should have said it was her mission for both of them to stay here. But it was too late now—the lie had caught her this time.

The day came when all the trenches had been dug and filled again and the only sign of any of it was a low ridge of aluminum foil that made a circle in front of the house. Inside the circle were Katrin's father and Lars and Doggett and whichever of the other men had volunteered to go to the mountains, which was all of them, plus some tarp-covered bales of who knew what, and a lot of sheep not quite big enough to collapse under their own weight in normal gravity. Outside the circle was Katrin.

"How does it work?" she asked.

"It uses the principles of reality," her father said. "After all, yours was only a model."

Doggett stepped to the edge of the circle and held out his hand for her to shake. He still wouldn't open his mouth, so his face looked almost normal, but now that she looked closely at him for almost the first time she noticed that there was also something wrong with the arrangement of his eyes, which were placed so that he seemed to be staring at something behind her; she glanced over her shoulder in case there really was something there, but there wasn't, but while she was looking away from him, there was a noise like a thunder-clap, and when she looked back everyone was gone.

She was alone on the farm.

She could only conclude that, despite the shortwave's lessons, she had never really understood canals. She phoned her mother.

"How did you know there was aluminum foil under the house?"

"I put it there myself. It was part of an experiment."

"What kind of experiment? Is an experiment anything like a mission?"

"A long-term experiment. Everyone has exactly the same mission, Katrin, and that's to figure out anything at all."

"Mother—are you from the mountains?"

"Of course not. I'm from an island. Do you have enough food in the house?"

"Enough for what?"

"I'll send more."

Katrin turned on the shortwave and pored over some circuit diagrams, and in the afternoon an airplane flew over and dropped a crate full of food at the end of a parachute. She put the food away and felt calm sitting there listening to the shortwave as if everything were normal, but she knew that everything was not normal, and she wasn't one of those people who sit around pretending everything is normal when they know perfectly well that everything is not normal. She called her mother again, but there was just a beeping noise. The voice on the shortwave told her to design a shortwave transmitter, which she did, but then she also built the transmitter, which the voice hadn't asked her to do, and made a giant antenna out of the leftover aluminum foil. While she built it she thought about how her father had built a canal, which was another thing that the shortwave had talked about but not actually asked for, and wondered whether what she was doing was different from what her father had done, because after all they both sprang from lies. When she finished building she started broadcasting. At first she just asked for someone to come take her away, but nobody did, so instead she started talking about canals and antennas, sheep and world records, and then about young men with letter-box mouths, and about bones your mother leaves behind that aren't quite human. After that she talked about everything else she knew, which was nothing, but she was lonely enough that she figured out how to talk about it. Her mission never got any less complicated, and sometimes, if you tune your shortwave just right, and if you have the ear for it, you can still hear her—even from very far away.

what will become an ongoing portfolio, along with the freewrite we did together in class.

Reading—

Read Bernadette Esposito's "Speck of Light" (pp. 291–302)

Syllabus: Reading and Writing Obsession—
A *Conjunctions* Workshop

IN ADVANCE OF THE CLASS ON SEPTEMBER 24

Writing—

In the first session, we did a guided freewrite that explored the end-of-line litany form, based on Karen Lepri's "The Thief." During the course of the next two weeks, try another litany, using a new subject/vocabulary of obsession. You can continue to place your repeated terms at the end of lines, or at the beginnings, or in the middles, or you can move the placement about. Your litany may be poetry or prose (or a mixture of both!).

As will be the case throughout this workshop, you don't need to

Parts List Counted in Ogham

Karen Donovan

"the alphabetic system of fifth- and sixth-century Old Irish in which an alphabet of twenty letters is represented by notches for vowels and lines for consonants and which is known principally from inscriptions cut on the edges of rough standing tombstones"

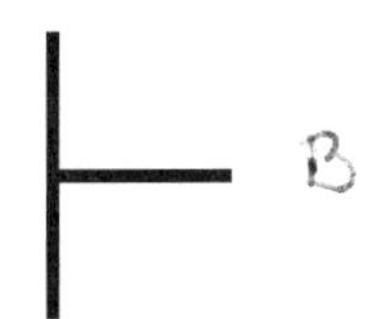

"a tufted marsh plant"

But I am already attached:
you, me, the nutsedge.

The way it unfolded from black loam
and July rain and spread sweetly once I cleared
rank jimson and panic grass.
Green blade, tell me, am I not to attach?
Oh, I am most pagan with respect to trees!
My confession: I have also refused to pull up
the velvet leaf and a twining pea.

Into haunted solitude: the weedpile
turning to straw, the yellow moon.

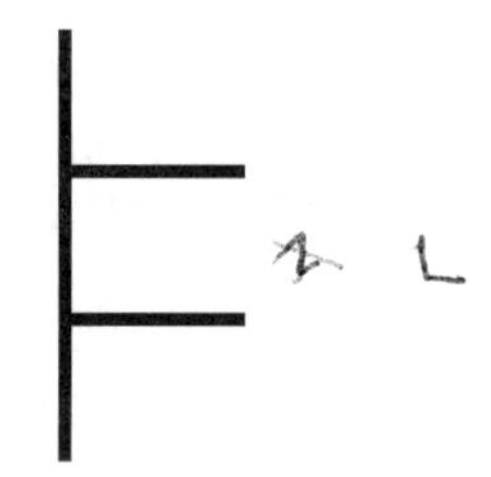

"an envelope of rays emanating from a point and reflected or refracted by a curved surface"

What I most love: the bright caustic,
rippled light on the ceiling as sun
breaking the treeline bounces off water,
incidental spectra painted on a wall,
or, there, that nimbus thrown from the lip
of your tumbler.

You do not know how to point to or define the meaning,
you lack any formula or image for it,
and yet it is more certain for you than the sensations of your senses

The nearly concealed dimensions of the everywhere.

"an arboreal chiefly nocturnal mammal"

And let us decide right now about the lemur.
Do we not love the lemur with our whole hearts and our whole minds?
Do we not also wish to return home soon to Madagascar,
where we will all speak the balanced, balletic language of the body?
What is the meaning of a bubble from the bottom of the sea?
the great mythologist of the psyche asks.

You must convince the lemur to give you the ring
from his storied tail.

Karen Donovan

"an insect that feeds on other insects and clasps its prey in forelimbs held up as if in prayer"

Regarding the mantis, let us at least be truthful
about the thrill of witnessing
the voracious grasshopper reverently dispatched
by a creature so suited to the task.
We are grateful
                    at a distance.
We are regretful
                    at a distance.
About the temptation to imagine ourselves at a distance.

It is impossible to prefigure the salvation of the world
in the same language
by which the world has been dismembered and defaced
As if the possibility of the act
of thanksgiving were sufficient to conclude
anything at all.

Karen Donovan

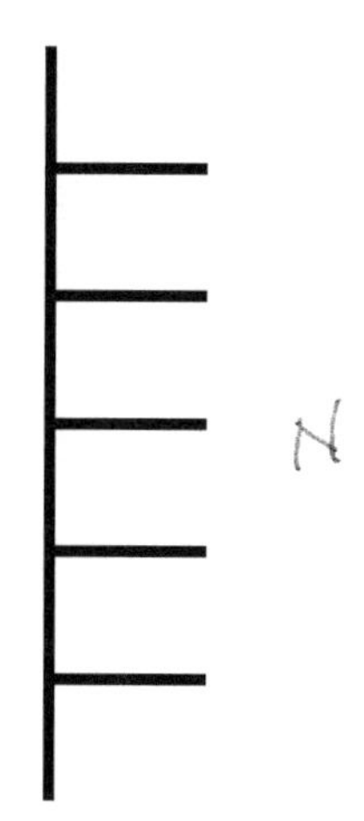

"an opaque cryptocrystalline quartz"

Mud, under pressure, crushes to sunset
multilayer cake, moss black, sienna, ocher, dark red,
splinters in slo-mo like brown bones
as the earth rolls its insides up.

This is how the jasper comes to me,
gravel in a plain Iowa riverbed,
ghost boats drifting downstream,
fishlines out, motor cut,

how you come to me
in a gesture common as sand,
the commonest gesture of the open hand,
warm wind in leaves, deep sigh
of someone sleeping.
Why may they not be the actual
turning-places and growing-places which they seem to be,
of the world—why not the workshop of being

As this fractured pebble, me,
final indivisible thing here, yours.

Karen Donovan

"any of various small fish that are less than a designated size and are not game fish"

Though they are
the calculus: minnow
then minnow then
minnow then minnow.
We are not persuaders
We are the children of the Unknown,

discrete linearity innumerably agreeing into

curves that stream through the eelgrass
on brackish late summer tides
and demonstrate closer to home
how the great mathematicians
solved the planetary orbits
by computing in fish flicks.

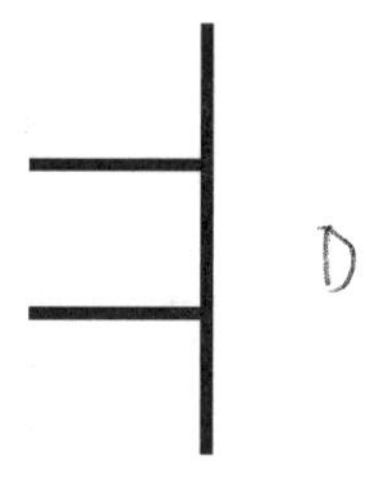

"fuzz especially consisting of fine ravelings"

And fast by hanging in a golden chain
This pendant world

Contrast: pocket lint.
Further reading: ontological shock vs. the circus catch.

The lack of consolation.
Whether postmodern materialism constitutes a second fall.

Exhibit notes: cyclades figures, votive statues, eye idols.
Dilmun the original paradise.

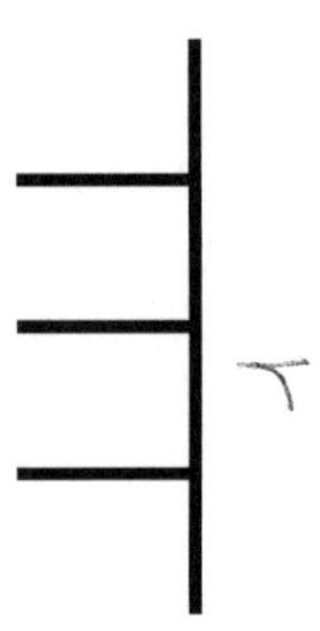

"radiation situated beyond the visible spectrum at its violet end"

Past the reef edge where color sifts out from all containers,
the abyssal, other side of depth, what the very ancients called
abzu, primeval waters,
sojourners to that ultraviolet would obtain
their tickets with proviso: You will not come back.
Thus I am now returned in Spirit as a Heavenly Spy
because I could not explain why
I knew there was someplace else to go,
someplace better,

because no stop sign is fail-safe.

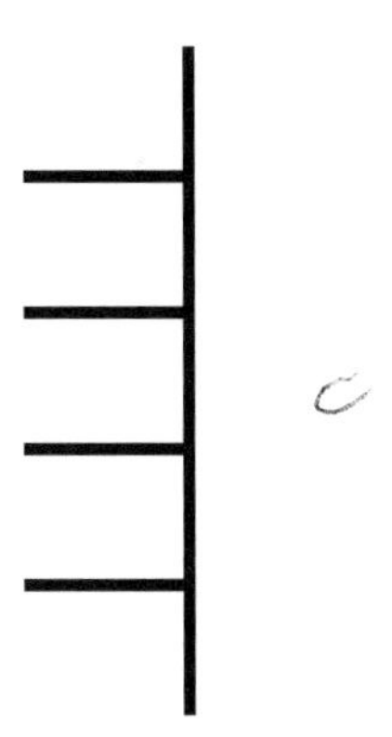

"a piece of mail that is undeliverable because [it is] illegibly or incorrectly addressed"

Virginia.
Heard today this definition of "nixie" will be deleted from all new editions of Merriam-Webster's Collegiate; thought you'd want to know. Went straightaway to my bookshelf to check, language being, as so much else in our overly policed age, basically use it or lose it. There it sits on page 800, a bit below "nitwit," still wheezing like a little appendix, unaware of the looming editorial scalpel that will excise it from the body textual. For now, they are leaving in the first definition, which you will appreciate. *It would seem to be something very erratic, very undependable—now to be found in a dusty road, now in a scrap of newspaper in the street, now in a daffodil in the sun.* This leafboat my messenger.
Regards.

Karen Donovan

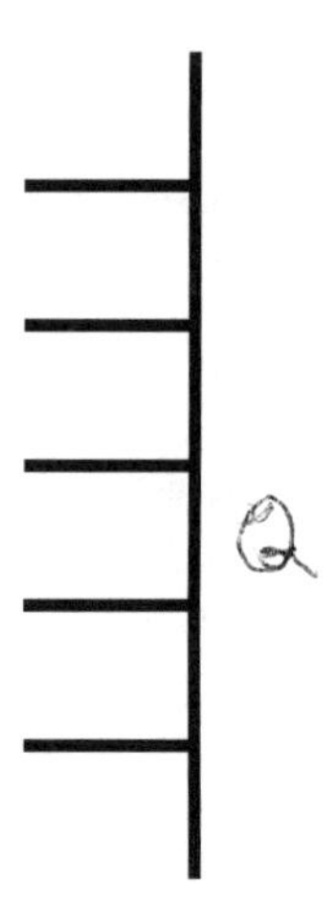

"a mythical animal having the power to endure fire without harm"

O salamander, my shepherd,
is it true? *The disciple simply burns his boats and goes ahead*
The drunken alchemist claimed you
became the flame and so were not consumed
but revealed most perfectly to being
of the same substance fundamental of the cosmos,
dark edge of dark ponds, that substance
we last breathed through lost gills, far from home.

Old soul, I followed you
out of one cosmos and into another, discovering
how the body can be unmade
and remade also by maple light
and green rain falling steadily onto the earth.

Karen Donovan

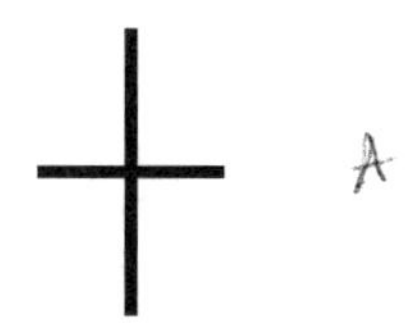

"a procedure for solving a mathematical problem in a finite number of steps that frequently involves repetition of an operation"

cirrus stratus cirrostratus
jack pine
tamarack
spruce
altostratus cumulonimbus
jack pine
tamarack
spruce
split pea split second
archangelic algorithm
Invisible wings are given to us too
tawee tawee tawee-tee-to
chick-a-dee-dee-dee
toooo tititi twee tititi tititi tititi
toooo tititi twee tititi tititi tititi
wicka wicka wicka wicka
chick-a-dee-dee-dee
chick-a-dee-dee-dee
spirogyra equinox
licorice dickcissel
jack pine
tamarack
spruce

Karen Donovan

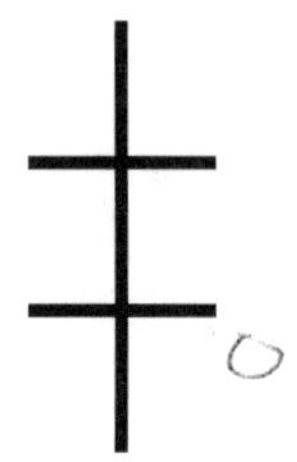

"any of family Ixodidae whose young cling to bushes whence they readily drop on and attach themselves to passing animals where they may produce troublesome sores or serve as vectors for disease-producing microorganisms"

Want the wood but not the wood tick?
Try ChemLawn.
Toxic to high-quality targets: weeds grassy and broadleaf,
sucker bugs that wreck the roses,
fish, bees, birds, the neighbor's pets, anyone's kids,
including your own. Got grubs?
Wild violet or nimblewill?
They're out there in the dark. Listen:
All those things men tell of down in hell,
far under the earth, are right here in our lives

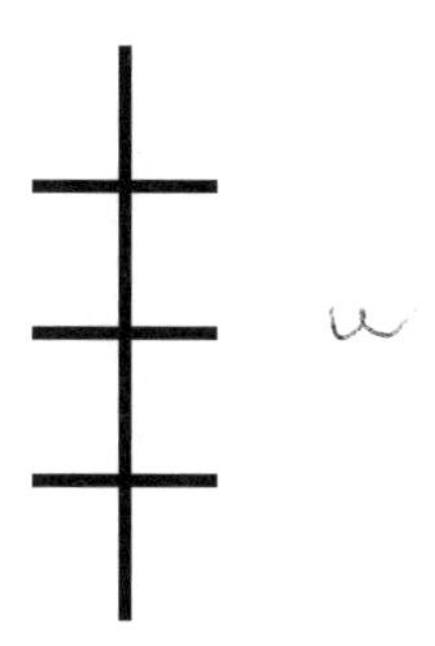

"the star of the northern hemisphere toward which the axis of the earth points"

The sense of a construction more enduring than the self.
No less of a construction but the chiefest
of made things. The sense of a floor.

A conviction the landscape carries,
for instance, masterfully turning us
under Polaris no matter which door you step from.

The ethic emerging in the struggle
has as its main theme not prudence but existential courage

A construction, if it were possible, a sense
of the floor, an allegiance
to it, and if it were possible then, liberty.

Karen Donovan

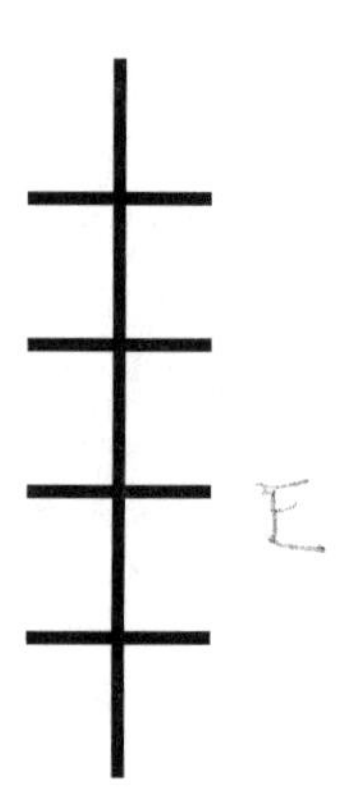

"a dense variously colored and usually lustrous concretion"

First the error,
then the bludgeoning,
then the pearl.
First the imagining,
then the pavement,
then the language.

New tortures have been invented
for the madmen who have brought good news

The above, the below,
the dividing line.

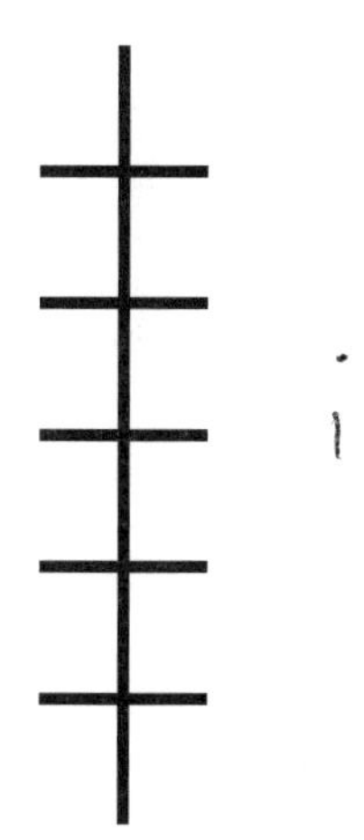

"a hill or ridge of sand piled up by the wind"

April. Cold dune.
Soon the clouds gathered and opened
to show what was gathered beyond.
A dog barked from a lawn
down the beach. A gull mewled.
I do believe that you can deepen
your own orthodoxy
if you are not afraid of strange visions
When I made a request,
it was not: Lead my army.

Reversing the way back
through the park, I leaned to study
catkins strewn over the path,
then the door to the porta-john slammed
and sparrows chorused rose briers, my license
to love the world finally
as much as I could or be damned.

Karen Donovan

"moisture condensed upon the surfaces of cool bodies especially
at night"

They also say of dew: It falls.
As though from the sky, iridescent on the grass
at dawn in halos around the bent places
where we slept together,
out under stars that pierced us with old light,

it fell like dew
on the rocks and the blossoms,
on us, till we woke soaking wet,
no longer dreaming, and shivering
embraced as if for the first time.

And then we who are not all wise think
that everything which we have undertaken
was all nothing

Looking back at myself in your eyes
I could see it had fallen on us
like knowledge, that food we would need
to learn how to eat on the way, the long walk
it would be.

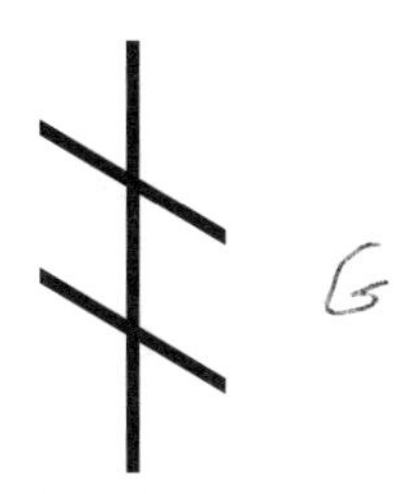

"an inscription or drawing made on some public surface"

Graffiti as tattoo, as surgical scar.
The symbol squats on a fact.

Are you living or just buying?

A labyrinth has no dead ends.
        [Now you tell me.]

You might consider your pain as a focusing tool.
        [I might consider YOUR pain as a focusing tool.]

A rhetoric as a collection, a thicket of skipperlings.
He left an ichthys in the urinal.

Karen Donovan

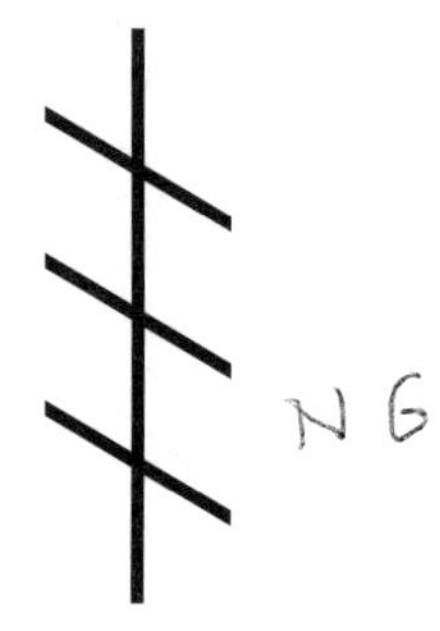

"a venomous or reputedly venomous snake"

So if the future is a viper
coiled at the bottom of an onyx jar
and in we must reach, why imagine

another future? *Every angel is terrifying*
Or if the bronzed ribbon tangled

in lavender this morning flicks its forked
tongue, look at us, already flooded
with namelessness.

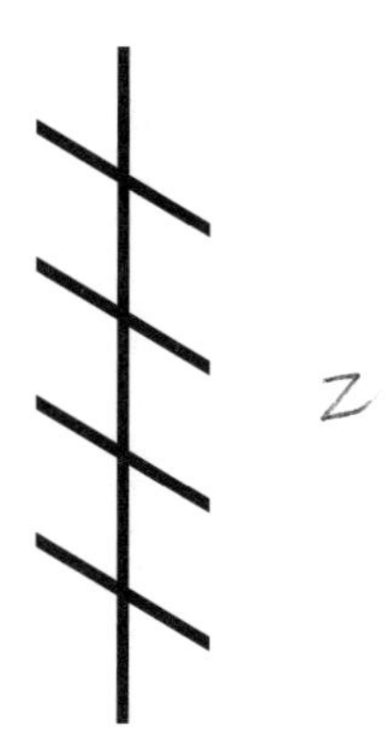

"a low heavy continuous reverberating often muffled sound"

in this stillness   the light blinds
what we imagine is coming
what the silence means   what the stillness
of what is coming
this   rumble
tumbling the darkness of it
listen for it listen

stillness the dark   the blind will
but what silence means   what the
surroundings will say in this stillness
of what awaiting
O   listen
is just the unspeakable
silence of the silence

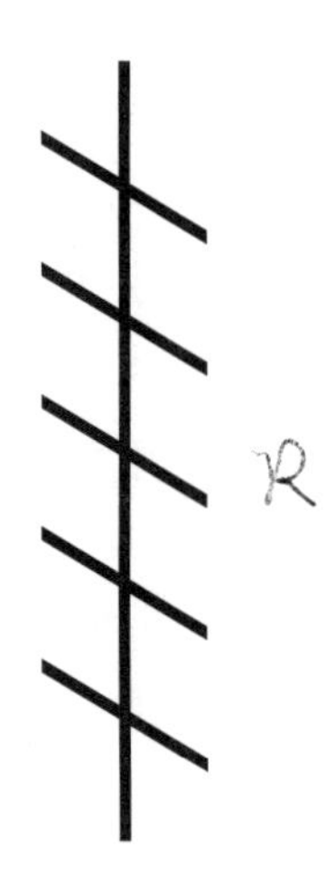

"a very small pool"
"a bed or receptacle prepared by a bird"

"any of a family of colonial hymenopterous insects with a complex social organization and various castes performing special duties"

"an open bowl-shaped drinking vessel"
"an injury to the body that involves laceration or breaking of a membrane"

"an unstressed midcentral vowel"
"the seedy edible fruit of various brambles"

puddle | nest | ant | cup | wound | schwa | blackberry . . .

There was only one thing to be done: Call out,
start the alarm, set the heather on fire

NOTE. Italicized quotes are borrowed from: Paul Tillich, Martin Buber, Joseph Campbell, Wendell Berry, William James, Thomas Merton, John Milton, Jane Lead, Virginia Woolf, Dietrich Bonhoeffer, Denise Levertov, Lucretius, Mary Daly, G. K. Chesterton, Flannery O'Connor, Julian of Norwich, Anonymous, Rainer Maria Rilke, Søren Kierkegaard, Margaret Sanger.

Some Remarks on Teeth
Adam Weinstein

I.

Meddle not with a hollow tooth.
—Sancho Panza

TEETH HOLD THE SUBSTANCE of our unknown selves. When we are born the teeth are inchoate. As we grow so do the teeth fill with infant dreams of indulged and withheld desire, of obsession and fantasy. The pulpy root crowds and tangles with unsound thinking; like a pearl it is slowly encased in layers of protective enamel.

These stratified layers are entirely personal. Their number reveals our age. Their articulation describes us: our past, our present, and, according to some, our future. Consider the ancient art of divination through the study of the teeth. By mapping the tooth's features, the secret self is discovered.

The tooth may first be described by its shape, which yields our basic characteristics and disposition: The Elementary (or Large-Toothed), The Necessary (or Spatulate), The Artistic (or Conical), The Useful (or Square), The Philosophical (or Knotty), The Psychic (or Pointed), and The Mixed.

If very narrow in the centre it may betray deceit and avarice—close-fistedness, while extremely wide it betokens foolish expenditure; but a change to width *beneath Mercury shows a tendency to economy in old age.*
—Henry Frith

Then, of course, there are the mounds and lines of the tooth. Of the mounds, one will notice that a molar, in particular, is usually divided into four quadrants. These are the mounds of Mercury, Apollo, Saturn, and Jupiter. No two mounds are the same shape or height.

> *A spot upon the mount always indicates an evil fatality, the cause of which must be sought for upon the lines of head or of fate.*
>
> —Ed Heron-Allen

The lines that run between the mounds and then those that whorl about the face of the tooth may be of varying degrees of intensity, length, steadiness, etc. These are usually the more popularly known and studied characteristics. Novice fortune-tellers often amuse guests at dinner parties by reading the life and marriage lines found there. When the mood strikes, the dental mirror, stashed in some miscellaneous boudoir drawer, is ferreted out; the mark arranges himself prone on an Oriental rug, mouth open, supplicant, but also both secretly wary and excited to have his future produced from his molar display. The amateur *odontomancer* begins his showy reading.

The major lines are: Heart, Head, Life, Saturn, and the Hepatic or Liver Line. There are also minor lines, such as The Girdle of Venus (*Cingulum Veneris*), and The Lines of the Sun.

> *This line, fortunately not universal, may be taken as a whole, to be a* bad *sign, indicating a tendency to debauchery, which it is extremely difficult to conquer.*
>
> —Ed Heron-Allen

The reading of the inner, stratified layers can only be done if a tooth is lost, or after death. Here the tooth is split open and the very fine layers are read according to thickness, color, material, etc. In some traditional death rituals, the fragments are placed in a teacup with a mixture of potent herbs and scalded with water. The draft is sipped by a medicant until only the dregs are left, and are read according to a series of diagrammatic charts; then a kind of obituary is spoken at a telling-event celebrating the life, death, and beyond of the recently deceased. It is especially remarkable if the fragments of teeth remain afloat.

When a deciduous tooth is lost—so called because they are shed in adolescence—the child may place her tooth beneath her pillow as a symbolic* exhalation of adolescent fantasy; the tooth is procured from

*It is worth emphasizing the symbolic play of the "lost" tooth. If one looks closely at the mire of evacuated gum, one will just be able to make out the naked white tip of the emerging replacement, permanently anchored in the jawbone.

under her pillow in the dead of night, and a token is left behind to symbolize a future of good fortune.

> *The first thing they do is to bring an obol and put it in his mouth, to serve as payment to the boatman for passage.*
>
> —Lucian

While deciduous teeth may give some insight into the early life, they are not good predictors, and the information revealed must be taken with extreme lightness.

> *The last piece of paternal dentistry that was ever performed on my teeth came about in a purely accidental way on my part, and is perfectly green in my memory, to this good day. It was at the breakfast table, and it had been about three weeks since my folks had had the pleasure of pulling one of my teeth; they were becoming impatient over the long wait, and when they discovered I had another loose tooth there was great joy in the family.*
>
> —*Joe Sap's Tales*

There are so many unfortunate occasions when the predictions are read as absolute, and the parents take an unwavering hand with their child's future.

It also goes without saying that there are cases of teeth being stolen in the night: To know or even seize another's fortune is a powerful measure.

> *His venom tooth will rankle to the death:*
> *Have not to do with him, beware of him.*
>
> —Queen Margaret

There have been cases where the teeth of the famous or fortunate dead (and sometimes living) are pilfered, and screwed into the mouth of an overambitious conniver, who then assumes the corpse's fortune. In the late days of the Qing dynasty in China, the Empress Consort Cixi became empress dowager—a position of great authority—when her husband, the Emperor Xianfeng, fell ill and died. Xianfeng had appointed his son, Zaichun, barely six years old, to take his place; he also appointed a group of eight regents to oversee the young emperor's future. Yet the empress dowager, in a coup, overthrew the Sunchun and consolidated power around herself. When Zaichun took ill and soon after died at the age of nineteen, Cixi further concentrated her power by appointing her two-year-old nephew, Guangxu, the new emperor.

As the young emperors fell ill, their futures purloined, they exhibited signs of wasting, dementia, and discoloration; truly, their very life forces were being drained. And so we read the apocryphal footnotes of a truer history: that of the empress dowager's theft, the stolen star-mapped destinies, the co-opting of the young emperors' teeth as her own.

The empress dowager's corrupted anthropophagism, capturing and baring another's teeth, suggests the history of Lycaon, an Arcadian king who was said to have boiled and eaten the flesh of his servants. As punishment, Lycaon was transformed into a wolf, made to forever bite the human form, from which he had been excluded. The empress dowager soon realized the consequences of her Lycaonian dabbling. She may have secured her position as mighty empress; yet within the tooth is the draft of the inner self, a dark phantasm. She bit of her own flesh, and so she was herself transformed: the haunt of subconscious plague.

She is said to have spent hours staring out at the frozen, manicured landscape surrounding her palace. She shunned company, expecting complete silence. One wonders at the babel she must have internalized, the tower that shook inside her mouth and fractioned apart and spoke with so many voices that she herself had nothing left except the ambition that seethed from her heart, poisoned her mind, and finally had no direction except its own annihilation. She died a mere day after Emperor Guangxu, who had been cannibalized throughout his lifetime, acting only as a prop, dying with a bloated, yellow tongue.

But the sons of the kingdom will be cast out into outer darkness, where there will be weeping and gnashing of teeth.

—Matthew 8:12

Teeth—small treasures that they are—remain an endless pour of mystery.

II.

But sometimes the teeth are damaged. This may be due to an unforeseen blow, an unexpected fall, or a long and protracted illness. These are natural abrasions, usually not threatening, and some disruptions are even said to add character. Many of these discontinuities may be repaired with little or no lasting effect.

The teeth are also acted upon by the bacterium *Streptococcus mutans*, or Tooth Worm, which was first identified by J. K. Clarke using complex systems of microscopes. Clarke suggested that tooth deterioration—or *dental caries*—results from the accumulation of these bacteria around the tooth and gums. The bacteria feed off the remains of starches and sugars, and when left unchecked, produce high levels of lactic acid. The acid eventually dissolves away the enamel, leaving small holes and exposing the psychic root.

> *and his coffers sound*
> *with hollow poverty and emptiness*
> —Lord Hastings

It is from these holes that the cache of desire leeches and resurfaces, and, when left unchecked, becomes an effective poison. Talking, chewing, eating—these activities only exacerbate the problem as the memories are drawn and reabsorbed. One will notice that, in the instance of a particularly obnoxious toothache, the thrum of the tooth overwhelms our focus. We can see nothing, feel nothing, hear nothing besides the throbbing pain. Over time, memories that should have remained calcified confuse the mind. Dementia results. Voices are heard. And the mind may be corroded until, in more extreme cases, the patient becomes psychotic.

> *We have come to regard the infection of the teeth as the most constant focus found in our patients. Without exception the functional psychotic patients all have infected teeth.*
> —Henry A. Cotton, MD

Affected patients begin to speak incoherently; are subject to sudden fits and bursts of obscenity-laden rage; lose the command of extremities, especially the hands and fingers; are restless, often wandering hallways and corridors, dictating minutiae; are in constant vocal tremors; and fall into terrible, unspeakable depressions, or moments of heightened acceleration (logorrhca).

> *He began talking in a way that he could not control. Later he spoke to me in a voice so like my mother's that her St. Bernard dog, which hitherto had not noticed him, got up and went over to him and smelt his face in seeming recognition.*
>
> —Albert Le Baron, communicated by Professor William James

One of the clearest early symptoms of *dental caries* is the contamination of sleep with tooth imagery and sensation. The most common dream is that of the loose tooth. Suddenly, a tooth is bothersome and irks us and we worry that it will fall out. We may place our hands to our mouths in an attempt to hold the tooth in place, though this will certainly do no good. In fact, the mere touch evokes a further weakening. The more we grasp, the more likely it seems that the tooth will come out.

In another familiar dream, the lower incisors become hooked over the uppers in an underbite fashion, which cannot be undone—doing so would, seemingly, pull the front teeth from their sockets. We can feel the pressure of the lower teeth against the upper, feel the gums caving, feel the teeth wiggling there, and yet we are impotent of action.

Within the dream state, however, we are almost never aware of the tooth as a manifestation of its real-life correlative. As such, we have no language to describe it, and are passive to its claims. This is why dreams of death are almost always plagued by senseless shouting.

It is seldom that the tooth is actually pulled, in which case the dreamer might feel a sense of relief. The scourge would be removed, and the soft hollow left behind would be a pleasant sensation. One would run one's tongue over the empty socket, feel the latent desire trickle out and over one's lips to be spat upon the ground, and the soul would be cleansed. Psychological malfeasance would be purged and the dreamer would be able to speak clearly of what he both knows and understands. What bliss!

Sigmund Freud argues that repressed (especially sexual) memories are impediments to a healthy psyche. His "talking cure," a forerunner of psychoanalysis, asks the patient to discover rooted imagery and vocalize it—whereby the patient is no longer held captive by unconscious memory. Tooth psychoses are, after all, the nebulous memories of childhood—the incomprehensible, and therefore unvocalized, trauma of early life.

A key to Freud's talking cure is the patient's dream life: a tapestry of symbols signifying defeated or overindulged infant desires.

> *He was being treated by two University professors of his acquaintance instead of by me. One of them was doing something to his penis. He was afraid of an operation. The other was pushing against his mouth with an iron rod, so that he lost one or two of his teeth. He was tied up with four silk cloths.*
>
> —Sigmund Freud

Women tend to dream of teeth less, though it is not an impossible occurrence. Instead, they dream of the mouth or lips, or some such analogue.

> *She was putting a candle into a candlestick; but the candle broke so that it wouldn't stand up properly. The girls at her school said she was clumsy; but the mistress said it was not her fault.*
>
> —An Innocent Lady Dreamer

During lengthy talking cures between patient and analyst, the patient comes to understand the repressed memories of which the tooth is made and gives those memories shape—concrete language. Here the tongue plays an important role: It shapes the vocalized breath in the formation of words, and it is an itinerant, aimlessly roving the mouth, loosing the other preformed words hidden in the mouth's recesses, its caves and fissures. The tongue tongues; it turns the teeth over and digs into their roots, finding the goblin hoard of the psyche. The tongue flings the words forward, exposing them to the pure light of reason.

Throughout the process, the patient gains insight into his memories and past experiences, bringing about resolution and achieving catharsis—from the Greek κάθαρσις: the cleansing and purging of the tooth.

Yet what of the patients for whom the dreams continue, who begin to experience excursions wherein a tooth is involved, on a more routine, or even nightly, basis, who are well on their way to irreparable psychic damage? Might they need to seek more aggressive means of correction? In the most extreme cases a patient first becomes psychotic, experiencing the above-mentioned symptoms until he eventually suffers a lapse of consciousness altogether. There is no more wakefulness, no more conscious life: The patient becomes catatonic, and it is unlikely that he or she will ever wake again. Catatonia owes its etymology to the Greek words κατά (down) and τονία (tone). Literally, the patient is silenced.

In response to observations of the routine condition of psychotic patients' teeth, Dr. Henry A. Cotton, MD, developed the practice of tooth leukotomy as a drastic, and, in comparison with psychoanalysis or other less aggressive actions, one might argue, more permanently effective treatment. By isolating and removing the rotten teeth, the infection is thwarted, and the patient, if not already too ravaged with psychosis, recovers.

> *So in order to rid a patient of focal infection a very thorough job must be done and no suspicious teeth allowed to remain.*
>
> —Henry A. Cotton, MD

Early experiments focused on injecting formalin or alcohol as a sclerosing agent into the tooth to destroy infected tissue. Yet this method was imprecise and unpredictable. Sometimes the acid would destroy healthy parts of the tooth as well.

Alternatively, ice-pick leukotomies focus on complete removal.

> *The only instrument that is ideally suited resembled the ordinary ice pick. . . . A light tap with a hammer is usually all that is needed.*
>
> —Walter Freeman, MD

With his delicate dental hammer, the doctor gives the tooth a small tap where the tooth and the gums overlap, and the tooth pops from the socket in its entirety without affecting the teeth on either side.

In a matter of minutes the dentist may remove all the teeth of the lower jaw. The patient requires only a topical anesthetic, and can go home the same day.

> Doctor: *Do you have any of your old fears?*
> Patient: *No.*
> D: *What were you afraid of?*
> P: *I don't know. I seem to forget.*
> D: *Do you remember being upset when you came here?*
> P: *Yes, I was quite upset, wasn't I?*
> D: *What was it all about?*
> P: *I don't know. I seem to have forgotten. It doesn't seem important now.*
>
> —Discussion between Walter Freeman, MD, and Mrs A.H.

Of course, shoving a household ice pick into anyone's jaw and removing teeth is barbaric. This is the kind of back-alley dentistry that casts a pall over legitimate dental leukotomy. The expected disasters that follow such operations—the loss of the ability to speak altogether; the pronounced depression; the black, sullen eyes; the aimlessness and purposelessness; the destruction of the short-term memory—these are not part of the world in which the careful practitioner operates.

Further, if the operation is not executed cleanly, fragments of the infected tooth may remain.

> *Failures to get results from removing infected teeth are frequently due to the fact that the diseased, infected, necrotic bone is left and absorption continues even after the teeth are extracted.*
>
> —Henry A. Cotton, MD

In a mere four years of leukotomous experiments, the exemplary Dr. Cotton worked with close to fourteen hundred patients, carefully honing and crafting his technique. The reports were favorable.

> *As a further indication of the results of treatment, 380 cases were admitted in 1918 and to-day only 50 remain in the hospital, nine of these being criminals.*
>
> —Henry A. Cotton, MD

Recently, however, ice-pick leukotomies have given way to the Moniz leukotome—modeled after an apple corer—which is then rotated to make cores within the tooth: The pernicious tissue is excised, and the empty, neutralized tooth is allowed to remain (thus eliminating the need for costly dentures).

Of course, like many successful clinical procedures, there is also the potential for abuse. There have been a handful of patients who have undergone elective leukotomies, and have had all of their teeth removed and replaced with denture plates. They are tempted with thoughts of permanent states of elation—and though this may be the case, it is clearly not what Drs. Cotton or Freeman intended. Alarmists write that soon the world will be without teeth, all for the sake of doing away with doubt and fear. *Do we not need some measure of doubt?* one might wonder. *Is this not what makes us human?* Yet what would such a place be like? A world without anxiety. Where smiles are, so to speak, fixed. Would it be utopia?

Other critics deemphasize or even resist the relationship between teeth and memory as a binary, going so far as to argue that the teeth are not repositories meant to safeguard memories, fixations, etc. The wearing down, chipping, and gapping of teeth is a function of growth, and slippages in conversation are an essential feature of heterogeneous discourse.

> *I'm now making myself as scummy as I can. Why? I want to be a poet, and I'm working at turning myself into a* Seer.
>
> —Arthur Rimbaud to Georges Izambard

It is only in the Police State, these critics argue, that the displeasures and darknesses of the soul are to be corrected, that the wisdom teeth are excised, ensuring homogeneity.

And yet the work of Drs. Cotton and Freeman has given rise to a great many other interesting practices.

There are, of course, other physical structures of the body related to mental states, disease, and psychosis. Before the results of tooth leukotomy took shape, Dr. Cotton had already begun analyzing both the uterus and cervix of psychotic women, and had large success in *enucleation*—the removal of fibroids without removing the uterus. In males, he found that in infections of the vesicles, excision is the only solution. And most recently, he focused attention on the intestinal tract.

It is evident that the removal of the colon will not produce results in such cases and such patients have recovered only after the administration of serum.
—Henry A. Cotton, MD

Results have been mixed.

III.

Our closest relative, the chimpanzee, displays physical and emotional characteristics remarkably similar to those of humans. Yet there are also marked differences: our relative hairlessness; the Mongolian eye fold; a higher relative brain weight; shortened toes, which result in the inability to grasp and handle objects with the foot; a thinness of bones; a longer period of infancy; variations in tooth structures; etc. As such, one notes the closer resemblance between adult humans and juvenile ape species.

This discovery—the human/juvenile ape link—supports a theory of *neoteny* (becoming child-shaped). Neoteny posits that humans are descended from juvenile ape species who were, because of some evolutionary mishap, sexually mature. And *their* progeny displayed similarly underdeveloped characteristics. Neoteny is also displayed in other species, such as the axolotl, a species of salamander that, unlike its amphibious relatives, reaches sexual maturity at the juvenile stage; and it does not metamorphose: It remains aquatic, retaining its gills.

Because humans display neotenic characteristics, one wonders if humans will further evolve toward a more childlike physicality. Note that the typical depictions of extraterrestrial life forms—always evolved (cognitively, socially, metaphysically, etc.) beyond humans—resemble infants more than adult humans.

An acceptable theory of neoteny then would posit human evolution beyond teeth. We would, eventually, remain toothless throughout our lives, the fleshy, unerupted gums the sign of a purified ambivalence. Though we cannot possibly imagine the materialistic consequences of such progress—i.e., what or how humans might eat—we can, to some degree, speculate on such metaphysical conditions as language ability and psychology.

*

Adam Weinstein

In most historical instances, a lack of teeth is equated with wisdom. Consider the tale of Perseus, who is instructed to find the sisters of Graiai.

> *Over their worn and wrinkled faces stream tangled masses of long gray hair; their voice comes hollow from their toothless gums, and a single eye is passed from one to the other when they wish to look forth from their dismal dwelling. Seek them out for these alone can tell thee what more remaineth yet for thee to do.*
>
> —Hermes to Perseus

Hawthorne too speaks of the gummy old woman.

> *I do not deserve a listener half so well as that old toothless woman, whose narratives possess an excellence attributable neither to herself, nor to any single individual.*
>
> —Nathaniel Hawthorne, "An Old Woman's Tale"

Consider that a typical feature of defensive posturing is the baring of teeth and we understand that it is, of course, teeth that ultimately separate us: They confound speech with subjective experience and create an impermeable division between what we say and what we mean. As long as we have teeth, the sign will always be ripped from the signified.

Though corrective dentistry (orthodontics, and especially tooth whitening, etc.) seemingly rights these differences, whereby we become a more coherent species, the corrections are merely cosmetic: In their roots, people guard the jewel of dark self. The whitened smile merely emphasizes aberrance.

> *This elusive quality it is, which causes the thought of whiteness, when divorced from more kindly associations, and coupled with any object terrible in itself, to heighten that terror to the furthest bounds. Witness the white bear of the poles, and the white shark of the tropics; what but their smooth, flaky whiteness makes them the transcendent horrors they are?*
>
> —Herman Melville, *Moby-Dick*

On the other hand, we also recall the deviant smile of Mr. Hyde, himself the pure *id*, with a mouth full of the yellowest and foulest teeth, his face a burst of profanity, the perfect signs of his unfettered selfhood. There is no attraction there either.

Freed of the teeth—not simply leukotized or broken or eroded, but with the pinkest, most perfect, unerupted gums—one would speak with the voice of all human beings. Our unbitten words—infantile, yet informed by a fully developed consciousness—would recoup their universality.

> *And the Lord said, Behold, the people is one, and they have all one language; and this they begin to do; and now nothing will be restrained from them, which they have imagined to do.*
>
> —Genesis 11:6

If history is our example—as it clearly is—it would be none other than a return to the Edenic state, so tragically taken from us when the incisors of our forebears broke the skin of that serpentine fruit.

What might a world without the limitations of incised language, as we know it, sound like?

Story, Story!

Chinelo Okparanta

IT IS A STORY THAT NNEOMA has told before, three times before, in the church on Rumuola Road.

The church is not the same one she attended as a child—not that small one out in the village, with hardly more than a dozen benches in it; not that old one where she used to sit, long ago, worshipping alongside her mama and her papa.

Her mama and papa had hoped that she'd one day get married in that small church, but it was now evident that Nneoma's was a life that refused to converge with hopes. Nneoma's only consolation was that at least she'd tried. This failure of her life to merge with their hopes, with even her own hopes, was certainly not owing to any fault of hers. She reasoned it this way, as if that settled it. But she would continue to try.

In any case, the last time she told the story was a long time ago now, perhaps two and a half, nearly three years ago. It was to a visiting woman she told it. The woman was fine, that is, very pretty, and her cheekbones were as high as Nneoma's own. The woman's eyes were sharp, penetrating; she might have suspected all along. Or perhaps she had not at all suspected. Perhaps it was that she was just that kind of woman—sharp—but merely on the superficial level: sharp eyes, sharp jaw, a very sharp fashion sense.

Indeed the woman was fashionable. She came wearing gold earrings. Her bangles dangled up and down her wrist, and her lipstick glowed red. She had painted a mole on her face, just above her lips. For the mole, the woman used the same black pencil that she used to line her lips. At least Nneoma suspected she did. Only the woman painted the mole far darker than the lining on her lips. It was the fashion, Nneoma knew. A mole, but some called it a beauty mark.

From the woman came the scent of something fresh, something not quite like perfume, or perhaps an adulterated sort of perfume, because, of course, she could not help but sweat. It was warm that day, and even warmer inside the church.

Before that woman, Nneoma told the story to two others. These two were visitors to the church also. They were not fine women, but ugly ones whose jaws were not as square as the jaw of the fine woman. These ones wore no earrings, no lipstick, no beauty marks. It was as if they had given up altogether, as if theirs was a conscious decision, this refusal even to feign beauty. Perhaps it was a mockery of beauty. Their blouses were plain—not made of lace, and both were a little foul smelling, something like the scent of fish.

These two women were separate instances, of course, which is to say that Nneoma did not tell both of them the story even nearly at once. There had been at least a two-year gap between the telling of the story to each one.

Nevertheless, Nneoma told the story. Three times she'd told it. And she intended to continue telling it, because she was after all the one who found Ezioma on the bed. Ezioma, just lying there in her yellow nightgown, with the blanket pulled up to her chest. Ezioma, eyes closed, sleeping as peacefully as ever. And the baby in her womb was by then sleeping as peacefully as she was.

Now, Nneoma enters the church. Being a city church, it is rather large. Sometimes she's thought how it appears a little like a cake—a wedding cake, because it is circular, and has two layers (two floors). And just like a cake, its top layer is a smaller circle than its bottom.

But it is no cake. The walls throughout the church are made of cement, not batter. The stairs connecting the layers, too, are of cement, and they spread out evenly all around the church, three or four cases of them.

Because the church is large, there are many benches in rows—neat, circular rows—and fans fill some of the spaces between the rows. Even with the fans, it is warm in the church. Perhaps the heat of all that fervent worship.

It was on those benches, and in that heat, that Nneoma told the story, the three times she told it. She told it in bits, in the breaks before and after and during the worship. She made sure to tell it only to visiting women, because the sudden absence of a regular member would surely be noted by the pastor, and by the congregation as a whole. And this would arouse more attention than Nneoma cared to have.

The sun has found the openings along the sides of the church. It has laid itself in long, tapering streaks, leading from the openings to the inside of the church. Nneoma walks to the row of benches closest to the perimeter of the church, closest to its walls. This row is at the very top of the church—in the smaller of the two layers. It is where the ushers stand, handing out the daily bulletin. Nneoma collects a bulletin and then finds a seat there. The fan near where she sits rattles and buzzes, and its metal frame glimmers where the sun lands on it.

The woman next to whom Nneoma sits is new to the church. Nneoma can tell. Hers is not a face that Nneoma has seen in all her years at the church. The woman is neither beautiful nor ugly. Her eyes are big, and round, and a little tired looking. Her nose barely rises from her face, but her lips are full, doing all the rising that her nose refuses to do. She smiles. Like the previous three women, this one is pregnant and shows.

Beads of sweat form on the woman's forehead. Nneoma takes out her handkerchief from her little handbag and offers it to the woman. "Were akwa," she says. *Take the cloth.*

The woman's smile widens. "Da'lu," she says. *Thank you.* She takes the cloth.

Nneoma folds her arms in front of her, above her handbag, which rests on her lap. She traces the seams of the handbag with her fingers. Her eyes find the woman's protruding belly. She allows them to settle there long enough that the woman is aware of the eyes on her belly. Then Nneoma turns abruptly away, as if flustered, as if embarrassed by the staring. She's done this before.

"Iwere umu nke gi?" the woman asks.

Nneoma shakes her head. No, she says, she does not have any children of her own.

The woman nods sympathetically. They both sit silently for a while.

A long time ago, when she was just beginning at Staff School (she must have been twenty-four then, having just finished her Youth Service), Nneoma had the impression that she would marry. Because Obinna—Mr. Nkangineme—the headmaster, had kept watchful eyes on her. His eyes on her had been more watchful than with any of the other teachers. Nneoma could tell. More watchful even than with Ezioma, who had started at the school the same year Nneoma started.

Before him, no other man had showed interest in her. She was shy, and awkward socially, could no more hold a conversation than a gaze. And she did not fill out her dresses the way the other girls did.

Perhaps all this was why. But even when she began to fill out her dresses, it appeared it was already too late. Not during that time in secondary school, not during her years at the university, certainly not during her Youth Service did any of the boys pay her any mind. She watched as the other girls put on lipstick, fussed with their dresses and hair, as they fervently went out on dates.

In any case, that was how Nneoma ever began to hope. Because Obinna would sometimes come into her class after school had been dismissed. He would take the seat across her table—they'd sit facing each other. Sometimes he leaned into the back of the chair.

The first time he came, she was rummaging through papers in the drawer of her desk. There was the scent of dead roaches coming from the drawer, and so she lowered her head into the drawer to find the roach. She was sure that there'd indeed be one or a few there. She was new at the school then, but the desk was old. Its wood was chipped at the seams, with bite marks where mice appeared to have chewed on it. It was an ashy brown, but Nneoma suspected that it had once been a richer shade of brown.

Opposite her desk, across the room, was a wall with a large window. Her desk faced the window. She wanted it that way, so that she could look outside and watch the plantain trees, so that sometimes, while the children worked silently in their notebooks, she could gaze at a vanishing point somewhere beyond the window, beyond the orange and guava and plantain trees whose leaves rustled in the morning breeze. She could look beyond the patchy field of green and yellow grass, beyond the tombstones in the cemetery across the Staff School compound. And she'd fade away into mindless thoughts, thoughts that dissolved instantly as soon as a student made any noise.

She did not see him coming, even with the window, because she was after all immersed in her search for dead roaches. He startled her, and she gasped loudly. Then she chuckled softly, embarrassed by her fright. He asked if he could help her find what she was looking for. She straightened up, smiled politely at him. Her desk was near the door of the classroom. He did not have to walk much to arrive at it. He was wearing a beige agbada with gold trimmings at its front. The agbada came down to his knees, about half the length of his sokoto. His hair had just begun to gray then. He held a hat in his hand. He fussed with it as he walked toward her. He brought with him a sweet smell, the scent of plantain leaves warmed by sunlight.

The chair on the other side of her desk was where students sometimes sat when she called them to have a one-on-one conference with her. He sat on it, leaned into the back of the seat, as if to create more space between them.

"Are you settling fine?" he asked.

She nodded.

"Be sure to let me know if you need anything—chalk, paper, pens, and pencils. Any supplies."

She nodded. "Thank you," she said.

He got up, reached his hand across her desk, held it up there, for a shake. She reached over with her hand. They shook hands.

That was how that first meeting went. He might have done the same with Ezioma, and in fact with all the other new teachers who had gained employment at Staff School that year. There were four of them in total. He might have gone to their classes and offered chalk, paper, pens, and pencils. And afterward, he might have shaken their hands. But Nneoma suspected that he didn't. She was sure he'd taken those extra steps just for her.

All around them voices rise in waves, crashing into one another, rising then settling, then rising again. Slowly it subsides and then there is no sound at all.

Nneoma leans over to the woman. "The pastor will soon begin," she says.

The woman nods.

Nneoma looks at the woman's belly, without any pretenses this time. "How far?" she asks.

"Seven months, almost eight. Counting down the weeks now."

Nneoma smiles. "I had a friend," she says. "Ezioma." She fusses with her hands, tangles and untangles her fingers above her handbag. There is a silence.

The woman clears her throat. "Your friend," she says, "she was pregnant too?"

Nneoma smiles gratefully. She nods. "Yes, she was pregnant. She used to come to this church."

The woman nods, as if to signal Nneoma to continue.

"She liked the church," Nneoma says. She pauses thoughtfully. "You know, here the pastor tells us to greet one another; and we do—by shaking hands, you know. We used to hug, but one day he told us to stop. Only to shake hands. Because he was afraid that all the hugging and embracing was scaring off the visitors. Makes sense. I suppose it can be a scary thing to have to hug a stranger."

This time it is the woman who appears thoughtful. Nneoma watches her. "Yes, handshaking seems a good enough greeting," the woman says.

"Ezioma thought so too," Nneoma says, "that handshaking was enough."

"You didn't?" the woman asks.

Nneoma shakes her head. "It's different for me. I liked the hugs, even looked forward to them. It was the only time anyone ever hugged me." She clears her throat. "But, yes, handshaking is good too. Handshaking and smiles."

By now the pastor has climbed onto the stage. He looks small in the distance, but Nneoma notices when he raises his hand and taps the microphone, the way he does every Sunday—to check that it is working. He taps it. She listens to the sound of the tap; they all listen; it is something like static on a radio.

"This is the day the Lord has made," he says. "Let us rejoice in it!" His voice is strong and merry. Convincing in its boldness. It makes Nneoma feel uplifted, and hopeful, and secure, the way it always does.

The pastor retreats to the corner of the stage, and the liturgist—one of the members of the congregation—comes up to the microphone and announces the call to confession. Everyone rises. He is wearing a white shirt, like an oxford, no tie. Black trousers. He says: "If we say we have no sin, we deceive ourselves, and the truth is not in us. If we confess our sins, He who is faithful and just will forgive us our sins and cleanse us from all unrighteousness."

A murmur rises—quiet, harmonized prayers. Nneoma feels the tears well up in her eyes. She is penitent, and wishes she could stop with her sins, with that particular one.

The liturgist finishes with the prayer of confession. Nneoma wipes her eyes, swiftly, so that the woman seated next to her does not notice.

There is a lull in the time that the liturgist leaves the stage, in the time that the pastor replaces the liturgist at the microphone. The pastor takes his time flipping through the sheets of his sermon. He always does. Nneoma knows this. She leans over to the woman.

"I found her in her bed," she says. "Just sleeping like a baby."

"Who?"

"Ezioma," Nneoma says. "It's been years now, but the memory is still so fresh."

"Sorry," the woman says sympathetically.

Nneoma nods.

"And the baby?"

"Gone with her." Nneoma shakes her head fervently now, because the pain is real, the feelings are true. She wipes her hands with her eyes. The woman watches her; Nneoma can feel the woman's eyes on her. Soon the woman touches Nneoma on the arms. She rubs Nneoma's arms gently. It is soothing, and is perhaps the reason why Nneoma remembers.

She remembers that it was after service that she invited Ezioma for lunch. They had planned that the lunch would turn into dinner. Ezioma's husband was a contractor for Shell, and work had taken him out of town. Not that he ever attended church, but he would have at least been home on a normal Sunday, and Ezioma would have had to return home to him.

Not that Sunday. And so, Nneoma invited Ezioma over. She had known for a while that Ezioma's husband would be away. (Ezioma had been married a year by then. She still continued her work at Staff School. She and Nneoma must have been twenty-seven or twenty-eight at the time.)

They planned it all—jeloff rice with chicken, ogbono soup with garri—both of these were main meals, but they wanted it that way, so that one dish would be for lunch, and the other for dinner.

Nneoma offered that she'd make them all. Ezioma would bring some meat pies and chin-chin for snacks. Between the meals, and even during the meals, they would sit on chairs on Nneoma's veranda. They'd talk about the sermon at church, about work—Staff School, about the baby and baby names, about Ezioma's husband, and they'd eat the snacks.

This last bit—Ezioma's husband—was painful for Nneoma to talk about, because, after all, she did not herself have a husband. Had she had one, perhaps she would not have become the way she was—always wanting a husband, always longing for a child of her own. (This was partly the reason she enjoyed her work, because it allowed her some time to play mother with her students. Still, when she went home, she was alone again and the longing resumed. Sometimes the longing became physical, like hunger pangs. She could feel it within the walls of her stomach, and sometimes it was so intense that it caused her to cry.)

In any case, Nneoma prepared well for her meeting with Ezioma. She even visited the dibia—the witch doctor—down in the village of Ogbigbo. She took the bus all the way there. So that she could go about the transaction in the best way possible. This was why she insisted that she would be the one to prepare the main meals.

Nneoma turns to the woman. "Di-gi, o no ebe?" she asks.

"Home," the woman says. "He's at home putting together furniture. Arranging the house. We're still unpacking. But by next week, we should be settled, and then he'll join me in church."

Nneoma nods. "It's good to have a husband," she says. "Makes things easier."

The woman lets out a laugh, but she nods too. "Yes," she says. "Some things it does make easier."

By now the pastor has begun his sermon, and so these little exchanges between the women are merely whispers. Now, Nneoma resigns herself to her thoughts, and it seems to her that the woman resigns herself to the sermon.

She thinks of Obinna, of those years when she was sure that he'd be the one. He might indeed have been the one. She was not quite sure how things could have gone so wrong.

He had allowed her to call him Obinna those first few years—Obinna, instead of Mr. Nkangineme. He had never objected to it until that day: He had again come into her classroom to ask if teaching was going fine.

He was wearing just a regular shirt, button-down, tucked into his trousers. A tie hung down from his neck. A belt wound itself around his waist. She was just sitting at her desk, gazing out the window. Sometimes she thought she heard small sounds in the classroom, like creaking. But the building was concrete. The creaking might have just been the pitter-patter of lizards and mice.

He came in and took that same chair on the other side of her desk. He was smelling sweet again, like heated plantain leaves.

He brought with him a box of chalk. A blackboard eraser. "This should do for the next few weeks," he said. "But let me know if you need more."

She nodded. She allowed her fingers to touch and linger on his as she accepted the package. He eyed her curiously. She noticed this.

Now, when she thought of it, she knew that there were things she should have considered before going ahead with her plan. Practical things, like, was he already married? Like, was he in fact interested in her, or was it the way he treated all his other employees, the males and the females? Was he just performing a duty, just handing out supplies so that his school would run smoothly? After all, by that time, he was only stopping by her class every other week or so, and he'd usually bring supplies with him.

But it did not even occur to her to consider these things.

She accepted the box of chalk, along with the eraser. She placed them on her desk. She looked at him—at his hair, his face, his eyes. His hair was mostly gray by then, but his face retained its youth. There were crow's feet visible at the sides of his eyes, but only when he smiled widely. His teeth were bright and crooked, but in a way she found endearing. His skin was a rich brown, like cacao, the very opposite of her own yellow skin.

She took in all of his features as he stood in front of her, took in all of it as he asked, "Is there anything else I can do for you?"

She shook her head.

He nodded and then turned to leave. Just as he had turned, she shouted, "Wait!" It came out like a gasp.

He turned back around.

She was giddy with anticipation. It occurred to her that soon she would be able to make the announcement to her mama, to her papa, to everyone who mocked, who doubted. She would be able to say, "I'm getting married." Or, "Here is my husband-to-be." And she would present Obinna to them.

She was wearing two layers of wrapper, both tied at the side of her waist. Underneath she did not wear a slip, like she often did, like most women did. There were concentric designs on the wrapper—circles and spheres of different sizes, two or more of them meeting at the middle. The blouse she wore that day was lace and short-sleeved. Its neckline came down just below her shoulders. It did not draw attention to itself, because it was the style. Those were the kinds of blouses that many women wore with their wrappers then, especially for special events—weddings, birthdays, funerals.

She had tucked the hem of the blouse into her wrappers before tying the wrappers at her side. She had then pinned it to the wrapper with safety pins, all around the circumference of her body. The hem of her wrapper—the longer one—was tucked beneath one of the legs of her desk, just one small portion of the wrapper's hem. She had seen to it that this was so.

She rose up from her seat then, abruptly, as if to announce to him what it was he could do for her. She felt the tug of the desk's leg on the wrapper, and the wrapper's tug on her blouse. The wrapper slid down her waist, still covering her body, but it pulled the blouse with it farther down below her shoulders so that it exposed half of her chest, that smooth yellowness of it, smooth but not flat, because there was of course the matter of her breast, which was small but round and full, which rose and tapered into a nipple the color of lumber wood. The nipple was nearly a perfect circle, she knew, and at the very tip of it—at the very tip of the other one too—was that tiny opening, from which she desperately hoped that milk would one day flow, enough to nourish her child.

Obinna gasped then. "Miss Enwere!" he exclaimed. "Cover yourself!"

Nneoma stood where she was, just looking at him.

"Miss Enwere! Do you hear me?"

Finally she said, "Obinna, don't worry. Everything is just the way it should be." She pulled the wrapper from underneath the leg of the desk then. She held it—held the portion that she had latched on to as she pulled. She walked over to him. Her blouse still hung down her chest.

When she reached him, she took his hand in hers, placed it on her chest, just above her exposed breast. She sighed with satisfaction. There was release, a blissful lightness in the mere touch of his skin on hers. She breathed deeply.

"I want this," she said. "I want *you*. Don't you want me too?" Why had she even asked this last question? At the time, she was sure he wanted her too.

He jerked his hand away. It startled her. His face was angry. She did not understand.

"Obinna," she said. It was hushed, both an exclamation and a question.

"Pull yourself together, Miss Enwere!" he said. "Do you value your job? *Do you value your job?!* If so, I suggest you pull yourself together, or you will soon be out of a job!" He turned to leave the room. At the door, he stopped. "And, from now on," he said, "it is Mr. Nkangineme to you."

He was tall—a full head above her. But it was nothing new, this height of his. He had always been tall, all the time that she'd known him. But she noticed his height then, as if noticing it for the first time. It was overwhelming. Luckily for her, he turned again and left.

For the months afterward, it was an embarrassment to see him, even from a distance—at morning assemblies and such. He stopped coming to her classroom to drop off supplies. Or, rather, he must have dropped them off late in the evenings after she was gone for the day, or early in the mornings before she had arrived. But he was a professional, and she knew that word of the incident had not spread from him. She was thankful for that.

Months passed, and she remained at the school, because she had been unsuccessful in finding other work. Eventually, it seemed he forgot the incident and began again to bring her supplies. They remained professional about those brief encounters. She called him Mr. Nkangineme.

Now the pastor calls for silent prayer, and the church is quiet for a minute or two. He finishes off with the Lord's prayer, first in Igbo, then in English. The congregation recites along with him. The voices are loud and fervent. Next, the choir begins to sing, and the ushers come around carrying those round, gold trays in which the tithe money is placed. Nneoma digs into her handbag. She places her money on the tray, more than a few Naira bills, in multiples of a hundred, more than enough to buy a loaf of bread. The woman next to her digs into her purse too; Nneoma watches. The woman places some Naira bills into the tray. Nneoma smiles approvingly at her; the woman smiles back.

When all the money has been collected, the ushers gather in front of the stage. The pastor moves forward to collect each tray. The choir sings even louder. *Praise God from whom all blessings flow. Praise him, all creatures here below. . . .*

The pastor delivers his closing address. "Go in peace," he tells the congregation. "Return no one evil for evil. And in all things, seek the good."

The choir sings briefly, just a refrain. And then members of the congregation begin to rise, their voices along with their bodies.

Nneoma turns to the woman. "My friend Ezioma," she says. "I met her at work. I teach at Staff School, in Abuloma."

The woman nods.

"It was thanks to my invitation that she ever even started to come to this church. I invited her, you see."

"Ah, I see," the woman says, nodding.

Nneoma skips the part about the dibia and the potion. She jumps right to the lunch and dinner get-together. She tells the woman again that Ezioma was pregnant and showing by that time. Eight months, just like the woman. Perhaps Ezioma ate too much that day, Nneoma tells the woman. Because the next day, Monday, she did not show up at the school. On Tuesday, she did not show up either. On Wednesday, Mr. Nkangineme held a teachers' meeting early, at 7:00 a.m., an hour and a half before the students arrived. All the teachers gathered, sat around that long oval table in the headmaster's office. He had been unable to contact Ezioma by phone, Nneoma tells the woman. And Ezioma's husband was apparently still away on the work trip, and so Mr. Nkangineme had also been unable to contact him on the phone. He asked for suggestions on how to progress from the teachers. Had any of them heard from Ezioma? Mr. Nkangineme asked.

Some teachers said that she was probably just ill, and maybe just too ill to contact the school. Others nodded and said that, if she were in fact ill, one of them should pay her a visit, to let her know that she was on their minds, in their prayers.

But it should be someone who knew her well, they agreed.

"Who was closest to her then?" the headmaster asked.

Eyes scanned the room. Most of them landed on Nneoma. By then, the teachers knew that Ezioma and Nneoma had grown close, that they sometimes walked home together after school. They'd heard that Ezioma sometimes attended church services with Nneoma on Rumuola Road.

Nneoma complied hesitantly. She asked the teachers when they thought was a good time for her to go.

The teachers responded that she should go as soon as possible. "Now," many of them said.

And so it was that Nneoma went, only pausing to hang her handbag around her shoulder.

She tells all this to the woman now.

The gate to Ezioma's house was locked. There was no gateman, or at least not at the time Nneoma arrived. She was forced to get on the tips of her toes. Then she reached inside the gate with her hands, manipulated the latch until she managed to open it. Lucky for her that there was no padlock on it.

She entered then, walked across the front yard, toward the front entrance. The door was wide—a double-leaf door—made of glass on the top half, wood on the bottom.

She knocked. Her heart had begun to beat fast by then. She could feel the moistness in her palms. She continued to knock, each one louder than the one before. She turned the knob as she knocked, but the door was locked. She shook it, frantically. Finally, it occurred to her to try to pick the lock. She reached for her hair, took out one of the bobby pins that held her hair in a bun. She inserted it this way and that, inside the keyhole, to the side of the door where the bolt and socket met.

Finally, she turned the knob once more, shook it. The door opened. Her heart beat even faster. She could feel its thumping in her palms. She entered. In the parlor, everything was calm, as perhaps it should have been, except for the buzzing of the ceiling fan. But the air smelled moist, musty. When she breathed deeply enough, there was something in it like rotten soup. Paintings decorated one wall—in them, pictures of women carrying buckets on their heads, of men at work in the farm, bent over at the hips, their axes high over their heads. Mere silhouettes. A picture of Ezioma and her husband hung on another wall, smiling faces. Her husband wore an agbada like the ones Mr. Nkangineme sometimes wore. It was a light-green color, but its front was trimmed in gold. He had the look of an Oga, which perhaps he was, all that traveling he did. But there had been no gatemen guarding the gate, like big men often had. And there were no housegirls to be seen. In fact, the house itself was modest at best. Perhaps he too was modest—having the money of a big Oga, but not feeling any desire to demonstrate his wealth. But no matter, Nneoma thought. She turned from him in the picture to Ezioma.

She scrutinized Ezioma's face in the picture. She decided that Ezioma had the soft look of a submissive wife. Nneoma felt the envy then. How she wished that she could have had the opportunity to be somebody's wife, even a submissive one.

She walked down a corridor, toward the room. On one wall hung a calendar. Down, on the floor beneath the calendar, was a broom, the native kind—stems of palm leaves bunched up, tied together with a bamboo string. Near the broom was a dustpan. It was clean—there was no indication that either it or the broom was currently being used. Near all of that was a small cluster of mouse droppings, and the dry brown shell of a dead cockroach. And then a kerosene lantern, also not being used—unlit. Not that it should have been lit—it was daytime and not so dark. And, by all appearances, there was electrical power in the house. The ceiling fan in the parlor had after all been turning.

There were two doors, one on each side of the corridor. There was a third door straight ahead. None of the doors was quite pulled closed. She pushed the one ahead first. She saw the toilet, a sink, the bath stall. Some towels hanging on a rack. She pulled the door back—not all the way closed, but just the way it had been.

She turned to her left. She pushed that door slowly. She felt her breath catch as she did. What if things were exactly the way she expected they'd be? She'd cry, she thought. She'd cry for poor Ezioma. But she'd be grateful to the dibia. And she'd be grateful for the baby. She'd not stopped to consider the fact that the baby's father would want the child. That he would wonder who had killed his wife and stolen his baby.

In any case, she pushed open the door. That scent of rotten okra soup was stronger then than before. She entered the room, and she could see the lump on one side of the double bed. She moved closer to it. There was a dresser to her left, with a mirror sitting on top of it. The bed was to her right. She did not notice much else. She went directly to the lump. She found Ezioma there, just lying down, her blanket pulled up to her chest. She was the lump—just sleeping as Nneoma suspected she had done all the nights before.

Nneoma began to cry then. All that emotion. The sadness of Ezioma's death. The happiness of having possibly realized a dream—of having finally wound up with a child of her own.

She flipped the blanket from Ezioma's chest, all the way down to the foot of the bed. There was that putrid scent, rising as a result of the disturbing of the sheets.

Nneoma touched Ezioma's arm. Ezioma was stiff. Ezioma's belly, too, was stiff. She touched Ezioma's belly again. She bent her head to be closer. She listened for signs of life in Ezioma's stiff belly. She could not have been sure, but somehow Nneoma knew then that the baby had not survived. She moaned. She imagined Ezioma being buried in that cemetery across the Staff School compound. She imagined the baby being buried with her. It infuriated her, the thought. She screamed. She pounded her fist into the side of the bed. She curled into a ball at the side of the bed. She cried, loud wails that could have startled anyone who heard. But there was no one to hear.

She remained there on the floor, in that little corner, where the mice must have scurried through, where the cockroaches must have sometimes crept by. The sadness became guilt. Guilt that she had wasted Ezioma's life. She had sacrificed Ezioma for the sake of getting Ezioma's child but had wound up with no child at all. Perhaps she had not been careful enough, she reasoned. Perhaps she should not have waited all these days to come check up on Ezioma. She should have suggested the headmaster's meeting far earlier than he called it. She should have suggested it the very Monday following her and Ezioma's meal together. She should have gone to see Ezioma then, because chances were that by then Ezioma would already be dead, but perhaps the baby would still be living.

It must have been afternoon by the time she picked herself up from the floor. She wiped her eyes with the hem of her blouse, which had by then sneaked out from underneath her wrapper. She did not have to look for the phone. It was there, sitting on the bedside table, on the other side of the bed. She picked it up, dialed the school. Obinna picked up. Mr. Nkangineme. She told him exactly how it was. Almost exactly, anyway. She told him of the way she had found Ezioma—still sleeping in bed, only more than sleeping: dead. She told him that she had gone into a sort of shock, that she had been curled up, crying by Ezioma's bed all this time. "Oh no!" he exclaimed. "My God!" Then, "Miss Enwere, I'm so sorry. Sorry for the loss of your friend. So sorry for your loss." His tone was sympathetic, the same sort of tone that the woman was taking with Nneoma now. Because, of course, Nneoma was telling the woman the story the same way she had told it to Mr. Nkangineme—nothing of her plot, her motivation. Nothing about her role in any of it. Nothing about the failure of the potion. Just the part about finding Ezioma in bed and mourning her loss. All of that was a little over a decade ago. Twelve years, to be exact. Nneoma was twenty-seven or twenty-eight at the time.

"I'm sorry," the woman says now. She moves to embrace Nneoma. Her eyes are sad, compassionate. "Ndo." She repeats it, whispers it. *Sorry.*

Nneoma leans into the embrace. She breathes in the musty scent of the woman. She remembers the days after she lost Ezioma and the baby, how she thought she heard people talking about her, gossiping about her being unmarried, about her being childless. The truth was that she had heard them talk even before she lost Ezioma and the baby. But all their talk was more painful, and therefore more memorable, after the incident with Ezioma and the baby.

They called her an old maid, an empty barrel—Mgbaliga, Nwanyiiga. She heard these names as she walked down to the market, as she rode the bus on her errands, even in school she heard the whispers.

Her mother was whispering those days too, each time Nneoma stopped by to visit them in the village. She'd shake her head disappointedly, not just her mother, but her father too—they'd shake their heads, arbitrarily—at the most unexpected times, for example, her mother, as she molded her garri to dip into soup; her papa as he munched on groundnuts and flipped the pages of his newspaper. She'd pass by, and he'd appear to shake his head. And it seemed to her that he murmured. She was sure the murmur had to do with her—because she was in fact becoming an old maid. Because she was of childbearing age, but childless. Sometimes her mama would say as much to her, not in a whisper, but loudly, frantically: "All your friends are leaving you behind. Won't you do something about it?"

She remembers all this now as she allows the woman to embrace her. She feels ashamed. She begins again to hear the whispers, only they are a paradox of whispers this time—not small voices, not tiny chirps as of birds. No, they are instead loud and booming but still mocking in their loudness.

She shakes her head slightly, trying to shake the voices away. Her thoughts land on the pastor, on his ban on hugs, on embraces. He had a point, she thinks now. Visitors rarely came to the church anymore, let alone pregnant visitors. How lucky she was, then, to have wound up with this woman. She exhales.

The woman is saying something, but Nneoma does not at first hear. Because she is instead thinking what she always thinks around now: that it will work this time. That she will love and nurture the baby and never take her eyes away from it. That she will name the child Ekwutosina, as an answer to her critics, as a response to their murmurs, to their mockery. Ekwutosina, she will call the child, if it is a girl. *Cease your gossiping.* And if it is a boy, Chukwuemeka, as an expression of gratitude. Chukwuemeka, meaning, *God has been very generous toward me.*

The woman parts a little from Nneoma, just watches her. She says to Nneoma, "You should allow yourself to move on. Do you have any other friends? You should make new friends. That will allow you to move on."

Nneoma nods fervently. "Yes-o," she says emphatically. "You're right. I don't have any close friends. Not like Ezioma. Maybe I should try to make some."

The woman says, "What are you doing this evening? You can drop by my house. I'll prepare food. We'll eat. My husband will be busy working on the house. He won't disturb."

Nneoma nods, accepts. "Dalu. Imela," she says. *Thank you.*

"Anytime is fine. I'll be expecting you—"

Nneoma nods. But her thoughts begin drifting again. This time she thinks of the dibia, of her visits there, of the potion, of all the failed attempts. She thinks of Ezioma. After Ezioma, Nneoma had not immediately gone back to trying. She thinks of this now. It had been six or seven years before she thought to try again with another woman. Perhaps she should have gone back to trying right away, she thinks now. Perhaps those years between Ezioma and the next woman were wasted time, wasted opportunities.

The woman taps her on the shoulder. "Are you all right?" she asks. Her voice is soft, concerned.

"Yes," Nneoma responds. "I will come this evening. I will come." But as she says it, she becomes agitated. The potion failed with Ezioma. It failed with all the women who followed, all three of them. They had taken their babies along, like Ezioma.

Suddenly Nneoma is angry. She wonders if she should even bother with visiting the woman. This anger is not, has never been, part of the plan; it grows in her, but she does her best to hide it. "No," she says to the woman calmly. "Maybe I won't make it after all. You see, I'm suddenly not feeling so well." As she speaks, she rises from the bench. Her intention is to head out of the church—to find one of its staircases, to find one of those open doorways that lead outside, to breathe in a sharper, more penetrating air than is in the church. Perhaps she will find that air calming. But beneath her the floor appears to shake. She sits back down on the bench. Soon, it appears to her that the walls of the church are collapsing all around. A crumbling cake. She hears loud screaming and thuds of racing feet. She thinks to run too, but her legs refuse to move. She reasons that all this is a figment of her imagination. She shakes her head as if to shake the sounds away.

"Are you all right?" the woman asks again. Nneoma watches as the woman reaches over with that same handkerchief that she offered the woman earlier. Nneoma feels the woman dabbing her forehead with the handkerchief, wiping her sweat away. When the woman is done wiping, Nneoma nods gratefully, but she is still angry, and dizzy with all that anger. Her heart beats fast, faster. It is a struggle to catch her breath. She grasps at her chest, where it appears that all the pain of the anger has collected. She yields to the anger, surrenders to its pain. And then all she can think to say is, "No, no. I cannot be your friend. I will not visit you. Not this evening. Not ever."

She says all this very boldly, because she means every word of it. But even as she says it, a part of her hopes. It is a deep-seated hope borne of nothing more than habit. It is a desperate one, this hope. It is the hope that the woman will insist.

Foreign Correspondent

Joanna Howard

FOREIGN VS. HOME

I AM A CORRESPONDENT. My subjects are very particular, and usually domestic, frequently feminine in the most conventional sense of that word: home and hearth, heart and health, sense and sensuality. Teased from common desire or collective lack: Find the things that fill the voids, and then find their variations. Which is to say, much of my life's work is built on replications rather than reversals. On the products of a market economy. On the expected rather than the disruptive. On creature comforts close at hand. This is Johnnie James, with subtle tips for quality lifestyles. This is Johnnie James, reporting the fine details from local haunts. This is Johnnie James from the intimacy of your kitchen.

This is no apology. For some time, I've been seeking the analogous, the symmetrical, the pieces that go together. I prefer to compare rather than contrast. Even in traveling from town to town, I am keeping it regional and representative. Rupture, exposure, or things held in precarious balance are the territories of another department.

I admit that my thoughts of late turn to violent distant subjects. I dream of becoming a foreign correspondent, but breaking into this takes some doing. To begin, I'll report from the field, and then lengthen slowly outward. Next, I'll take up my pen name, Ute Brynstock. Ute Brynstock, reporting from the aftermath. Ute Brynstock, on the trail of the assassin.

FOREIGN BODIES

I am on the way to Alphonso's house for field reporting and notation. He is a great philosopher and photographer and greater traveler. He is said to live among the most spectacular treasures of art and of nature, in his refuge for exotic creatures. He has an aviary, an apiary, two aquariums, several constructed ponds with burbling mechanical falls, and an expansive library of lofty texts, both in terms of their content and their position on soaring shelves. He has many bedrooms, offices, and areas for repose and contemplation. And yet, he is never there. He travels the world. To catch him at home is a rare treat. Rarer for me, as I am only the friend of a friend and so a casual acquaintance, with little to offer in the way of holding his interest.

In related news, I've recently begun corresponding with a semi-retired cage fighter called Scooter MacIntosh, the Bricktown Butcher, a welterweight boxer and grappler. My reasons are not professional, far from it. I am an avid fight fan. He is violent and imposing, but also scrappy and approachable. He's roughly my age and holds two nicknames, personal and professional. Also, I fell in love with his voice in a radio interview. We come from the same region, and he holds a cadence that has been almost entirely lost. I cling to these trappings of home, since I am so far from it. Scooter raises something in my mind that attacks all my senses at once. His letters are terse and guarded; mine are acrobatic and exhaustive. Having experienced a decent amount of fame, he values his privacy and a certain peace of mind. My goal is to cut through to the tender interior. He values respect, which I try to deliver in a kind of ecstatic catalog of his fight skills and good looks. (Alphonso writes that respect is about deference to the limits and boundaries of another person. I am lousy at this, and Scooter is cottoning on.) In any case, I have a lightness of spirit as a result of these exchanges, as I jostle down the lane to Alphonso's house, the image of two compact male bodies tangled inextricably inside a cage hovering always just beyond my eyesight. I am lucky on these days when I can hold a world in my head that is equal to but not in competition with the world outside it.

OCCUPIED TERRITORIES

Alphonso's house is laid out in pods, with decks and bridges, like a spa or a bathhouse, with pools and rivulets running between. In this way, it reminds me of the hot springs in Iceland where the water steams up from the pools against the frozen cup of the mountain, and the bathers, moving lethargically, their faces coated in white volcanic clay, pass as ghosts visible only in the gaps in the mist. Or so I saw depicted in an article.

In an adjoining side yard, just off Alphonso's kitchen, there is Misha, the Victoria Crowned Pigeon, in iridescent indigo, with lacy head crest and bright-red eyes. He approaches with some trepidation.

I wonder why he doesn't begin his salutation? Alphonso asks. He will greet you, Al assures me. I wonder as well, and step back, perhaps to make the bird feel less threatened, or perhaps because I am a little threatened. I'm not sure I can bear up under the rejection of such a creature, and burbling pleasantries, as I am in his direction, I am starting to feel more than a little foolish. I step back from the porch into the kitchen. He crosses the threshold. Then, all at once, he bows to me, and bows again, and repeats this, with deep, cooing calls, his crown feathers brushing my sneakers.

I can't deny that part of me is highly put off by this type of social contract. I should wait for him to approach, no doubt, as if I am taming a fox. I am often waiting for such recognitions from such wild creatures. The occasional undaunted address would be nice, less of this sidestepping. However, that said, if you announce your desires too quickly, you become equated with a list of wants, and little more.

Successfully assimilated, as I am, I have neutralized the more unattractive and soppy aspects of desire through deportment, good manners, ladylike behavior. This is useful in my field. It allows me to float along, engaging with different personality types while remaining a charming blank. If asked about it in an interview—for instance, if I was interviewing myself—I would probably sound smug. The fact is that it is very hard work to keep up such a skill, and I am often giving myself away. These are fraught times we find ourselves in: where managing to appear bubbly but not too, sincere but not too, intellectual but not too, political but not too, edgy but not too, flirtatious but not too, etc., and being able to keep up this balance either over an imported cheese wheel or a chili cheese dog is a skill that can carry you. But, secretly, I'm doubtful. I am very doubtful. I often think of my region, and what is lost and found there, in isolation, in what is called rural even if most of where you go is paved or air-conditioned. I am doubtful of what this skill will do to me over time in overuse. What if once again that syrupy sense of repletion, of satisfaction in a successful transaction, uses up what little's left of—what? Spark of life? Emotional juices? Genuine mojo? Occasionally in life one meets someone who can't be assimilated into such ritual courtships. Oh, and the havoc they are likely to reap on an otherwise stable organism. Euphoria, rapture, rupture, and in little time I am back in the thick of the world. Hence, I fly to you, Scooter.

Joanna Howard

BODIES OF KNOWLEDGE

Scooter's path as a mixed martial artist has been unusual, mysterious: He stopped at the highest point of his career. He left the best fight club in California, and returned to our home state, which is itself in a state of decline. In a letter, he says to me simply that there was supposed to be another fight, but then there wasn't one. In my exchanges with Scooter, many questions remain unanswered even after I've done my best to ask, and he's taken pains to explain. (Or, I can read some interview and learn the details of his tumultuous life in a way that certainly makes him feel exposed.) For me, the learning curve is steep, and every step a potential misstep. I know that my time in this correspondence is limited.

I spend much of my free time imagining scenarios of what my first real-world encounter with Scooter might be like. I travel by car to his region. I arrange an interview time. I arrive at his home with my stenographer's pad, and also a device for recording his voice. It's late on a warm, close evening such as are chronic in our home state in the summer months. Standing on the porch of his house (which is in a kind of dilapidated Victorian style, built close upon other such homes), I can already hear the sounds of the interior, the window fans that are trying to move the heavy air, the television that is playing a popular show about vampire romance, the voice of some female whose miraculous proximity to Scooter fills me with admiration but also a choking dread. How have I managed to seek out something so unfathomable? Scooter opens the door, bare to the waist in his low-slung gi pants, his slender and sinewy frame pale in contrast to his tattooed breastplate, which demands, pictorially, that we remember the dead but look toward the hope of the living. It is a banner of adornment on the body, one that is no doubt popular with fighters. Fighters like such succinct wisdoms, codes to live by. The look of Scooter makes me gasp, but I try to smile and act nonchalant. He does not smile.

Did you run here? he says, with considerable contempt, because you sound out of breath.

With this he turns his back on me, and I recall that I have used professional pretenses to gain entry into his home, and although I have been invited in, I am not yet, and may never be, welcome.

Such Victorian homes, of course, are nonexistent in our region. They come to my mind no doubt the detritus of another memory of another place.

Joanna Howard

ANOTHER BLANCHED FIGURE/VICE VS. VERSE

Scooter has a very high threshold for pain, and so he does not mark it so carefully as he should. Perhaps for this reason he has a spinal injury, one that will not be easily resolved. And one that, I assume, makes it unpleasant for him to hunch over a laptop, in his reading glasses, crafting his blunt compliments and his truisms. I have no business knowing about his reading glasses, except that he has appeared in them on television. I can't help it that I am trained for investigative research. But it concerns me that Scooter is someone who understands holding guard, not simply from a grappler's perspective. I sometimes feel that I am wielding information against him, not simply those things that I have learned about him illegitimately, but many things that I have learned for myself in fairly legitimate ways, such as facts about our region, including root-beer floats and river parks.

In our intensities, the internal often has a powerful effect on the external. There is the vulgar way practicality gets used against us for our own subjugation: under the guise of protections, preservations, safety first. Or, instead, we make our bodies vulnerable, or others make their bodies vulnerable to us. I think I'm on board for this part. It's how it has to be. Something solid has to shoulder the brunt of so much abstraction. Often that shoulder is way outside us, maybe even across the room.

A finer line is making use of someone versus making someone feel used. (What do you want with this guy? my friends have been asking about Scooter. That seems like a question that has an answer.)

Scooter says, in two different interviews, "I'm tired, I'm tired, I'm running out of words." Probably because the interviews seemed interminable, and the interviewers not so bright, not so prepared. In any case, two indications of exhaustion in two separate encounters with his voice.

Scooter, in his letters, often makes statements about heart: how we need more of it, and how we get it or keep it, or demonstrate it. Heart is pretty big with fighters. Heart is what takes over when the body is really exhausted but the fight is still happening. I have to be a little careful about listening to Scooter's interviews. The longing to know him becomes so great I can feel something happening inside my rib cage. Explosion, like the formation of a star, to generate heart where extra heart is needed? Implosion to fill the cavity with my own bones? Whatever it is, I have no doubt this gets well in the way of my ability to correspond.

SHIP TO SHORE

I never subscribed to any religious leanings. I have my personal tendencies, though, and can bring a lot of fervor to the subject of my obsession. I like the sea. In the fanciful engravings of nautical charts, I have seen sailors ascending a spiral staircase rising from the sea. This passageway to paradise is oft depicted as a corkscrew of stars. Such imagistic flourish on a map might communicate the presence of a deadly whirlpool, an impenetrable strait, a patch of sirens, a corridor wherein death awaits. Or it might simply mean the edge of the world. The picture really talks. Both the stairs and the stars are notable: For sailors it must have been hard to imagine any voyage that wasn't precarious, but alluring.

LEXICAL BODIES

From the deck, I can almost gather enough communication frequency to make contact with my friend Johni, because I learned long ago the importance of taking council from a comrade of the same name.
Dispatch:

Johni, I'll be frank. No word from the Bricktown Butcher for sixty-two hours. I'm adrift, Johni. Awash, afloat. I write to you from a tomb of despondency. As of today, Johni, there are suddenly many new photographs of Scooter MacIntosh—available in the digital ether—looking quite a bit more devastatingly handsome than in any previous image I have seen of him. He appears to be sporting hair (possibly shorn with a piece of glass) and a hearty salt-and-ginger anarchist's beard. I have been looking at images of Scooter for three months, no changes, and now suddenly, in a matter of hours, he looks like he has been roaming the highlands in battle! Several of these photos were taken in some sort of tiki bar. He wrote to me recently that he had "NO TIME" for writing to me due to excess craziness in his life, but apparently there is still plenty of time for wasting away in Margaritaville? I am so in over my head. No saucy anecdote in the world can measure up to that level of rugged masculinity photographed in the dim light and overhang of the plastic palm fronds of a tiki bar! I am so utterly doomed.

What do you think? Would a photograph of me sitting on the back of a Harley-Davidson holding two chain saws seem like I was trying too hard?

Yrs, Johnnie

MIXED ARTS

The street-smart, practical-minded sportswriter for the local gazette is a martial artist in his own right. He's been studying boxing and grappling for over a year since he figured out men's fitness freelance was more lucrative than coverage of local soccer meets. He writes articles with titles like "Get Ripped with Killer Complexes" and "Chemical Warfare: Winning the Fight with Lactic Acid Training." We often get together and compare notes before going to press. We are both trying for a different audience. He reckons on taking on my softer, more artsy style for the slick intellectual men's magazines targeted at vain urban professionals. I'm ready to bring the pain. I don't mention that I spent last spring reporting on skinny slacks.

I don't mean to stereotype, I tell him, but dudes are more into their bodies than they used to be. Ladies are less into their bodies these days and more into their things.

Dudes are into their bodies and their things. I have to get versatile with this, he says.

It's true, I feel like I could nail your demographic.

Yeah, well, I feel like my demographic likes to get nailed. And probably does get nailed pretty frequently.

I get that. I'm looking for something less fluffy. I think I can seriously transition this year.

I remember Scooter, you know, he says. He had such fast hands. Why are you trying to write letters to that guy? He's probably punchy. If you're going to write letters to a fighter, you should write to Mac Danzig. He seems smart still. He's a photographer when he's not in the cage. Wonders of nature, canyons at sunset, and shit like that. Wolves and bear cubs snuggling. You two would have more of a common-ground base.

Scooter is not punchy! And we are from the same region!

Not anymore, he says.

He lives in the town where I had my first adult thoughts. I can picture him walking around in parking lots where I've been standing in the distant past in short-shorts.

As long as it's strictly professional, I guess.

Why does everyone say that? It isn't remotely professional.

Why would you want to do this to the guy?

That's the other thing everyone asks. Why does everyone ask that?

Because it's valid.

I have been thinking about it. I think it's because he's the visceral next step in my thus-far frilly existence? Or possibly because I'm all mind, but he's all body?

That should sell him.

And he's got all this stuff. Like, he's kind of skater punk but kind of motorcycle club also. I'm branching out. I'm going long.

This will not end pretty, Johnnie.

Why do you say that?

Because he won't play your game.

My game is I think he is awesome.

There's your first problem. That is not grounds for correspondence.

ASKANCE YIELDS THE IMAGE

In many ways, Scooter, who is compact and fair skinned with a cleanly shaved head, reminds me of a ghost. Partly because when attempting a comeback, in a television interview, he said, "I was dead, but now I'm trying to make a future." But it is much more likely that I am the ghost in this scenario. We who haunt bring attention and focus to our subjects. We bring a kind of obsession, one that is inevitable and fixed, but that is inexplicable and ethereal. Our subjects may feel overwhelmed by our attentions, they may recoil. The living may be unable to see the specter in all her depth and complexity due in part to an incapability of the eyes. We ghosts appreciate luminescence as the attribute that improves recognition of the self. When we glow, we are seen. Ghosts must remain resilient, we must be prepared to take different tactics to most effectively connect with the haunted; we focus on eliciting emotional responses where emotional response is not necessarily preferred. We are not as likely as the living to abandon a place, because we are aware of unbreakable ties to location that the living overlook. Females who haunt often haunt from sorrow, or from love. We make the most of our feminine wiles because we can now pass through material unscathed.

PVP: PUBLIC VS. PRIVATE

Location, our region, the past we hold in common. The present moment of our lives in difference; when it comes to Scooter, I am approaching a foreign body of knowledge, and must pick my shots carefully. I don't understand why this contact raises such a fighting spirit in me: the desire to force his response.

There are some things that I want to discuss with Alphonso, which I do not yet deserve to discuss. The same goes for Scooter, and the process must be longer, combative, if he's willing to engage me, to stand up and trade.

I awake quite early. I write on a scrap of paper—the same that is so lightly hinted with some former fragrance—a sentence or two for Scooter: "So perhaps now you're waking, and warm with sleep, twisting your body in the blue glow of dawn, and perhaps are alone, and hard as a fist, and near to bursting, and if so, Bricktown, think on me." Flowery, but fairly direct. There is a part of me that worries that he won't get the message I'm sending. But if he hasn't gotten my message at this point, he doesn't want it, which is worse to consider. I secrete the scrap in my duffel. I know better than to send off this text, for it will likely catch me the cold shoulder. And, oh, what a shoulder to turn against me!

THE PERILS OF HALF SLEEP/TOWARD OTHER MIXED ARTS

On the advice of the sports reporter, I joined him at his gym for a day of grappling. Strictly for the purposes of hands-on research, of course, very professional, totally aboveboard. Arriving in a part of town I associated with loading docks and heavy machinery, we parked, crossed a rubble lot, and entered through a garage door on a building marked as a body shop. (And indeed it was! A body shop of sorts, though there were no cars around.) In a class made almost entirely of large men, in air that seemed to hang with a mixed paste of sweat and testosterone, many pairs of bodies were rolling and twisting together in a violent, animated snuggle on a sea-blue wrestling mat. The soundtrack was Curtis Mayfield. There was only one other girl—

part pinup, part comic-book vixen—already locked in fierce combat with a man three times her size, and I was told she was the instructor's special lady friend. It was hard to know how or where to jump into the mix. Finally, under the generous auspices of the instructor—an intimidating creature with a great depth and breadth of exposed, tattooed chest and a black eye—I was paired with one mustachioed, slender, and highly skilled warrior who seemed mostly unfazed by the fact that I was a girl. He pulled me, gently, by the waist, into his leg guard while explaining the most basic escape technique from this hold.

There are so many things in this world that we are not really supposed to touch. Artworks, sleeping dogs, celebrities, raw poultry, strangers on a train. Some of these things are pretty touching in their own right, which makes it harder. Throw a couple of bodies into a room together and you can cut the decorum with a knife. Ideally, tact serves some reason other than fascist, repressive, communal norming, right? That's what I've been told anyway. Tact in practice is about finding the right tone of approach.

He locked his ankles around my lower back. His voice held the markers of a specific New England accent, one that connected him undeniably to a region, but a region different from my own.

It will be easy to learn where to hold on to me, he said, placing my palm on his hip. I'm a little fella, so you can feel my bones. (And indeed I could! And the tight tendons connecting his leg to his torso.)

You want to press really hard there, he told me, and try to bruise it if you can; that's going to give you more control.

MACGUFFINS

Complacency and anxiety. When I haven't had a letter from Scooter for a couple of weeks, I tend to take drastic measures. Passionate declarations followed by suggestions of how many men are vying for my attentions. Highly constructed narratives of the glamour of my daily existence as a domestic, and potentially foreign, correspondent. Once, I staged an elaborate, flattering photo shoot; lucky for me, in this field, photographers are drifting around just dying to capture a pretty basic-looking girl as if she's a movie star through careful manipulation of light, space, and modern technologies. I posed with the handsome sports reporter while he was eating a sandwich. I posed against a floral backdrop that complemented my wardrobe and eye color. I posed on a park bench in a pear grove where in moments of quiet repose I have often drunk a coffee and even, although I know better, smoked a cigarette, while mulling over thoughts of my fantasy future subjects: political intrigues, a getaway car, global crisis, a painting by Vermeer or a painting *thought* to be by Vermeer, following an assassin to a windmill in the countryside, one that has been partially ruined by fire and whose spiral staircase has been exposed to the elements. A strong wind picks up and begins to turn the paddles of the mill, which in turn spins an axle in the center of the spiral stair. Presumably somewhere a turbine is attached, out of sight, or perhaps below ground.

A tall, polished gentleman with pomade in his thinning hair appears on the stair in a leatherette trench coat. He levels a Walther PPK at my heart.

How did you track me? he asks.

I watched you leaving the palazzo. You paid for your coffee in foreign coins.

Brynstock, I have no quarrel with you.

How did you discover my name?

I am fFolliet! We are on parallel trails, you and I. We have been for some time.

fFolliet! The first "f" silent, of course! I had an ancestor called fFolliet. . . .

But he was executed.

Yes!

Blood relations, I assure you. We were together as children in the house in the highlands where the water was the color of the peat it ran through, and so, you may recall, as a tiny child you mistook the water in the cut-glass decanter for whiskey and so avoided it, but instead gulped the gin. It must have burnt your throat terribly, so you began to cry, and to soothe your tears, I sat you on my lap, and read you the Kipling story of a valiant young mongoose. My hair then was still golden, and my guardian . . .

PERSON TO PERSON

Dear Johni,

Help me to dig my way free of this!

Devastating Stalking Error #1: I discovered a way to prowl Scooter's posts to underground Mixed Martial Arts forums, where I could read rabid debates between him and other fighters and fans in which he pleads with his cohorts to fully recognize the death counts, begs them to approach the sport with some semblance of humanity, respect, and critical thinking, also asks bluntly, "I really wonder what draws me to this violent sport. . . ." He asks for respect for himself and for other forgotten fighters, describes the fact that boxers are prone to Parkinson's and grapplers to strokes due to constriction of the arteries of the throat during choke-out. At times he rails against the youthful upstarts. All of this in his manner of writing, his manner of typing, the manner that I love so well. As I began to sift through these postings—admittedly none from recent months—it was as if my heart were breaking open, I literally lost my ability to breathe. It took eight hours for me to gather myself to prepare for the final devastation of Stalking Error #2.

Devastating Stalking Error #2: Scooter's fight club posted photographs of the Ta-ta's Bar and Grill Car and Bike Show at which Scooter was the special guest star. I looked at pictures of Scooter in a winter coat. Pictures of Scooter having a large soda at an outdoor picnic table on the Ta-ta's parking lot despite the obvious chill in the air. Scooter gesturing warmly to overweight hometown teens in hoodies while standing in front of a minivan with neon ground effects. I could tell exactly where he was, given a prominent salad-bar landmark in the background. I could have walked there from the mall, or from my brother's apartment, if anyone ever walked anywhere in that town, if there were sidewalks. Scooter's winter beard is a bit ragged and graying. One of his fighter cohorts might have been missing some teeth, but perhaps I am too quick to typecast. The show seemed lightly attended. There were no pictures of him snuggling with the Ta-ta's girls in their short-shorts and strappy tops, but I do suspect that might just be because his fight club is a family-oriented business. Whatever semblance of my sanity remained, it has now been obliterated. I told the universe that if he didn't write to me by today I would become catatonic. He did not write to me today.

I have written a very long and crazed letter to him that is desperate, which I can't even show you because it is even more desperate and crazed than this dispatch, which is already clearly problematic. I am writing you this desperate and crazed dispatch in the hopes that it will draw me to my senses and stop me from sending off the desperate and crazed next letter to Scooter MacIntosh Ultimate Human. It's actually a very beautifully writ letter, but the beautifully writ

letter of an insane stalker. Ah, Johni, where did I go wrong?
Expletives,
Johnnie

HARD BODIES

Where do things stand with the punch-drunk pen pal? the sports reporter asks me on one of our drives to his gym.

Disastrous! It has now been over thirty-six hours since I have had a communication from him.

Yeah, it's probably over.

No, this is bad. I reread my last missive and found as few as five as many as seven grave tactical errors of correspondence, counting, of course, his lyrical misattribution of a Social Distortion song to Bad Religion, a minefield in which any comment or none meant certain doom. Beyond this I, 1) failed to praise his fighting style as adequately as I had done in previous missives; 2) talked about myself on too many occasions, forgetting the purpose of my mission is to bolster and support Scooter; 3) confessed that I found him easy to talk to—

Whoa, nightmare.

—4) presumed that further exchanges would follow rather than begging him to respond to me as I had done in previous missives; 5) described a work of digital art that involved animated butterflies, and additionally, or finally, 6) I made several unladylike bawdy puns at the end of the e-mail that I thought might be able to pull me out of the pitfalls of Strategic Error #5 (digital butterflies).

Yeah, guys hate sexy banter. If he got that far in the letter, anyway. It sounds long.

I do believe that Strategic Error #6 is a gray area, since I find it hard to believe that an ultimate fighter would hold tasteless humor against me, unless he wasn't getting the puns. Beyond the whole thing just being too long, too boring, and sent off too soon, I also failed to respond to the extremely moving story of his bad divorce, which he kindly shared with me. I fear I am at an end with Scooter. Is there any way to escape this tragedy?

The answer to that one is easy: Don't put yourself in it to begin with.

Joanna Howard

FROTTAGE, COLLAGE, REPORTAGE

When Scooter writes to me, he offers me one small piece at a time.

He writes, our hometown is the same place in some ways, but very changing in others.

He writes, being known is very difficult.

He writes that it seems the days are going too fast.

He writes that because his eyesight is damaged, he seldom reads.

He writes that everyone starts with a blank slate with him.

He writes that he had to write me back, but doesn't know why.

It is not as though Scooter is entirely a closed book. I look at this, and I've got only words to go by. I tell myself that if I could see his face, I could better understand his meanings, I could see what I might have said, and what I should not have said in my correspondence. I might not ask, "What did he mean?" so often. I began with words because it's what I could begin with, but words separate the meaning from the patterns, the forces of things, the action we might be taking, the action we hope we are taking, the action we seek to report.

I look at photographs of Scooter signing his autograph for his fans. I look at the posture in his torso and neck and imagine it responds to my correspondence—his attention to my reportage. It will do for the moment, but really, enough of this asynchronous fantasy making! I ask him questions, many questions, because I am begging to be told something, but asking a question is not supplicating. It appears to be brought in earnest, humble terms, but Alphonso knows it is already a command, an imperative. Questions demand attention. And they should be entered into with a certain integrity, a certain sincerity, and should not be just about absorbing the remaining bit of a man's already depleted resources. And yet I ask, and I ask, and I cannot stop myself.

LEAD WEIGHTS ON FISHING NETS/ TO THE PERILS OF WAKING

In execution of the classic armbar maneuver, one opponent captures the arm of the other and straightens or torques it to a degree that indicates to his victim that he is seconds away from snapping the arm at the elbow, or even tearing the limb from the body, thus giving the opponent time to tap out, submit, and save the limb.

It's like the animal kingdom, the sports reporter tells me as we walk into grappling class. You have to fend for yourself. If I help you too much, the others won't want to grapple with you. It makes you seem runty.

Uh-huh.

The instructor is the alpha. You don't talk when he talks. The skinny one with the trucker mustache: He is the second in command. You don't look him directly in the eye unless he invites it.

Uh-huh.

If he gets your arm or your throat, you tap, and you tap quick. Got it?

Got it!

And Johnnie, war face, OK? Concentrate. No giggling.

Every emotion a vertigo, Alphonso says. And by some miracle I find myself in the hands of someone whose intention it is to indicate that he can injure me, but that he won't do so unnecessarily. Such trust is twofold: He must also believe that I will actually communicate the point at which some part of me is ready to break.

MADAM, WE HAVE A SHELTER DOWNSTAIRS

I know my bag of tricks is small, but I am trying to use my skills as best I can to accomplish new feats of information exchange where Scooter is concerned. I should have learned long ago you can't force someone to correspond with you. Every effort is naturally destined to fail if invested only in the desire to extract something coherent and revealing, something later to be recorded, organized, and documented. Even if the reasons are personal rather than professional. And yet, I am still hopeful, even pigheadedly so.

To Scooter, I write, "I am trying to give you space to get your breath and recoup, to show you that my interest is honest, and not shallow. I am seeking your response, although I have no right to it. I'm seeking your attention, but I have no right to that either, which is probably why I am seeking it so desperately, as we sometimes scramble for things we shouldn't have." Even as I drop the letter in the mailbox, I imagine Scooter, in an azure gi, in the locker room of his gym, opening, scanning, and recoiling from my missive: Is this bitch off her rocker? I image him saying to his grappling companion. Dude . . . , his friend is saying, that shit is crazy. She is totally stalking you. Don't write back.

On other days, when I am feeling more confident, I imagine him, still in his azure gi, still in the locker room of his gym, but now seated alone on a long bench, perusing the words, grinning his imp grin, grinning at my catalog of his charms. On such days, I return, undaunted, to my correspondence.

Alphonso writes that the figure outside us, whoever he or she might be, that distant foreign body, unapproachable, across a great gulf of time or space, in another country entirely, or in a region we recognize but can't return to, this figure becomes a tinderbox or an open floodgate for our enthusiasms. I spend some time thinking about these possible descriptors. The first one consumes and destroys. The other can be opened or closed as needed to control the flow of a body. A restraint or barrier against the outpouring, or a sluice, through which it might pass.

Misadventure

Nicholas Grider

THIS IS NOT NECESSARILY a proclamation of anything. Though I thought perhaps you should know, being remote and discreet yet knowing all of the main players in the narrative, that is to say, all of us men in the apartment complex on San Vincente Boulevard. My recent correspondence has been full of false cheer and misleading matters and now is the time to set things right so you have a clear view of what transpired and can apply your own consideration to the matter.

Q. Whom is Martin addressing in his message(s)? Q. How would the recipient know all of the friendly neighbors at the apartment complex? Q. Why does Martin now feel compelled to report what has "transpired"? Q. What might be some reasons why his diction is so stilted and formal?

REPORT #1 (AUGUST)

I need to acknowledge both the paucity of my reports and their brief nature but inform you that much has happened that has been difficult to relay. Things have become as complex as they have become tenuous in certain regards concerning all of us now. I do not wish to delay reporting the matter with Bob. I do not hasten to it either. It's important to get right to the main line with what happened to Bob. First, however, I must point out that even given what happened, Bob's recklessness could not possibly have been Andrew's influence, Andrew now always dragging himself through the breezeways of the complex, always now alone, forlorn, bereft, such that you could stop him and give to him a hey what's going on and he would exchange it for silence. That's Andrew and Andrew's lot and this is not an acknowledgment that I had any influence over Andrew or how he might be thornlike to all of us with his malcontent by pulling us back into the unfortunate past after the catastrophe or that he may have been willful in his dolor even before the incident and neither can I try to explain or justify the thin smile that remained fixed to his blushless face as he drifted throughout the complex on the internal two-tiered breezeway that ringed the pool declining various offers and condolences from all of us. We've all taken things hard but it is not for Andrew to play the martyr. I wanted to make things clear to you. I don't want you to believe that Andrew played the main part in what happened but you should know that Andrew was closest to Bob, like brothers, as they say, almost like twins, and that each one of us has weaknesses of personality and that those weaknesses can, when searched for, be easily found. It could be said that there was an element of us egging each other on during the incident and now in handling the present and that Andrew thwarted the latter.

Nor is this an apology. I don't feel that it's mine to give. I did my part in what happened in the incident, which was on the surface pure misbehavior by all parts as you must soon concur, but in any event my part was but a part and nothing more. I was a participant. This is not a confession of guilt although I do feel remorse because it would be inhuman not to feel something over what happened to Bob, by which I mean the drowning, but the authorities are sure, I want to let you know, that it came to nothing like anyone, even Andrew, holding Bob's head under the water or willing into actuality what took place. The death was ruled misadventure. I played my part and the rope belonged to me, but I didn't purchase the liquor or even suggest the exercise, which in fact was suggested by Bob himself having spied a documentary on the Navy SEALs in which what we improvised is a strenuous test of athletic ability and willpower and quite beyond us and beyond even our intentions when Vincent said well if you want to prove you can do it let's find out, no time like the present.

As I've already indicated, the authorities concluded it was an accident. We've come to an agreement that it was negligence due in part to our drunken state and that we all share the guilt (such as it is) among us, those of us distracted by the fireworks display while Bob plunged, saying, and I can still hear his voice clearly, guys watch me I can really do this I was a champion swimmer at Indiana State. But we can't blame the alcohol any more than we can blame our agreement with Bob that this would be a good bet, and I'm disinclined to say whether in my heart I thought it was the right thing to do, because I must admit my thoughts had not touched right or wrong that festive night, much less safe or unsafe.

I was the partygoer poolside with the rope, however, rope I still had in my closet from hauling a mattress on my Honda a few weeks prior, a new one to replace what happened to its predecessor when Alex stayed over and things got out of hand. Which is an incident I will pass over to spare time and embarrassment. I supplied the rope that bound Bob's hands and feet, or rather wrists and ankles, but I did not prepare the rope or do the actual tying, which was a task left partly to Vincent (the ankles) but primarily to Adam (the wrists and the cutting of the rope in proper lengths) and it was our intention that we would take turns, each of us trying to prove himself in the manner of a Navy SEAL after a certain jesting fashion. I want to assure you that it was all meant in good fun and was not planned in any part beforehand and even, as I mentioned above, was Bob's suggestion, though we had all viewed the documentary on the Learning Channel a few weeks earlier at Bob's place in the complex, having chipped in to order a large deluxe pizza.

It may help for you to understand if I explain the exercise. SEALs in training were, in a certain segment of the documentary, bound hand and foot (hands behind the back) and directed to dive into a deep swimming pool and retrieve swimming goggles that had been placed there by the instructors. The intent of this challenge was, I believe, for the SEALs to demonstrate both mental toughness and physical strength and dexterity though a test of lung power might also have been at play; I don't remember the program clearly though I do remember Bob pointing to the screen and saying that looks easy, I could do that, and the rest of us telling him no, that it was more difficult than it looked, that if the prospective SEALs were having difficulty with it then it would be far beyond the literal and metaphorical reach of an ordinary civilian, even if he used to be a champion swimmer at Indiana State. But back to the program: The SEALs dove down headfirst, bound, and retrieved the goggles either with their toes or with their teeth; I must confess we were inebriated when we watched the program so my memory is not clear. What I can relay to you is that when Bob brought the subject up again poolside on July 3 during our party it was Bob's idea that he should use his teeth, and as we didn't have swimming goggles we would use a piece of the rope tied to a small donut-shaped weight, and I am not sure how the weight materialized but I believe it belonged to Andrew. No one claimed it after the incident.

And I don't feel as if I should belabor you with every detail but instead simply give you the report, so that you should know and hence come to your own conclusion. All six of us were inebriated; it was approximately 9:30 p.m. when Bob made his suggestion and I fetched the rope and scissors and Andrew(?) fetched the weight and Adam and Vincent tied the rope to the weight and let it sink at the pool's deep end and then led Bob up to the diving board, at the base of which his wrists and ankles were bound. He then, with a slow shuffling motion given his restricted stride, moved to the edge of the diving board and although it was darkening at that point and our complex is not very well lit I recall him turning back to us and smiling and saying here I go. And of course, mentioning again his swimming prowess. After that he plunged headfirst, bouncing himself off the board and into the deep in a wide arc. Just then, however, a fireworks display celebrating the holiday commenced very near to our complex and we all turned away from Bob to watch. After a few moments, and I can't quantify how long those moments were, Andrew called back to Bob to give it up and come watch the fireworks, which incidentally were magnificent and lasted an initially jubilant half hour. There was no sign of Bob, however, and Andrew turned back to watch, assuming Bob would rise up without the weight. After several more moments, given Bob's disappearance, several of us turned back again to spot Bob, who was still in the pool. Andrew and Adam and I moved from where we were on the deck chairs to get a closer look, and what we found was Bob, in a tilted column, floating head side up close to the bottom of the pool, motionless. Adam and I dived in to lift him out of the water, each of us at an elbow, and after doing so we bent his still-bound body over the pool's edge, positioned him, and after a few rudimentary shakes we were certain that Bob simply wasn't playing a cruel joke so Alex began CPR as Vincent dialed 911.

Of course things did not turn out well for us that night, not least of which for poor Bob, but when the EMT summoned the police and they questioned us we told them about the program and the boast and they (and we) all agreed that it was odd that he didn't even at least rise to the pool's surface but that in any case it was an accident. Death by misadventure, rather. And of course all of us in the complex who knew each other well enough to hail the others as friends felt deeply distressed and aggrieved about the entire situation, and all of us rehearsed scenarios in which we could have persuaded him not to go through with the boast, or, if you would have it differently, the dare. I should mention that the funeral was solemn and ostentatious and that all of us participants and friends attended and were acquitted of blame by Bob's family, with Bob's father even saying we always knew Bob was reckless, and that when he went it would be this kind of thing, though of course everyone had been hoping for a long life and a death by natural causes with only a few reckless acts to share as stories told to Bob's friends and family and future life partner and children, were he to elect to have them. This is to say that in a certain sense Bob's death was to be expected, but that nevertheless it shook us all.

Q. Why doesn't Martin feel the need to apologize? Q. Why does Martin describe Andrew at such length? Q. What could have contributed to the others' willingness to help Bob perform his stunt? Q. Even given the fireworks and the drunkenness, why did the group suddenly become so unobservant? Q. What is Martin trying to achieve in reporting everyone's agreement about Bob's recklessness?

REPORT #2 (OCTOBER)

One report following hard upon another is a decided strain, but I must inform you of what happened to Andrew last week, poor Andrew, wounded the most of all of us by Bob's death although he was not the main player in the sorrow of that holiday night. One day, approximately six weeks after Bob was buried, Andrew stopped attending our frequent social functions in the complex, both casual and formal. At first we thought he was nursing his grief privately and we gave him due space. In time, though, we became concerned because Andrew's car was never seen to move from the complex's lot, yet when Alex knocked, nearly pounded, on Andrew's door there was no answer. After a day or two of knowing the facts of the car and the lack of answer we decided to call the landlord and report our collective concern about the welfare of our friend and that he wasn't answering his door. The building manager let us in to Andrew's apartment and it was in the bathroom we found him having hung himself with the rope of our terrible night from the steel support beam of the shower. The building manager remarked that he must have suffered to go slowly like that and told us that he would take care of things and that we should wait outside the apartment.

The police arrived again, and again we explained the Bob incident and the origin of the rope and ventured that Andrew might have hung himself bereft for lack of Bob and remorseful over the whole enterprise and the small part he played in it. Of course we were all shaken badly. There was no explanatory note. And I will pass over the description of Andrew, poor slight Andrew, dangling from the shower support beam, lower legs bent against the ground, but I should impress upon you that it was a sight that won't soon leave my mind or the minds of our friends. Indeed, some of us began musing aloud about moving out of the building, a building with too many bad memories, two sorry deaths, and though Adam, for one, suggested he was thinking seriously about relocating, I decided to stay because of the on-the-main convenience of the location and the knowledge that surely things would end with Andrew, after the funeral, at which he had explained the Bob incident to Andrew's tearful mother and stoic younger brother. At the complex we began to meet less frequently for social occasions and so I was compelled to develop new relationships, both with others in the complex and with men I met online.

For a while, then, there was some resettlement, but things continued somewhat as they were during Andrew's curious absence, and inasmuch as all of us privately harbored thoughts of having reached out to Andrew or in some other way done something to save him from his terrible fate there was simply nothing any of us could do but move on and, as with Bob's incident, become more watchful over ourselves, our friends, and our collective behavior. I do, however, recall a passage of conversation with Bob before his decease during which he confessed that he had misgivings about Andrew's mental health, and that conversation still gives me qualms, primarily because it had the import of the hushed passage of key information, yet neither of us acted upon what we knew, Bob obviously being unable to do so after his death. Briefly, then, for a short while, things returned to a semblance of normalcy while we individually were put upon to consider our own lives and directions and try to understand what drove both Bob and Andrew to their distinct but still unfathomable decisions.

Q. Why does Martin pass over the "details" of the suicide itself? Q. What might be some reasons this report is much shorter and in a less formal diction than the first report? Q. Does it make sense for Martin to stay in the building if it holds so many bad memories? Q. Why doesn't Martin adequately account for his feelings about the suicide? Q. Why is the report of Andrew's funeral passed over?

Nicholas Grider

REPORT #3 (MARCH)

This, now, after a considerable length of silence, is less of a confession than a simple addition to the file on the course of our fates here on San Vincente, a report to give you the uncensored story of my own actions within the context of the deaths and what transpired in the weeks and months following Andrew's funeral. The hints of moving rendered themselves into facts, and, over the next months, all of our usual gang save myself (the others from whom you may have heard individual reports) left the complex to resettle at nearby complexes or duplexes in the city. This unfolded gradually, and there were promises made that we would all stay in touch, but those promises faded with the ensuing weeks as what once was a circle of friends brought together by proximity loosened until it dissolved entirely. This is not to say that I don't still hold occasional phone conversations with Vincent, Adam, or Alex but that things now are merely incidental to our collective past fellowship. There is a quality of strain in our asking after each other's activities and outcomes. And of course our salutations are becoming less and less frequent as the days whisper by us and we drift into our diverse futures. Hence this is not a confession of guilt or insinuation of error but rather a report meant to deliver you the entire as they say unvarnished truth of what is happening now that my proximal friends have slid quietly away and I am still seeking to understand the incidents, Andrew's less than Bob's because of the relative lack of mystery on Andrew's part other than direct motive but it is not for us to know, entirely, you must concur, what blossoms in the minds of others, as hard as we might try. And try we must.

After my contact with my old friends became tenuous, I began to forge new friendships via the Internet. As you are of course aware, I am relatively young and modestly comely and I strive to maintain an athletic build, and I sought the company of a number of men in the months following the end of our formal social circle. At first these were simply matters on the level of so-called first dates, nothing of them to relay other than that they proceeded with all the awkwardness and hesitation, explicit or implicit, any first date carries. And it should be noted that there were many first dates and no second or third dates. This was by intent. A relationship was not what I was seeking, even given the pleasure and promise I found in a few of the men with whom I had dinner or accompanied on varieties of taking-the-pressure-off day outings. Gradually, the encounters became more exploratory. At first I began to invite men back to my apartment in the complex for drinks after dates and I would casually tell them an "acquaintance" who had lived here had drowned, bound hand and foot, and I would supply this as a topic for conversation, probing the innocent men variously according to their personalities and inclinations as to how it must have felt for dear Bob and what must have gone wrong so badly to induce Andrew to suicide. These conversations were somewhat difficult, not least because it was an awkward subject to introduce. Most of the men merely remarked at what an awful thing it must have been to have witnessed the events at close hand, and offered the polite empathy of strangers before bidding me farewell.

Finally, then, in what for me was an admittedly bold move, I dispensed with the formality of the dates and bought some rope, a swimsuit resembling Bob's blue Speedo, and the brand of swimming goggles he wore. I roamed a different set of websites catering to different male needs and asked other varieties of men over to my apartment, informing them exactly of where my interests lay. I didn't get a great many responses, but the ones I received were filled with eagerness, and so commenced my investigation of the incident in earnest, queries made in order to know and report what goes on in the minds of other men. After what happened to unfortunate Bob, however, I was reluctant to go near the swimming pool other than to pass by it, glancing elsewhere, on my way to my one-bedroom abode, so when the men arrived at thc gate and I ushered them in to my apartment and invited them to disrobe and then don the swimsuit and goggles, I used the rope I had bought to bind them, wrists and ankles, and sat them in a chair with their ankles tied to a crossbar beneath the chair and their wrists tied together behind the chair back and down to the same crossbar. Then, I must report for the sake of being comprehensive, I told them I was planning to hold my hands over their nose and mouth for a few seconds on and off, ten or twelve seconds at most, nothing dangerous, and ask them to inform me how they would feel if they were bound like this and about to drown. Some of the men balked though I proceeded anyway, and some were more imaginative than others in giving me the diverse and often surprising answers I sought, but all of them, to the last (and this was nearly a dozen men) told me, in one form or another, pull down my swimming trunks and take hold of me and I'll tell you anything you want to know.

Q. Why does Martin feel obligated to report such personal information? Q. Why do you suppose Martin mentions his early dating? Q. Why might Martin have gone to such elaborate lengths to reenact a scene and oblige the men sexually? Q. Is any part of what happened in all three reports possibly eroticized for Martin? Q. What do you suppose are some of the things the men told him after he allowed them to breathe again?

Speck of Light

Bernadette Esposito

THE PSYCHIC FAIRS WERE HELD one Saturday a month in the ballroom of various Sheratons and Hiltons across suburban Chicago. Organized by a mother-daughter team named Jade and Journey, the fairs featured clairvoyants, palm readers, hand-writing analysts, iridologists, past-life readers, aura readers, astrologers, and numerologists. By the time TWA Flight 800 exploded over Long Island Sound, I had had everything from my natal chart to my Social Security number read.

The astrological synastry between my chart and TWA Flight 800's showed an excellent aspect for a union, love at first sight, in fact. As water signs on the cusp of fire signs, we would be drawn to one another like magnets. We would stimulate, vitalize, motivate, and believe in one another. And though I might be met with ambivalence, 800 would need my love and affection. The square between Jupiter and Pluto suggested that it might even try to change my way of viewing life.

"Your challenge number is *zero,*" said the numerologist. "You've struggled through the challenges of all the other numbers and now you are rewarded *free will.*"

I nodded.

"The responsibility of a zero challenge is tremendous," she added, taking both of my hands in her own. "Do you understand?"

I shook my head.

"You're a sponge. You collect frequencies." She paused to gauge my response. "It's like a radio," she said. "You can change the station. But you can also turn it off. Your challenge is to turn it off."

At the time of takeoff the natal chart for Flight 800 showed Pluto, ruler of death and explosions, entering Sagittarius, ruler of air travel. The ascendant moved into Aquarius. The angles of opposition closed in between Mercury and Uranus, auguring unexpected news. In my own chart, Saturn, the planet associated with limitations, restrictions, fears, and father figures, was positioned in the eighth house, the most powerful in the zodiac. Historically, Saturn's eighth-house placement in what ancient astrologers referred to as the House of Death warned of an unspeakable passing, possibly preceded by life-long suffering. Today astrologers take an enlightened approach, commonly referring to the eighth house as the House of Things Over Which We Have No Control.

I was working the late shift at Shoetown when I had my vision. The question of when Shoetown would be replaced by a more fulfilling minimum-wage job was a regular one at the fairs. Before Shoetown I scooped ice cream and handed out fliers dressed as ICEE Bear, a furry, eight-foot polar bear out of whose mesh and crinoline mouth I navigated the mall, shaking hands and handing out coupons to crying children.

"Beth," I said, moving from the Easy Spirit display. I picked up the Windex, spritzed it over the glass, and began wiping down the windows.

"I dreamed Karla and Julie were in an accident. First I saw the funeral, then there were the cars, then there was a hospital." It was like a reel rewinding itself until it got the story right. Like seeing a puddle of milk on the floor, then seeing the glass tip over, then seeing the glass caught before the milk spilled.

Beth looked at me.

"Maybe you were abducted," she suggested after we found out Julie and Karla were in the hospital recovering from the accident. I recalled earlier that year, on our way to Florida, the family had passed around Whitley Strieber's *Communion*, a nonfiction account of what Strieber believes was his abduction by nonhuman entities. My mom, who had been ruminating over a recurring dream in which a herd of deer stood over her supine body on their hind legs, said she almost felt relief when Strieber noted that some abduction memories come in the form of animal dreams.

"Are any of you dreaming of animals?" she asked.

My youngest sister, who was only three, dreamed that a big, round airplane picked me up in the field behind our house in the middle of the night and she had to walk home alone. "Oh, Lord," my mom said, remarking that not long before, the two of them were in the dentist's office and Kiley had open on her lap a feature article in *National Geographic* filled with photos of dead and dying deer. When my mom tried to close the magazine, Kiley protested. "No, mom," she said. "I love the dead deer."

Animals had not found their way into my dreams, but plane crashes had. In them decapitated engines and broken wings fell from burning fuselages. Fiery jet fuel streaked the twilight sky. Silhouetted bodies left hazy imprints on the ground below. Then, on the afternoon of July 17, 1996, TWA Flight 881 took off from Athens, Greece. Ten hours later, it arrived at JFK to warm weather and clear skies. That evening, after several maintenance inquiries, TWA Flight 881 became TWA Flight 800. Biblically speaking, the number 800 marks omega, the end of the divine alphabet, but I was not surprised to learn that 800 had a previous incarnation in 1964 as a crashed Boeing 707. Carrying seventy-three passengers and crew *to* Athens, the plane's Number 2 engine failed during takeoff. When the crew responded by aborting takeoff, the plane did not slow down quickly enough. It veered right, hit a pavement roller, and caught fire. Fifty people were killed. That the industry had not retired Flight 800, a gesture made out of respect for surviving family members, seemed an audacious revolution of the karmic wheel.

For all its impartiality, the airline industry is not above observing some rituals and superstitions when it comes to numbers. Taking stock in the number eight, conventionally believed by most cultures to be one of good fortune, is not among them. But the number thirteen is. While the Egyptians believed the number thirteen represented immortality—with twelve steps on the ladder of life, taking the thirteenth step meant crossing over death and into eternal life—the Christians associated it with Judas Iscariot's unwelcome arrival at the Last Supper in which he becomes the thirteenth dinner guest. On Air France, Air Tran, Continental, KLM, Iberia, Cathay Pacific, and Thai Airlines there is no row thirteen. On all Nippon Airways there are no rows four, nine, or thirteen, because in Japanese the numbers four—"shi"—and nine—"ku"—sound like the words for "death" and "torture." I didn't believe that airplanes crashed because they were with or without certain rows, but dates and flight numbers left me suspect. Five different flights whose numbers were 191 had, over the course of three decades, crashed, killing a total of 460 people.

All of this eerily followed a palm reading in which I was told that I was not from here, that my soul—a very old one, indeed—was connected to the stars, possibly Arcturus. "When you hear sounds in your ears or see little dots across your eyes," said the psychic, "it means the Star People are trying to communicate with you." Then he said, "Your lifeline is long. Your headline is strong. This line means you have a strong will, but little self-control. Make a fist. You can't let go. I see someone with dark hair and light eyes. He won't make it. You see auras. You knew him in a past life. Ask the ghost what it wants. Light white candles. Sprinkle salt around the outside of your house. Burn cedar incense. Ring a bell.

"You are a stream jewel. Streams are mediators. They like to counsel people. Jewels are analytical, methodical, cut-and-dried, logical. Your grandma *on the other side* says he ain't no damn good. You are here to burn a debt. You bottle everything up until you explode. I see someone with sand-colored hair and light eyes. He's holding a newspaper. I see someone jumping up and down reaching. He's angry. Uri Geller could bend metal with his mind. You can too. Your card is the Chariot. Your number is seven. Your motto is 'I perceive.'"

In an industry where thirteen is considered middle-aged for an airplane, eight hundred was old. Many of its internal systems, including the miles of high- and low-voltage wires held together in thick bundles, had gone unchecked since their installation twenty-five years earlier. Given the complexities of airplane wiring, routine inspections are not performed. With the exception of some fatigue cracks that did not play a role in the breakup sequence, 800 was structurally sound and healthy: It had given no warning of mechanical failure.

That evening at 6:00 p.m., when passengers at JFK began to board, the tarmac was hot. The corneas, ice packed in Styrofoam and stored in the cockpit, were ready for transplant. On their way to Paris from a Baltimore eye clinic, they could survive up to thirty hours. As the cockpit crew prepared for its 7:00 departure, a notification arrived from the terminal: Bags had been checked, but the passenger could not be found. Since the bombing of Pan Am Flight 103 over Lockerbie, Scotland, in 1988, FAA regulations stipulate that a plane can only be cleared for takeoff after all passengers with checked luggage have boarded. For a total of two hours and twenty minutes, air conditioners, located beneath a near-empty center wing tank, kept the cabin comfortable. Then, at 8:02, because of the corneas, air-traffic control declared TWA Flight 800 a "lifeguard" flight. At 8:19 p.m., it was cleared for takeoff; the missing passenger had been on board all along.

Thirteen minutes after the captain took Flight 800 into the sky,
Two minutes after the flight engineer turned off the cross-feed switch,
Thirty seconds after the second officer increased thrust,

At 13,800 feet,

Between the wings, beneath the business class, where Susan Hill and Judith Yee, Daniel Cremades and Matthew Alexander and Deborah and Doug Dickey sat, where newlywed Monica Omiccioli rested her head on her husband's shoulder,

The floor lifted: Tearing metal. Snapping cables. Shattering glass. Tiny fractures raced up the walls. Overhead bins popped open. The forward lavatory ripped loose chunks of the plane's belly.

The sound took fifty seconds to reach land. When it did, it caused plates to rattle on shelves twelve miles away.

Those in the forward lavatory did not know the plane had been severed. Those in the rear saw twilight where the front of the plane should have been. Some passengers were shaken free. Others, their seats ripped from the mounting tracks, were tossed out. Deborah and Doug Dickey, sucked through an opening in the bottom of the plane, fell nearly two and a half miles, smashing into the ocean at 120 miles per hour.

Passengers seated in the rear of the plane were pushed back in their seats when TWA Flight 800 continued to climb fifteen hundred feet. The right wing folded up. The left wing snapped off. As the plane lost momentum and began to drop, these passengers were forced forward. The farther the tail section of the plane fell, the faster it went, colliding with the ocean at four hundred miles per hour.

A wide, fiery curtain. An acrobatic dive. A speck of light pitching down.

Of the nineteen people who survived the explosion, some lived through the fall, and some, briefly, survived the plunge into the Atlantic.

Not Daniel Cremades. His face was damaged, his bones fractured.
Not Susan Hill or Monica Omiccioli's husband. They were torn to pieces.
Not Judith Yee, though some of her bones were recovered.
And not Matthew Alexander, though some fragments of him
Remain.

Hundreds of people heard what they variously described as an explosion, a boom, a roar, a thunderlike rumble. Hundreds more—some on beaches and in boats, others who were looking out windows of airplanes and restaurants—described what *seemed* or *appeared* or *looked* like a white light, an orange ball of light, a ball of flames, a hot-pink flash, fireworks, a flare, a shooting star streaking upward against the twilight sky. This was an era when airplanes were frequently conspiring against their crews and passengers. Every few months a new catastrophe, more spectacularly conceived than its predecessor, fell from the sky and covered the newspapers. In 1996, the most deadly year for commercial air disasters on record—1,187 people lost their lives—TWA Flight 800 outdid them all. It became the nation's worst next to the 1979 crash of American Airlines Flight 191. It surpassed the mysterious 1991 and 1994 Boeing 737 crashes about which investigators were still baffled by the sudden lateral roll and subsequent drop each plane took from the sky on approach to its respective airport. It even upstaged the ValuJet crash in the Everglades two months earlier, in which federal regulators, the day before TWA Flight 800 exploded, moved to restrict oxidizers that feed fire in the absence of air.

But Flight 800 didn't dive nose first or roll out of the sky. An uncontained fire did not erupt beneath the cabin. Its Number 1 engine did not separate from the pylon. And its crew did not encounter an uncommanded rudder hardover from which it could not recover. How an otherwise healthy twenty-five-year-old airplane—that had logged 16,000 flights and 93,000 hours, weighed in at a hefty 590,441 pounds at takeoff, and was valued at eleven million dollars—exploded was about to become the top news story of the year and the fourth most closely watched story since 1986. One reporter, alluding to the four-year, $400 million investigation that would ensue, noted that it might have even caused the same national obsession as the O. J. Simpson trial, "if there were something akin to Court TV—something called Hangar TV, featuring blow-by-blow, you-are-there presentation of the evidence as it goes before a jury of scientists, engineers, and law enforcement agents all trying to reach a verdict on what caused the plane to explode."

I was working at a coffee kiosk when ABC broke the news. "A 747 taking off out of JFK carrying 230 passengers to Charles de Gaulle Airport in Paris exploded in midair. The Coast Guard is reporting no survivors, and eye witnesses reported 'a big fireball with pieces coming off of it.'"

The anchorman paused.

"It is at this point," he added cautiously, "that we begin to enter the realm of speculation."

Coffee customers were abuzz with theories. Randy, a clairvoyant, cited a surge of UFO activity over Long Island Sound replete with reports of tubular-shaped objects blinking green and blue. MuRasha's beings of love and light indicated that 800 had intersected with an invisible temporal axis, the result of a top-secret government experiment involving Einstein's unified field theory, the particulars of which included a vortex between Montauk and Philadelphia and a rift in the space-time continuum.

"An FAA source has told ABC News late this evening that there was no distress call," the anchorman said. "'Under those circumstances,' said our source, 'there are only two things that could have caused the plane to explode in midair: an explosive device—that is, a bomb—or a collision with another aircraft.'"

The anchorman went on to reassure the American people, who in less than seventy-two hours would be treated to reports of the FBI's activation of a joint terrorism task force, reports of a telephone call placed to a Tampa television station by a member of a jihad, reports of a letter warning of an attack signed by the Movement for Islamic Change, reports that the FBI had received 750 calls from its toll-free information line, reports that showed an "errant blip" falling with the plane on the radar tapes, and reports of a preliminary examination of a wing fragment for bomb residue by the Bureau of Alcohol, Tobacco, Firearms, and Explosives turning up what was anonymously described as a "borderline reading."

But terrorist activity, hijackings, and shoot downs never counted for me as crashes. Neither did the *Hindenburg* nor the Space Shuttle *Challenger*, which I watched explode on TV in sixth grade. Smaller aircraft disasters such as those connected to Cessnas and Beechcraft, the Learjet and the Concorde, while having made interesting survival stories and educational tools, held little interest. Moreover, cargo jets like the flower-laden 747 that crashed near the Colombian capital, killing two on the ground, or the El Al Air carrying "consumer goods" and Israeli military equipment that crashed into two high-rise apartments in Amsterdam, killing the four pilots and thirty-nine tenants, did not pique my curiosity. When Randy and MuRasha asked why, I told them that my concerns were *accidents*: unforeseen mechanical failures, pilot and air-traffic control errors, weather, bird strikes, design flaws, and lightning affecting those airplanes carrying 1.09 billion passengers on eighteen million flights per year. I also told them that the crash of TWA Flight 800 did nothing but wrest my numerological misgivings: Bad things happen with the number eight.

Almost a decade had passed since TWA Flight 800 exploded when on August 8 I boarded Air France flight 7685 to Paris. Add seven and six and eight and five, and you get thirteen and thirteen. Add thirteen and thirteen, and you get twenty-six. Add two and six, and you get eight—the number representing death and resurrection. Flight 7685 had been delayed. I sat in the terminal reading *The Letters of Abelard and Heloise*. When I finally took seat 22F on an over-wing window, the summer sun had dropped below the horizon. The blinking lights along the starboard wing spread out before me. The engines hummed. The slats retracted. A few moments later we muscled into the twilight sky. Just as our heading brought us over the Mediterranean a loud boom shook the plane. The engine, obscured by fire and smoke, clung to the wing of the Airbus. By then, TWA Flight 800 had been dredged from Long Island Sound, reconstructed in a Calverton hangar, and brought to the NTSB training center, where it was to begin a new life as a teaching tool for air-disaster investigators.

At the time the *Onion* had run an article uproariously and inappropriately titled, "TWA Flight 800: Rebuilt, Ready to Return to Air," in which fictitious Director of Safety Walter Gorman implores the audience to "turn tragedy to triumph" and "give Flight 800 a second chance—we're confident you'll like what you see." The article complimented what looked like a haphazardly executed diorama: jagged lines, mismatched pieces, dangerous edges of pitted metal and exposed beam. If the irreverence of the photo somehow belied the scrupulousness with which the ninety-foot section of fuselage was salvaged and reconstructed, it was quickly allayed by the byline touting it as the most "complex recovery and reconstruction effort ever undertaken in the history of aviation." Even if you know nothing about dredging and reconstructing twenty thousand shattered pieces of a 747—some the size of a quarter—the photo is a sobering reminder that the first requirement for such an undertaking is not the thirteen trawl lines scouring forty miles of ocean floor, the tethered underwater robots linked to a ship by an umbilical cable, the side-scan sonar, the laser-line scanning equipment, or the EGIS supersniffer, capable of detecting as little as one-billionth of a gram of explosive. It is an initial explosion so immense it had fused the DNA of those passengers seated over the wings.

Survival Factors is a branch of air-disaster investigation. Rarely involved with the cause of the accident, its job is to document *Substantial Damage* to the aircraft and impact forces and injuries to passengers and explain them in the context of the accident. Before entering the hangar where two hundred tons of the 800's reconstructed fuselage reside, Jason, a member of the Survival Factors Group, delivers a talk on TWA Flight 800, an *Accident* the group has designated *Not Survivable*. He doesn't want to say, Oh by the way, ignore the charred remains of Flight 800 sitting over there. He has a knack for making light of the macabre. About a surviving passenger of American Airlines Flight 1420, an MD-80 that overran the runway, caught fire, and broke in half, killing eight passengers and one crew member, he says, "And this guy, ejected from 3B, managed to crawl one hundred feet still strapped to his seat. We called him Turtle Man."

The term *Accident* falls under a federal regulatory code describing "an aircraft having undergone *Substantial Damage* or a person suffering *Death* or *Serious Injury*." *Substantial Damage*, or "damage that affects the structure or the performance of the aircraft, or damage that requires major repairs or replacement of parts" might include a broken propeller or a broken rudder. *Substantial Damage* is sometimes, but not always, coupled with *Death* or *Serious Injury*. Turbulence, which has its own severity index, can cause *Death* or *Serious Injury* to unbuckled passengers without causing *Substantial Damage* to the aircraft. In 1997 turbulence encountered by United Airlines Flight 826 killed one passenger during level flight and left three others *Seriously Injured*. For an injury to qualify as *Serious*, it must require hospitalization for more than forty-eight hours within seven days of the *Accident*, result in a fracture, cause hemorrhaging, damage nerves, muscles, or tendons, or involve an internal organ, second- or third-degree burns, or burns covering five percent of the body surface. In some cases if you prevent an injury, you will prevent an accident. Engine explosions are not considered *Substantial Damage* and are, therefore, not *Accidents*. These are called *Incidents*, "occurrences other than *Accidents*, associated with the safety of the operation of the aircraft." Not all *Incidents* are noteworthy. Those that are are called *Reportable Events*. From a Survival Factors perspective, an *Incident* becomes a *Reportable*

Event when there is "a sustained loss of power by two or more engines, an in-flight fire, when the event requires the evacuation of a multi-engine aircraft necessitating the use of the emergency exits and inflatable slides, when a force transmitted to occupants through the seat and restraint system exceeds the limits of human tolerance, or when the structure in the occupant's immediate environment does not remain substantially intact." *Limits of Human Tolerance* and *Substantially Intact* are not defined under federal regulatory codes.

Survival Factors takes a quantitative approach to survivability, one whose boundaries are as distinct as mathematical proofs: A crash is *Survivable* when no passengers die, *Not Survivable* when no passengers survive, and *Technically Survivable* when at least one passenger survives. Technical Survivability is tricky. It means that the crash itself was survivable, but poor communication, lack of preparedness, and insufficient evacuation plans resulted in the loss of lives. One example is the US Air Flight 1493 crash at LAX in 1991 in which nineteen passengers died of smoke inhalation after two passengers in a fistfight over who got to jump first obstructed an emergency exit, while others obstructed aisles trying to get luggage out of overhead bins. Another is United Flight 232, whose survivors were seated between the three breakage points. Those who watched live coverage of the crash of United Flight 232 as it tumbled over the runway, broke into four pieces, and landed upside down in a cornfield, killing 112 passengers, remember thinking that the survival of the remaining 184 aboard, including the pilots, was not only against the odds, but downright miraculous. Leslie Roth, whose three children were flying alone on Flight 232, recalls television commentators asserting, "Nobody could survive *that*." When Roth was later told that at least two of her children had survived, she said, "What does that mean? What *is* survival?"

Jason says a whole day might be spent naming crashes that are *Technically Survivable* and only a fraction of a day naming crashes that are *Not Survivable*: ValuJet 592, Swissair 111, Egypt Air 990, US Air 427, American 191. TWA Flight 800 is an exception. It's here at the training center to teach investigators how to use reconstruction techniques to solve and prevent future accidents. When he asks if anyone in the room worked the crash of Flight 800, three men from the Federal Aviation Administration quietly acknowledge themselves. If the FAA has anything to offer, they should please speak up. To the rest of the room, he asks:

Why do you remember TWA Flight 800?

The FBI and the NTSB battled each other on TV, says one of the Boeing people.

The media got involved, says a quality assurance instructor.

The government got involved, says Boeing.

Terrorists planted a bomb in the passenger cabin, says a Southwest Airlines Regulatory Analyst.

The navy hit it with a missile, says a cabin safety inspector.

The center wing tank exploded, says a senior air-safety investigator.

Jason affirms all of these by stating that the investigation into the crash of Flight 800 was not at all typical. A typical accident investigation is led by the National Transportation Safety Board, an independent federal agency made up of five members who are nominated by the president and approved by the senate for five-year terms. When the NTSB arrived the morning after the crash with the intention of ensuring that it would not be overlooking a mechanical failure, the FBI had begun a criminal investigation. Unbeknownst to the NTSB, it had also begun documenting what would become fifteen hundred pages of eyewitness accounts. The accounts would not only become evidence suggesting that *something* had been used to bring down Flight 800, they would generate enough public interest for it to become necessary to determine exactly *what* those witnesses saw.

A witness was defined as anyone who reported, firsthand, hearing or seeing something in the sky in the general vicinity of the accident at the approximate time of the crash. Of the 755 potential witnesses, 736 fit the definition. Of these, 670 were classified as "sight witnesses." "Sight witnesses" were further classified as "streak of light" witnesses and "fireball" witnesses. A "streak of light" was defined as an object moving in the sky that could variously be described as "a point of light, fireworks, a flare, a shooting star." A "fireball" was defined as "one or more balls of fire in the sky that appeared in the sky after the streak of light."

Jason projects onto a screen a time-lapse computer model simulating

800's initial ascension and explosion at 13,800 feet. The nose breaks off. The forward fuselage breaks off. The engines still powering the plane cause it to ascend at least fifteen hundred more feet for nearly thirty seconds before the wings break off and the rest of the plane falls two and a half miles into the sound. What cannot be seen is the tiny fractures traveling at about six thousand feet per second, so fast the entire event took less than two minutes:

8:31:11 Center wing tank explodes.
8:31:15 Plane banks left. Front section breaks off. Fuselage continues up, banks left.
8:31:25 Fuselage rolls right, falls toward water.
8:31:53 Left wing breaks.
8:32:05 Fuselage hits water.
8:32:50 Front section hits water.

Two hundred and fifty-eight witnesses saw a streak of light. Five hundred ninety-nine saw a fireball. Two hundred saw the fireball split in two. Four hundred sixty-nine of them were on land, one hundred ninety-four on boats, forty in aircraft, and ten surfing or swimming. Not one of them realized that what they had just witnessed was a plane crash.

Craquelure
Ryan Flaherty

THROUGH MY WINDOW, THE CURVING river is like the rim of a door, slightly ajar—coming in at the bottom left before oxbowing halfway up and across the glass, around the marina and then on toward the enormous, empty mills. The river is frozen and cracking and in the low moonlight a shadow seems to haunt the edges like the draft between a door and its frame. The tide drains out from under the creaking carapace of ice, the edges crackle inward, the rims glint like spittle on the frozen dead.

Outwardly, I look calm (I can see myself faintly reflected in the glass), but within, an animation is picking up and collapsing. I had tried to fall back asleep, but every few seconds it churned, two armies crashing together in an anxious geography of foreshortened wills. Metal and mud-thick shadows, muscles losing grip, something plunged into the long flinching neck of a horse, its wide orbs, black as always, but crazed with ground slipping out from under. The body both real and abstracted. Its violences and illnesses close as wool to skin. The dark angle the body cuts into catastrophe. I blink and it starts again—an inverse breathing that seems endless, the imagination agape before the wide scales of death.

Two nights later, something in the wind wakes me and the commotion starts up again—a conscription, a peasant mass funneled both against and toward empire. It plays for a time in my head and collapses. Bolstered with the certainty that lingers on from dreaming, I am certain that this war is somewhere in an opaque Chinese century. I get up from bed, go into the study, and click on the lamp. The window is a dark mirror, then a bath of reflected light.

Ryan Flaherty

From the stack of books on ancient bloodletting that I took out of the library—the Crusades, the Mongols, the Spartans, the Visigoths—I pull *Medieval Chinese Warfare 300–900* by David A. Graff. I skim the index for "banditry," "conscription." I find "An Lushan; rebellion of" and read:

> The rebel army was well supplied with horses. . . . It encountered no effective resistance as it swept down through Hebei toward the Yellow River, covering an average of about twenty miles a day. . . . With a hastily raised army of sixty thousand conscripts and volunteers, Feng Changquing attempted to block the rebels' advance at the Hulao Pass, the same strategic chokepoint where Li Shimin had halted Dou Jiande in 621. On this occasion, however, the terrain advantage was not enough to compensate for the qualitative imbalance between the two sides, and Feng's untrained rabble was trampled beneath the hooves of An Lushan's veteran cavalry.

Above this text is "*Map 19*, North China during the An Lushan rebellion, AD 755–63."

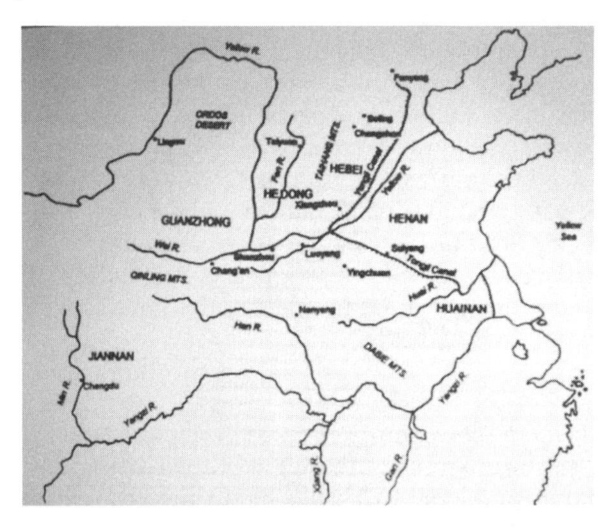

I squint to lose the names and whether the lines are of rivers, shorelines, or Great Walls, until it looks like the page has shattered. I close the book, thinking of feet marching in rhythm before breaking into dissonance, before becoming an undifferentiated thunder. I turn off the light. Outside, the powdery grains of snow shift, the wind twists, holds off, and again bruises into my window.

*

I warm in bed and continue refining the scene. A morass of men clogs the high plain, awaiting the thunder of An Lushan's rebellion to be squeezed through the narrow gap of the Hulao Pass. They watch the high ridge to the north, where the bare-rocked mountains dip down, waiting, though the rebels aren't expected until tomorrow or the next day. The Imperial Army is making a last stand in a series of last stands. Fires dot the formless, undulating mass of men, smoke drifts, the weight of ash drifts, rice congee boils and is ladled out. The few professional soldiers, with their padded leather armor, are showing the peasants how to hold the lance, how to parry.

Two days later, still researching, still refining, and the snow has settled as a fine crust over the backyard and in the joints of the trees. The sky is a clear, hard blue glaze. I want to get close to the river. I follow the path I have worn to the compost pile but veer left and across the bowl of deep snow that tops my boots. Under the limp and yellow willow tree, there is an opening in the bushes where a ramp drops down the five feet of bank to the river bottom. There, tree roots strain in the exposed mud, and flat, colorless rocks slope gently toward the reeds, and then the channel.

The ramp is a narrow foot wide with a rough foot of snow following the contours of the slope and the ribs of cross slats. I step on the edge, and when my feet start to slip, I drop to my haunches and grip the sides with my bare hands. Cold blisters and shunts up my forearms. I slide from cross slat to cross slat, feet plowing a trough, arms now straight out to steady me, waving around for balance. As the ramp descends, it twists—my hands are red, my feet feel drugged with cold. Halfway down, I start to skid more off the edge than down the incline. I try to jump the rest of the way before I am dumped off, but my left ankle catches on the ramp, and when my right foot lands, it immediately slips out from under me.

I land, back first, in the river bottom's cushion of snow. I pull myself out of the imprint my fallen body has made and scuff through the drift the wind has swept onto the shore. I want to see the ice. Near the edge, where a fine dusting foothold of snow still clings, the ice is brittle, more like a heavy frost. Then tectonics, sheets pushed up from under, scaffolding of frost heaves, broken jaws, bleaching and clouding grays.

Near my foot, a leaf is either half swallowed in the ice or is being pushed out like a spearhead from a body. I peel back the thin ice sheath with its mirror image of the leaf, the rib curving and veining. The warmth of my thumb and the warmth of my forefinger bore through the ice until they meet. I hold it up to the sky and look through the hole: clarity surrounded by a blurring refraction. I spin it around my finger until it breaks apart from momentum, catching half in my left hand as the other half skids frictionlessly over the ice. On my tongue it melts a seeping musk of winter, a coldness. The orange nibs of grass all lean downstream like parted, thinning hair. It is easy to imagine the landscape as a body in magnification and exposure. Flaking, chapping, a boil bursting where the skin of ice has been pulled taut over a boulder. A body in repose.

On my hands and knees, I look into the capillary patterns of ice. Cracks, deep and shallow, shatter and corkscrew. I trace the wandering lines, wondering if I am mistaking divisions for binding seams. I look past the white craquelure between pores on my numb, red-pinched skin to follow the lines in the ice up, around, choosing the left fork, then the right, an endless peripatetic unraveling, looping out and back to where I started. The body in decay.

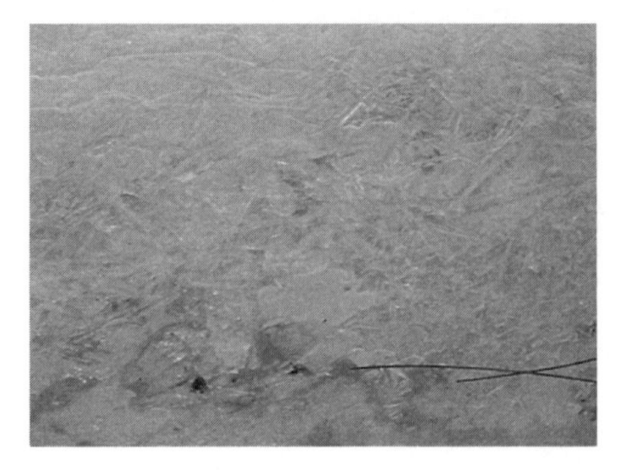

The blade of the pike is like a scythe, so the peasant feels less alone. With one end of the six-foot pole braced between his feet, the heavy blade swings above him, and he has to be vigilant that some quirk of momentum doesn't drop it on the head of one of the men standing around him. This awareness keeps him preoccupied and distracted from the cold and how his fingers feel like short, useless stubs of twine. I imagine rising above him to look across the field of tightly packed men, pikes eddying like reeds, all facing one way: the exit of the Hulao Pass. Sixty thousand mostly silent men—shifting from foot to foot because of the cold and an almost impenetrable fear that keeps threatening to paralyze them. Listening for it. From the few horses, men yell orders into the wind, and the immense distance dwarfs the tiny radius of their voices in the mass. Every one of them is terribly alone, staring toward the still-empty pass where reverberating hoofbeats are just starting to avalanche down on them.

Beyond the fracturing near the shore, the ice firms up and marbles mud and milk and a dark crystalline. I test my way farther out, tapping the ice, stepping and waiting to see if it holds. Under me a series of deepening dusks bruise and creak. I lie down on my back and stare straight up at the dome of blue. Space. In my periphery, I can see the wiry black fingerings of tree limbs along the river, briars stitching, desiccated ferns, and shadows tilting toward me. It is easy to imagine eternity. We do it every day, constantly. It is our normal mode of passing from morning to night and through the night to morning. Every day is wide with our imagined unendingness, our willful ignorance. Even when shocked by some dead end of future metastasizing toward us, we cannot recover for a time our equilibrium. Like now. A loved one is ill. Or not. I am ill, or not. Dying, or not. Calls and appointments await while deep in the body pain calcifies its hard shell. Calendar books stretch ahead into next year, but locally moment to moment seems insurmountable. Illnesses real and imagined and unknown bring the present to the present.

It seems that lying still on the ice is a perfectly reasonable response to all of this. Just as, earlier, on the bus, I was thinking about the unstoppable momentum of hooves. It was crowded and I stood, hung really, with both arms stretched above my head, gripping the metal bars that run the length of the bus. The seats were full and the fluorescence from the faint lights pressed like a migraine. Silent faces on either side stared past me, their knees touching my legs as we were all rocked in the bus's accelerations and stops. Behind me and before me, others stood, and there was no way not to brush an elbow along the small of a back or feel a knee press against a knee. The compactness, the claustrophobia seemed accurate to waiting in the crowded mountain pass. I tried to imagine a sudden vaulting into violence. I closed my eyes and imagined swinging body into body until chaos triumphed and self was lost. I imagined myself becoming diffuse, the ground coming up to meet me as gravity lurched. The bus tumbling over and over. Like a glass bead a disoriented peasant had been holding for luck, until the hooves started driving the men back, and in a panic he dropped it under foot and hoof and mud.

In an archaeological compendium of statues, buildings, vases, and elements of filigree, *Asia: Forms and Styles*, I find, in the China section, a pattern partially titled "The mystic or endless knot."

For some time this morning, I traced the central figure over and over, a never-ending progression. I am continually surprised by its representation and persistence. Periodically, my finger and eye coordination slipped and I found myself following one of the additional loops and ribbons to a dead end. I wondered why they were there, strange tails and parentheticals. Were they camouflage? A nod toward hard realism? I sat looking and tracing for an hour, the endless figure, the odd additions, and the implication of its title.

427
The mystic or endless knot (or entrails)

The ice's zero Celsius is absorbing into my hands, into the backs of my legs, and my hatless head, where a thin, battling buffer is oscillating between the heat of my skull melting the ice and the ice refreezing and gripping strands of my hair. The sun is warm against my closed eyes as it ticks toward the horizon. Under me, the ice bellows and moans apocalyptically in the glacial current and tide. The philosopher Mo Tzu from the Warring States Period says about war: "It exhausts the people to an immeasurable degree," and I am exhausted by warring. I dare the ice, decide now: Either open under me or don't.

The field is now still. The heat of battle and blood has dissipated into the elements. A tiny wind slips through manes, beards, flaps of skin, loops of intestines, hoof-crushed folds of brain. All is finality for a time before the chemical reactions of decay start the unraveling. Even the carrion eaters haven't yet arrived. No witnesses and nothing living to witness. A brief clarity, a round hole bored into a jagged and insistent continuum like the ice I spun on my finger. And for a moment I slip just into sleep. A passage of time glides down the river, and right over me, past my closed eyes, over my form, as if I were any other incongruity of ice or riverbank or tree. It goes unrecorded. Until a chill shivers me awake. A second of surprise as my mind backtracks and remazes to me, here, on the river. When I realize that I am on ice, becoming ice, I push myself up and draw my legs under me. A deep whine shudders and the ice shifts noticeably against my frantic weight. I freeze, awaiting the verdict. The sun is falling behind the hill where houses and mills hunch; a shadow is creeping across the ice. Panic sweeps through me as my head seems less and less mine and more like an inanimate slab pitching forward. I flatten onto my stomach, my numbed limbs moving a half second after my thought, my fingers clumsy as I push myself back to my hands and knees. Light catches on three hairs the ice has pulled from my head, a thievery I didn't feel as I can't feel the back half of my skull. I crawl like a beetle toward shore and when I finally stand, I sway, searching for equilibrium. The back half of my head feels like stone dragging me backward. I slip and stagger up the ramp and stumble across the yard.

Inside, I run first cool and then increasingly warm, painful water over my hands. I drink a glass of tepid water from the tap, not wanting to wait for the kettle to boil, the tea to steep. Had I been tired enough, I think, had the creeping chill fused more quickly to my slumber. I rub my damp hair and cold scalp, and it feels like a pile of wet abandoned twine, certainly like it is the flesh of someone else. Blood thumps in my temples and slowly the disconnect is being bridged with the tingle of needlework, threads of warmth drawn from bone to surface and back to bone. I sit, watching the still landscape out my window sink into purple and more obscuring dusk as my head goes from frozen and not mine to spark under the skin to fierce pain to immolation to raging fire to awareness, until I am once again alive and, once again, mine.

The Thief

Karen Lepri

Jealousy is an equation involving three permutable (indeterminable) terms: one is always jealous of two persons at once: I am jealous of the one I love and of the one who loves the one I love. The odiosamato *(as the Italians call the "rival") is also loved by me: he interests me, intrigues me, appeals to me (see Dostoevsky's* Eternal Husband*).*

—Roland Barthes, *A Lover's Discourse*

The thief came into the house, and came and came into.

The thief came into the house and there was nothing but red tulips hanging from the ceiling. Nuts hidden by squirrels. My fist crashing into his nose.

The thief came into the house. You were sleeping, no I was.

The thief came in, suddenly our neighbor, knocking, I let him.

The thief in our house after seventeen weeks training for the army—everyone knew he was leaving any day.

The thief came into the house and cats devoured him.

The thief came in and let me pummel every part of his body that seemed made of granite and the rocks were laughing. He was in no hurry.

Karen Lepri

The thief came into the house, me.

The thief came in and received directions to take the elevator to the fourth floor.

The thief came into some wealth so he ate shrimp with sauces of ground chilies, nuts, and spices from the cabinets.

He came in and sat and I slept and he slept. In our dreams we attended the same festival or wedding or some celebration where we did not know each other but tried hard to understand how we might.

The thief, he returns.

The thief came and went and came and went regularly like a festival or parade such that we began to prepare for his arrival. Tulips in every color.

The thief entered, and instead of stopping him, I just kicked her in my sleep.

The thief came into the house and we stripped down to the bones, our blood a deluge over everything we owned.

He came, and she mumbled, and I huddled closer.

Once, a thief came into the house. All he took: an empty vase and some blood in a jar.

A thief entered the house, sat on my chest, said threatening things, and I just lay there, yelling at myself, Wake up, there's a thief in the house, you fool.

The thief came into the house and started up the record player. I could hear Pergolesi but we were still at the party where the host didn't understand why we'd come empty-handed.

He came in through the front door, porch door, basement door, windows, skylight, and the big hole around the pipe under the kitchen sink.

The thief came into the house and finished painting what we'd started. Then he took what we'd started, what he'd finished.

The thief came into the house and the authorities came into the house and then the thief came in again.

We set up cameras to study his ways, figure out why we fumbled the keys each time we came in.

The thief came in ghostlike, so we could see him and through him, and his form bumped along the edges of ours, up and over or around if we crossed his path.

The thief came into the house like always. He knew where everything we lost was hiding.

The thief came so we pulled out the script, put on our wedding costumes, and slowly paraded the halls, chanting promises that echoed alien in our ears.

Karen Lepri

I'd told you to seal it up, that my dreams were entering not through the pipe but the hole that went all the way around it.

He came in and no part of our bodies was precious enough to leave whole—bone samples from the arch of our feet, bile of our guts, the tip of a branch of your left coronary, my right—he snipped, muttering about starfish and roses, his prizes for grafting.

The thief came in hungry and sucked clean every peel of papaya we had—the green edge hardly bitter on his tongue.

The thief came into the house and our machinery failed—the semiautomatic jammed, the rifle bulletless, the blender cord frayed.

He came in and nothing appealed to him, not even the gold of my labia or the silver in her teeth. He wanted to talk about painting, wanted lessons on how to create tension in the surface.

The thief came into the house and we were already tied to the bed, well you were, I mean me, this seemed memorable but for some reason—

He slipped in while we slept, which was always in winter, never in summer. He'd heard us chatting over dinner—What time you gettin' up tomorrow? Oh, I dunno, never, you?

He inched in between the thin wooden crossbars of the windows, removing each square of glass, but in leaving, he first removed the frame.

In the interviews, I tell them, I have no idea how he got in. Yes, I know what he looks like. No, I didn't see or hear him come in.

The thief came into the house and closed the windows. Outside the air grew toxic with night—we would have choked, we would have died had he not sealed us in.

He came in. Did you come? Yes, I came, she says.

The thief came into the house and all you can say to me is, have I seen your gloves, which of course I haven't seen, we've been sleeping, gloveless, for almost three weeks without waking.

The thief came in, a bouquet in each of his hands for each of our mouths while he showed us his good side.

The thief came in not to read but to do his job, however once he started reading he couldn't stop, and the pillows grew flat beneath his elbows.

The thief came into the house on schedule—simple, we just called ahead and his free slot lined up with our free slot.

The thief came in and stood before the mirror with Spanish tiles and punctured aluminum framing the glass, and picked the unplucked hair growing through the mole on his chin.

The thief came into the house because the basement was filled with dormant daffodil and tulip bulbs just waiting to be tricked back to life. Something about a receipt with our address on the bottom, something I returned that you wanted.

The thief came in singing, "It's spring, ladies, time to spring!" but I could have sworn it was the bluebirds braiding my hair with tokens of oak bark.

The Healing Machine
Shena McAuliffe

NEBRASKA

MAYBE IT WAS SUMMER. Call it hazy July 1935. Emery took a break from his mother's bedside and walked the hills. Grass and sand, roots anchoring it all so loosely, but for such a long time, and below that the aquifer, quiet and dark and invisible. In low spots the water seeped through, forming ponds and swamps. The toes of his shoes grew damp.

The cranes were his company, with their back-hinged knees, their stalk legs and black-tipped feathers—gray, soft, and draping—their red eye patches. Had he missed them when he was away? Had he thought of them? Their long necks and those wings that could wrap a man and hold him, if only the birds were less shy? A five-to-six-foot span—overwhelming. What did they sound like, the cranes? A ratcheting squawk, like something wooden was caught, rattling in their throats. And that step-step-wild hop-flap of a mating dance. The approach. The circling of the desired. The endless cavorting.

From above, nowadays: irrigation crop circles and perfectly straight roads. Nothing to go around. Nothing to go over. The sandhills roll like tumors (try again). Like goiters bubbling from the earth, but rippled and waving, those empty, endless, grassy dunes (try again). They move like pelts.

He would bury his mother there, in January. Chip away at the frozen soil of Custer County and heap it back again. And later, he would bury his father there too. Stomach cancer took his mother. Lung cancer his father.

PHOTOGRAPH #1 (circa 1972)

Emery Oliver Blagdon sits at a table. The soft, filthy brim of his cap is folded upward. Yellow light comes through the window behind him and his eyes gleam with the reflection of it. His beard, shaggy and white, overwhelms his face. Tools hang on the wall behind him. The counter is heaped with boxes and tins, loops of wires, crumpled paper, a heap of dirty rags. Squinting, you can make out the label on an old canister of Nestlé Quik. His face is tilted downward, but his eyes meet yours, quiet and certain.

By the time of this photograph, he had lost both parents and three siblings to cancer. He leased his two hundred acres to his younger brother for farming, but he lived in the house and built his Healing Machine in the shed. When he died, in 1986, his body too was riddled with cancer.

PHOTOGRAPH #2 (circa 1979)

Shoelaces untied. Grinning and unbuttoned. Gray-white beard, overgrown and frizzy. Scaly elbows. Blocky brow. Thin line of hair on his chest. Suntan fading midsternum. His belt is buckled, but the end, untucked, curls back. On his pinkie he wears a thick silver ring. Wide, knobby-knuckled hands—one pressed against his stomach, the other hanging at his side. He is not wearing the copper bracelets meant to relieve joint pain (blood was thought to absorb the copper by osmosis, through the skin). Daubs of paint mark his forearms. Around him hang various wires and paper pieces of the Healing Machine.

Born in Callaway, Nebraska, in the Sandhills, Emery rode the rails during the Depression. Looked for gold in California. Visited home now and then. His eight maternal aunts and uncles were scattered across the Garfield Table in their nearly identical houses. His was a family of e's: Edward and Emma. Ethel, Emery, Edward, Jr., Edna. He fixed tractors and bicycles. Built mechanical toys with moving parts for his nephews and nieces. Painted the kitchen wainscoting silver. Grew his vegetables in an unwieldy garden. Concocted peanut butter–watermelon cakes. Loved the Fourth of July and his own birthday. As he aged, his eyebrows softened and his hair grew long.

LABELS

Folk artist. Outsider artist. Self-taught. Working class. Builder of vernacular environments. Visionary. Tramp. Naive. Primitive. Intuitive. Shaman.

He called himself a scientist. Channeling electromagnetic energy through wire and glass beads and wood and paint and scrap metal. And salt. Most important, those mineral salts.

IN *MR. WILSON'S CABINET OF WONDER*

At first all you've got is a few disconnected pieces of raw observation, the sheerest glimpses, but you let your mind go, fantasizing the possible connections, projecting the most fanciful life cycles. In a way, it's my favorite part about being a scientist—later on, sure, you batten things down, contrive more rigorous hypotheses and the experiments through which to check them out, everything all clean and careful. But that first take—those first fantasies. Those are the best.[1]

DEFINITION: MACHINE

A machine is an expedient remedy. Does it necessarily have moving parts? Does it use or transfer energy? A stapler is a machine for hinging pages. An eye might be a machine. The way it gathers and condenses light. The way it flips the image. The eye is an expedient translator. Is a mattress a machine? The way its coils return equal and opposite pressure against the [resting] [tossing] body? Is it only a machine when the body presses against it? Does it make expedient sleep? Is a sweater a machine? All those interlocking fibers trapping and pocketing body heat? A bobby pin, inserted into the hole on the clothes dryer (which is certainly a machine) where the start button fell off and disappeared into its own hole, might successfully start the dryer, but there may be a few sparks. Some smoke and burned plastic. Is a cat a machine? For its pistons and joints, its many moving parts, its balls and sockets and tendons and claws? This transference of energy is an expedient remedy for loneliness.

---

[1]Tom Eisner, quoted in Lawrence Weschler, *Mr. Wilson's Cabinet of Wonder* (New York: Vintage Books, 1995), quoted in Leslie Umberger (see Source Note).

COPPER IS A SOFT CONDUCTOR

Emery wore a bracelet on each wrist, copper being said to ease the pain of arthritis. He was double cuffed. He had terrible arthritis. The fluid in his joints—where did it go? A leak somewhere and the fluid seeping out, leaving the bones, the cartilage, glancing off each other, too close. Wearing away. A knock or two. The quiet drag and scrape. Then the swelling.

AS DESCRIBED BY EDNA

Sure, he wore overalls a lot, but so do most of the men around here. Sleeves rolled to the elbow. Always a button or two missing, or just left unbuttoned. He could be careless like that. Haphazard. Floppy. Maybe that's the word for it—there was a floppiness to him. After the buttons fell off his shirt he'd keep it closed just by tucking the tails into his waistband. Pants rolled in big cuffs—a little stiff 'cause they were so dirty. Yeah, he was always kind of dirty, but he did his own laundry once a week. I brought him a plate of food once in a while, and he ate dinner over at our place pretty often, but mostly he took care of himself. Dried his pants on the line. His beard? Yeah, well, I cut his hair for years until he got strange about it. The last time I cut his hair he fainted dead away. Fell right down on the floor in a heap. Fear, I gucss. He was so afraid of the pain when the scissors cut through his hair. And he thought his hair had power. Like Samson in the Bible? When he heard the blades he just fell right over. Poor thing. That was the last time. He just let it all grow after that.

COINING THE CHARGES

It was [Benjamin Franklin] who coined the terms positive and negative charges. He defined the negative charge as one which is similar to the charge produced by stroking hard rubber with fur, and a positive charge as one similar to that produced by stroking glass with silk.[2]

[2]In the 1970s, a local teacher gave Emery a science textbook, *Matter and Energy*, by Arthur Talbot Bawden. It is from this book, a copy inscribed in cursive with the name "Edith Pritchard," that this quotation was culled.

PHOTOGRAPH #3

In the kitchen, starting at the ceiling light fixture, he painted a radiating series of red concentric circles across the room, filled with alternating green and yellow bands of color. He treated the kitchen wainscoting with silver radiator paint and the walls above with a shiny pale pink, with green half circles where those walls met the ceiling at the corners, and he detailed the light bulbs with stripes, dots, and other shapes.[3]

He baked bread. He stood at the stove, stirring a pot of soup, boiling an ear of corn. He took off his shoes. He scuffled along in his underwear.

WHILE HE WAS BUILDING THE HEALING MACHINE

Nikola Tesla was dead and had been dead for nine years, plenty of time for his orderly hair to lose the grooves of the comb, for his mustache to stop growing, and his skin to shrivel and decay and bare that thin skull. Time for the electricity of the brain to fizzle out and depart (to where? all that trickling, itinerant energy). In Emery's kitchen the radio fizzed and popped and spoke the news to him while he baked. (Radio: a machine. Antenna extended, it captures only those waves to which it is tuned and lets the others float by uninterrupted.)

[3]Leslie Umberger, "Emery Blagdon: Properly Channeled," *Sublime Spaces and Visionary Worlds* (New York: Princeton Architecture Press, 2007).

Eisenhower was elected president. Alaska and Hawaii became states. Kennedy was elected president. Kennedy was shot—the bodies in the convertible ducked and sprawled. Kennedy died. The United States continued hushed entanglements in Vietnam. LBJ took over the presidency. Heaps of papers were signed (the pens, now steeped in the magic dust of history, were given away as tokens, framed, and hung above fireplaces). LBJ was elected. Hushed entanglements roared. The marchers on Selma were blasted in the streets with high-pressure water hoses, yanked by arm, by leg, by neck. They were struck with billy clubs. The girls were burned in the church.

Andy Warhol had an old warehouse space—the Factory—papered with foil and spray painted silver. *A good time to think silver,* he said. Foil. Knife blades. Photographs. The mechanized production of Elvis, over and over.

Millions of veins were cauterized. Over twenty thousand people were lobotomized. Electroconvulsive (Shock) Therapy gained and lost popularity for treating depression, mania, general psychosis.

Nixon was elected. Ford was elected. Carter was elected. Reagan was elected.

AFTER HIS FATHER DIED

Emery started tatting wires. His pretties. Twisted wire shapes that he hung side by side from another wire. Mobiles. Wind chimes. Parts of machines. Some like the coils from the insides of old mattresses. Baling-wire doilies. Wrapped and knotted and dangling. In Edna's living room he tatted. Beside him Edna knitted.

PHOTOGRAPH #4

Rows and rows of wires. Copper-wrapped boards. Waxed paper–aluminum–waxed paper sandwiches. Little scrolls of tin. Snarls and snags. Drifting squares of salvaged metal. Bright beads, glass and plastic, paint.

INSIDE THE HEALING MACHINE

He built it in the barn first, but the roof collapsed, pulled down by the pretties and nails and paint and magnets and jars. He salvaged the wood and built a two-room structure, low ceilinged, the work space and the healing space side by side.

It was kind of comical watching him do something; he'd wiggle around there a while, [and] sometimes he'd [lay a piece] down and leave it right where it was, pick it up, and pretty soon he'd start tinkering with it again.[4]

Sometimes people said they felt it—the energy—healing them, buzzing through the wires. Your arm hairs rippled if you stood in the middle of the shed. Goosebumps rising across the surface of your skin: right arm, small of the back, up the spine, nape of the neck, down the left arm, wiggle fingers. In the soles of your feet: the hum of the earth, the soil, the heat, the aquifer. You knew it was there. You were engulfed by twinkling lights—cheap, twisted Christmas strands—and the wood, so splintered and warm. There was the scent of paint and dirt and oil. Wire-wrapped jars. The taste of copper on the tip of your tongue. Your knees loosened a bit, as if the ligaments had been untied, then retied in a floppy bow instead of a knot. Your stomach touched your shirt when you breathed, the kiss of cotton and skin cells. The buzz moved through your neck, out your skull, into the tip of each hair on your head. You might want to lie down, press your cheek to the painted board, but then you might rather conduct the energy. Conduct it, as if a symphony, the flutter of electrical current coursing through your raised arms, the braided energy of the earth passing through your hands and out the end of your baton, filling the room. You, a lightning rod.

Maybe it was Emery's energy they felt—the hours he put into painting the wooden panels with those muted bright colors, gluing beads to the panel, twisting, twisting, wire after wire after wire, attaching this bent fork, that tin plate, hanging a vial of salts, emptying crystals onto a glue-smeared board. Bending a coat hanger. Cutting his thumb on the serrated edge of a can. Mousetrap, pie tin, baling wire, ribbon, and wax circuit board.

But some people felt nothing. They saw the paint on the boards, the light glinting against glass and wire, the spinning, sharp-edged tops of coffee cans. And they felt nothing.

[4]Ben Fox, interview by Dan Dryden, November 1987, quoted in Leslie Umberger.

HE WENT TO THE PHARMACY

He said, "I'd like to buy some earth elements."

He was so intent on his inquiry that I took him seriously—which, to look at the man, you wouldn't really. "Elements" is a broad category, I thought. I tried to ask him what kind of elements he wanted, what he was doing with them. He said he was building machines—magnetic machines—machines that had electrical activity. So I thought the only elements I know, per se, having any electrical activity are simple earth salts—mineral salts. This guess turned out to be accurate . . . I offered to give him some. I went back to my wets-and-dries counter and filled up various vials with these powders—salt powders, crystals, sodium chloride, maybe some sulfur and a few other inorganic compounds. I labeled these—he was very happy to receive these. His face brightened up, and he was getting very talkative.[5]

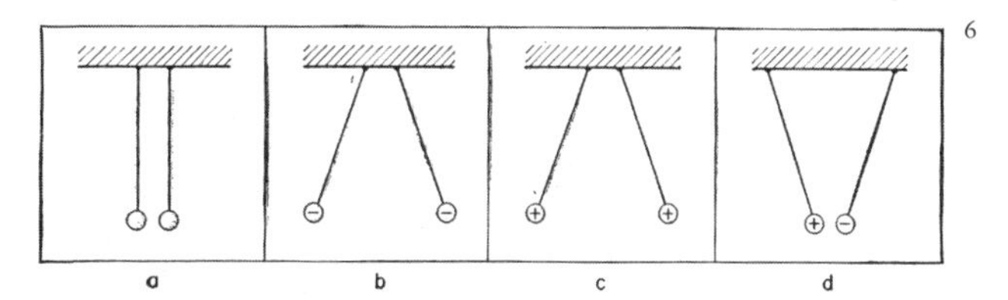

[6]

Fig. 23.1. Attraction and repulsion of charged bodies.

THERE WAS A GIRL ONCE

She lived on the neighboring farm, but her father didn't approve of Emery. His vagabonding. His sixty-mile-per-hour tractor. The way he loitered at the soda fountain and didn't work that much. The man didn't know responsibility, and besides, the way the children liked him—wasn't it a little creepy? But they liked him for fixing their bikes, for asking them questions, for catching lightning bugs with them, in jars, and after they fell asleep beside that lantern of bugs, Emery always let the bugs out. When they woke the jar was open and

[5]Dan Dryden, "Emery Blagdon Recollections," 1987, quoted in Leslie Umberger.
[6]From *Matter and Energy*, Arthur Talbot Bawden (New York: Henry Holt and Company, 1957).

empty. The bugs were off sleeping, or doing whatever it is that lightning bugs do during the day when their lights don't shine against the darkness.

ETHEL DESCRIBES THE HEALING MACHINE

He invited her into the machine, of course. *Nothing doing,* she said. *I didn't want to go in there. It was a lot of wires and stuff.*[7]

ITINERANT IS A HARD WORD

Metallic and knocking. It is often applied to traveling preachers, but means, more generally, movable. One who roams. Does the wanderer have a home somewhere? Some place that holds him? That he thinks of when he is away? Is he always trying to return, or is he trying to escape? He is always longing for another place.

Try *vagabond*. Why does he leave? Over and over, he is always leaving. Does he lose track of himself, leaving a fragment in each place—an eyelash in Nashville, a tooth on the boxcar, his gullibility in San Francisco? Or is he overwhelmed by the places he takes with him? Such heavy baggage: the green ocean wave, the beckoning limbs of the Joshua tree, the pale child offering her glass of lemonade, the bed with cool white sheets, the gray morning light and a pillowcase printed with yellow roses that smelled of another's hair? Is his body his only home?

Try *nomad*. Is the firmest self the one independent of opinions? Free from conversations that thread years? From the expectations of other people? Is the firmest self the one that washes away? The one who says: *There is no self*?

Try *hobo*. He collected places like Easter eggs.

ON THE QUALITY OF LIGHT SURROUNDING THE AVERAGE MACHINE

Cold. Mechanical. Inhuman and, possibly, inhumane. Think *robot*, for example, and likely you think silver, cold toned. But the Healing

[7]Ethel Blagdon Sivits, interview by Don Christensen, October 1990, quoted in Leslie Umberger, but sonically adjusted here.

Machine was copper and gold and bronze and—yes—silver too. Glinting. The wood was old and streaked and maybe half rotted. Paint, wood, warm-toned metals, the yellowy twinkle of Christmas lights, the wax paper like layers of skin, like a well-peeled sunburn.

(But what about the cotton gin? What about the printing press? Those are machines and they are not cold toned or metallic. What about the way you want to eat the letter-press stamps, or more, to press them to your skin, wear an "R" in Garamond on the soft inside of your wrist, an "E" in Palatino Linotype on your cheek?)

WHAT THE CITY SAID

He refused to cut his hair and paid little attention to what he wore. He looked like a scary old vagrant. Now he can be seen as a great rural American shaman.[8]

OTHER MACHINES: THE MODIFIED SNOOPERSCOPE[9]

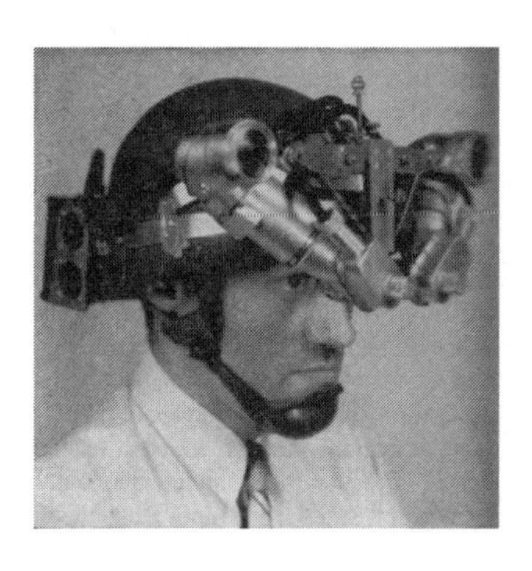

Fig. 31.2. A modified version of the snooperscope tube to give binocular vision for night driving. It runs off of the vehicle's power system. (Radio Corporation of America.)

HE PICKED UP ODD JOBS

The sawmill and the lumberyard smelled of sawdust and sometimes a little like burning wood from the friction between buzzing blade

[8]Ken Johnson, "Emery Blagdon: Flights of Fancy from the Artist as Medicine Man," *The New York Times*, January 10, 2008.
[9]From *Matter and Energy*, Arthur Talbot Bawden (New York: Henry Holt and Company, 1957).

and board. A little oil kept things turning smoothly and occasionally smelled like popcorn. Emery wondered aloud: *Is sap tree blood?* Sawdust collected around his nostrils. He blew opaque white snot onto his handkerchief, stuck it back in his pocket. He wore gloves but the splinters dug into his flesh anyway, festering, pink and swollen, blotching his forearms and the skin between fingers. Tweezers were useless. Edna squinted through a pair of reading glasses and pushed at them with a needle. Emery squeezed his eyes shut. *If a tree could grow from a sliver,* he thought. If a tree could grow from his arm it would be worth it. A tender-rooted sapling ready for transplant. A new solution of sap blood in his veins.

Baling hay was no better. Still the scratches on his arms. The grass was named timothy. The hot dust in his eyes. The men whistling and opening lunch pails. He whistled too, looping and low. Windmills cut the sky with their bony limbs. Their flayed fingers sliced and gathered wind. And down in the dirt the water pumps nodded. Prayed to mud and grass and spit their bounty into ladles, into pails and troughs. For lunch he had two chicken wings and a leg and a wide slice of rhubarb pie.

ON HAIR AND OTHER INANIMATES

Hair was dead, of course, and brainless, but he feared for it nonetheless. That the snip would hurt it. All that energy that would escape from the cut, invisible, but gushing like blood from a wound, electricity from a live wire. Feared that *things* had feelings.

He considered the sensitivity of a piece of pie, the crust separated from itself, the juices running. Of the broken shoelace, gray and fraying, marked by the black rings of metal eyelets. Of a page no longer blank, its surface scratched by a pen running dry, the marks accumulating, pressing faintly through to the other side. The communion between the wire and his swollen joints. In everything a sensate buzz.

The human body walked through the world like a spindle, the invisible energy winding upon it, tighter and tighter. Like the sputtering fuse on a stick of dynamite. To feel oneself as the spindle, or as the circuit between aquifer and sky. To live in the space between catgut and fret, absorbing the vibrations. This was the purpose of the Healing Machine. To shake loose the pain, to carry it to the next thing, to release it, but also to be the knot, the fuse, the loosened gnarl.

MILES AND MILES OF NOTHING

There was the house, faded gray in the yellow grass. There were the cornfields. In the dark, crickets. In the day, cicadas and rustling. The front steps were flanked by two overgrown junipers. Musk thistle and small, twisted sunflowers tangled along the walk. An eastern red cedar half blocked the steps. *Emery,* Edna said. *Your house looks abandoned.* Anyone who mattered would know to go around back, he said. Or knock on the door of the Healing Machine. And they did. They knocked. They waited.

Afternoons in summer the sky turned green. Tornadoes. Hail. But when the lightning storms blew through most nights in July, Emery watched the strikes roll across the hills, marching toward him, forking and flashing. He felt them in his hair, in his fingers, in the copper bracelets around his wrists. The buzzing heat in his throat and in his knuckles. The crickets and bats fell silent. The cattle pressed against the barbed wire and lowed. Their coarse hides prickling. They bellowed and the rain fell on them. A loose board banged somewhere out back. The curtains snapped but he never bothered to close the windows. He liked the puddles under his feet in the morning.

PHOTOGRAPH #5

A newspaper photo. Blurry and cropped to a portrait. A laughing cloud of beard fills the dark frame. Pixelated wrinkles. And his eyes—where, in the other photographs, you see the spark—are lost. Is he wearing glasses? Over and over, the accompanying article calls him "The Old Farmer."

THE BODY IS NOT LIKE A PHOTOGRAPH

Simplified, the aura of a work of art is that clingy trace of the maker, the nonmechanical quality, like a halo, the smudge of humanness. We can print photograph after photograph and they will look identical. The body is a closed system of one-way roads. Every penis exactly the same when it comes down to the two tiny veins, pinched off when the arteries rush. But the small intestine, framed by the orderly large intestine, loops every which way, a different bouquet in every body, a haphazard mess of ruffles. The small intestine is unique in its heaping.

Machines that read the output and rhythms and shorted circuits of the body: the X-ray. The ultrasound. The blobs of color on a nuclear image, marking the place where the blood slows and gathers, indicating the clogged artery at the entry to the heart. The seismic blips of the EKG.

Emery avoided doctors. Did he feel the tumors gathering within him? Like cumulus clouds, all billow and rise? Did his arthritis go into remission, his body distracted, producing something new? Each day he pressed his cheek to the painted boards of the Healing Machine. Each day standing perfectly still, feeling the twinge and the currents.

CONSIDERATION: HEALING

1. Skin knits itself together and scabs over.
2. The scab falls off, leaving behind a purplish spot.
3. Scars are also called *cicatrices*.
4. We opt for the easy term that is less beautiful and more closely resembles its sign. "Scar" slices and steams when spoken.
5. The body heals around shrapnel when necessary.
6. The heart reroutes the blood if the usual route is defective. Say you were born without a particular artery. If you are lucky the lub-dub will go on. The body improvising.
7. It is the overproduction of collagen that leaves a scar.
8. Smear it with vitamin E.
9. After gastric bypass the skin remains six sizes too large, draped over the shoulders, dewlapping the triceps, skirting the body.
10. You want to heal, but to heal means to incorporate the shrapnel, to minimize the overproduction of collagen.
11. Who wouldn't want to feel the vibrations, the electrical currents?
12. A suture, too, leaves a scar.
13. A Band-Aid is a plastic suture. You get to peel it off. The sticky black outline of lint stuck to glue is not a scar because it washes off.
14. Cauterization. Amputation. These, too, "heal."

THE MAKER IS NOT CLUMSY

Emery hammered at a piece of tin, denting it flat. He punched a couple of holes in the corners and stuck a bit of wire through. He changed his mind, pulled the wire out. The holes remained. He looked up at Edna, who was standing in the doorway. "Dinner," she said. "If you want it." She was holding a plate with a pile of greens and cooked carrots and meat. He stood up and wiped his hands on his pockets. He took the plate from her. He said, "Crumpled tin will never look new again, no matter how you press it and smooth it."

THE PHARMACIST ON THE HEALING MACHINE

It depends upon what you mean by healing powers. If you mean is there an emotional, psychological impact that can affect your outlook, I would say, Yes, it definitely has powers of some kind.[10]

WHO IS HEALED?

The maker? The looker? The writer? The one who stands absolutely one hundred percent motionless on the painted, salt-smeared panel? Right here: under these twisting wires. Under this chandelier of painted baby-food jars and plastic beads and copper coils. Right here: where the energy fields converge.

Emery hopping in excitement: *Stand here,* he said. *Do you feel it?*

OTHER MACHINES: THE SCENT DISTILLER

A small copper pot—about two inches round—that collects an air sample, then distills and concentrates the scent of that parcel of air. These scent molecules are compressed into a tiny block, like a bouillon cube, and vacuum sealed. To regenerate, add water and simmer over low heat.

Air scent sample distilled in Salt Lake City, Utah, at 1001 E. South Temple on November 21, 2010: salt, algae, sulfur, car exhaust, coal

[10]Dan Dryden quoted in Joe Duggan, "The Healing Machines of Nebraska," *Lincoln Journal Star*, January 7, 2006.

dust, copper, copper by-products (mostly alkaline soil), leaf meal, cut grass, soiled kitty litter, singed hair, cooked pork, spearmint chewing gum, lavender, sweaty gym socks, coffee, rubber of a bicycle tire, bicycle-chain lubricant, Simple Green biodegradable cleanser, cedar soap, dirty wool (how long will you leave that pile of clothing before taking it to the cleaners?).

Air scent sample distilled in Callaway, Nebraska, at the corner of Third and Main on July 13, 2011: crane excrement, sunflower pollen, corn pollen, nitrate fertilizer, Roundup Ready, diesel, popcorn, car exhaust, paper pulp, cattail, burned matches, asphalt, wet concrete, sweaty gym socks, coconut sunscreen, pine sap, tarpaper, varnish, apple-pie potpourri, paraffin, honey-baked ham.

A RIDDLE IS A CONUNDRUM OR ENIGMA

By the time Emery died, his body was riddled with tumors. The doctors guessed they had been growing for ten years. That grain of sand in the oyster, growing precious. Then a rhizome with running roots spidering the soil. A potato with so many eyes. The doctors had not seen him in town. Not at the clinic. His only medicine had been the Healing Machine.

THE PHARMACIST, DRIVING

The high-school class reunion was in North Platte, twenty miles west. Dan and his high-school friend Don sped along I-80, the fence posts stuttering past like a film. Dan's hands at ten and two.

It had been years, Dan said. What—six or eight? Since he had given Emery the elements and then, curious, driven out to the hills to check out the Healing Machine. That way somewhere. (He took a hand from the wheel, gestured at the hills.) Maybe ten miles north. Just this totally unassuming shack. You'd never know from looking at it.

The interstate cut a corridor between the hills.

We should stop, said Don. You've been telling me about this kook and his magic salts for years. The G and Ts will wait.

Yeah? You want to? Dan said.

There was no one at the farm. The hem of a kitchen curtain was pinched in the window sash, flipping in the wind. They walked up to the porch. A bill was posted on the door.

Emery Blagdon had died. The estate would be auctioned. The woodstove. The windmill. Lots of fancy wire work. Some painted boards. Some jars. Homemade toys. Pie tins. Paints. The list was long—the Healing Machine would be sold piecemeal. More than four hundred individual components.

THE GAVEL AND THE AUCTIONEER

Each shining jar of salt held like a scope against the sky.

Andwe'vegotsomemorewires.What'llyougiveforthesewires.CanIget fifteen?Fifteen.Seventeen.Seventeen.Twenty.Twenty.Twentyfive.And Twentyfive.Thirty.Thirty?Thirty.CanIgetthirtyone?Goingonceat thirty.Twice.Soldforrthirty.Andwe'vegotanotherboxofjars.

Dan Dryden and his friend Don Christensen purchased the Emery Blagdon works at the sale of his estate in 1986. They bought all four hundred pieces. The shed was torn down.

PHOTOGRAPH #6

A man and woman, wearing green latex gloves, tinker with a piece of the Healing Machine balanced on a table. Fluorescent light and gray industrial carpet. They bend their heads. They wield brushes and tweezers. They breathe mint and wear aprons. They do not look up for the photograph.

SOURCE NOTE. Throughout the entirety of this piece I have quoted, stolen from, and mercilessly appropriated words and information from Leslie Umberger's essay "Emery Blagdon: Properly Channeled," *Sublime Spaces and Visionary Worlds: Built Environments of Vernacular Artists* (New York: Princeton Architectural Press, 2007). I credit her with most of the information found here and with none of the inventions, fabrications, mistakes, misquotes, or careless imaginings. I am an unreliable source, making various assumptions and projections. You can put these pages down but the words will still be here, the ants parading. My voice, their voices, stored in ink or electricity. I am no scientist. I am barely responsible enough to pay my cell-phone bill on time.

Jo's Murder Game
Urs Allemann

—Translated from German by Patrick Greaney

THERE WEREN'T ANY SUBMACHINE GUNS, at most gardening shears. There was murder nonetheless. It's claimed nonetheless that there was murder. When flesh got stabbed, it bled. Flesh, two fleshes; there weren't three. When the man and woman murdered each other, the kid always happened to be at the circus. He made his appearance in the circus, he walked the tightrope, he fell to his death from the tightrope. When his neck broke, the applause from one half of the audience swelled up as the applause from the other half of the audience ebbed away. No one except Jo was able to appreciate the dynamic equilibrium of silence and applause. Jo wrote, "I don't know if it's the kids who are cheering because they have one less kid to fear from now on. Maybe it was the geezers who fell silent, moved by the thought that the kid would never grow up to be a geezer. What did the women's clapping, less and less inhibited by the minute, mean, what about the men's quasipremortuary (utterly silent! utterly silent!) pause. Et cetera or vice versa. I'm amazed, dear Svetlana or whatever your name is, by the acoustic fire of hands gunning down the peace and quiet. I'm amazed by how peace and quiet swallows up the most powerful eruptions, explosions, exaltations. Let's meet for tea today. You can have Cointreau if you want. Whenever I say, hear, think, or even just write the word Cointreau, coitus comes to mind. Did you know that you too are the delayed product of coitus. Call me. I may have locked the telephone in the wardrobe, but I can still hear it. Luckily for me, but even more so for you, I hid the wardrobe key in the nightstand drawer. Don't get your hopes up that I'll find it again, you know how bad my memory is. So just come over. Go ahead and buzz! go ahead and buzz! at the entrance to the building, I promise you, I won't let you in. The fact that I'm naked, that's so easy to explain. The old clothes I threw out the window, the new ones are hanging in the wardrobe. Better the clothes than me, I comfort myself with that when I'm freezing and jiggling the wardrobe door. I hid the key in the old water closet in the attic. No one, not even me, will ever find it. Write me sometime. Did I already write you that I went to the circus today. Fatal outcome, like always. Send me a telegram, like always, as a sign of your grief. See you Thursday. You can have a martini if you want. Whenever I write, smell, or taste the word martini or even just see it jump out of the trash can into my mouth, murder comes to mind. Did you know that every murder presupposes the coital act whose delayed product is the murderer as well as the coital act whose delayed product is the one who's murdered. Whereas the *conditio sine qua non* of suicide is a single coital act. Don't be sad. See you Wednesday. Your Jo." If the kid didn't come home from the circus by eight, the man and woman knew they had to make a new one. They always had to make a new one; the old one never came back from the circus. The man was never allowed to enjoy, the woman was never allowed to enjoy a summer evening in the beer tent on the lake or a fall evening in the wine tent on the illuminated bridge over the river or a winter evening in the pennant-covered glogg tent in the snowy mountains or a spring evening! a spring evening! the woman was never allowed to enjoy, the man was never allowed to enjoy, a spring evening in a tent, in which tent, the man was never allowed, the woman was never allowed, to figure out which of the innumerable tents was being set up in springtime, which of the innumerable drinks was being drunk in the tent in springtime, he sometimes spoke sadly of the spring tent, she sometimes spoke longingly of spring drinks. At 8:05, at the end of the mourning break, the man, sighing, unzipped his zipper. At 8:10, at the end of the longing break, the woman, groaning, lifted up her skirt. If they had spent the afternoon naked they could have spared themselves the drudgery, now that the end of the day was nearing in all its glory, of each having to bare, before the sweat of each of their respective brows, their sexes. There was no one there to give them that good piece of advice. The kid who was begotten by the man 270 days ago at 8:15 and given birth to by the woman at daybreak today! today! always happened to be at the zoo to feed on the lion. It, the kid, squeezed through the bars into the empty cage. It had figured out early on that the victims it sought always happened to be away. It bent down to the ground. With the magnifying glass, the birthday present from the woman out of whose belly the white attendants had just pulled the kid an unimaginably short time ago, it was looking for lions that quite possibly could have been microscopic. The kid would have been naked if it hadn't had its white diapers. They covered up its sex, which otherwise would have been defenselessly exposed to the zoo visitors' gazes and the lions' teeth. From the undeniable absence of the large lion the kid had originally wanted to feed on, it quite correctly did not infer the absence of the tiny lion that it would in fact feed on in the end. The only thing that worried it was the far-too-weak magnifying power of its magnifying glass. It wondered if the stinginess of the woman out of whose belly it had just fallen onto the stone tiles of the birthing room an unimaginably short time ago was just barely forgivable or enough to be unforgivable. One thing was certain, it said out loud, for the pathos of truth tore its mouth open, and that's that the inference, based on the absence of the lion under the magnifying glass, of the absence of the microscopically ohwhat-amisaying optical microscopically ohwhatamisaying electron microscopically demonstrable lion would be a logical fallacy beneath my! my! dignity. By the time the kid's neck broke the zoo visitors had long since gone home to look up on the scope of work form what the evening had in store for them. It's the fuck, the doctor said and unswaddled the bank clerk, taking her out of her workaday rags. It's the fuck, the judge said as she unbuttoned the social worker's everyday bib. It's imaginable that the social worker ripped the white coat off the doctorial body. It's imaginable that the bank clerk was burrowing around under the judge's black robe. But no such claim is being made. The fact that the lion didn't feed on the kid went unnoticed by them at first; then it surprised them; then it bored them. Whenever they left and dwelled, in the subway or commuter train or tram or on a motorcycle or in a car, on the bus, on the trolley bus or on a boat! on a boat! on the question of whether the lion would really go ahead and devour the kid in the evening or wait until daybreak, the lion devoured the kid. It broke the kid's neck; the lion found it beautiful to resolve the dissonance of diaper and loupe and perennial babbling, no matter how carefully articulated the babbling might be, to death's final consonance. No one except Jo was there to appreciate the lion's aesthetico-practical perspective. Jo was the only one to stick it out right there in front of the cage's bars. Jo wrote: "See you Tuesday. Don't get too excited too soon. You may have preferred that the lion impregnate the kid instead of killing it. No one knows what was hidden under that white diaper. Did you too wear white rubber pants in your day. Did you too, in your day, whip out binoculars in search of missing giants. Did you too go around singing when you were waiting for me in your garret. I'm not going to come. Do you like chicken, I'll bring you some chicken. I'll lay the dead chicken out for you in front of the garret door. Did you know that dead hens lay no eggs. I'll call and explain it to you. Don't pick up when it rings, I'd hold a sock or handkerchief in front of my mouth but you'd still understand me. You've always understood me, thank you so much, go ahead and lower the rolling shutters. It won't be of any advantage to you, with a ladder and an ax I'll still reach my objective. Do you like fish, I'll send you a box of fish sticks. You'll be able to tell from the smell that there's mail from me. I was at the zoo today. Fatal outcome, like always. Don't forget to put the pack of decomposing fish in the freezer. I'm amazed, Tatjana or whatever your name is, by the truly gigantic dimensions of your forgetfulness. Like always I ripped your congratulations telegram to shreds without reading it. I chewed up the shreds, my sense of taste told me it was from you. Let the bathwater run, lie down in the water, then it won't hurt. See you Monday. Don't forget to slit lengthwise, dear, and not under any circumstances crosswise. I'll dump wood splinters and the shards of glass in the trash can. I'll put the dead hen in with the dead fish in the freezer. I'll tidy up. Not even you, not even I, not even my archenemies can deny that I was always the most efficient when it came to tidying up. You're not going to be hanging in the wardrobe, I'm telling you that to your face. Maybe I should eat an apple now before I go into the bathroom. The kid, if the lion hadn't fed on it, would surely have starved. Don't be childish. Why would you hide the bathroom key in the nightstand drawer. With an ax I'll still reach my objective. I'll sweep up the splinters and dump them in the trash can. I'll lean in disbelief! in disbelief! over the edge of the bathtub. Why did you ruin everything. Why are you spoiling my fun like always. Why am I not allowed to ask myself the question I painstakingly prepared for myself, whether I should lift you out of the tub and lay you to rest with the dead fish and the dead hen in the freezer or get the dead hen and the dead fish out of the freezer and inter them with you in the tub. Don't think that I will infer, based on your corpse's absence in your tub that was, as expected, filled with water, that your corpse is present elsewhere in your garret full, as expected, of the stench of decomposition. You didn't suffocate in the old water closet in the attic, that I'd swear. Hanging over the edge of the tub inconsolable! inconsolable! I'll ask myself the backup question I painstakingly prepared for myself, whether the reciprocal shattering of actuality by possibility and possibility by actuality includes or excludes the reciprocal triumph of possibility over actuality or actuality over possibility. While I'm inconceivably quietly but inconceivably clearly whispering to myself the answer I painstakingly prepared to my backup question, you'll break my neck with the blunt side of the ax. It'll still be lying by the bathroom door, don't you remember. Just don't worry about consonance and dissonance anymore. Just in case death occurs before I'm able to utter my, you know this already, inconceivably clearly but, you know this already, inconceivably quietly whispered answer to my backup question to a degree of completion! completion! that would convince even my archenemies, even me, even you, I wrote down the answer on a piece of paper for you. Rip it up, it's enclosed, chew up the shreds, you'll always understand me. See you Sunday. Shall I let you in on a secret. You have to check off Includes, not Excludes, darling. Nothing is ever excluded. Everything is always included. Go ahead and swallow the key, with an ax I'll still reach my objective. Tell me, would you let yourself be impregnated by the bank clerk if you were the social worker. Or another question altogether: Would you let the doctor break your neck if you were the judge. Be so good as to write down the answer for me on a piece of paper. Have a great death. I won't be able to have anyone come by to get the piece of paper. We're all busy. Your Jo." Since the kid hadn't come home from the zoo by eight, the man and woman knew it was necessary to make another one. They had kept the evening open just for that. At daybreak, like always, the woman tossed today's kid to the white attendants. At daybreak, like always, the man dreamt the first draft of today's nightmare. After breakfast, this was not the time to report what was served, the man called in the second draft of today's nightmare to the work friend, male, and work friend, female, in the turret. The man was never able to learn if the voice on the other end of the line, with its towering Babylonian silence, belonged to the male work friend or female work friend or maybe even both of them. It's imaginable that the male work friend and female work friend, as the voice on the other end of the line dictated the second draft of today's nightmare, conjointly performed, with their sexual tools, the drudge work that according to the scope of work form was to be performed with these tools and not with any others on this morning like every other morning. But no such claim is being made. In an inconceivably loud but inconceivably garbled voice the man bellowed the second draft of today's nightmare into the earpiece's beloved diaphragm. The sight of the completely scentless! completely scentless! earpiece approaching the man's mouth moved the man to the brink of tears. He'd have cried if his task on the scope of work form hadn't been to bellow. While the man's voice, inconceivably garbled and inconceivably loud, bellowed the second, slightly improved draft of today's nightmare into the bewitchingly porous, girlishly tender, perforated earpiece, the man's brain tried in vain! in vain! to calculate, based on the tension between bellowed bellowing and unwept weeping, the factor determining his telephonic hollering's aesthetico-practical propulsive force, he could have called it XX, he called it XY. Like always he dialed the right number. Like always he renounced biting into the earpiece whose defenselessness vanquished him. What did he do, this man! this man! He bellowed: "The head's lips move incessantly. It's the head of a woman. The woman is made of rock. The rock is in the desert. The desert is empty. No one is playing in the desert. The dark streak on the horizon is made of wood. The rock is cracked. One rock. Two rocks. There aren't three. The third rock was just cleared away. No one tidies up in the desert. The desert is empty. The ocean is empty. The woman's torso is lying in the water. The woman's head is standing up in the sand. The rock's lips are moving incessantly. No one plays in the ocean. No one tidies up in the ocean. The dark streak on the horizon is made of wood. It's low tide. The woman's torso is lying in the sand instead of in the water. It's high tide. The woman's head protrudes out of the water instead of out of the sand. A plastic chicken, blue. A plastic fish, red. Tidy up! tidy up! please. No one says anything. No one hears anything. The lips move incessantly. The ear is made of sandstone. The lips crumble away incessantly. It's low tide. The sand trickles from the lips into the sand. It's high tide. The lips trickle from the lips into the water. It's low tide. The ear trickles from the ear into the sand. It's high tide. The words trickle from the lips into the water. The words are the lips are the sand. It's a very old rock. The sand is the ear is the lips. It's a very young rock. It's low tide. The word biddy trickles from the lips into the sand. It's high tide. The word girl trickles from the lips into the water. The head crumbles away incessantly. The wind is picking up. The desert is empty. The storm is brewing. The torso crumbles away incessantly. The ocean is empty. It's windless. The waves move incessantly. The waves are made of sand. The sand is made of rock. The rock is the sand is the water. The dark band on the horizon is made of wood! wood! did you get that. End of the second draft. Too bad you're not familiar with the first draft. It was bursting in anticipation of the second draft, which is bursting with reminiscences of the first draft. The biddy's head was made of granite. Nothing crumbled. The ocean couldn't be seen. The biddy's words were jeeps speeding around the sandbox. Jeeps are naked little animals, and the boy who dug them tunnels was one of them. There weren't any submachine guns, at most rat poison. All of them tried to climb up on the granite head from all sides. They all tumbled back into the sand. O the naked little jeep stomachs. The boy knew he shouldn't feel bad about leaving his comrades in the lurch because their type is hopeless. The poison was already working, o the minicramps. The rock's lips moved incessantly. The boy had made it pretty far for himself. The jeeps' flesh wheels weren't moving anymore. The boy analyzed the situation, they're dead, I'm up here on top. He crouched in the rock ear, took a break, paused. I'm great-grandmother's word that wandered into great-grandmother's ear. A sentence, a pause filler. The attempt to move from analysis to poetry failed. While trying to peck his way into the inner ear, the boy took a fall. Down below in the sand, before he died, he pulled his notebook out of his diapers. The other jeeps didn't have exercise diapers; he did, though. The rock's lips moved incessantly. The boy just had to take notes. The holes in the rock are made of rock! rock! did you get that. Over and out. That was the errant draft. Good thing you aren't familiar with the first draft. You will never be able to record it on your miserable tape. I dreamt it at daybreak, Hans. Except if you're Irina. Keep at the fucking. Noon is already looming over the hills." After breakfast, now is not the place to report what was cleared away, the woman had gone to kindergarten like always. The kids were standing around the flower beds. Their thighs were trembling in anticipation of the verdict. They were manuring away virtuously with what they almost already were. Only the gardeneress's kid was standing off to the side. The kid knew since daybreak that its pensum was noted on a special death certificate. Since it was its nondelegable task to leave, by means of its absence, a lean, mean, streamlined stamp on the man and woman's afternoon, it was safe from the antemeridian transubstantiations. Before the kindergarteness sprayed, she read the liturgical instruction manual's appellative chapter out loud to the children, her fists folded like always. "You shall all become beautiful black humus. But it wouldn't hurt to exert yourselves a little. Only with practice does dust return unto dust. All you high-performance moribunds, consider yourselves sound chattel whose sentence has been commuted to soundlessness. Don't sound your bugles anymore, the firm will be taking them back. Death, good gracious. It's the telos of every composition but it must also be fully integrated into the composition, that's the tricky part. It'll be impossible to compost you all if you don't dissolve your (individually! individually!) prescribed infanticide in music for my ears. No talking.

Give form, gardeners, may your death be but a breath. Praying's always good. Weeding too, but that can wait. Here's a transcription for you, made specifically for this occasion: Praying, weeding will set you free. Dear attendees. Dear decomposees. It's all much too much for you. Maybe you should just stop breathing. Maybe you should just take a really deep breath. In the place where we all want to go the firm's formula obtains. Vapor comes before nonvapor but non-vapor has priority. Understandable, understood. Not parriable, parried. The boss's boss for the boss to the boss o boss. And now the youngest, all of you, in the final chorus, each in his own furrow. Whether your lung is empty or it's full / What matters is, you're dead, how wonderful. Start off slow, get your decay off to a conscientious start. Start off deep inside. Then by and by! by and by! proceed from the inside outward. The firm thanks you and kindly requests it. No flowery talk, the bulb principle. We'll cross our fingers for you until you're nice and black. Help us. Help yourselves. Cross your fingers for yourselves. No doubt you shall be nice and black." After lunch, no one wants to know what was cleared away, what was served, the lonely hours of lonely murdering had come, like always. One flesh; two fleshes. The third flesh always happened to be at the movies. It was planning to tumble down from the screen. It was planning to feed on the screen. It was planning to perform, on the screen, an operation on the spectators. Not anymore. There were only gardening shears. There was murder nonetheless. It's claimed nonetheless that there was murder. Aren't you also of the opinion, the man asked as he scratched the woman's finger with the gardening shears, gently initiating the murder game, that considering our considerable, ever more considerable need for gardening shears that our ever more inconsiderable supply of gardening shears seems sheerly insufficient. Doesn't it make a mockery of your notion of justice, the woman countered as she slit open the man's toe, gingerly keeping the murder game going, that in a world in which millions ohwhatamisaying umpmillions ohwhatamisaying umpbillions of garden shears are incessantly produced and pulped and produced again and pulped again that we! we! of all people we! own only one! one! pair of garden shears. Wouldn't it be better, the man chimed in circumspectly as he rammed the garden shears quick as an arrow into the flesh of the woman's arm, giving the murder game its expected turn, instead of going back and forth begrudging each other our most precious possession, our garden shears, even disputing the other's right to them, yea even resorting to violence, to resolve contractually of our own free will, each for the benefit of the other, to renounce the garden shears, each ceding to the other the other half of our most precious possession, so that, at any one time, one of us owns exclusively! exclusively! one half, the other exclusively! exclusively! the other half, of our most precious possession, the garden shears. Alas, we shall never, with our bare hands, the woman hastened to respond, as she leisurely dug the garden shears into the flesh of the man's leg, testing out anew the murder game's ancient peripeties, succeed at separating, halving, or even only breaking apart into unequally sized or, alternately, unequally heavy or, alternately, unequally well-whetted pieces what truly titanic specialized expertise together with truly titanic specialized labor in addition to truly titanic specialized assiduity once joined together, according to the will of the garden shears' fathers and mothers, as indivisible garden shears. Would it even be permissible, the man, truly moved, threw out for discussion as he hacked up the woman's cheek, temples, auricle! auricle! and eyelid with the garden shears, as weary of the murder game as ever, to refer to our previously undivided garden shears' two parts, once separated and considered individually, even if they were to be separated from one another by the very best garden shear specialist, as garden shears! shears! and not as garden daggers! daggers! Time to mop up, the woman said briskly, after looking at the wall clock, interrupting the dialogue undulating between husband and wife, as she drove the sharp garden metal, be it dagger, be it shear, into the man's heart, which was not exactly clearly marked by the yellow wool cross on the yellow wool sweater, thereby bringing the daily postmeridian murder game to a conclusion that was a bit abrupt but still followed all the rules of the game, come on and mop up our blood into the bucket, the woman insisted, our blood we both once again so copiously spilt, since we'll need it again tomorrow at the same time for our daily postmeridian murder game, oh there over the hills, don't you see it, night is already upon us. It'll be the fuck, the man said. He mopped the blood up into the bucket, filled the bottles in the bucket, corked the bottles, uncorked the bottles, looked around on the floor for flesh-wafer tidbits, found some, sampled blissfully, set the dinner table. It'll be the fuck, the woman said. Cheers. To the kid. Bon appétit. She panted sorrowfully, did it for the kid, at that moment it always happened not to be there, the little hick, and cleared off the table. It was eight. The kid hadn't come home. It had! had! spent the afternoon at the children's hospital. Its plan was to do a complete job. First the doctors, then the nurses, then the patients, then me. It was hoping for an audience, reserved the Large Auditorium, tore open the doors to the operating theater. The public sphere! it screamed. Tathandlung! it screamed. Self-actualization! it screamed. Debestialization! it screamed. The only thing it was concerned about was the choice of weapons. The garden shears weren't available, they were needed at home. Rat poison had been put out elsewhere at another time by others for others. The spray can was empty, nothing was inexhaustible on this earth. The ax! the ax! where was that ax? There weren't any submachine guns, at most electric razors. At most straight razors. At most the old straight razor from the broom closet. Of course there was still the question of whether the patients also, the nurses also, the doctors also had old straight razors. Operating on the defenseless, that was a thought the kid was able to bear, even if it brought it to the verge of tears. It wasn't interested in be it determining, be it naming the coefficient determining the moral-practical thrust of its future, its past, its present actions, based on the completely missing tension between its hypertrophied yet paralyzed sense of justice and its unwept weeping that nonetheless pattered down as conscientious downpour on the system of its inner sensations. It tried to climb up on the table from all sides. The ladder! the ladder! where was that ladder. The white nurses' lips moved incessantly. Doctors, nurses, patients; they crammed into the auditorium. Them, fit as a fiddle on the periphery, me in the middle even fitter than a fiddle. The kid had made it pretty far for itself. Judges, bank clerks, social workers—those types were there too. The kid didn't care. It was crouching on the operation table. Succinct analysis of the situation. Mind! it cried. Style! it cried. Future! The applause from one half of the audience swelled up. The applause from the other half of the audience shrank. Exaggerated crescendo, exaggerated decrescendo; both premature. The kid didn't care. Me! it cried. Revolution! It swung its straight razor. None of the extras seated on the stage or in the audience had a straight razor, just the kid. Kakthanalogon! To prepare itself for the critical moment's pangs of consciousness, the kid unswaddled itself. It put the diaper over its eyes, nose, mouth. Its attempt to break its neck with the straight razor failed. The kid's comment: too rushed; couldn't have gone well; time for a little break. Attempt to cut its way into the inner ear with the straight razor. No comment this time. The only one who would have been able to appreciate the fiasco's equilibrial dynamics was Jo. Jo would have written. Jo didn't write. Jo was lying in the tub. Jo's blood mingled with the water that wasn't Jo's water. Jo tried to think things over. Jo tried to die. Dying, Jo thought over the fact that dying's one thing, thinking things over another. Jo died thinking things over. 8:20. End of the pleasure break. Sigh. The woman brushed the wrinkles out of her skirt. 8:25. End of the exhaustion break. Groan. The man zipped up his pants. 8:30. Her: That was the fuck. Him: That was the fuck. Turn the radio on. Today's nightmare, third draft. Severely abridged. Carefully censored. Slightly mangled.

NOTES ON CONTRIBUTORS

Swiss writer URS ALLEMANN is the author of *Babyfucker* (Les Figues). "Jo's Murder Game" is from the collection *Öz & Kco: Seven Telephonic Deliria*, which is forthcoming from Dalkey Archive Press, as is Allemann's *The Old Man and the Bench: A Five-Month Twaddle.*

The most recent books by MARTINE BELLEN (www.martinebellen.com) are *GHOSTS!* (Spuyten Duyvil) and *2X*[2] (BlazeVOX).

GABRIEL BLACKWELL is the author of *Critique of Pure Reason* (forthcoming from Noemi Press). He is the reviews editor for *The Collagist* and a contributor to *Big Other.*

JONATHAN CARROLL has written sixteen novels and lives in Vienna, Austria. In June, Subterranean Press will release his collected stories, *The Woman Who Married a Cloud.*

BRIAN CONN (www.brianconn.net) is the author of *The Fixed Stars* (FC2) and a co-editor of *Birkensnake*, a fiction annual.

KAREN DONOVAN is the author of *Fugitive Red* (University of Massachusetts Press), winner of the Juniper Prize for Poetry. She is the former coeditor/publisher of the journal *¶: A Magazine of Paragraphs.*

JULIA ELLIOTT's fiction has appeared previously in *Conjunctions*, as well as in *Tin House, Georgia Review, Puerto Del Sol, Mississippi Review, Best American Fantasy* (Prime Books), and elsewhere.

BERNADETTE ESPOSITO teaches math in Laramie, Wyoming. Her essays on plane crashes have recently appeared in *Best American Essays 2011* (Mariner), *North American Review*, and *Hotel Amerika*. She was the Winter 2012 Jack Kerouac writer in residence in Orlando, Florida.

ROBERT FERNANDEZ is the author of *We Are Pharaoh* and the forthcoming *Pink Reef*, from which the poems in this issue are taken (both Canarium Books). He lives in Iowa City.

RYAN FLAHERTY's first book of poetry, *What's This, Bombadier?*, won the 2011 Lena-Miles Wever Todd Poetry Prize (Pleiades Press/LSU Press). He lives and teaches in New Hampshire.

PATRICK GREANEY is the translator of Urs Allemann's *The Old Man and the Bench: A Five-Month Twaddle* and cotranslator of Heimrad Bäcker's *transcript* (both Dalkey Archive Press). The author of *Untimely Beggar: Poverty and Power from Baudelaire to Benjamin* (University of Minnesota Press), he teaches at the University of Colorado at Boulder.

NICHOLAS GRIDER is a writer and artist currently living in Milwaukee.

LYN HEJINIAN is the author of numerous books, including *The Book of a Thousand Eyes* (Omnidawn), *The Language of Inquiry* (University of California Press), and *The Wide Road*, written in collaboration with Carla Harryman (Belladonna).

JOANNA HOWARD is the author of *On the Winding Stair* (Boa Editions) and *In the Colorless Round* (Noemi). She lives in Providence, Rhode Island, and teaches at Brown University.

SARAH LANG was born in Canada. Her first book, *The Work of Days*, was published by Coach House Books.

KAREN LEPRI is the author of the chapbook *Fig. I* (Horse Less Press). Her poems, translations, and reviews have appeared in *Boston Review, Chicago Review, Denver Quarterly*, and elsewhere.

FIONA MAAZEL is the author of the novel *Last Last Chance* (Farrar, Straus and Giroux). Her new novel, *Woke Up Lonely*, will be published by Graywolf in 2013.

SHENA McAULIFFE's writing has been published or is forthcoming in *Western Humanities Review, The Collagist, Black Warrior Review, Alaska Quarterly Review*, and elsewhere.

ANDREW MOSSIN is the author of two collections of poetry, *The Epochal Body* and *The Veil* (both Singing Horse Press), and a book of criticism, *Male Subjectivity and Poetic Form in "New American" Poetry* (Palgrave MacMillan). "I Get Her Up in Daylight" is excerpted from *Through the Rivers: A Memoir of Theft*.

SIGRID NUNEZ has published six novels, including *The Last of Her Kind* (Farrar, Straus and Giroux) and, most recently, *Salvation City* (Riverhead). She is also the author of *Sempre Susan: A Memoir of Susan Sontag* (Atlas & Co.).

JOYCE CAROL OATES's most recent books are the novel *Mudwoman* (Ecco) and the forthcoming *Evil Eye: Four Novellas* (Mysterious Press/Grove Atlantic). She teaches at Princeton University and is a 2011 recipient of the National Humanities Medal.

The most recent book by STEPHEN O'CONNOR (www.stephenoconnor.net) is the short-story collection *Here Comes Another Lesson* (Free Press).

CHINELO OKPARANTA's first novel, *Too Much Wahala*, and debut story collection, *Under the Udara Trees*, are forthcoming under the Portobello imprint of Granta UK and from Houghton Mifflin Harcourt in the United States.

Work by photographers ROBERT and SHANA PARKEHARRISON (www.parkeharrison.com) is in the permanent collections of the Los Angeles County Museum, the San Francisco Museum of Modern Art, the Whitney, the National Museum of American Art, the Boston Museum of Fine Arts, and elsewhere. Recent exhibitions include group shows at Mudam Luxembourg, Jack Shainman Gallery, and the Nobel Museum in Stockholm, among other venues. In 2012, their work will be shown in Mediations Biennale in Poland and Lille 3000 in France.

ELIZABETH ROBINSON's most recent collection of poetry is *Three Novels* (Omnidawn). *Counterpart*, a new collection, is forthcoming in 2012 from Ahsahta.

RYAN RUBY teaches philosophy at York College in Queens. His writing has appeared in *The Baffler*, *More Intelligent Life*, *n+1*, and elsewhere.

MICHAEL SHEEHAN is the reviews editor and an assistant fiction editor for *DIAGRAM*. A former fellow of the Wisconsin Institute for Creative Writing, he is currently working on a novel.

The most recent book by CHRISTOPHER SORRENTINO (christophersorrentino.com/), *Death Wish* (Soft Skull), is a critical study of the film of the same name. He is completing a new novel.

ADAM WEINSTEIN lives in Salt Lake City and teaches at Westminster College. "Some Remarks on Teeth" is from his recently completed collection *The New Commonplace Book of Custom and Use*.

After the Apocalypse
Maureen F. McHugh

THREE MESSAGES
AND
A WARNING

PUERTO DEL SOL
a journal of new literature

AGNI
TESTING THE EDGE
SINCE 1972
WWW.AGNIMAGAZINE.ORG
CODE PN06 FOR 20%
NEW SUBSCRIPTONS